LEAP of FAITH
Second Chance at the Dream

Crossroads Collection, Book 1

Shannon Winslow

Cover design by Micah D. Hansen

For **Bob**, **Brian**, and **Kyle** –

three of the most important men in my life.
With all my love…

Soli Deo Gloria

Leap of Faith

Author Acknowledgment

When I first set out to write this story, I thought I knew quite a lot about baseball. After all, I had been watching games for years. I understood the rules, positions, and how to keep score. But I quickly discovered that I knew next to nothing about the behind-the-scenes stuff I needed in order to portray what life would have been like for my protagonist, Ben Lewis, a struggling young baseball player trying to work his way up the ladder.

Then Chris Rosenbaum came to my rescue.

I was hunting for helpful source material on the internet when I stumbled across Chris's blog: *Looking Through the Mask – a unique perspective on professional baseball....* And it really was a unique perspective. While other pro ball players were blogging about how their games had gone and endlessly obsessing about their stats, Chris was giving outsiders a wider view on the day-to-day existence of an athlete pursuing his dream in one of the most competitive sports on the planet. Yes, he wrote about what happens on the field but also what happens off of it – living arrangements, workout routines, dealing with high stress and low pay in the minors, etc. In other words, exactly the sort of thing I needed to know. I read Chris's blog from one end to the other, and then I took him up on his open invitation for readers to contact him with questions and future blog topic requests.

I cannot say enough about his willingness to help and his generosity with his time and expertise. Chris not only answered (with care and in detail) several specific questions I had run up against while writing, he went above and beyond when he agreed to read the entire manuscript for technical accuracy. Nothing could have made me prouder than hearing him say afterward that *Leap of Faith* perfectly captured so much of a ballplayer's feelings and attitudes.

Thank you, Chris! I am very grateful for your help. This book wouldn't have been the same without you.

(Don't miss Chris's baseball retrospective at the end of this book.)

Leap of Faith

PRELUDE

"So, what do you think of our newest specimen, Dex?" asked the forty-ish brunette lounging on a canary-yellow chaise. She gave a nod toward the monitor displaying a good looking, athletically built young man pacing his room like a caged lion. "Personally, I like the look of him."

"I'm not surprised," muttered her associate, a thin man of a more mature vintage. He stood at attention, tapping his pen against his jaw as he studied the screen. He barely heard the nasal twang in Cora's voice anymore. After so many years of successful partnership – professional as well as personal – he had grown as accustomed to her idiosyncrasies as she had to his.

"It is far too soon to venture an educated opinion," he continued in his clipped, aristocratic accent. "However, Mr. Lewis must have shown *some* promise or he would not have been referred to us."

"His bio's impressive – smart, talented, disciplined, loyal to the core, and a real team player. Plus, look what he did for the Ellerton boy. You have to admire someone who goes out of his way like that to help a kid. Ben's good at heart, I believe, just down on his luck."

"My interpretation of his character is rather less sympathetic. I shall endeavor to keep an open mind, but something tells me this one's going to be a tough nut to crack." Pursing his lips, he pondered a moment. "I'll test the waters first, shall I? Then you can tidy up whatever mess I make and smooth things over with your charms, like always. I think you had better use your alter ego this time. The pre-arrival evaluation indicates the subject will respond best to a woman his own age. Besides, with the quantity of science fiction books and movies this young man has consumed, he will no doubt be expecting all the high-tech bells and whistles we can throw at him. Best foot forward, eh?"

"Of course." Cora sat up and stretched her long, cat-like limbs. "I think I'll be a blonde this time," she declared. "I'm going to have to adjust the pitch on the voice modulator too. The higher setting I tried last time was a disaster. I could hardly stand to listen to myself. And the poor client... I swear he winced every time I opened my mouth."

"Well, we all have our off days." He extended a hand to his colleague and ran an admiring eye over her form as she rose. She stood nose to nose with him in height and, with her well-rounded figure, probably outweighed him by a few pounds. "It turned out right in the end, though," he added. "I checked in on Mr. Carson only the other day, and he's adjusting nicely to his new life. I believe we can count it as another resounding success."

"I'm glad to hear it. Same approach this time?"

"Yes, I believe that will be best. I do hope this one won't be too obstinate," he said, finishing with an exaggerated sigh.

"Come on, Dex. Your complaints don't fool me for a minute. You thrive on the more challenging cases. The others bore you to tears."

"How well you understand me, my dear," he said, squeezing her hand. "Of course, you're perfectly right... as always."

Part One:

Ben's Log

Leap of Faith

-1-
A Lucky Man

What would the average guy give to turn back the clock and set his life straight? Probably anything short of his right arm… that is if he'd made as much of a mess of things as I have. I hit bottom in September of 1997. Then, just when I thought I couldn't go on, when I was at a point so low I had to look up to see outfield grass grow, I received a genuine, world-class do-over. Now I'm praying I still have time to salvage it.

It came as a gift. No charge. And I appreciate how lucky I am. Except I'm discovering there *is* a kind of cost after all, which I'm belatedly paying.

To be fair, I was forewarned. A year ago, I barely thought twice about exchanging my lackluster past for a chance at resurrecting my dream. But now that they're at risk, I suddenly realize some memories from those discarded months and years are too precious to part with: the satisfaction of helping one of my students succeed, friendships with Jeff and the others at the Center, and most importantly, every mental picture of Abby from a time she knew and loved me. The thought of those treasures being sucked irretrievably down a black hole…

Well, I simply can't let that happen. While I'm still able, I have to write down how I got to this point – what took place the first time around and everything that has changed since. But where should I begin? With my past, which hasn't happened yet and now won't? With the future, which I lived once but now is subject to reinterpretation? Or with the odd people and place that made it all possible?

Time is the issue, and now time is my enemy as well. With every tick of the clock, another valuable scrap of my memory is stripped away forever. But it's not only my original history that's at stake. My entire future hangs in the balance as well, and this time it's going to be permanent. No more do-overs, so I can't afford to blow it. This log will be my guide going forward. I'm depending on it, and I don't have a minute to lose.

~~*~~

September, 1997
Swedish Hospital, Seattle, Washington

I floated, half asleep in an anesthetic fog. The only thing that cut through the haze – besides the excruciating sensation in my gut – was a pair of voices hovering nearby.

"Your husband's a lucky man, Mrs. Lewis. If we hadn't gotten him into surgery when we did, he might very well have died from complications. I know he's been dreading the possibility of this operation but, under the circumstances, surely even he would agree that it's preferable to the alternative. There's every chance the colostomy can be reversed later too."

"I know you're right, doctor…"

Ah, that sweet, familiar voice. A wave of peace flooded up from my toes and out in every direction, pooling in my scalp and fingertips.

"…It'll be a shock to him at first, I suppose, but I'm just so grateful Ben's going to be okay. That's all that matters to me."

I heard the words, but their meaning didn't fully register at the time. The reassuring sound of Abby's voice sent my medicated mind spooling backwards to a less complicated world – to my youth, when I led something of a charmed existence. Not that I recognized it at the time. It's just the way things were in the suburbs in the 80's. Life revolved around family, school, and for me, sports. It seemed like there was always some kind of game on in the neighborhood: pick-up basketball in the cul-de-sac, an impromptu football scrimmage at the park down the road, or a few kids knocking a baseball around on the vacant lot.

School was okay, but athletics is where I really excelled. And it's what I loved too. All kinds of sports, but particularly baseball. The happiest hours of my childhood were spent on the diamond, and my dream was to make it my permanent home – a dream that had seemed within reach. I had all the necessary tools. A good left-handed bat is always in demand, and my arm and range made me a natural in center field.

College and pro scouts followed my progress from an early age, and I was drafted right out of high school. At my parents' urging, though, I passed up the possibility of jumping directly to the pros to accept a full-ride athletic scholarship at the University of Washington instead. Dad thought it would be best for my career in the long run, and Mom just wanted me to get an education "to fall back on." I had my own motives for choosing college, not the least of which was the appeal of a coed dorm with my girlfriend Jessica just a floor or two away.

All was going according to my grand plan, and then I got sick.

I was more lucid when I surfaced the next time. Although I couldn't remember much, I was pretty sure of two things, equally upsetting: I had unforgivably picked a fight with Abby earlier, and I was now in a hospital bed instead of my own. Opening my eyes just a fraction was enough to confirm the second part. There on the ceiling was the telltale steel track encircling the bed, the curtain suspended from it pushed to one side. Above my left shoulder dangled a bottle of colorless liquid, dripping steadily into the tubing that snaked toward my hand. The dark eye of a television stared back at me from its high perch across the room, and the acrid odor of disinfectant hung in the air.

It was night, I gathered, but far from quiet. A relentless beep chirped from within my own room. I could also hear muffled voices, the distant clatter of cabinetry, and some kind of machinery droning back and forth in the hallway. When my head cleared, I risked a more thorough look around the room. Other than an array of monitoring equipment, I was quite alone.

But what was I doing there? I took the ache in the pit of my stomach as my first clue. My free hand gravitated to the site, where I felt unfamiliar bindings and apparatus through my hospital gown. Then fragments of the conversation I overheard earlier shed added light: surgery… operation… colostomy.

Colostomy! Oh, God, not that horror. Anything but that.

I wish I could say that I soon plucked up my courage and stoically faced facts, finding a way to look on the bright side. But it wouldn't be true. I didn't feel brave or even nobly resigned to my fate. I felt angry and hopeless, like I'd been dropped into an inescapable pit a second time, and there abandoned. Major insult had been heaped on top of serious injury. My body, which had been my best asset and friend for the first twenty years of my life, had betrayed me all over again, first with the illness itself, which had ruined my baseball hopes, and now this. I wasn't counting my blessings. I wasn't searching for the silver lining. I didn't like the program, and I was looking for the exit.

A fresh shot of pain rocketed through my midsection. I hit the button clutched in my left hand. That was supposed to help. At least I thought I remembered someone telling me to use it when the "discomfort" became too great. That euphemism didn't do justice to the fire raging in my belly, but I pushed the button all the same. The morphine pump did its job; the drugs mercifully kicked in and I faded back into oblivion.

-2-
The Light of Day

Daylight streamed through the hospital windows when I next opened my eyes.

"Good morning, Mr. Lewis," boomed a formidable nurse whose name was Rosanna English, according to her plasticized hospital ID badge.

"What time is it?" I croaked.

"Six AM. Sorry to wake you, but I have to check your vitals."

Before I could ask which of my "vital" parts she had any business inspecting, the woman stuck a thermometer in my mouth. She took my pulse and ran the pressure in the cuff on my arm up and down. After scrutinizing the monitors and making notes in the chart, she gave me a critical once-over.

"You're looking considerably better than when they brought you in yesterday, young man. I don't suppose you remember, but you were in a pretty bad way. Doctor says you're lucky to be alive."

"Yeah, lucky," I mumbled when she removed the thermometer.

"Your kidneys are functioning splendidly."

I grimaced, seeing that what interested her was apparently a bag of my urine clipped to the side of the bed.

"We'll have that catheter out as soon as you're up and can get to the bathroom on your own – probably later today. Now, let me take a look at the surgical site."

Ms. English, with professional efficiency, folded back the bed-clothes and my generic hospital gown to expose my mutilated physique. But I couldn't bear to see what they'd done to me; I just closed my eyes and groaned.

"Are you in pain, Mr. Lewis?" asked Nurse Rosanna. "Give that button by your hand a nudge, dear. You'll feel better in a minute. I'm all done, so you can go back to sleep. Your wife said she would be in to see you around eight."

But sleep eluded me. Instead, I tortured myself by dredging up memories of the past and how I wound up in this mess.

I'd met Jessica Martinelli in high school, at a party following a football game. She was exactly my type: drop-dead gorgeous with long, dark hair and smoky eyes. And, lucky for me, she had a thing for athletes. Instant chemistry.

Our first two years of college flew by. Jessica majored in journalism and I inched my way toward a teaching degree. Neither of us actually expected to earn a living in those professions, though. Our heads swelled with bigger ideas – a lucrative pro contract for me and an upscale lifestyle for us both. College was simply the means to that end.

Anyway, I worked my tail off on the ball field and it was paying dividends. In my junior year, I began to consider turning pro sooner rather than later. Barring anything unforeseen, I knew I'd be drafted again that spring. And if I had another very good season, I'd probably get an offer I couldn't refuse.

The trouble started during winter quarter. At first I thought I'd picked up a bug in Mexico where my family and I had vacationed over Christmas. "Montezuma's revenge," I joked to my friends to explain another hurried trip to the restroom.

I started downing Pepto tablets by the handful and hoped for the best.

I got worse instead. Yet I hesitated to see a doctor or talk to the team trainer, knowing that even the rumor of an injury or illness can damage a player's market value.

I couldn't hide my deteriorating health forever, though. One day in the weight room, I almost blacked out when I stood up after a set of leg presses. I grabbed one of the machines to keep from collapsing on the floor as stars popped up before my eyes.

The trainer saw it and rushed over. "Lewis! What's the matter with you? You're white as a ghost."

"I'll be all right in a minute," I lied. "I'm just tired. Pulled an all-nighter to get ready for midterms. You know how it is." I did my best to sell it, but Mr. Keller wasn't buying. He escorted me into his office and closed the door.

"Sit down, Ben. I think it's time we had a little chat. I've been watching you, and I don't like what I see. You're pale. You can't lift like you normally do. And it looks to me like you've dropped a few pounds. Now, what's going on? The truth this time," he warned.

I had no choice but to confess.

Keller listened to my story. Then he called in the coach, who called the team doctor. They packed me off to see a gastroenterologist who scheduled me for a couple of unpleasant tests.

"There's no doubt about it. It's Crohn's disease," said Dr. Bingham at the follow-up appointment.

I'd never heard of Crohn's, but I already didn't like the sound of it.

"It's an autoimmune disorder which can cause inflammation and ulcerations anywhere throughout the digestive tract. In your case, it's confined to the colon."

To illustrate his point, the doctor handed over glossy, color photos from my colonoscopy. One glance was all I could stomach.

"The exact cause of Crohn's is unknown," Bingham continued in monotone, "although there's probably a genetic link since it tends to run in families. Any history among your relatives?"

"Not that I'm aware of."

"Well, never mind. We'll get you started on a strong anti-inflammatory drug right away, along with a couple of other prescriptions. I won't lie to you, Ben. Currently, there's no cure for Crohn's, and it's often a real challenge to control. Occasionally surgery is required. I wouldn't worry about that, though. In most cases, the disease can be managed with medication, and the patient leads a pretty normal life."

"But I'm an athlete!" I protested. "I have to be in peak physical condition, not just 'pretty normal.' My entire future depends on it."

The silver-haired physician hemmed and hawed. I suppose he didn't want to make promises he couldn't keep or remove all hope either. He neatly avoided both, saying, "The course of the illness varies a great deal from one patient to the next. Some people have one bout of the disease and it never raises its ugly head again. Perhaps you'll be one of those. There's no way of knowing at this point. Here." He handed me three prescriptions and a thin paperback book. "Read this when you get home," he instructed. "Give me a call if you still have questions. Otherwise, I want to see you back here in two weeks."

I scanned the title of the booklet: *Living with Inflammatory Bowel Disease – Crohn's and Ulcerative Colitis.* "Fascinating reading, I'm sure," I muttered with heavy sarcasm.

It was a stupid thing to say, but milder than what I felt. I wanted to yell or put my fist through a wall – preferably both. Instead, I grunted an apology and left thinking, "Why me?" What had I done to deserve this? Was this some form of bad karma coming back at me, or was it God's idea of a joke to zap an elite athlete with a debilitating disease?

When a brief wallow in the deep end of the self-pity pool failed to improve my situation, I changed game plans. I embarked on a campaign to restore my health with the same dedication and discipline that made me successful in sports. I took my medications as directed, followed my dietary recommendations to the letter, and got plenty of fluids and rest. Within a few weeks, my symptoms were completely gone. I was thrilled. Dr. Bingham expressed cautious optimism and gave permission for me to resume my training regime.

I worked harder than ever to make up for lost time and felt nearly at full strength when the baseball season began. A month later, though, the old symptoms flared up again. This time the drugs took longer to tame them. Between the illness itself and the side-effects of the medications, my performance clearly suffered. I had a pretty good season, but not a great season. I played well by normal standards, but not nearly well enough to earn the juicy contract offer I had hoped for. No need to panic, though. I still had one year of eligibility left in my college career, one more year to prove myself.

Crohn's disease continued to dog my heels, however, spoiling my senior season as well. No big contract. I wasn't even drafted. The dream was officially dead.

So I holed up in my apartment, marinating my sorrows in alcohol and seeing no one. A week into my self-imposed isolation, though, Jessica pushed in without an invitation.

"Hello?" she called, peering through the gloom as she entered.

I was sprawled on the couch, vacantly staring at the TV. "Over here, Jess."

"This place is a cave!" She flipped on the lights and flung open the drapes.

My hand flew to my face, too late to shield my eyes from the explosion of sunlight. It was worth it, though, to see Jessica in all her splendor. A mix of pride and desire warmed me. I reached toward her, saying, "I'm glad you're here, Babe. I really need you."

She took a hard look at me and stopped at a safe distance, hands on hips and wrinkling her nose. "I've missed you too, Benji, but you're crazy if you think I'm coming any closer. You obviously haven't shaved in days. And when was the last time you took a shower?"

With a huff, she grabbed the wastebasket from the kitchen and started collecting the junk-food wrappers and beer cans strewn in a semicircle around me. "Disgusting," she said, making a face at the three-day-old mac and cheese cemented to a paper plate on the coffee table. She used a copy of *Sports Illustrated* to shove the whole mess into the garbage, dropping the contaminated magazine in after it.

I should have tried to stop her or at least gotten up to help. But I didn't.

When Jessica finished, she spent two full minutes washing her hands before returning. She then stared down at me, shaking her head. "I know you've had a setback, but don't you think this has gone on long enough? You can't just lie around on that ugly couch forever. You've got to pull yourself together; get back on track!"

"I thought you'd be more sympathetic," I said, dragging myself to a sitting position. "Don't you understand, Jess? This time it's really over. I'll never get to play pro ball now. We can kiss that dream goodbye once and for all." I dropped my head into my hands and rubbed my throbbing temples.

When I glanced up again, Jessica looked stunned. She sank into a nearby chair. "I know that's what you said, but I thought... I thought you were exaggerating. Isn't there still a chance, when you get better, I mean? What about all the plans we've made?"

Leaning forward, I took her limp hand. "Don't worry, Jess. We'll be all right. I'll figure something out, I promise."

"But no more baseball?"

"No. Dr. Bingham talks about some promising new treatment they're testing for Crohn's. But even if it's a miracle cure, it won't be in time to save my career."

"So, what *are* you going to do?" she asked, a hint of hysteria rising in her voice.

"I don't know. I suppose I'll have to finish my degree and teach."

"Teach?" she repeated in a tone of disgust, drawing her hand away. "Is that the best idea you've got?"

I shrugged and slumped back into the couch. "I haven't really thought the whole thing through yet."

After a minute of unsettled silence, she went on. "What about me? Am I supposed to just accept this? I've been expecting a certain kind of life, Ben. You know – all the stuff we've talked about. And now? Well, now I'm not sure I can count on you anymore."

"You can. We may have to scale back our plans a little, but we'll still have each other."

Another uncomfortable pause.

"Look," Jessica said, getting to her feet. "It's been great, Ben, and I'm sorry things have turned out badly for you. Really, I am. But put yourself in *my* place. You know I have my sights set pretty high. It was fine as long as we were heading in the same direction. Now, though... well... there's no reason we should *both* be miserably poor, is there?"

I gaped at her. I couldn't believe this was the same girl who had been by my side for over four years; who had laboriously mapped out every detail of our wedding and our future together; who had already named our three unborn children.

"What are you saying, Jess?" I asked, bracing myself. "Don't you love me anymore?"

"I don't know. Maybe I never did."

R-r-r-rip. I felt my guts spill out onto the floor. Jessica trampled them in her hurry to reach the door.

With her hand on the knob, she looked back over her shoulder. "You've really let me down, Ben."

Those were her parting words.

I hoped it was only a temporary rift, but when I tried to contact her, Jessica wouldn't answer the phone. A few weeks later, I heard she'd taken up with Derek Williams, a teammate of mine who had a brighter future.

I had been teetering on the brink before, and Jessica's desertion sent me right over the edge. Still, I couldn't hate her. No one should be judged too harshly for abandoning a sinking ship, and I was definitely going down.

For help, I rifled through my mental catalog of Star Trek episodes – a reliable source of all-purpose wisdom. As I saw it, I was like the Enterprise set on self-destruct. But even though I'd seen that scenario successfully overcome more than once, this was different. I was no Captain Kirk. I had no clue how to cancel the countdown and save the ship.

-3-
Abby

"Ben? Are you awake?" asked a feather-soft voice at my hospital bedside.

I opened my eyes enough to glimpse her angel face. "Abby," I whispered.

She laced her fingers through mine. "You're still tired. I shouldn't have woken you."

"That's okay. I'm glad you did. I wasn't sure you'd come, actually. I wouldn't blame you if you were still mad after that argument. I was a total jerk."

"It's already forgotten." She kissed the back of my hand and hugged it to her cheek. "Don't think about it anymore."

I winced as I shifted position.

"Are you in a lot of pain?"

"No. It's not so bad." I tried to smile, but all I could think, looking at her, was that she could have married anybody. And I... "God, I'm such a mess," I moaned, turning away from her. "You deserve better, Abby."

"Don't say that, B-bear. Everything's going to be fine."

I didn't answer. At that moment, it seemed impossible that anything could ever be all right again.

"There are a lot of people praying for you. Your friends send their love. I've even heard from a couple of your students. Zac Ellerton wants to know when he can come see you."

"Not now, for God's sake. He has enough to deal with. The last thing Zac needs is to witness me like this, a preview of what he might be in for down the road."

"No, I told him you couldn't have visitors yet. I don't think you need to worry about scaring him, though. He seems to have adjusted really well to his illness, thanks to you."

"Zac's a brave kid. I didn't do much."

"It may not seem like much to you, but I know it meant the world to him – and to his parents – that you took him under your wing."

We lapsed into silence, and I rested my eyes closed. As I felt the heaviness of sleep pulling me down like quicksand, I clung to Abby's hand. She was my lifeline, but I went under all the same.

~~*~~

I met Abby the summer following my meltdown over losing Jessica and my baseball career. I'd finally made another appointment with Dr. Bingham for some help, and she was there. She opened the door to the waiting room that day and called out my name.

"You're new," I observed, following the waif-thin blonde down the hall.

"I'm working here part time now. I'm a nursing student at U-Dub."

"Really? I go there too. I don't think I've seen you around campus, though." This girl I would have remembered.

She laughed. "That's not surprising. With thirty-five thousand students, you can't expect to run into everybody. Besides, I spend most of my time in the health sciences building. You?"

"More like the sports complex."

"So you're an athlete. What's your sport?"

"Baseball mostly. At least it used to be."

"I like baseball." A wistful look crossed her face. "When I was little, my dad used to take me to the games at the college where he worked, but I don't claim to understand the finer points. Here's your room, Ben. Have a seat and roll up your sleeve, please."

"It's a more complicated game than most people realize," I explained as she wrapped the blood pressure cuff around my arm. "There's a lot of strategy involved. A guy's got to stay alert all the time – think ahead, anticipate what the other team's planning." When she finished and took the stethoscope out of her ears, I continued. "Most people assume that batting's the biggest thrill, the chance to be a hero every time you step up to the plate. For me, though, scaling the fence to rob the other guy of a home run is just as much fun as hitting one myself."

23

She was grinning at me.

"Sorry," I said. "I guess I'm kind of running off at the mouth."

"Just a little. Sounds like you really love the game."

"I do. I did, that is. I don't play anymore," I said, dropping my eyes.

"That's too bad," she said as if she really meant it. "Well, it was nice meeting you, Ben. Dr. Bingham will be with you in a few minutes. See you around."

"Yeah." I made a quick check of her name tag: Abigail Albright. "See ya, Abby."

She turned back toward me and flashed a dazzling smile, one almost too big for her small-featured face to contain. "That's what my grandma used to call me. I'm Gail to everybody else."

"Why is that?"

"Oh, my Aunt Abigail goes by Abby, and people thought it would be too confusing if I did too. So they've always called me Gail instead."

"Which do you prefer?"

"It's been a long time since anybody called me Abby. I kinda like hearing it again."

"Okay. Abby it is. I'll remember."

It was the most important conversation of my life, although I didn't know it then.

I saw Abby twice more that summer in Dr. Bingham's office. On the surface, nothing significant happened. I didn't even think about asking her out initially. She wasn't my usual type, and I was still smarting from my breakup with Jessica. Abby gave me something to look forward to, though, a little spark of sunlight in the middle of a dark time.

Other than passing my classes, I had two goals that fall – three if I'm honest. I needed to forget baseball, avoid Jessica… and accidentally run into Abby again. I failed miserably at the first, but managed to pull off the other two.

I started parking in the underground garage between Mountlake and Pacific at the south end of campus, which gave me an excuse to walk past the enormous UW Medical Center and Health Sciences complex every day. I figured Abby was in there somewhere, and sooner or later she had to come out.

Weeks of perseverance paid off. One day I saw her and quickened my pace so that our paths would intersect. I carefully studied the tree-covered knoll across the street as I walked, pretending not to notice Abby until she was right in front of me.

"Hey, Ben. Remember me?" she said with the same brilliant smile as before.

"Oh, hi! Sure I do. It's Abby, right? What a coincidence, running into you like this," which, of course, it wasn't. "It's good to see you again," which it really was; she looked great. "Where are you headed?"

"I was going out to find something to eat. Cafeteria food doesn't appeal to me today."

"Can I give you a ride? My car's right up here in the garage."

"Thanks, but I'd rather walk. It's such a beautiful day."

"Oh. No problem. Well… I…"

"Do you want to join me?" she asked. "I'd like the company."

That's how it started. We had lunch together, talked for hours, and began dating. Abby was like no one I'd ever met before – smart, funny, full of energy and optimism. She had a child-like innocence that made me want to take care of her too. I fell for her fast and hard.

I still have no idea what Abby saw in me; I was no great catch. Oh, I'd been popular all through school, but this was the post-jock era. Even if I didn't deserve her, I wasn't about to let her go – not if I could help it. Maybe it was my dogged persistence that won her in the end.

Anyway, after we both graduated, we got married and settled into a tract house south of Seattle, less than ten miles from where I grew up. Abby started work in the pediatric unit of a Tacoma hospital, and I took a job teaching English at the local high school. I actually liked teaching, as it turned out, and I did some coaching on the side.

It was a good life. I see that now, looking back. Ordinary, but good. Abby loved me, and it shouldn't have mattered what I did for a living. Yet, I could never shake the feeling that I'd been cheated out of what was rightfully mine, what I'd worked all my life to earn: a shot at the big leagues and the lifestyle that came with it. I suppose if a guy's never had prime rib, he might be satisfied eating hamburger forever. But I'd tasted success only to have it ripped out of my mouth and something more mundane substituted. It was an enormous come-down to swallow. Years later, it still stuck in my throat, choking me bit by bit.

Every week, some new reminder of what I'd lost surfaced. The argument just before I wound up in the hospital was a case in point. Abby came home that night bursting with excitement. She told me her parents had decided that, rather than trade in their two-year-old BMW, they'd give it to us.

"It's all paid for, and it's all ours!" she announced, throwing her arms around my neck.

I peeled her off and set her down. "Abby, there's no way we can accept it."

"Why not? They really want to do this for us, Ben, and you know you'd love driving around town in a classy car. Don't let your pride stand in the way."

"Pride? On my salary? I can't afford pride... or a BMW."

"But it's free!"

"Nothing's free. Do you have any idea how expensive it is to maintain a car like that?"

"Not really," she admitted, contracting her brow.

"The license, taxes, and insurance would probably bust our budget. Then, if it ever needed any serious repairs, we'd practically have to take out a second mortgage on the house."

"Oh. I didn't realize," she said, the joy draining from her voice.

"What? That when you married me I would be so totally incapable of..." I broke off and turned away.

"Never mind about the car," she soothed, massaging my shoulders. "I just thought you would enjoy it. I certainly don't need a BMW to be happy."

"But it wouldn't hurt, would it?" I accused, spinning to face her again. "Paul, the doctor, would have been able to buy you a decent car. That's probably what your parents were thinking."

"Don't be ridiculous! This has nothing to do with Paul. Why does it always come down to money with you?"

"Hey, those are the rules. 'Money makes the world go round,' or hadn't you heard?"

"No, what I heard is that it's *God's* job to keep the world turning. Is money your god, then, Ben?"

I had no answer for the anguish I read in her eyes. What a change from only a few minutes before. She'd come home beaming, thrilled to share her good news with me. What had I done? I'd thrown cold water on her enthusiasm and picked a fight to boot. Unforgivable. I grabbed my jacket and went out for some air before I could do any more damage.

That's the last thing I remember before waking up in the hospital, tethered with tubes and wires like an experimental lab rat. The damned illness had stolen my baseball career and even tainted my marriage. Now this surgery. It was the final blow. I felt like I was drowning, and I was inexcusably dragging Abby under with me. Even our kids, if we dared to have any, would be under the curse since they would stand a higher risk of getting Crohn's too because of me. I couldn't bear thinking that would be my legacy.

Not very heroic, but I have to be honest. That's how I felt. I was tired of grieving the past, of suffering the present, of worrying for the future. I couldn't help wishing it was all over, that I wouldn't have to deal with it any longer.

Sleep promised a temporary escape. As I drifted off, I remember noticing that the perpetual beeping from off to my right finally stopped. Instead, I heard an alarm sounding somewhere… far away.

-4-

Poindexter

I woke up – God only knows how much later – in an empty, white room. It was nothing more than a box, really, about twelve feet square. No doors or windows. No furniture except the couch I lay on – also white. Soft light and soothing instrumental music filtered in from somewhere, and a current of contentment overwhelmed me like a drug.

Curious rather than alarmed at the unexplained change in my surroundings, I sat up and took stock. White sweat pants and T-shirt had replaced my hospital gown. My skin seemed a little pale, but at least the needles, tubes, and monitors were gone, along with any pain. In fact, not a single thing remained as evidence of my recent medical crisis.

I waited patiently at first, still cocooned by an unexplained feeling of well-being. I fully expected someone would soon come to tell me everything was fine and that I could go home. But as time passed and my artificial calm began wearing off, I grew increasingly restless. There was nothing to do except pace, so I wore a path back and forth on the tile floor until I heard a noise to one side of me. With a swoosh, a seamlessly integrated door slid open in the wall, and a thin man with a pasty complexion entered through it. Anything alive should have stood out against such a plain, static backdrop, but this guy nearly disappeared, thanks to his white suit.

The odd little man looked familiar, although I was sure I'd never seen him before in my life. I couldn't put my finger on what it was about him... Then his salt-and-pepper mustache twitched and I knew. I once kept an albino rat named Roscoe as a pet, and this guy reminded me a lot of him.

Silver clipboard in hand, the man stepped forward, saying with businesslike formality, "Good day, Mr. Lewis. I trust you are feeling better now."

Although "Mr. Clean" didn't seem all that warm and friendly, it was still a relief to have someone to talk to. I said, "You bet I am. I'm glad to be out of that hospital, I can tell you. Or was that whole thing some kind of weird dream? I don't seem to have a mark on me."

"It was no dream, but it's over now, just as you wished, and you need never return to it." He paused a moment. "Please do sit down, Mr. Lewis. We have a number of things to go over, and you may as well be comfortable."

I did as he suggested. "So, when can I go home?"

He focused his watery blue eyes on me. "Home? What home would that be, Mr. Lewis?"

"Oh, I guess I thought you'd have all my records from the hospital. I live in Edgewood with my wife, Mr...."

"Poindexter; the name is Andrew Poindexter. You must pardon me for disagreeing with you, young man, but you no longer live in Edgewood."

"Of course I do," I said with a nervous laugh. "I'd know it if we'd moved."

"Mr. Lewis, you mistake my meaning. What I am endeavoring to make you understand is that you do not reside *anywhere* on earth at present."

My mouth fell open, but no words came out. I couldn't believe I'd heard him right. Did he mean I was homeless or... I jumped to my feet again. "Hey! What are you trying to pull, Poindexter? Are you saying I'm dead? Cuz that's just crazy! Besides, this doesn't look much like heaven to me."

"Do try to calm yourself, sir. You may correct me if I'm wrong – although I hardly think it likely – but during your recent hospitalization, you expressed the most serious dissatisfaction with your lot in life and a desire to avoid continuing it under those circumstances."

I blinked. "What? Well... maybe I did, but..."

"Then, there you are."

"Oh, come on. You don't really think I meant I wanted to die!"

"That is not for *me* to say, and strictly speaking, you are not dead – at least not yet."

"Then, what the hell's going on? Where am I?"

"*Please*, a little decorum," Poindexter said, wagging his head at me and pointing me back to the sofa with his pen. "If you will allow me to explain?"

What choice did I have? I obediently sat and waited to be enlightened... or preferably for the nightmare to be over instead.

"Now, then, this is what you might call a holding area, a way station of sorts, between your former life and the next. There are many paths that lead from here, some back to points in the world from which you came, and some to the world beyond. Where you travel next is largely up to you. You have been given a great opportunity, Mr. Lewis. The Almighty has heard your pain and granted your wish to be removed from it. I believe a little gratitude would be in order."

I felt like I'd been run over by a three hundred pound lineman: too stunned to reply.

"I see you are having a little difficulty grasping what has happened," continued Poindexter with a disapproving frown. "Sadly, it is often the case, in my experience. Human intellect and imagination are so very finite. Nevertheless, you must make an effort to accept what I have told you. It will be impossible for you to move forward otherwise." He paused expectantly.

I continued to stare at him, dumbfounded.

He sighed. "Really, Mr. Lewis, I am surprised at you. I was told you were one of our brighter candidates. That remains to be seen, I suppose. In any case, I must be getting on." He began making hurried notes on his clipboard as he spoke. "There are other important matters requiring my attention; I cannot afford to stand about idling. Perhaps Cora will have more success with you."

"Cora?" I asked, regaining my power of speech at last.

"My associate. She will be joining you shortly." He drew in his eyebrows as he looked at me. "Do try to pay close attention to what she says. When I see you next, I hope to find you more coherent and capable of forming some kind of plan for your future."

With that, he hustled from the room, the automatic door sliding open and then closing behind him to blend into the wall again. Preferring even Poindexter's company to solitary confinement, I attempted to follow. Whatever sensors reacted to his presence refused to respond to mine, however, and the door didn't open. I grasped and fumbled for a hidden mechanism but came up empty. I was trapped.

Don't panic! Whatever you do, don't panic, I ordered myself, retreating to the couch once more. My heart should have been pounding, and sweat breaking out in all the usual places. Yet my palms and forehead were dry and eerily cool. Stranger and stranger. It had to be a bad dream, I decided, but willing myself to wake up did no good.

-5-
Cora

Despite my altered state of body, my mind seemed to function normally. At least I was rational enough to see that, if Poindexter told the truth, this was the most extraordinary thing that had ever happened to me... to anybody, as far as I knew. *If it's true?* I couldn't believe I was actually considering the possibility.

Of everything Poindexter told me, though, the idea that I'd brought this on myself shocked me the most. Had I really wanted to die? I remembered thinking it, but in the same careless way I might say "I could kill you" to my brother when I was angry. I hadn't meant it – at least I didn't think I had – and I certainly never expected anybody to be listening in on my private thoughts. Let alone acting on them. If I had known, I would have been more careful.

I leaned back against the angular couch and closed my eyes.

"Hello, Mr. Lewis," said a sultry female voice.

I jumped. When I shot a glance around, no one was there, at least not in bodily form. Then something drew my attention across the room. As I stared, the wall seemed to come alive, flowing and shimmering like the surface of a lake on a bright summer morning. From it, the three-dimensional form of a young woman emerged, stepping into the room on four-inch heels.

"Hello, Mr. Lewis," she repeated, slinking toward me in a tight red bodysuit. "I'm Cora. It's my job to facilitate your successful passage through this Crossroads station. How may I help you?"

"Uh..."

Recent Stargate episodes should have prepared me for coming face to face with a real live hologram, but I could only stare with my mouth hanging open. This being, who called herself Cora, was a mesmerizing balance between the earthly and the ethereal. So human, yet I suspected if I tried to touch her, she would disintegrate into a thousand bits of stardust… or pixie dust… or something equally unsubstantial.

Whoever designed her had done an excellent job, though; she was *very* easy on the eyes. And her voice? Rich and smooth as melted chocolate. I could have listened to her talk for hours. Besides, I was desperate for company… and information.

"You can start by telling me where I am and what the hell's going on," I barked. "Sorry, I guess I'm a little upset."

Cora paused a few feet away, arms loosely crossed. She smiled at me, unperturbed. "A certain amount of disorientation is quite natural. Lean back and try to relax while I explain. I'm here to make this transition as easy for you as possible." I complied, and she went on. "Now, as I said before, I'm Cora," she cooed, sitting down at the opposite end of the sofa and draping one arm across the back. "May I call you Ben, or do you prefer something else? We're going to be spending a lot of time together, and I'd like you to think of me as your friend."

'Friend' was stretching it, but I said, "Ben is fine."

"Good. As to where you are, this is the Crossroads Center."

"Is this place part of heaven or…"

"No, no. We get that question a lot. This station is not associated with either heaven or hell in any way, except that ultimately we all operate under the same supreme authority. Crossroads is an independent agency set up for an entirely different purpose."

"You said 'this station.' Is it some kind of space station, then?"

"Not really, Ben. It's hard to explain, but it would be more correct to call it a time or dimension station. From here, we are able to access alternate realities and different points in time for our clients. That's why you're here. You were very unhappy with your former situation…"

She waved her arm toward the same wall she'd entered through, which retained its fluid form. A picture of a hospital room – *my* hospital room, I realized – appeared. I saw my body in the bed, hooked up to all the monitors and tubes I remembered. Then I heard my thoughts from that moment as clearly as if I'd spoken them aloud:

I don't have the strength to go on like this. I wish I could just go to sleep and never wake up. It was an accurate representation, I had to admit.

"...and so you were lifted out of that life and brought here," Cora continued. "Very few are chosen. It's considered quite an honor."

"Look, Cora, I don't mean to seem ungrateful, but I think there's been some mistake."

"Oh, please don't say that," Cora interrupted, suddenly looking worried. "It's important that you keep Mr. Poindexter on your side, Ben. Nothing upsets him more than accusations of error or wrong-doing. He takes great pride in his work here at the Center, and he's very efficient at his job. I'm sure that when you fully understand, you'll have no reason to question the decision that brought you here. You have been given a great gift, you know."

"That's what Poindexter implied, but I still don't think..."

I trailed off, my attention yanked back to the screen which continued to play the ongoing scene at the hospital. An alarm had sounded, and I saw nurses and doctors rushing to my bedside. They worked furiously over my body, injecting pharmaceuticals into the IV, performing CPR, and ultimately bringing out the defibrillator paddles.

"Is that really happening?" I asked Cora.

"Time is relative here, but it would be simplest to say it has *already* happened. What you see now are the events immediately following your exit from your former life, the moment you were lifted out of that place and brought here. If you find it distressing, I can discontinue the display," she offered, starting to lift her hand toward the image.

"No! Leave it."

I couldn't take my eyes off the spectacle. I stared with the same macabre fascination as someone witnessing a house burning to the ground or the aftermath of a train wreck. Only this was far more personal. As I watched, the workers continued their heroic efforts to revive me for several more minutes. At last, they gave up. A doctor called out the official time, and everyone began packing up their equipment.

"So I *am* dead," I said as I continued to look on.

"You shouldn't think of it that way, Ben," Cora soothed. "It's merely that your life force no longer exists in that time and place. Your essential being – your soul, if you like – is still very much alive. That's all that matters."

I was about to disagree when I heard – as did the medical team in my hospital room – a voice wailing from beyond our view.

"Ben! Ben!" the woman cried out. "Let me go to him! I have a right to see him."

Everyone stopped and looked at each other. The doctor in charge said grimly, "I'll take care of it." He left the room, and the others went on about their work, silently and methodically.

Another burst of anguish issued from the hallway. I knew who it was, of course. It was Abby, and she had just been told I was dead.

-6-
Options

"That's enough," I shouted, getting to my feet.

Cora turned off the display with a flick of her finger. "You seem upset, Ben," she remarked, unruffled.

"Of course I'm upset!" I stalked up and down the room. "Can't you do something for my wife? And my parents! Oh, God, this is going to kill them. Send me back! I don't care what happens to me, but you have no right to put my family through hell by hijacking my life."

Cora tipped her head to one side. "I'm sorry, but our work here only concerns *your* well-being. The client's friends and relatives are completely beyond our jurisdiction. Your loved ones will grieve for a time. Then they will go on. People do, you know."

"Just put me back the way I was, and we'll forget about the whole thing. No harm, no foul, okay?"

"I can't do that, Ben," she said evenly. "We follow strict protocol here at Crossroads. I'm afraid no exceptions are allowed. Don't worry, though; none of this is necessarily permanent. Even what you saw on the monitor may change depending on the choices you make from here on. You'll feel better once I clarify your options."

I closed my eyes and rubbed my forehead. Yet I couldn't erase what I had just seen and heard. I'd been so wrapped up in my own problems that I hadn't thought about how all this would impact others. Supposedly *I* could go on; *I* had "options." But what about my family? They had no choice. They would suffer and not even know why.

"Oh, what have I done?" I moaned.

"Ben?" said Cora gently. "Would you like me to explain?"

I lifted heavy eyes to her and relented. "All right. Let's get on with it."

"Yes, of course. Please sit down again."

Cora didn't continue until I obeyed.

"Now then, there are three primary pathways open to you. First, if you've had enough of the world and have no desire to return to it under any circumstances, you can move directly from here to the afterlife. This is a popular option with older folks who have already lost most of their family and friends, but I'm guessing it won't appeal to you."

Cora raised her eyebrows and waited.

I shook my head. "No thanks."

"Second, you can return to the world in a totally different existence – a different person, a different place, and even a different time period. You might choose to be present when the Magna Carta was signed or the Declaration of Independence framed; to fashion a new life for yourself in Botswana or Brazil; or even take your chances in the future. If you like, I can provide you with a menu of upcoming vacancies for whatever time, place, and situation interests you. The possibilities are endless. Of course, you can't expect to go back as a billionaire playboy or the king of an independent country. Those openings are few and far between. But we will come as close to your preferences as possible."

Once again, Cora paused for my reaction.

I shrugged. "I don't really think that's for me either."

"Very well. Your third option – and this one I think you'll like – is returning to your old life, but with the opportunity to make a change. Most people elect to go back to some critical point in time so they can undo a mistake or make a wiser choice for their personal or professional future – to avoid a disastrous drunk-driving incident for example, or perhaps to stay in school instead of dropping out. But you could change some characteristic of your body or personality instead, whatever you believe will give you the best outcome. In a recent case, one of our clients went back to his life, minus his life-long stutter, and began a very successful public speaking career. What do you think, Ben?"

"You mean you could make me… What? Taller, or smarter… or *healthier*?"

"Now you've got the idea," Cora said, returning my conspiratorial smile.

I was on my feet again and pacing, a million possibilities racing through my head. Yet it all boiled down to one thing in the end. "So, let's be clear about this. Could I choose to go back to college and pick up my life before I got sick, only this time I wouldn't get sick? Is that what you're saying?"

"Exactly."

"And everything else would stay the same: my abilities, my family, my friends?"

Cora nodded.

I looked her straight in the eye. "So what's the catch? It sounds too good to be true."

"No catch. You just have to agree to live with the consequences of your decision. Once you go back, you're pretty much on your own. Your success or failure will be up to you, and there's no guarantee that you'll be happier in the long run."

"I don't need a guarantee. Of course I'll be happier without Crohn's than with it; that's a no-brainer."

"Still, you must think your decision through very carefully, Ben. As I've said before, you have been given a great opportunity. Use it wisely."

Cora went to the wall that provided the visual display. A small panel slid open at her touch, revealing a compartment. From it, she pulled a tray holding what looked like a sheet of glass about ten inches square and half an inch thick. When she handed the tray to me, however, I could see that the object on it was not rock solid after all – more like a slab of super-thickened gelatin. I touched it with the tip of my finger, and the mass quivered in response, emitting a low hum.

"In your terms, it's a remote control for the wall screen," she explained. "When you rest the palm of your dominant hand on this plasma block, the organic microprocessors imbedded in it will sync with the electrical impulses generated by your body. It reacts to your thoughts and your slightest movements, directing the display in front of you. This system is here for your use, Ben, to help you research possibilities and make your plans. You can view any place or time you wish. Since you want to return to the past of your former life, I suggest you use it primarily to review events leading up to that point – to prepare yourself and to choose the right spot for your reentry."

I couldn't resist; I sat down to try it. My hand hovered just above the surface of the plasma a moment before touching down, then sinking into the cool gelatin as it conformed to the contours of my skin. The wall screen leapt to life with wild images and noise.

"Whoa!" I exclaimed, jerking my hand away. The screen went blank and silent again.

"Try again," Cora encouraged. "This time, quiet your mind first and focus. Start with something simple – some calm and peaceful experience from your past."

I closed my eyes, and a perfect example came to me.

I must have been about fifteen when my father woke me early one Saturday with a surprise invitation to go fishing, just the two of us. Careful not to wake my younger brother, I pulled on some clothes and tiptoed out of the house. Dad was loading the gear into the old Rambler station wagon he drove back then. I remember he was wearing his "lucky" hat and that awful, quilted flannel shirt Mom kept threatening to throw out. We grabbed a quart of milk and a box of doughnuts at the all-night grocery and reached the lake before dawn. With the morning mist swirling around us, Dad motored our skiff out to the middle and cut the engine. We just sat there in silence, drifting and watching the sun come up.

A decade later, I could still picture it clearly. I even heard the hum of insects and the water lapping at the sides of the boat. When I looked up, I found it had all materialized on the screen, complete with sound effects. It only lasted a few seconds. The instant I lost my concentration, the image swirled and vanished.

"Cool," I said, feeling like a kid with a new toy.

"Yes, you'll do fine, Ben," said Cora. "And you can spend as much time as you want with the system later. Set it aside for now, though. It's time you got out of this room and met some of your fellow travelers, don't you think?"

-7-
The Commons

Cora showed me how to operate the door to my room, and then she pointed down a long corridor. "Turn right at the end and you'll find the commons," she said. "It's a gathering area for all the clients at the center. Right now, we have twelve others in transition besides you. You're the newest arrival."

"Which makes me lucky number thirteen," I said. "Good thing I'm not superstitious or anything." In the doorway, I glanced back. "Are you coming, Cora?" I knew she wasn't exactly *real*, but at the moment she was the closest thing I had to a friend.

She smiled. "No, Ben. You go ahead. I'll see you later." With that, she strolled to the wall-screen and stepped through into it. As I watched, her form melted into the surface, becoming just as indistinguishable from the rest as a cup of water poured into a pond.

I was on my own, but I *was* glad to get out of that stark white room. Someone had taken a little more trouble with the décor in the commons where a colorful assortment of furniture had been set out in casual groupings.

As I entered, a dozen curious faces turned to look at me, actual human beings with welcoming expressions. I noticed we all wore the same uniform too (our white sweat pants and T-shirts), so I felt like I was about to meet my new teammates.

Before I could join the huddle, Mr. Poindexter intercepted me. "Ah, Mr. Lewis, there you are. We have been expecting you."

"We?"

"Yes, I informed the other residents of your arrival, and they are most anxious to make your acquaintance. It is quite an affable group. And our research shows that the sense of community provided by shared experience eases the clients' stress and disorientation. You understand."

"Sure. 'Strength in numbers' or 'misery loves company' – that sort of thing."

"Well... yes, I suppose so. At any rate, now that you have completed your first orientation session, you are free to move about our center as you please." He said this with a sweeping gesture of his arm.

I scanned my surroundings and wondered if I was missing something; there didn't seem to be much space for exploration. "So, what else is there to do here? With your technology, I bet you have an awesome entertainment system."

"Really, Mr. Lewis," Poindexter said with a sniff, "this is *not* a carnival arranged for your amusement. We do serious work here. I hope you will try to remember that." He cleared his throat. "Now, as I was saying, you may remain in the commons as long as you like and return to your room when you are ready. Time is relative here. Still you may find – as indeed do most of our clients – that adopting a fairly regular schedule is most comfortable. Although in your current state you have no physical requirement for food or sleep, the preference for routine over randomness is deeply ingrained in the human psyche."

He looked at me narrowly, daring me to disagree.

I shrugged. "Makes sense."

"Good. To assist our residents in this, the lights, both here and in your rooms, are dimmed for a recommended period of retirement to simulate normal patterns of rest and wakefulness. Naturally, it is only a suggestion. You are by no means obligated to abide by this schedule, but please be considerate of those of your fellows who do."

"Okay. Was there anything else? If not..."

"Only one more thing, Mr. Lewis. I believe you have already formed an opinion about your next move – which option you will select and how it should be arranged most satisfactorily."

"Yes, I know exactly what I want, and the sooner I get started, the better."

"You are to be congratulated on your decisiveness; this represents a great deal of progress since our last meeting. However, as much as I might personally like to oblige you by swiftly sending you on your way, we are both bound by certain constraints. It is my responsibility to ensure that Crossroads protocol is strictly observed, and the procedure manual is very clear on this point. A minimum of five cycles – we shall call them 'days' for the sake of simplicity – must be spent here pondering your choice. It is an irreversible decision and, therefore, not to be taken lightly. 'Act in haste; repent in leisure,' as the saying goes. Although I'm sure you know your own mind as well as anyone, Mr. Lewis, you will be expected to abide by the same guidelines as everybody else. Is that clear?"

"Perfectly. Don't worry about me, Poindexter. I can put up with your... your 'protocol' for five days if I have to."

He kept me standing there while he made an entry – for his eyes only – on his ever-present clipboard. Although I was a head taller and outweighed him by a good fifty pounds, he had an annoying way of making me feel like a kid in the principal's office again.

"Very well, Mr. Lewis, I think we are finished for now."

Dismissed, I left Poindexter in favor of my "fellow travelers," as Cora had called them. Rather than approaching the main group, I headed over to join a couple of guys who looked nearer my age than the rest. I hadn't even introduced myself, though, when a scraping of chairs and shuffling of feet began. The others left what they were doing to rearrange the furniture, forming one large circle to include me, the obvious focus of everyone's interest.

When they got settled again, an older woman spoke up.

"Welcome, young man, we always start with introductions when someone new arrives. My name is Mrs. Jensen. I'm seventy-six, and I was brought here to spare me a painful cancer death. I've selected option one. In fact, I'll be leaving tonight to join my husband in the afterlife," she finished with a flush of excitement.

The group clapped enthusiastically.

The man on Mrs. Jensen's left followed.

"I'm Richard Fegals, thirty-five. I was a messed-up addict. I'm goin' with option three 'cause I wanna get back to before I started using cocaine. You know – to see if I can make somethin' of myself this time." The others applauded their support, the same as before.

This continued all around the circle, each person telling his or her prior circumstances and future plans, if decided, all without apology or embarrassment. Like me, most intended to return to improve on their former lives. Two others were planning to use the second option to try something completely different. The remaining three, including Mrs. Jensen, were headed directly for the afterlife. At last, it was my turn. And even though I was still pretty sure this whole thing was bogus, that it would turn out to be a dream in the end, I decided to play along.

"Uh… I just got here, so this is all pretty new to me. Anyway, here goes. I'm Ben Lewis, twenty-seven. I had a disease that really screwed up my life. I intend to go back to when I was in college and live out what should have happened – would have happened – if I hadn't gotten sick."

I hoped that would be enough to satisfy their curiosity. It wasn't. After an encouraging round of applause, Jeff Kendall, a middle-aged former plastic surgeon, wanted to know what my illness had been. Other questions followed his. Had I been married? Any children? What was my profession? And, how did I expect my life to be different this time around?

My chance of rekindling a baseball career raised a lot of interest.

"You know, Ben," said Mr. Rutland, an elderly man on his way to the afterlife. "There was a time – long before you were born, it would have been – when I wanted to be a ball player too. Wanted it so-o-o *bad* I could feel it in my bones. Not for the money, mind you, because of course back then nobody was giving million-dollar contracts to kids still wet behind the ears, not like they do nowadays. No, I just loved the game, and I suppose I thought I was pretty hot stuff too. I was gonna show the world how baseball ought to be played." He shook his head, irony tugging at one corner of his mouth. "I sure had a lot to learn."

"What happened," I asked. "Did you ever get your chance?"

"Nah. The war came along about then, you see – the big one, WW2. Suddenly, baseball didn't seem so important after all. I enlisted right out of high school and got sent to fight in the Philippines. Won the Purple Heart. Picked up a little shrapnel in my leg there too – another permanent souvenir," he said, wincing in remembered pain as he flexed his knee. "When I got home, nothing was the same. The world had changed. *I* had changed. War does that to people." Mr. Rutland paused. "None of that matters now; it was all water under the bridge a long time ago. But I hope *you* get your shot, young fella, if that's your dream."

The conversation went on for what may have been hours, and I ended up telling those twelve former strangers about every important facet of my life. I felt as if, rather than a team, I had just joined a family.

When the lights dimmed and the gathering broke up, we parted with a clasp of hands or a hug. The most poignant goodbyes went to Mrs. Jensen. As I understood it, she would be spirited away during what passed for night around there, and we wouldn't see her again. The others seemed both happy she was getting what she wanted and sorry she was leaving. I didn't know her as well, of course, but I got choked up all the same. Plus, I couldn't help feeling she might have made the wrong decision.

I stopped her in the hall. "I'm curious, Mrs. Jensen. You could have chosen to go back and start over, to live a different life, to be young again. Why didn't you?"

"Yes, to be young once was wonderful. I still remember. But, for me, it would never be the same without my dear San. His name was Sanders, you see, but everybody called him San. He was the best part of my life. We'd been married over fifty years when he died. I've been lonely for him ever since, like the most important piece of me had gone permanently missing. You said you were married, Ben. Did you love your wife?"

A jolt of fresh pain reminded me how much. "Yes."

"Well then, you know what I mean. When I could be with San forever in heaven, starting tomorrow, why would I choose anything else?"

"I don't know. People around here keep saying what a great opportunity we've all been given. It just seems like kind of a waste not to use it."

"Oh, but you're looking at it all wrong. Just because I chose something different, doesn't mean it's any less valuable. I suppose I could have decided, as you have, to go back and never get sick with cancer. But why? It would only postpone the inevitable. I would just die of something else instead – maybe something even worse. No, don't be sad for me. I was ready to move on, and now it's like… Well, it's like instead of an economy-class seat on a long flight with six miserable stopovers, I've been given a non-stop, first class ticket." With arms posing as wings, she glided to her room, saying, "It's smo-o-o-th sailing all the way!"

Back in my room, I stewed over Mrs. Jensen's words. She – and Mr. Rutland too, for that matter – seemed so philosophical about dying, about crossing over to the afterlife. I couldn't understand all that cheerful resignation. I wanted to *live*, and on my own terms too.

But then, they were old and I was young. I supposed that accounted for the difference in how we viewed things.

I could relate to the old lady's talk about missing her husband, though. I ached for Abby, and I grieved for her suffering on my account. It made me more determined than ever to build a better life for us. Abby deserved to be taken care of. She deserved what I could never afford to give her on a teacher's salary. This time, I would make sure she had the best of everything.

-8-
Meditation

"Did you love your wife?" Mrs. Jensen had asked. It was an innocent question, yet one that haunted me. Abby and I had only been separated, what? – the equivalent of a day or maybe two? We'd been apart longer than that before, but this was different. The impenetrable barriers of time and space divided us now. Mrs. Jensen expected to be reunited with her soul mate that night. Who knew when I would be?

I'd been riding an emotional roller coaster. First, I discovered I was dead. Then, I found that wasn't necessarily true. My life was over... or was it just beginning? I thought I'd lost Abby forever. No, it turned out I had the chance to go back and make things with her better than before. The whole scenario was incredible; I'd say unbelievable except it was happening. It was a lot to take in, and I was exhausted.

Although genuine sleep was impossible, I lay down on the couch and got comfortable with the help of some brightly patterned pillows that had shown up while I was out. I tried to let my mind relax and drift, not thinking about anything in particular. I figured some kind of mantra would help, but all that came to me was, *There's no place like home. There's no place like home. There's no place like home.*

I'd grown up revering the opposite principle, as defined by the Star Trek mission statement (*To explore strange, new worlds... to boldly go where no man has gone before*, etc.). The fact that I was now channeling Dorothy instead of Captain Kirk was seriously disturbing. So, I gave up meditation and turned to mastering the display screen instead.

With the control tablet on my lap, I gently set my hand on its gel surface. This time, I was prepared for the chaos that first filled the screen. I stayed with it, though, focusing my mind on a pleasant memory of me and my kid brother, Scott, when we built a fort one summer in the woodsy vacant lot next to our house.

I recalled how we chose a strategic location between two giant cedar trees near the road. From there, we could covertly observe all enemy movements, having a clear line of sight to spy on our neighbors' houses as well as our own. For walls, we set out to appropriate several abandoned hay bales. Each one, we discovered, weighed approximately a ton after absorbing a month's worth of rain like a giant sponge. Scott and I had to give up the idea and substitute other materials – begged, borrowed, and stolen.

Initially, only flashes of this targeted memory materialized before me, interspersed with random impressions. One flinch of a finger or a distracted thought would break the flow. With practice, though, I learned to hold the picture in place for longer and longer periods, until I could watch an entire scene play out.

After working on our fort for nearly a week, it was almost finished. "All we need now is a roof," I said, surveying what remained of our scavenged resources. "There's nothing here that will work."

"We could use a whole bunch of branches," Scott suggested.

"That's a dumb idea. Branches would sag too much, and they wouldn't keep the rain out." I looked at the trees overhead. "I know. Let's tie those lower limbs down to the corners of the fort and stretch a tarp across them. Hand me that rope." He did, and I cut it in half with my pocket knife. "And bring me the ladder."

"It's too heavy for me," my eight-year-old brother whined.

"All right. I guess I'll have to do it myself. Sometimes I wonder why I let you into my fort, Scott; you're such a baby."

"I am not!"

"Yes, you are. Now, run back to the house and get the tarp. It's in the corner of the garage by the freezer. And don't let anyone see you. That's an order."

"Do you have to be so bossy?"

"Yes, I do. I've told you before, Private, giving orders is a general's job."

"When is it *my* turn to be the general?"

"You? You're too little to be a general! So you'd better do what I say, or I'll kick you out of the army and never let you play in the fort again."

Scott blinked back tears and obeyed.

I'd seen enough; I removed my hand from the controller and let the screen go blank. It was only then that I noticed Cora standing off to one side. This time, she was dressed in a blue sequined number.

"Where did you come from?" I asked.

"Oh, I just slipped in. I didn't want to interrupt. You were doing so well. Why did you stop?"

"There's something wrong with this thing," I said, indicating the controller. "It's supposed to read my thoughts, right?"

Cora nodded.

"But, what I was seeing – that's not how I remember it at all. I'm sure I was never that mean to my brother."

"I can explain. Your conscious memories are imperfect, Ben. This technology retrieves the accurate version of events from your brain's subconscious. That's what you saw just now – what really happened, not your distorted recollection of it. It's one reason we always advise our clients to review past events before returning to their old lives. The exercise can be very helpful in giving perspective and correcting misconceptions."

"You're saying I have a warped view of the past?"

"Everybody does."

"If this is a typical example, I guess I'll have some apologies to make when I see Scott again."

"You must decide that for yourself. I'm not here to judge; I'm here to assist. Now, do you need anything? Do you have any other questions or concerns?"

"Oh, thanks for the pillows, by the way. And I have been wondering something. When I go back, will I remember all this – what happened the first time around and about coming here, I mean?"

"An excellent question, Ben. I can tell you've put a lot of thought into this. The answer is yes; you will have your memories of the way your life originally unfolded and of what you experienced here, at least at first. All that will gradually fade away, though, until it seems like nothing more than a distant dream. The system is set up that way to spare our clients any long-term regrets over how things turn out, and also to maintain the confidentiality of the Crossroads operation. If people knew that such a place existed, they might become preoccupied with praying for a second chance rather than doing their best with the life they've been given."

"I see. Well, what about other people? Will they remember me or anything about my former life?"

"Everyone you've already met – everyone you met before the time you choose to return to, that is – will know you and remember what has gone before. But they will not share your familiarity with events beyond that point in time. For them, that's the future. It hasn't happened yet. You shouldn't attempt to explain your second chance to anyone either. It would only create confusion or worse. Think about it. Before experiencing it for yourself, what would you have said if one of your friends told you such a story?"

"I would have said he was crazy."

"Exactly."

"Okay. But, what about my wife? Abby and I didn't meet until later. Are you saying I'll be a total stranger to her? She won't re-member me? She won't remember that she loves me?"

"That's right."

"Then how can I be sure she'll want to be with me again?"

"You can't be absolutely certain. There are no guarantees, as I told you earlier. Still, you'll have a lot going for you. Your wife will be exactly the same person who learned to love you before. And this time you already know everything about her – where she will be and when, all her tastes and preferences, and what it was about you that attracted her in the first place. The odds are strongly in your favor."

"I suppose so," I agreed, but the whole idea made me uneasy just the same. I wasn't all that sure I *did* know why Abby had fallen in love with me the first time, let alone if I could reenact it. The laws of probability might be on my side, as Cora suggested, and yet it was something else that stuck in my mind. She'd said it twice now; there were no guarantees.

-9-

Retrospect

When Cora left me, I returned to the screen. I was hooked by then, yet almost afraid of what I might find out after the incident from my childhood I'd viewed earlier. It wasn't all bad, though – more of a mixed bag. The past turned out to be less idyllic than nostalgia had made it seem years later. But there were plenty of good times, especially with my brother – hours sitting on the floor together constructing Lego spacecraft and pirate ships or manipulating our favorite Transformers; secret military maneuvers ranging across the neighborhood's back fence lines; general mischief.

I gained a new sympathy and respect for my parents as I faced up to some of my bad behavior. A stray memory conjured up a day when I had been torturing poor Scott worse than usual. I must have been around fourteen and he was ten or eleven, judging from what I saw on the screen.

"That's enough!" Mom ordered at last. "Ben, go get your gear together. It's time to leave for swim team."

Her grave look communicated the fact that I was in trouble. I figured the inevitable lecture would come once we got into the car and I couldn't escape. We rode along in silence for several minutes. I sure wasn't going to say anything, and when Mom finally began, she was surprisingly calm.

"Ben, you weren't being very nice to Scott back there."

"I couldn't help it," I complained. "He gets on my nerves, always following me around like he does."

"Do you know *why* he does that?"

"Just to bug me."

"No, that's not it. Scott wants to be with you because he admires you, Ben. It's very natural for kids to look up to someone older who knows more and can do things they can't. Remember how you trailed after your cousin Chris at the family reunion last summer? You thought he was so cool because he had his driver's license already."

"I wasn't 'trailing after' Chris. We were hanging out together."

She gave me one of her "get real" looks. "Well then, keep in mind that your brother wants to hang out with you the same way. When you tease him like you were doing today, it hurts. How would you have felt if Chris treated you like that or told you to get lost?"

Mom let me ruminate on that uncomfortable question while she maneuvered through traffic. I couldn't justify my behavior... or even understand it. Although I would have rushed to defend my little brother against any outside threat, I reserved the right to bully him myself when it suited my mood.

"Look, Ben," she continued when we pulled into the parking lot at the pool, "There's nothing brave or clever about picking on a little kid. Besides, if you push Scott too far, you could permanently alienate him. That would be a real shame too, because, whether you know it or not, your brother is your best friend... and always should be."

Mom had it right back then, I reflected. Scott was still my closest friend, and he had been best man at my wedding.

That brought my mind around to Abby. With the controller still engaged, the thought instantly translated to an image from the day we were married. Suddenly, Abby beamed at me from the screen, transporting me back with her to that moment. I stood facing her at the altar again, holding her tiny alabaster hands in mine. Lord, she was beautiful... inside and out. I repeated the vows, barely hearing them. But I never forgot the way her sapphire eyes glistened, looking up into mine, and I can still smell the honey scent of the gardenia she wore in her hair.

A choking lump grew in my throat. Yet, I clung to the vision as long as I could, not daring to blink or breathe lest I accidentally dislodge it for something far less precious. The spell broke when the room lights flared to daytime brightness. I reluctantly set the controller aside and watched Abby's face slip away.

~~*~~

When I poked my head out of my door, I saw that the others were already streaming toward the commons, as if they couldn't wait. Funny how such a diverse cast of characters harmonized so well away from the world, whereas back in it, we'd have struggled to find any shared ground: the church lady and the tattoo artist; the doctor and the drug addict.

"Good morning, Ben," said Jeff Kendall passing by. "Are you coming?"

"Yeah, might as well." I joined him.

Stationed at the end of the hall, Poindexter checked us off as we entered the commons. "...Mr. Harris, good morning. Mrs. Cuthbert, nice to see you. And Dr. Kendall, very good. Mr. Lewis, yes..."

"He's taking attendance like we're a bunch of first-graders!" I whispered to Jeff. "I'd sure like to get a look at that clipboard of his. What secrets do you think he's got written there?"

"Search me, but he seems to know what he's doing. I find that reassuring."

"I guess. There's something about the guy that rubs me the wrong way, though."

Poindexter spoke out to the group. "I shall hold the daily announcements until everyone has arrived. Mr. Fegals, might I have a word? The rest of you may go about your business."

"So, how are you adjusting to all of this, Ben?" Jeff asked as we settled into seats across from each other. "You looked pretty shaken yesterday."

"It's a lot to take in."

"True. I've had more time to get used to the idea. This is my tenth day here."

"Really? I thought five was standard."

"That's the minimum, but you can stay longer if you want. I'm in no hurry. I have a lot of material to review and options to weigh."

"You said yesterday you planned to go back and take a different career path. Are you considering something other than medicine?"

"No, quite the opposite, as a matter of fact. I want to get back to the reason I became a doctor in the first place, before I got sidetracked. I went to medical school because I wanted to help people. Somewhere along the way, it became all about the money instead. I ended up performing nose jobs and breast implants for society snobs instead of using my training to ease human suffering. What a waste! I hope to do something more worthwhile this time around, to make a real difference. The only question is where and how I can do the most good. That's what I've been wrestling with. From here, I have access to information about places doctors are needed worldwide, past and present. The possibilities are endless."

"Wow. That's impressive. My goal is just to improve things for myself and my wife, not the whole planet."

"Sorry. I guess that sounded pretty pompous, that I think I can somehow change the world. I didn't mean it like that. I should have put my education to better use. That's all I'm saying."

"Yeah, that's cool. I get it."

Poindexter interrupted. "If I could have your attention, please, I have just a couple of announcements. For those of you who have inquired: yes, Mrs. Jensen did leave us last night, and I have received confirmation of her safe arrival at her destination. Also, we are expecting a new client soon – a young woman by the name of Hope O'Neil. She will be joining you tomorrow if all goes well. And lastly, let me remind you that anyone planning to depart tonight must see me now so that the necessary preparations can be made."

There was a collective pause. Then all eyes turned toward Kerri Andrews as she pushed her heavily pregnant body out of her chair and solemnly made her way toward Poindexter.

"Well, well," Jeff murmured. "Looks like Kerri's finally decided to take the plunge."

53

-10-
Another Possibility

"What's going on?" I asked Jeff in a whisper.

"I believe Miss Andrews is informing our Mr. Poindexter that she's ready to leave us. She's been here a lot longer than anyone else, trying to make up her mind about what option to take."

"Didn't she say she meant to do something about her unwanted pregnancy?"

"Yes, she was on the verge of suicide because of it when she was brought here. But she's been torn about the best solution."

We all waited in hushed suspense for Kerri to finish her business with Poindexter at the far end of the room, gathering our chairs a-round her when she returned.

"Well, Kerri, you've been awfully quiet the last couple of days," Jeff began. "Do you have some news for us now?"

Kerri, with her freckled, girl-next-door looks, appeared even younger than her twenty-one years. She smiled and averted her eyes. "Yes, I finally decided what I'm going to do."

"That's great," said Mrs. Cuthbert, and some of the others chimed in with encouraging words.

When everyone quieted down, Kerri continued. "Most of you know what a bad situation I came from – broke, pregnant, and alone. The only thing I was sure of when I got here was that having this baby would be a disaster. Since then, I've considered everything from starting over in a different time and place, to the obvious – turning the clock back nine months and taking preventive measures. I could never have an abortion, but I thought if I could cancel out the conception, that would be different.

"The thing is…" Kerri paused, rubbing her protruding belly with both hands. "The thing is, even though I could undo the pregnancy, I couldn't undo my knowledge of it. Maybe no one else would remember that this baby girl ever existed, but I would. That would haunt me, no matter where I went. Our memories are supposed to eventually fade, but wanting to forget seems like getting rid of her all over again. You see?"

Sympathetic heads nodded around the circle.

"So in the end, I decided to go back and pick up where I left off. I'm going to have the baby after all."

A ripple of surprise spread through the group.

"Good for you," said Mr. Rutland.

"I'm so glad, dear," added Mrs. Cuthbert.

Richard asked, "You gonna give the child up for adoption then?"

"I don't know for sure," Kerri answered, giggling with excitement. "I haven't figured that part out yet. I just know that I want this little girl to live." Her voice faltered. "And I'm not afraid anymore."

The group rallied around Kerri, offering support, information about agencies that might be able to help, and stories of similar situations with happy endings. Later, when Poindexter called her away to fill out the necessary paperwork, I pulled Dr. Kendall aside.

"Hey, Jeff, I didn't want to say anything in front of Kerri, but can she do that? Returning to pick up exactly where she left off, I mean? I thought that wasn't allowed."

"I'm not sure. A case like this hasn't come up since I've been here, and I never asked about the possibility myself; it wouldn't suit my needs at all. Kerri must have cleared it, though. Why? Are you interested?"

"Me? No, I was just wondering."

"You'll have to ask Poindexter about it then, or better yet, see Cora."

"Yes, I'd much rather see Cora." I gave a long, low whistle. "She's a real looker."

Jeff broke into hysterical laughter.

"What's so funny?" I finally asked.

"I'm sorry, Ben. I agree Cora's a fine specimen for her age – very nicely put together, as a matter of fact. But I would have thought she was a little too... too 'mature' to catch *your* eye. Or do you have a secret thing for middle-aged women?" he teased.

"Middle-aged?"

"She's got to be forty if she's a day."

"No way!" Then I understood. "Oh. So when she appears to you, she's..."

"...a well-seasoned brunette with a saucy little twang in her voice."

"I prefer my version: a sexy twenty-something blonde."

"To each his own, I guess. It's all part of the personalized service."

Jeff and I joined the others again, and eventually Kerri reappeared as well. I was too distracted with my own thoughts to focus on the conversation around me, though. I kept wondering how soon the lights would dim, signaling a breakup of the conclave. John "Bruiser" Harris was relating an anecdote from his former life as a professional wrestler when my impatience got the best of me. I shot to my feet, interrupting his colorful story.

"Excuse me," I said, "but I'm really tired. I think I'll head to my room a little early. Kerri, best of luck with the baby and all. Night, everybody." I turned to go, and a chorus of goodnights followed me out of the commons.

By myself at last, I paced my room, head down in concentration. I'd told the others I was tired – the sort of excuse I would have used on earth, but it hardly applied here. In truth, I felt far more agitated than tired.

"Can you hear me, Cora?" I yelled, wishing I had a call button to summon her. She had always just appeared on her own before. "I need to talk to you, Cora!"

"There's no need to shout, Ben," said a buttery-smooth voice behind me. I spun around to find Cora already materialized and adjusting her impossibly short skirt. "I heard you the first time. Now, what's the problem?"

One look at her – this time in hot pink with huge, white polka dots – took the edge off my anger. It was her most outrageous outfit yet. "That's an... an interesting dress you're wearing, Cora."

"Do you like it? I picked it out especially for you. I also added a few things to your room to make it a little homier. Did you notice?"

I hadn't. Looking around, I saw the new coffee table and then the painting on the wall opposite the door. Pointing, I said in amazement, "That's the picture..."

"Yes, I know – the one you and your wife bought when you went to Victoria last year."

"For our anniversary, right. We found it in this little gallery and just had to have it. I don't know much about art, but there's something about this painting… the colors, or the clouds."

"It gives you a very peaceful feeling."

"Exactly."

"Which is why I thought you should have it with you now. You looked a little tense a minute ago, Ben. What's wrong?"

"Oh, yeah," I said, recalling my complaint and some of the anger that went with it. "I want to know why you lied to me."

"I would never do that, Ben."

"You told me when I got here that it's against official policy to put people back where they were before. Yet that's exactly what Kerri Andrews is planning."

"No, that's not quite correct. It's true that when you asked me to send you right back, I couldn't comply with your request. But the reason was because every client is required to stay here at Crossroads for at least five days before choosing when and where they want to go after that. I thought Mr. Poindexter explained the waiting period to you."

"He did, but…"

"Once you've fulfilled that requirement, you're free to return to your old life if you wish, to any point in time from conception to the moment before you were lifted out and brought here."

"You never explained that part."

"There didn't seem any need to. Once you heard your options, you knew immediately what you wanted – to return prior to your medical problems and pursue your lost baseball career. Isn't that so? If you'd prefer, though, you can go back at a later date and still be free of your illness. The difference is that instead of the disease being prevented altogether, you would be cured of it at that point in time, still avoiding the surgery that upset you so much."

"But by then, a lot of damage would already be done."

"You would know best about that, Ben, and the decision is yours entirely."

A whole new range of options – and excruciating choices – opened up as I considered the ramifications. If I went back before my illness as originally planned, I wouldn't be reunited with Abby for a long time, and I ran the real risk of losing her altogether. If I returned after Abby and I were married, I could be with her in just a few days, but I forfeited any chance of resurrecting my dream of playing pro ball. Anywhere in between, and I was just as likely to lose as to secure both the things that meant so much to me. Suddenly, I wasn't so sure of myself.

-11-
Deliberations

I looked at my dilemma from every angle, but found no simple answers – only more questions. Logic told me I should first focus on my career, and that everything else would fall more easily into place once I was successful there. Or was that a sign my priorities were screwed up? Was I being selfish? Maybe I should sacrifice my baseball ambitions once and for all. Would that be best for Abby and me in the end? Even if true, I wasn't sure I could ever be content knowing I'd thrown away the golden opportunity to try for a better life.

Tough questions with sticky moral overtones. I longed to talk them through with someone I trusted implicitly – with Abby. If she didn't have the answers, I had a feeling she'd at least know where to look. Although I hadn't always appreciated her strong views on God and right versus wrong, now I needed all the help I could get. I was in unfamiliar waters right up to my chin, and I didn't know which direction to swim. The thought of being free of my illness and with Abby again so soon was nearly irresistible. Yet it seemed cowardly – like taking the easy way out – to give up my dream and slink back home with my tail between my legs just because the alternative involved patience, hard work, and a little risk. Anything worthwhile was worth fighting for; I believed that was true.

I leaned first one way and then the other. Finally giving up the struggle, I turned to the video screen purely for distraction, letting my mind wander from scene to scene. If I hit on something useful by chance, fine.

As I rambled through my memories, up popped the first time I met Abby's parents.

We'd been dating steadily for a few months, and it was time. So Abby brought me home to dinner one night. I felt my shoulders tense as soon as I got a look at the Albrights' quasi-mansion in Seattle's Magnolia neighborhood.

"You never mentioned your family was so wealthy," I said as I parked my ten-year-old Toyota Corolla in the steep, brick driveway.

"I didn't think it was important."

"I hope you're right. Am I at all what your parents had in mind for you?"

She grimaced.

Not a good sign. "Come on, Abby. You'd better tell me, whatever it is."

She hesitated. "All right, but promise you won't make too much of it. I probably wouldn't have thought of it myself except for Valentine's Day being so near."

"Now you've lost me," I confessed, turning off the car.

"I guess I never told you about Paul."

"No. Paul who?" My built-in radar pinged wildly at the hint of a potential rival encroaching on my territory.

"Ruston – very close family friends. Anyway, Paul and I had known each other since we were kids, and our parents made no secret of the fact that they hoped we would end up getting married. That's all."

"Is that what he wanted too?" I asked, feigning casual curiosity.

"I guess," she said, dropping her eyes. "I didn't feel that way about him, though. Then he died – on Valentine's Day a year ago, hit by a truck as he crossed the street in front of the Health Sciences building on campus."

"Oh, Abby! I'm so sorry," I said, ashamed of the flush of relief I felt. I rubbed her arm. "It must have been awful for you. Was he coming to see you when it happened?"

"Apparently. It was just before noon, and he was carrying a boxed lunch for two along with a dozen red roses. If only…" Tears glistened in her eyes. "Look, Ben, I'd really rather not talk about it anymore."

"Of course," I said, leaning over to kiss her cheek.

"And you shouldn't worry about my parents," she continued, forcing a smile. "They're going to love you."

"Right."

Abby gave my hand a squeeze as we came up the front walk. I stole another kiss from her on the porch to further fortify my spirits.

"Better?" she asked, grinning up at me from within the fold of my arms.

"Yeah, I just needed a reminder of why I'm doing this."

Abby rang the bell to announce our arrival and then led me in without waiting for an answer. "Hello. We're here," she called out.

Mr. and Mrs. Albright only had eyes for their daughter at first, greeting her affectionately if more formally than would have been the case at my house. I was glad for a moment to take in my surroundings – a large, vaulted foyer with hand-textured walls and a floor tiled in some kind of expensive-looking stone. I suddenly felt underdressed in my jeans and polo shirt.

"Mr. Lewis," said Mrs. Albright, turning to me. Except for her subdued manner, she appeared an older copy of her daughter.

"Call me Ben," I said.

"As you wish. I'm Judith and this is Gail's father Franklin."

The name "Gail" sounded strange to my ear, even though I knew that's what Abby's family called her.

"Nice to meet you, sir."

Mr. Albright, a bear of a man, mumbled a civil reply and stuck out his meaty hand to take mine. His rock-solid grip and no-nonsense expression told me everything I needed to know.

"Well, dinner won't be ready for a bit yet, so let's make ourselves comfortable in the living room," suggested Mrs. Albright, showing the way up a broad, half flight of stairs. Her husband followed, and Abby and I brought up the rear.

At the top, we stepped into an oversized room at the back of the house.

"I want to show you something, Ben," Abby said, pulling me toward the wall of windows at the far end. A stunning view of Puget Sound and the Olympic Mountains spanned the horizon over the tops of the few trees that clung to the bluff below. "Isn't it wonderful? On a clear day, I could sit and stare for hours. There's always something to see. Look at that sailboat coming around the point. I'd love to try sailing sometime. Wouldn't you?"

"Actually, I get seasick."

"Oh, too bad! Well, we'll just have to enjoy the sight from solid ground, then. The sunsets from here are amazing too."

"I can believe it. It's a million-dollar view."

"More than that," Mr. Albright added dryly from behind me, "according to my property tax assessment. State must have its pound of flesh." He strode over to a polished mahogany cabinet. "Drinks, everyone? Ben, what will you have?"

"Oh, no thanks. I'm fine."

"You kids are over twenty-one. No harm in a little nip before dinner," he chided. "Purely medicinal, of course."

"Thanks, Daddy. Maybe a glass of white wine," suggested Abby.

"Coming up." Her father began pulling out bottles and glassware. "And you, Ben?" he asked over his shoulder.

"Nothing, sir, really. The stuff doesn't agree with me."

Abby and I sank into a sofa across from the armchair Mrs. Albright had taken.

"I suppose that's a carryover from your athletic training," she said. "Gail told us you used to be quite a good ballplayer."

"That's right; I used to be."

"College athletics. Stepping stone to better things, if you know how to cash in," said Mr. Albright. "That's how I got my start. Did Gail tell you?"

"Uh… no. I guess it never came up."

"But now you're going to teach," he stated, handing his wife and Abby each a half-full wine glass before sitting down in the other armchair with something on the rocks for himself.

"That's the plan – high school English… but I'd like to do some coaching as well."

A natural pause stretched into an uncomfortable silence. I scanned the room for something I could comment on intelligently. "This is a great place you have here," is what came out instead.

The lady of the house accepted my clumsy compliment. "Thank you. I'd be happy to give you a little tour before dinner if you'd like," she offered.

"Oh, Mom," Abby responded, "I'm sure Ben's really not that interested."

"Nonsense, Gail. He won't mind if I borrow him for just a few minutes. Shall we?" Mrs. Albright invited, rising.

Clearly no graceful way of escape. "Love to," I said.

"Good." She ushered me out. "You'll see the dining room in a few minutes, and I don't dare disturb Mrs. Avila in the kitchen. So let's start downstairs."

She showed me the enormous rec room (complete with home theatre, bar, and nine-foot pool table), and then the guest suite, followed by the office and gym. Most of the rooms opened out to the manicured back lawn and the view beyond. A spark animated Mrs. Albright's otherwise placid face as she explained her decorating choices, the importance of design, and the mystifying distinction between the various styles of furniture. It was all lost on me. She could just as well have been speaking in Swahili.

Back on the main level, the tour continued in the music room, where a shiny, black, baby grand took center stage. "Gail had lessons on this piano every week for seven years," she told me, sliding her hand along the closed lid of the instrument.

No dust, I noticed.

"I can't get her to play at all anymore. Still, I couldn't bear to leave this behind in Tulsa. I don't think a home is really complete without a piano. Do you have any musical talent, Ben?"

"Not a drop. My brother plays tenor sax, though."

"Now, our dear Paul…" She sighed. "He was a true artist. This piano never sounded better than when he played it. I suppose Gail told you what happened."

"Of course." I didn't add that it was less than an hour before.

"Just a year ago this month." She trailed off with another sigh.

I felt obligated to say something. "A real tragedy."

"Yes, it's such a senseless waste. Paul could have accomplished so much with his talent and his medical degree. This is his picture," she said, holding it up for me to see. "I like to keep it here on the piano to remind me of him. He was almost a member of the family… and *so* devoted to Gail. We all had very high hopes for them." She placed the sterling silver frame back in its place and turned to me. "I'm sorry. That was rather tactless of me, wasn't it?"

"It's okay. Sounds like he was a great guy."

"He was. Oh, but so are you, I'm sure. My daughter has excellent taste, and she seems very fond of you. Tell me more about yourself, Ben…"

We got through the rest of the evening without disaster. That's all I could have asked under the circumstances. I think the Albrights warmed up to me a little in the months that followed. With them, it was kind of hard to tell. If they were disappointed with Abby's choice to marry me, they never said so… at least not to my face.

-12-
Group Discussion

It was my third "day" at the Center, and I was familiar with the drill. The house lights came up, and the residents began spilling out of their rooms, flowing down the corridor, and pooling in the commons under the watchful eye of Andrew Poindexter. Once assembled – our number now down to eleven – he informed us that Kerrie Andrews had gone and that Hope O'Neil's arrival would be postponed a day. Announcements over, we were left on our own.

Since indulging in memories of Abby the night before left me no closer to a decision for my future, I planned to throw the question out to the group. My new friends gathered around and I spilled my guts. "…So you see, it isn't as straight forward as I thought," I finished.

"Basically, you gotta choose between your wife and your career 'cause you probably can't have 'em both," summarized Richard Fegals.

I felt my heart give a lurch, and I stared at Richard with my mouth hanging open. Is that really what it boiled down to? I hadn't even allowed myself to go there.

"No, no," objected Jeff. "As a matter of fact, I think Ben has a very good chance of achieving both. There's no reason to assume that the two goals are mutually exclusive."

Karen Altman, a thirty-something dental hygienist, joined the discussion. "I agree. If you and Abby are meant to be together, then it'll all work out."

"Yeah," 'Bruiser' Harris added. "You gotta take your shot, man. And when you make it big, you'll have your pick of Abby or any other girl you want. Chicks really go for athletes."

"Life is full of hard choices, Ben," said Mr. Rutland. "I hope you'll keep in mind that there are things far more important than baseball."

"Like true love," said Karen.

"And trying to make the world a better place," Jeff added.

"But Mr. Rutland, you must know how I feel," I said. "Didn't you ever resent losing your baseball career because of the war?"

"I would be lying if I told you I *never* did. On the whole, though, I don't regret it. Which do you imagine makes me proudest – my old batting average or knowing I saved lives on the battlefield?"

"I think you have to follow your dream," said former life insurance agent Ken Fielding. "Isn't that why we were brought here? Not to play it safe, but to do something bigger and better?"

"Nobody else can know what's best for you, Ben," said Mrs. Cuthbert. "Not one of us has all the answers. Trust God to guide you down the right path, and you'll do fine."

Everybody had an opinion, and they all meant well. Yet their lack of consensus only added to my confusion.

By the next day, nothing had changed. The fresh buzz that morning was entirely thanks to Hope O'Neil. Citing Crossroads' privacy policy, all Poindexter would tell us about her was her age: nineteen. We learned more when she joined us after finishing orientation with Cora.

"Hi, y'all. I'm Hope!" she announced, as if introducing herself at a beauty pageant. She would have fit right in – perky, pretty, and impeccably groomed.

"Welcome, Hope," said Jeff. "Have a seat."

She took the empty chair between Mr. Rutland and me.

"Thanks! This is so exciting," she gushed, looking around at all the new faces. "Isn't Mr. Poindexter super? And I just adore Cora. I can hardly believe this place is for real and that I'm actually here. What happens next?"

Mr. Rutland led off the introductions, which followed around the circle just the same as when I arrived. Hope answered with a believable "pleased-to-meet-you" after each person spoke. When I finished, it was her turn.

"Well, as I was saying, I'm Hope. I'm nineteen, and I was brought here just as I was about to die anyway. Apparently, in another millisecond I would have been clunked on the head with a chunk of blue ice the size of a picnic ham."

Karen Altman gasped at the news; others murmured their wonder and surprise.

"It's true," Hope confirmed.

"It is possible," said Ken. "Things like that happen. A gasket on an airliner leaks toilet water, which freezes at altitude, busts loose, and plummets to earth like a meteorite. In my business, you hear of every possible way there is to die, but the odds on that one are incredibly long, Hope."

"Leave it to me to find the most ridiculous way to expire known to man. My gym teacher always did say I was accident prone."

"I don't know how you can joke about it," Karen said. "It sounds awful, and you're so young."

"I didn't feel a thing. Besides, now that I'm here, I plan to cash in on option two – a completely new life. I don't have any family, or much else to go back to. Plus I've always felt like I was born in the wrong place and time. So, here's my big chance to fix up the mix-up! Is that great or what?"

Hope's attitude amazed me. She treated death like a day at Disneyland; no time to be sad that the *Pirates of the Caribbean* ride is closed for repairs when you're already anticipating the thrill of *Space Mountain*. "What kind of new life do you have in mind?" I asked.

"I haven't worked out the details yet. But I might try England – say around 1800 – you know, because I'm such a huge Jane Austen fan and all. The main thing is I want to finally be part of a real family. You're so lucky to have that, Ben. If I had family of my own, I wouldn't dream of leaving them behind. Both my parents died, though, and I don't have any siblings, a boyfriend, or even a flea-bitten hound dog to miss me."

Hope's story reminded me to be grateful for a life worth going back to. The question was still *when*?

~~*~~

Returning to my room that night, I found a collection of books added to the coffee table – Cora's doing, no doubt. I had the *Dune* series, a sampling of Isaac Asimov, and some *Tom Swift* (my childhood favorite), along with a Bible and a volume called *Scenic Washington State*. I picked up the last and absently flipped through the glossy photos covering everything from the Palouse country east of the mountains to the Long Beach peninsula on the southwest coast.

Shannon Winslow

As I dropped the book back on the table, Cora popped in. This time her outfit was strictly conservative... except for the outrageous hat (shades of Carmen Miranda after a pillow fight).

"Hi, Ben. I wanted to check and see if there was anything I could do for you."

It was hard to focus on her words with that tropical concoction of fruit and feathers bobbing up and down on her head.

"Tomorrow's your fifth day," she continued. "I hate to think you could be leaving us so soon, though."

"Yeah, I'll miss you too. I've never met anyone quite like you before, Cora."

"I'll take that as a compliment. Seriously, though, is there anything else you need? I've done my best, but I might have overlooked something."

"I have a feeling you don't miss much around here, Cora. You sure have my tastes nailed," I said, gesturing toward the books. "All I need now is to make up my mind, and no one can do that for me."

"I want you to be comfortable here, Ben, and to stay as long as you like. I brought you the departure request form for whenever you *are* ready to go, though. The video system can help you isolate the precise date and time that will work best for you, but there's absolutely no rush."

No rush, yet I was impatient to get on with it. Again I spent most of the night browsing through my memories with the use of the video display, hoping to stumble on a signpost to point me in the right direction. Maybe because of what Hope had shared about having no parents, I fell to reviewing recollections of mine.

One day, when I was sixteen, I came home on the athletic bus carrying some bad news.

"Hi, hon. How was your day?" Mom asked as I burst into the kitchen. She sat at her desk, paying bills.

"Fine." I dumped my backpack on a chair, poured myself a glass of milk, and grabbed a handful of Oreos from the cupboard.

"Did you have a good practice after school?"

"Yeah, I hit a home run off of Frazier. Man, was he ever pissed."

"Watch your language, please!"

"Sorry." I dropped my progress report on the table. "You need to sign this, Mom." She rose to retrieve the paper. "It's just my mid-

67

term report card," I said, already half-way out the room and bracing for what I knew was coming.

"What's this? Ben, come back here."

I headed for the stairs. Mom would have been right behind me except that luckily my father walked in the front door and intercepted her.

"What's the matter, Jan?" Dad asked. "Aren't you glad to see me?"

Safely out of sight on the landing, I stopped to listen in and learn my fate.

"Of course, dear, but we have a situation. Look at Ben's report card!"

A short pause.

"How did he explain it?"

"He didn't! He just left this on the table and went off to his room. I was going after him when you came in."

"Why don't you let me handle it instead?"

"If you'd rather. What will you say to him?"

"All the same things you would, I'm sure. Don't worry. I'll have a little man-to-man talk with him and get this squared away."

"There's no need to be *too* hard on him, I suppose. But he has to start taking his grades seriously if he's going to get into a good college. Ben has so much potential…"

I didn't hang around to hear any more. I was just relieved I'd be spared – at least for the moment – the look of disappointment on my mother's face. Dad, I could deal with. He knocked on my door fifteen minutes later.

"Come in," I said, figuring I might as well get it over with. I stood to face him.

"Hey, kid. How's it going?"

"Not too good if you've been sent to deal with me."

"No one sent me, but we do need to talk. Your mother is very upset about your report card, Ben. I'm sure that comes as no surprise. So, what's going on with your grades?"

"I don't know. I guess I've been a little distracted lately, with Jessica and baseball and everything. It's really no big deal, though. It's not like I'm shooting for valedictorian of my class or anything."

"True," Dad said, chuckling. "We'll leave that sort of thing to your brainy little brother. No one – except your mother, maybe –

looks for you to be an intellectual giant. What you've got going for you is far better. After all, it's the sports heroes, not the desk jockeys, who get the big bucks… and the pretty girls, eh?" he finished, giving me a nudge with his elbow.

"Right, Dad. As for college, I've been wanting to talk to you about that. It seems like a waste of time to me."

"No, now there I have to side with your mother. You've got serious talent, Ben. Anyone can see that. But you'll get better offers after a couple more years of seasoning and high-profile exposure. Besides, college is a great experience; best years of your life. Don't worry too much about your grades. Just keep them high enough that you're not risking your eligibility. I'll smooth things over with your mom. She wants you to get into a good school, and you've got no problem there. Colleges will be falling all over themselves to recruit you, with or without a stellar grade point. A-students are a dime a dozen, but athletic talent like yours is rare."

Dad was right, of course. The scholarship offers poured in despite my mediocre grades. By contrast, poor Scott was left pretty much out in the cold when his turn came, even with a far more impressive GPA and musical talent to boot. My brother protested against the injustice of the system, but I had no complaints.

In the class-sensitive climate of high school, I'd been popular. No mystery why; I knew it was because I was a star athlete, a jock. A hottie like Jessica wouldn't have looked twice at me otherwise. She told me so herself and later proved it by ditching me as soon as the promise of any further accolades evaporated. Without athletics, I was a nobody, at least to most people.

Abby had somehow managed to see beyond that – a credit to her character rather than to mine, I'm sure. Yet sometimes I wondered how long even she could be satisfied with such a painfully average existence. She deserved the good life. I wanted to be the one who provided it and shared it with her.

That's what my decision actually boiled down to. It wasn't only about me. It was about what was best for Abby, and for our future together. It didn't matter what I had to do, how hard I had to work, or how long it took. Abby was worth it. Making her happy would be my reward. And no obstacle would seem too daunting once my health was restored.

I'd nearly made up my mind; all I needed was confirmation. I glanced at the Bible on the coffee table. God and I hadn't been on the closest footing the last few years, but I figured if he'd brought me to this place for a particular purpose, He might be willing to give me a sign... for Abby's sake if not for my own. I took the leather-bound book in hand, and, muttering a little prayer first, I let the tissue-thin pages fall open somewhere in the middle. When I looked down, my eyes immediately caught on these words from the twenty-ninth chapter of Jeremiah:

"For I know the plans I have for you," declares the Lord, "plans to prosper you and not to harm you, plans to give you hope and a future."

The verse had a familiar ring to it, so I'd undoubtedly heard it before. And the message seemed a clear answer to my question. If God intended to prosper me, then why should I hesitate? Placing the Bible back on the table, I picked up the form Cora left and began filling it out, taking special care with the most important point: the exact place and time for my return. With that done, I felt a huge weight lift from my shoulders. I would see Poindexter first thing in the morning and be on my way by the following night.

-13-
Farewells

As usual, Poindexter supervised everyone's arrival at the commons the next morning. I discreetly handed him the departure request form, and, to my relief, he took it without comment. For some reason, I wasn't quite ready to make a public announcement about leaving. Maybe I didn't want anybody questioning my newly formed decision before it had a chance to fully solidify in my own mind. No rush. There would be time enough later to explain and say goodbye.

As I looked around the circle of now-familiar faces, I couldn't help regretting that this would be my last day as part of the group.

"You're awfully quiet this morning," Jeff, who sat to my left, remarked a while later. "A lot on your mind?"

"Exactly," I mumbled.

"Want to talk about it?"

"Not really."

A while later, Poindexter called from the doorway. "A moment of your time, Mr. Lewis, if you please."

I jumped out of my chair as if jolted by a cattle prod. Although I'd been expecting the summons, it still managed to startle me. Inquiring looks flew at me from all sides as I excused myself. Explanations would have to wait until I returned from my meeting with the man in the white suit.

Poindexter led me down a corridor running in the opposite direction from the one that gave access to the client rooms. His deliberate pace and solemn silence left me with the strange impression that I was being marched to my doom – the firing squad or the hangman's noose. Instead, he ushered me into his neat-as-a-pin office. As far as I could see, not a single file or paper clip was out of place.

"So, I understand that you have every intention of leaving us tonight, Mr. Lewis."

"That's right."

"Very well. Before you go, though, we have some paperwork to complete. We run a tight ship here at Crossroads – every "i" dotted, every "t" crossed."

"Exactly what I have come to expect from you, Poindexter: proper protocol above everything else."

The tone of my remark was not lost on the man. He had his revenge soon enough, handing me a raft of legal-sized papers with a smirk of satisfaction. The lengthy document, every inch of it covered with actual "fine print," read like a will and a release for experimental medical treatment combined.

"I'm supposed to wade my way through all this legal mumbo-jumbo?" I asked. "You've got to be kidding."

"Do I look like I'm kidding?"

He didn't.

"Come now, it won't be as painful as all that. Have a seat over there and get started. Most of our clients manage very well on their own. However, if *you* have difficulty, I will be more than happy to assist you. We want to get you on your way as soon as possible, now don't we?"

True enough.

When he saw that I didn't intend to give him any further trouble, Poindexter sat down behind a large desk and went about his business.

I likewise ignored him to tackle the task before me. Although the contract wasn't exactly an easy read, it turned out to be more manageable than I expected – pretty standard legalese stuff. *Whereas the party of the first part, henceforth known as "the client"* blah, blah, blah... *Being of sound mind, I do hereby give my informed consent... and agree to hold blameless the Crossroads Center and its agents,* etc. etc. Kind of pointless, I thought. It's not like I would have any way of filing a successful lawsuit against Poindexter or the Center if things went horribly wrong.

After the liability release, I came to the section outlining my specific wishes. The blanks had been neatly filled in, stating that I would be cured of Crohn's and returned to my former life on the exact date, time, and place I had requested, right down to the detail that I was to be dressed in my PJs and deposited in bed. I did the calculations in my head one more time to be sure the date was correct. Everything seemed in order.

Examining each article, clause, and addendum, I initialed where required as I went along. I didn't run into any problems until I read the last two conditions of the contract.

"What's this in article six?" I asked.

Poindexter looked up from his work.

"It says you are allowed to recall me to the Center at your discretion, should my presence 'ever be deemed necessary for educational purposes.' What's that about?"

"Yes, occasionally we do summon back a former client if that person is uniquely qualified to assist in transitioning one of our current residents. I think it quite unlikely in your case, though, Mr. Lewis. In all events, any interruption would be brief and non-disruptive. A reasonable man could not object, surely."

"And this last part, the non-interference clause?"

Poindexter sighed and began tapping his pen on the desk. "I should have thought that was fairly self-explanatory. It applies to all clients traveling into the past. It simply stipulates that you may not use your knowledge of the future for financial gain or in an attempt to change the course of history. Obviously, your own personal path will alter and inadvertently affect others to a limited and quite manageable degree. But no deliberate interference is allowed."

"How can you possibly enforce that? Is there going to be somebody following me around and reading my mind?"

"Although you will be completely unaware of it, your progress will be monitored, yes. Should it become necessary, you will be deprived of your memory to prevent any further policy violations of that kind. I expect even *you* can appreciate the need for such safeguards. There's nothing sinister about it. One client run amuck could do incalculable damage, and that we simply cannot permit." He paused, allowing his measured glare to carry his point home. "Do you understand and agree to these terms?"

"Do I have any choice?"

"Not really, no."

"Then I guess I do."

"Excellent. Please sign at the bottom." He came and hovered over my shoulder, waited while I scribbled my name one last time, and then triumphantly swept the completed paperwork out from under my pen. "We are done here, Mr. Lewis, and you are free to go. Cora will come round to your room tonight to be sure you are sent smoothly on your way, but you and I need not see each other again. I wish you a very successful journey. Goodbye."

He held out his bony hand, and I shook it.

"So that's it?" I asked.

"Yes, why? Were you expecting something more? Trumpet fanfare or perhaps a parade?"

"Of course not. But it *is* a pretty big deal."

"For you, undoubtedly so. Though you must understand that for those of us who work here, your departure is a routine matter. One client leaves us and another arrives; it happens every day. It would be absurd to treat each person as some sort of celebrity or to give way to sentiment when he or she moves on. Don't you agree?"

"Yeah. We wouldn't want you going all mushy on us, Poindexter. Still, I think it would be hard for some people to maintain their emotional detachment." I paused for his response. Nothing. "So I guess they found the right guy for the job."

An unreadable expression crossed Poindexter's face. Then he cleared his throat saying, "Quite. Well, good day, Mr. Lewis."

Had I seen a small chink in the man's Teflon-coated exterior? For a moment, I thought so. But I had been dismissed, so I went, went back to the commons where the group waited for me with a host of questions. They listened respectfully as I outlined my plans and the reasons for my decision.

"It's what I would have done in your shoes," said Ken Fielding.

"Right on, brother," Richard agreed. "Don't give up the dream."

Jeff gave me a thoughtful nod.

"I wish you all the best, Ben," said Mrs. Cuthbert. "And hang on to that verse God gave you, no matter what happens."

"We're going to miss you, my boy," added Mr. Rutland.

"You'll be leaving soon yourself, won't you?" I asked him.

"I expect so. I can't be much more use around here. Still, I'll be sorry to leave the place in some ways – the people, mostly. It's been a privilege getting to know each and every one of you."

I felt the same way.

I was glad when the conversation moved on; I'd been the center of attention long enough. Hope O'Neil assumed that place next without even trying. Her effervescent personality and quirky expressions made her an instant crowd favorite.

"I'm totally impressed, Ben, that you could put together such a logical plan for yourself," she said. "Me, I'm so gosh darn dazzled by all the possibilities, I can't think straight." She went on, addressing the group at large. "You know how I was saying yesterday that I was thinking about starting my new life in Regency England? Well, I got a list of potential openings with Cora's help. Isn't she just as cute as the knees on a honey bee, by the way? Now, tell me what y'all think about this idea..."

For the rest of the day, I talked very little and listened a lot, soaking up the humor and wisdom shared by those incredible people whom I now considered friends. Being thrown together in such an extreme situation had bonded us for life. At least that's how it felt. I supposed even that would fade along with my memories. It wasn't like we'd have any means of keeping in touch once we went our separate ways. Telephones couldn't yet reach across time or beyond the great divide into the afterlife.

Finally, the lights dimmed, and it was time to say my goodbyes. Although I intended to be stoic, I failed miserably. It was all I could do to keep from breaking down with each hug or clasp of hands. Jeff held back until the last. Then he caught me in his steady, brooding gaze.

"I hate to see you go so soon, Ben," he said, taking my hand after all the others had drifted off toward their rooms. "Are you sure you're ready?"

"Ready as I'll ever be. You didn't say much before. Do you think I've made the right decision?"

"What I think is that you're an impressive young man, Ben, with or without a major league contract. If you keep your head on straight, you'll be successful at whatever you set your mind to do. Just don't buy into what the world says success ought to look like."

"The wisdom of your experience speaking?"

"Exactly. I was prosperous by all the usual, external standards, but I was rotting away inside. I wouldn't want you making the same mistake."

"I'll try my best not to. What about you, Jeff? Are you going to take the plunge one of these days? I hope you haven't become so comfortable here that you never want to leave the place."

"I don't expect to be very far behind you. As a matter of fact, I've finally boiled down all the possibilities to the two options that interest me most. I discovered an orphanage in Zimbabwe that's full of children left alone and homeless as a result of the AIDS epidemic there. They've been functioning without a full-time physician on staff for five years now. The pictures of those kids... Well, anyway, I think I could do some real good there."

"They'd be lucky to get you, Doc. What's your other option? You said there were two you were still considering."

"Yeah. I'm also strongly drawn to the idea of going into research – to be on the cutting edge of science, to play a part in finding a cure that could benefit thousands. I only wish I could do both."

"Tough choice, but either way you can be sure your talents and education won't go to waste."

"That's what I'm counting on."

We self-consciously released our extended handshake and headed down the hall.

"Well, I guess this is it," I said when we got to my door.

"Yup. My very sincere best wishes, Ben. I hope you find what you're looking for."

"Thanks. You too, Jeff."

We clapped each other on the back and said a simple goodnight, which came far easier than the permanent goodbye it actually represented. I stepped into my room and the door slid closed.

Alone again, I swallowed hard. No more looking back. A new and improved future waited for me.

-14-
A Departure

What happens now? I wondered, leaning against the closed door of my room. The hum of anticipation inside me built to a fever pitch. It was hard to believe I would soon be off on the next phase of my journey – heading home, but with a difference. This time I would be wiser. I wouldn't take things for granted, not after feeling what it was like to lose it all.

"Cora? Can you hear me?" I called out.

She came shimmering through the wall screen moments later.

"So you *are* leaving us after all. And just when we were getting to know each other too," she said with a pouting lip. This time she wore an authentic Star Trek uniform straight out of the original series, which looked every bit as good on her as it ever had on Uhura. Cora understood my nod and smile of appreciation. "It makes me sad when people I care about go away," she continued.

"I thought you had to maintain a professional detachment in your line of work. That's what Poindexter said."

"I can't seem to help getting emotionally involved sometimes. And between you and me, Ben, Dex isn't as immune as he pretends."

"You mean there's a heart beating somewhere inside that scrawny chest of his?"

"Oh, yes. But he doesn't like to let it show, not to anyone. Well, anyone except me."

"Ah, I see how it is; you two are pretty tight."

"I wish you knew him like I do. He can be gruff, but he's pure marshmallow inside, honestly."

"I'll have to take your word for it, Cora, since I won't be sticking around long enough to find out for myself." She was probably right. There had to be more to the man than met the eye. Then it occurred to me, studying my pretty holographic friend, that I didn't know the real Cora either. "Will you do something for me?" I asked her.

"Anything, Ben."

"Will you let me see what you really look like? I'm very fond of this image you project, but I'd like to meet the flip side once before I go."

"The flip side isn't nearly as glamorous, you know. I'd hate to spoil your illusions."

"I'm a big boy. I stopped believing in Santa Claus a long time ago."

"All right, then, if you're sure. I'll be back in a little while as plain ol' me."

"Thanks."

While she was gone, I speculated about how I might be sent back to my life on earth. Would I be carried off by the Crossroads version of a transporter beam? That was the preferred method of travel on Star Trek, and I would have gladly given it a try. Maybe there was a genuine stargate on the premises that would take me where I wanted to go. Or would I be launched in some sort of capsule or pod? Over the years, I had eagerly devoured every Hollywood depiction of space and time travel. I could hardly believe that I was about to find out for myself how it was actually done.

As I pondered the question, I heard the telltale swoosh of the door opening. I turned to find a woman of about forty standing there, wearing the same costume I'd seen earlier. "Cora?" I asked.

"In the flesh, like you asked," she said, spreading her arms in a what-you-see-is-what-you-get gesture. "I hope you're not too disappointed."

She was undeniably older... and a little heavier. The hair and voice were different too, but the face and the personality seemed essentially the same.

"Not at all. You've got no reason to apologize. And being real has some advantage. Now I can give you a farewell hug, and I wouldn't have dared before."

"Good point," she agreed, looking pleased with my reaction.

"So, what do we do next? How do I get home?"

"Well," Cora began with a mischievous grin. "You close your eyes, think about Kansas, and tap your heels together three times. I'll wave my magic wand, and off you go."

"You've got to be joking," I said, adding with straight face, "That will never work without ruby slippers."

"I'll check my wardrobe, but I don't think I have any in your size."

We both cracked up.

"But seriously, Cora, how does it happen?"

"I suppose you're expecting something dramatic – a special effects extravaganza – but the process is actually pretty peaceful. You will watch the events of your life, from birth on, pass before you on the video screen. As you approach the point in time you've chosen to return to, you'll lapse into a deep sleep. It's similar to hypnosis and makes the transportation much easier on you. When you wake up, it'll all be over."

"Actually, I was kind of looking forward to experiencing it – conscious, I mean."

"I know. But it's better this way, believe me. The shock of the transition would be too much for your system to handle. It wouldn't be safe."

"I see. So, when do we get started?"

"Whenever you say. I'll stay here and monitor your departure, confirming that you've arrived safely at the proper destination and time. Then you're on your own. It's still not too late to change your mind, though, if you feel like you need a little more time."

"No, I'm eager to get started. Can I have that hug before I go?"

"Of course."

It was more awkward than I expected – like hugging an aunt that I only knew by correspondence. "Thanks, for everything," I said, letting her go.

"You're welcome, Ben. It's been my pleasure, and I won't forget you. Now, since I can't persuade you to stay any longer, I suppose we might as well get on with it. Are you ready?"

"Ready. Should I sit down for this?"

"Not necessary. Just stand facing the screen and relax. Don't try to hold on to any of the images you see. Allow them to flow by like a warm breeze. And don't worry; you're in no danger."

"I trust you, Cora."

"Good. Then we'll get started."

I nodded and braced myself.

"Relax," she reminded me.

"Oh, yeah. Sorry." I shook out my shoulders and arms, then let them drop loosely.

"Okay. Here we go," she said.

After one last look at Cora, I turned my attention to the video screen.

"Live long and prosper, Ben," I heard her say as the lights went out.

At first, the screen is black. Then unfamiliar light hits me from all sides. A cry of protest wells up inside my throat. A baby wails. People crowd around, unintelligible sounds spilling from their lips. My mother and father – so young. And this place I totter through? An apartment? The ceiling soars high above; the furniture towers. Another baby. They call him Scott and put him in my lap, red-faced and screaming. A new house. This one I know. My blue bedroom and the big back yard. Our dog Bogey. A yellow bus full of rowdy kids. A classroom, then another and another, all blur together. But the playfield stands out. A fall. Shocking pain. My arm wrapped in cold, wet plaster – so heavy. Exploring the woods and building a fort. A summer of baseball and fishing. An autumn of fifth grade and flag football. A funeral in the snow. Swim team. High school. First car. Jessica...

The years fly by, faster and faster. It all runs together and washes over me like a drowning wave. I can't breathe. Then I am falling, tumbling backwards and down... endlessly down.

That's all I remember.

FIRST INTERMISSION

"On his way then, is he?" Poindexter asked his partner when she sashayed into his office, heading for her favorite perch.

"Yes, Dex." She sighed, scooting back onto the corner of the desk and swiveling around to face him. "Unfortunately, he is."

He shook his head. "Cora?"

"I know, I know. 'Rule Number One: Maintain emotional detachment.' But this one was special."

"Need I recount for you the number of times you've said the same before?"

"That won't be necessary."

"I often think you really are too soft-hearted, my dear. And yet, I know that's part of the reason you're so good at your job... and so good to me." He took up her hand, stroked it once, and finished by bringing it to his lips. "Still, I wish I could spare you from feeling these departures so keenly. I try to look at it this way. We take excellent care of our clients while they are with us, but then we must be prepared to move on when *they* do."

"Sounds reasonable, but it's not always so easy to let go."

"Well, never mind. Work will soon set you right, and there's never an end to that here."

There was a knock at the door. Cora slid onto her feet again and turned to see who it was.

"Come in," said Poindexter. "Ah, Mr. Rutland."

"Pardon the intrusion, Mr. Poindexter, Ma'am," said the older gentleman, nodding to each in turn. "But if you're finished with me, I'd like to be getting back."

"Yes, yes, you can be off as soon as you like," said Poindexter, rising. "We needn't detain you any longer. Your contribution to the Center and your assistance with our young friend is much appreciated. You're under no further obligation, of course, but might you be willing to come again sometime if needed?"

"I expect so, if you think I can be of any use. I admire the work you folks do here, and I'm glad to help out. Still, I doubt anything I said to Ben made a speck of difference in the end."

"We haven't seen the end yet, Mr. Rutland," Cora interjected, laying a gentle hand on his shoulder. "I'm sure the wisdom you shared made a strong impression on Ben, since it came from your heart and out of your own experience. He may not always remember where he acquired it, but I believe it will stay with him."

"Thank you, Ma'am. It's right kind of you to say so."

"I think we've all done our best by the boy," Poindexter summed up. "The rest will be up to him. He will have to sink or swim on his own now."

Cora lamented Ben Lewis's departure for days, as did some of the others. Yet, as Poindexter predicted, the business of the Center carried on; the needs of the remaining residents demanded it. Cora assisted Mr. Rutland with his immediate departure. Mrs. Cuthbert followed the next day. Both Dr. Jeff and Richard Fegals worked to finalize their plans. Hope O'Neil continued to light up the commons with her colorful personality. And soon, new clients arrived to re-plenish their numbers.

"Dr. Kendall? A word, if you please," said Poindexter, poking his head into the commons a few days later.

Jeff excused himself and headed for the doorway. "What's up?" he asked the Center's diminutive director.

"Apparently there's been a little hitch in your plans," Poindexter informed him. "Cora will explain; she's waiting to speak to you."

Continuing down the hall, Jeff found Cora standing by in his room. She was decked out in body-hugging black leather from her ankle-high boots to her upturned collar.

"So, there's some kind of problem with my plans, Cora?"

"Problem or progress; it all depends on how you look at it. It seems the vacancy at the orphanage has been unexpectedly filled. There are other similar facilities in need of doctors, of course, but I know this was the one you were especially drawn to. I hope you don't mind too much making a change."

"I *am* disappointed. Still, I'm glad those poor kids will have some decent medical care at last. And that does make my decision easier, as a matter of fact." He paused, stroking his bearded chin. "Yes, the more I think about it, it probably has worked out for the best. I was badly torn before, but now I can choose to go into research without being haunted by the faces of those children, knowing I could have helped them and didn't."

"Good. I was hoping you'd feel that way."

Ten days after Ben Lewis left the Crossroads Center, Dr. Jeff Kendall also made the leap.

Part Two:

Ben's Second Chance

-15-
Homecoming

"Are you awake, Ben?" asked a soft, female voice.

"Abby?" Ben mumbled, struggling to clear away the sticky cobwebs that tangled his mind. Was he back in the hospital and the whole business at the Crossroads Center just a dream? He opened his eyes, finding instead his childhood bedroom and his mother looking down at him.

"Hey, sleepyhead. Do you have any idea what time it is?"

"Mom! Wow, it's so great to see you," he said, raising himself up on his elbows.

"Well, that's a better reception than I expected," she said with a puzzled expression. "Usually you just groan when I wake you before noon. Anyway, you'd better put some clothes on. Jessica's here," she announced, retreating and closing the door.

Jessica. That clinched it. It was 1991... again. Either this was some amazing illusion or the whole time-travel-second-chance thing was for real. Ben launched out of bed to take stock. Pulse and breathing, normal. Skin? Warm and flushed a natural pinkish-bronze color again. A few squats and flexes confirmed that his former, healthy muscle tone had also returned.

"I'm back! Yesssssss!" he cheered to himself, pumping his fist and breaking into a silent, victory dance. Cora had come through. He had his new-and-improved life as promised. For a few minutes, he couldn't focus on anything beyond that all-important fact. What a rush! He felt as if he really was going *where no man had gone before*... except, of course, he himself had been in exactly the same spot once, nearly seven years ago. Surreal.

When he was able to calm down, Ben reviewed his situation. If everything had come off according to his carefully outlined instructions, this was the first week of January and they'd all just returned from Mexico the afternoon before. Now he remembered that Jessica *had* come over that next morning to welcome him home. But how should he handle her? He hadn't really thought that part through. For her, nothing had changed, and they were still together. He supposed he should try to maintain the status quo for the time being; no wholesale changes until he had a chance to settle in for a few days at least.

Ben hurried through his morning routine. It felt at once both strange and comfortably familiar to be moving around his family home again, to be twenty for the second time, to be reliving history. "Totally déjà vu-ish," he muttered as he went out to meet Jessica.

He found her in the living room, posed by the window, her mane of dark hair shimmering and every dangerous curve set off to perfection by the light. His gut wrenched tight at the sight. He'd almost forgotten how superbly sexy she could look.

"Hey, Jess," Ben said with forced casualness, keeping his distance and both hands in his pockets.

Jessica came up and slipped her arms around his waist, running her fingers under his shirt and up the taut skin of his back. "Did you miss me?" she asked provocatively, going in for a kiss.

Warning alarms exploded in Ben's head. "Not now!" he protested. "Remember my parents."

"They're in the other room. Besides, I'm sure they're not as clueless as you'd like to believe. They have to know what's been going on with us." Jessica pushed her hips tight against his, leaving no doubt about what she meant.

Very deliberately, Ben began extricating himself from her grasp. "Even if they do suspect... you know... I'm sure they'd rather not have it thrown in their faces. Take it easy for now, would you, Jess? We'll have plenty of time to get reacquainted later."

"Reacquainted? You haven't been gone *that* long," she said, finally backing off. "So, how was Cabo anyway, and what did you bring me?"

When she had collected her loot and Ben's promise that he would see her later that evening, Jessica climbed into her banana-yellow Mazda and drove off.

Ben watched from the curb until her car disappeared around the corner onto Shaw Road. He sucked in a chest-full of frosty air and let it out again. Jessica was going to be a problem, he acknowledged heading back to the house. Although he would have been perfectly justified in making a preemptive strike (considering how ruthlessly she had ditched *him* the first time around), a gradual cool-down of their relationship was more what he had in mind. Unfortunately, there was nothing cool about Jessica. She might not – as Ben now knew – have given her heart, but she had given him everything else. In return, she expected what he was no longer willing to furnish.

Well, if she insisted on all or nothing, then it would have to be nothing, he decided. In this timeline, he and Abby hadn't even met yet, so technically he was free to date whomever he pleased. But Ben still felt very married – morally and emotionally committed to Abby on every level. Taking familiar liberties with Jessica now would seem like infidelity. The brief brush with his old flame just then had been enough to teach him that. He had vowed to be faithful "till death do us part" and nobody had died yet. So, the way he looked at it, the promise was still in force, at least on his side.

The fact that Abby didn't currently know he existed was beside the point. She wasn't even scheduled to arrive in Washington State until June. By then, Ben hoped to have another good season of baseball and a pro contract under his belt.

He'd thought a lot about how to hook up with Abby again. Even if he could stand to wait another year and a half, until they had originally met, he could hardly wander in to Dr. Bingham's office and introduce himself. Knocking on the Albrights' front door out of the blue didn't seem reasonable either. The most feasible plan he'd come up with so far was that he should arrange to bump into her on campus and strike up a conversation. People met like that every day, right? And it had worked for him once before. In the meantime, he intended to focus on baseball and getting his career off to a good start.

"Lunch," Jan Lewis called out from the other room.

Food! Just like one of Pavlov's dogs, Ben's mouth started to water. It seemed like ages since he'd last eaten. There were no meals needed or offered during his week at the Center. Before that, he'd been in the hospital with his only nourishment coming through an IV. No wonder he was ravenous. He headed for the kitchen, greeting his mother with a bear hug as he entered.

"What was that for?" she asked.

"No special reason. Where's Scott?"

"Oh, you know your brother. He got up early and went to the library – something to do with his senior project. He should be home soon, though. Do you two have plans?"

"Not for today, but I thought I'd see if he wants to go skiing tomorrow. You know; last chance to hang out together before I head back to the U."

"Uh-huh," she agreed as she set the last of the sandwich fixings on the table.

Ben saw the crinkle at the corner of her eye and her suppressed grin. "What?" he asked. "Did I say something funny?"

"Not funny exactly; nice. I was remembering a few years back. It used to be you couldn't wait to ditch your little brother."

"Yeah, well, things are different now."

Ron Lewis came in from the garage, and the three sat down to lunch.

Ben dug in greedily. But once the initial stab of hunger dulled, he slowed to savor every element of the meal. The multi-grain bread – although it undoubtedly came from Safeway – somehow had retained a hint of that just-baked aroma. Between the slices, Mom's tuna salad tasted even better than usual with just the right balance of creamy mayo, bite of green onion, and tangy pickle bits mixed in. Then, with the crack of the first bite, the glossy Red Delicious apple sent a splash of sugary juice over his tongue.

Ben stopped mid-chew, suddenly struck by how extraordinarily good everything tasted and smelled. Was it from going so long without food? No, more than that, because it wasn't just the food, he realized. Everything – the intoxicating scent of Jessica's perfume; the blinding shaft of sunlight he'd seen slicing through the clouds when he'd walked her out; the cut of the icy air plunging deep into his lungs; the satisfying burst of power that sprang from his muscles as he sprinted back to the house afterward – everything seemed somehow intensified over what it had been before.

"Ben," his father was saying in his gravelly voice. "Are you still with us?"

"Oh, sure, Dad. You said you needed my help?"

"Yeah, with changing the brake fluid on the Monte. Can you spare me an hour this afternoon?"

"No problem."

Working with his dad later, Ben was glad he'd chosen the time he had for his return instead of skipping over these few days at home to go straight back to school. He needed to be grounded by his family, to be reassured they truly existed in this version of his life. As it had turned out, he never was in any danger of dying and losing everyone he loved. But he'd believed it at the time, and the experience had changed him.

When Scott arrived, Ben had to fight the powerful impulse to rush up and hug him too. With his mother, he'd gotten away with it because she never turned down any kind of affection from her sons. Scott, on the other hand, would have thought it was "creepy-weird," one of his favorite expressions. So Ben played it cool. "Hey, bro. How was the library?"

"Full of books. What did you expect?"

Ben ignored the sarcasm, figuring he'd earned that and more by years of mistreatment. "How about making a run up to Crystal with me tomorrow? I checked the ski report. There's five inches of fresh powder and more expected overnight. It should be awesome."

"Sounds good, except I don't have any money. Spent it all in Mexico."

"It's on me."

Scott's eyes narrowed. "Why? It's not my birthday or anything."

"I don't need a special reason to do something nice, do I? I thought it might be fun to hang out together, that's all."

"Okay, who are you and what have you done with my real brother? Has he been abducted by aliens or something?"

Ben smiled at the suggestion. Closer to the truth than Scott could possibly imagine.

-16-
Burning and Building Bridges

Unable to resist a chance to hit the slopes, Scott soon came around, and plans for the next day were set. Ben looked forward to that appointment far more than he did the one with Jessica, which he figured could get ugly – fast.

After a family dinner, Ben headed out into the stormy January night for the twenty-minute drive to the Martinelli house. If he'd needed any more proof that he was back among the living, the reality of cold rain in his face and the wind clawing at his coat would have done the job. He hurried to his rusty Toyota and folded his tall frame once more into its cramped confines. Ben paused a moment to reconnect with this old friend. The "new car" smell came from the air freshener hanging on the dashboard, and the upholstery of the driver's seat was worn so thin he could see through to the padding beneath. But the little Corolla had served him well, and it had a solid claim to some permanent real estate in his heart. On nights like this, though, it was too bad the heater was so pathetic. Yes, a new ride with all the amenities would be top priority as soon as he got his hands on some serious cash.

As he drove the familiar route across town, Ben racked his brain for the right approach to take with Jessica. He intended to travel the high road – let her down easy, if possible. He had considered calling with some excuse to put her off for a while, theorizing that if he neglected her long enough she'd walk away on her own. Ultimately, though, he'd decided that would be cowardly... and unnecessarily cruel. Out of respect for their three-year history together, he had a duty to face Jessica, to deal with the situation directly and honorably.

Jessica opened the door when Ben arrived, greeting him with a quick kiss and pulling him inside out of the storm. Mrs. Martinelli joined them for a few minutes of stilted conversation in the tiny front room. "Did you enjoy your vacation, Ben?" "Yes, very much. The weather was great." "And how are your parents?" And so on. They'd known each other a long time, so there was nothing inherently awkward in the situation – nothing except Ben's own nervousness about what would come next. It took a tremendous effort to keep up the pretense that everything was perfectly normal when he knew he was about to change all that.

When Mrs. Martinelli left them on their own, Jessica led the way down to the basement, to a low-ceilinged family room of sorts. At the bottom of the stairs, Ben flicked on the lights, seeing again – for the first time in a long while – their old haunt. Not exactly the Ritz, but private. No one ever disturbed them there, so it had been the site of more steamy action than Ben cared to remember. Privacy was what he needed now too, for different reasons.

"Alone at last," Jessica said dramatically, throwing her arms around Ben's neck.

His back stiffened. "Wait, Jess, we need to talk," he said, peeling her off.

"What's up, Benji? Playing hard to get?" she teased.

"I'm not in the mood right now, that's all. Besides, like I said, we need to talk."

"But you're never 'not in the mood.' And I'm sure what you have to say can wait," she suggested, casually switching the lights off and pulling him close again by the belt loops of his jeans.

Old habits were hard to break. Ben felt his body responding to her raw sensuality as it always had. Nothing overt at first – just a pleasant drift of mind and a tightening in his gut. He lingered, though, rooted to the spot by visceral memory as Jessica's hands roamed deftly over him.

It would be so easy to let go.

Assisted by the darkness, Ben's carnal train of thought carried him ahead, taking him to the vivid image of Abby's body, warm and receptive in his arms. His whole being ached for her. He bent and kissed her hungrily.

"Now that's more like it," Jessica murmured.

Her voice startled Ben back to reality. He broke away, feeling guilty and fumbling for the light switch.

"No! I'm sorry, Jessica. I can't go back to the way things used to be."

"What is wrong with you?" she shrieked, her eyes flashing. "You're not making any sense, Ben. 'The way things used to be'? What the hell has changed?"

Ben gave his head a violent shake to toss off his confusion. "Come on," he said. "Let's sit down." He steered Jessica toward the shabby, brown couch against the far wall. She dropped at one end of it in a huff. He sat at arm's length, turning sideways to face her. "It's hard to explain, Jess," he began. "The truth is, for me, something *has* changed. I still care about you a lot, but I'm not sure we're meant to be together forever like we used to think."

"Don't you love me?" she challenged.

"What about you? Can you honestly say that you're in love with me?"

No answer.

"I didn't think so." He continued more gently. "Look Jess. I'm not denying that we have a… a strong attraction. I just don't know if it's enough to stake our entire futures on."

"So, you think we should break up. That's what you're really saying," she snapped, crossing her arms and looking away. "I suppose you've met someone else. Who is she?"

"No, this isn't about anyone else. I just think we've been moving too fast, that we should back off a little, to make sure what we really want before we get in too deep. We can still hang out together. We've been friends for a long time."

Jessica erupted from her seat. "Hang. Out. Together?" she spat back at him, one word at a time. "Are you serious? I have far better offers than 'hanging out' with you! Plenty of them. You might be surprised how many of your buddies have already tried to make a move on me. But I stayed with you because we had plans! And now, suddenly I'm not good enough for you? Me, not good enough for *you*." She laughed. "Oh, that's rich."

"I never said that, Jess."

Ben made no further attempt to defend himself; he just let Jessica rant. She was entitled. He'd damaged her almighty pride if nothing else, and it was totally her style to retaliate with claws bared. It had been naïve to think they might get through this without bloody chunks of fur flying everywhere.

When Jessica finally wound down her tirade and ordered him out, Ben offered one more apology before showing himself to the door. Outside, he sucked the cold night air deep into his lungs. He felt slightly maimed, but relieved.

~~*~~

The brothers got up at seven-fifteen, piled their ski gear into the family SUV, and headed for the mountains. They planned to arrive early and get a few runs in before the crowds showed up. Ben took the wheel and Scott, riding shotgun, served as deejay, selecting the music for the hour-and-a-quarter drive up to Crystal Mountain.

"Do you want to get something to eat?" Ben asked. "I'm going to stop in Enumclaw for gas anyway."

"Nah. I had a yogurt before we left, and I brought granola bars. Want one?" Scott offered, handing it to his brother.

"Thanks." They continued on in silence for several minutes before Ben asked, "So, have you decided where you're going to college next year?"

"Probably WSU, but I won't make it final until I see what kind of financial aid they offer me. Whatever it is, it won't be as good as the deal you got."

"Sorry about that. I know it's not fair. You've worked just as hard as I have, and academic excellence should be rewarded same as athletic talent."

"Exactly! But I never thought I'd hear you admit it."

"Yeah. Well, it takes me a while to figure these things out sometimes." Smiling, Ben added, "You gotta cut me a little slack; athletes aren't all that bright, remember."

Scott smirked and shot his brother a sideways glance. "You can say that again."

The brothers arrived at the ski resort in time to snag one of the last parking spots in the small, upper lot, which they considered a major coup since it so rarely happened. They began the familiar, pre-ski routine without a word. Sitting side by side on the tailgate, they booted up, then hauled out their skis and poles, and made their way to the ticket booth. Ben paid for them both, and they attached the day-passes to their jackets. After that, a flight of metal-grated stairs and a short hike took them to the first lift.

They made a warm-up run on Quicksilver before heading to the top via Chair One and the new high-speed Rainier Express. The view from the summit was breathtaking. The Cascade Range, so often shrouded in thick clouds, stood out clearly for miles in both directions with Mt. Rainier rising up right in front of them, larger than life. They might have stayed longer to enjoy the scenery but for the biting wind that whipped along the ridge. Besides, fresh powder beckoned.

"Race you to the bottom," Ben called over his shoulder as he shoved off toward Lucky Shot. Scott followed right on his heels.

When it came to skiing, the brothers, though different, were evenly matched. Whereas Ben's approach was simply to throw himself down the mountain with more regard for speed than style, Scott was a technician, choosing the better route and negotiating the descent without an ounce of wasted motion. They made it to the base of the lift in a dead heat and skied right onto the chair with no wait, both flushed and gasping for breath.

"Woohoo!" shouted Ben as they were swept off their feet into the air. "Great run, Scott."

"You too. The snow's primo."

They simultaneously reached overhead, swinging the safety cage down in front of them and sliding their skis onto the footrest for the long ride back to the top.

"For sure. I'm glad we came today. This is the perfect way to finish off our Christmas break. Tomorrow I have to head back up to the U, you know."

"Are you and Jessica driving together?"

"Somehow I doubt that. I'm pretty sure she never wants to speak to me again."

Scott jerked his head around to look at his brother. "Why? What happened?"

"I, uh... I kinda broke up with her last night," said Ben, sheepishly.

Scott gave a long, low whistle at the news, his breath trailing a jet of fog into the freezing air. "Man, I didn't see that coming. Big mistake too, cutting a hottie like that loose. You can't possibly have anything better than Jessica waiting in the wings."

"In a way, I do," Ben said, thoughtfully, "although she's not exactly waiting for me; it's more like I'm waiting for her."

"What's that supposed to mean? Who is this girl, and when did you manage to hook up with her anyway?"

"Can you keep a secret?"

"I suppose so."

"Okay, then, I'll tell you this much. Her name is Abby. She's amazing, like no girl I've ever met before. But if I told you when I met her, you'd think I was crazy. I guess you could say I had a dream about her – a very long and detailed dream." A gust of wind whisked a shower of snow crystals off a fir tree alongside the lift. Ben watched them sparkle in the sun. "Do you believe in fate, Scott?"

"I don't know. I haven't given it much thought."

"Well, I do. A year or two from now, after Abby and I get together, you'll remember what I told you today. That will make a believer out of you."

"What's up with you anyway, Ben? Did you hit your head or get religion all of a sudden or something? You've been acting really weird ever since we got back from Mexico. It's kind of creeping me out."

"Not religion exactly, but I do feel like I've been given a clearer picture of what's important. Traveling to foreign lands – the more alien the better – can do that for you sometimes," Ben said, laughing at his private joke.

The boys wore themselves out with several more aggressive runs – mostly on the intermediate and advanced trails of the Green Valley basin – before breaking for lunch. Afterward, they returned to the slopes for a more leisurely afternoon. The crowds were thicker and the lines longer by then, forcing a slower pace. Ben and Scott had plenty of time to shoot the breeze while doing their sidestep shuffle in line, riding up on the chairlifts together, and on the drive home. Their improved camaraderie nearly carried Ben to make some kind of formal apology to his brother for past behavior. It would have been a relief to unburden his conscience before leaving for school. But clearly Scott had already noticed a change in him without going that far. Best not to freak him out completely by getting too sappy, Ben decided.

-17-
Back on Track

The parting words of advice from Ben's parents the next day differed along predictable lines. His mother urged him to drive carefully, eat right, and not neglect his studies. His father's counsel focused more on the upcoming baseball season with appeals to "make me proud" and to "knock 'em dead." Not that Ben needed a pep talk from either of them; he already brimmed with confident anticipation for what lay ahead. Knowing his health wouldn't betray him this time made all the difference.

As he headed north toward Seattle, everything seemed fresh, a-live, and new, seen through the eyes of his second chance at life. A change in the weather couldn't dampen his spirits. The blue skies of the day before were long gone, replaced by a more-typical steely, January gray. Yet, passing Boeing Field on I-5, the city beyond looked magnificent, even through the steady drizzle and intermittent wipers. The mistiness softened the coarse contours of the industrial zone and gave the high-rise buildings in the distance a dreamy qual-ity, as if they had recently coalesced out of the clouds.

The Kingdome came up on his left. Although Ben knew its many detractors viewed it as a concrete atrocity, to him the home of the Mariners was hallowed ground. Some proposed tearing it down to make way for a new, retractable-roof baseball field and a separate open-air stadium for the Seahawks, but that possibility was still years in the future.

Ben took the 45th Street exit and made his way through traffic to the converted three-story house on 19th Avenue that held his studio apartment, along with five others. It wasn't much – less than four hundred square feet – but he had it all to himself. Two years of dormitory living had convinced him he needed more privacy. Now he was particularly glad he'd made the change and grateful that he'd resisted the invitation to move in with Jessica. What a disaster that would have been.

After hauling in his bulging duffle bag, Ben checked the place over: the pocket-sized living area by the front windows, its dimensions further dwarfed by his monstrous couch; the L-shaped kitchen with its three-quarter scale appliances; the drop-leaf table that served as a spot both to study and to eat; the corner in back where his double mattress rested directly on the hardwood floor; a small closet, charged with the task of holding nearly all Ben's worldly possessions; and a bathroom barely big enough for him to turn around in. Everything seemed just as he had left it two weeks before... or six years before, depending on how he looked at it. It was going to take some time to adjust his thinking.

Suddenly he remembered Kyle Rosier. It would be great to see him again. In his previous life, Ben had lost track of his college buddy and teammate after graduation. But now, he should be just a floor away. They had discussed rooming together until they found this house, where they could each get a separate unit for little more than the cost of sharing a two-bedroom somewhere else. And the location worked – within easy biking distance of campus, even walkable in a pinch.

Ben returned to the common hall, took the stairs two at a time, and knocked on Kyle's door.

"Hey, dude," Kyle said, letting him in. "You just get here?"

"A few minutes ago." Ben flopped down on the gold plaid, hand-me-down couch just inside the door, as if nothing out of the ordinary had taken place since they'd last seen each other. "You?"

"Oh, I've been here since noon. I couldn't wait to get back to the city after two weeks with nothing to do but play video games and stare at my father across the kitchen table. Not much action in the big town of Davenport, and none of my friends were around."

"That's rough, man."

"You don't know how lucky you are having a brother."

"Yeah. Scott's pretty cool for a kid. Hey, you wanna go get a pizza or something? I'm starving, and I haven't restocked my fridge yet."

"Sure. Giovanni's?"

"Sounds like a plan. I'll meet you downstairs in five."

Ben fetched his Gortex coat from his apartment and stepped out onto the stoop to wait for his friend. It wasn't as cold as the day before. The damp marine layer served as an insulating blanket whenever it rolled in off the Pacific. Ben sucked in the heavy, water-logged air. A spicy olfactory cocktail singed his nostrils: salt and a hint of decay from the distant waterfront blended with the oily scent of wet city streets. That, plus the background static of the bustling metropolis, helped to plant his feet firmly in the current time and place – far from the muted, suburban life he'd fallen into before with Abby and light-years removed from Crossroads. Ben closed his eyes and drew in another lungful.

"You okay, Lewis?" Kyle asked, emerging from the front door.

"Never better. Let's go."

They walked the few blocks north to the Italian café they had discovered shortly after moving to the neighborhood the previous fall. It was clean, cheap, and not as crowded as the more popular hang-outs near campus. This time, the restaurant was almost deserted. They picked a table and placed their order.

Kyle rocked his lanky frame back in the bentwood chair, hands behind his head and elbows spread. "So, are you ready to resume the daily grind, then – classes, workouts, and all?" he asked idly.

"I can hardly wait," Ben answered, rubbing his hands together. "You can't imagine how much I've missed it, especially baseball. And now, every day will bring me a little closer to my goals."

"See, dude, that's where we differ."

"True. You have no goals," Ben teased.

"I have goals, man," Kyle objected lazily. "I'm just not in such a panic to reach them as you are. I plan to chill and enjoy the ride. After all, there's no guarantee that what's ahead is better than what we've got right now. Look at us. Today, we're big men on campus, cruising along on scholarships – nothing to worry about. A year or two from now, who knows? Some serious shit could come down and bury everything. So where's the rush to jump into it?"

"Hey. That's almost profound, Rosier. I never knew you were so deep."

"Yeah, well… proves you don't know everything after all."

"You're right about one thing, though," Ben added soberly. "The future is unpredictable. I don't take stuff for granted anymore." He downed a gulp of his Coke. "I have a really clear vision about where

I want to be in five years, though, and I mean to do whatever it takes to get there."

"Good for you, Mr. Overachiever. Just try not to make the rest of us look like total slackers while you're doing it, okay? Then, after you're some hotshot, big-league ballplayer, I'll be proud to say I knew you when you were ugly, poor, and humble. Well, ugly and poor, at least."

~~*~~

When the new quarter started, Ben hit the ground running. A man on a mission, he got up every day at six to spend time in the weight room first thing. His classes – the minimum required to maintain his full-time student status – were grouped together in the morning to leave the afternoons free for baseball workouts. Then, in the evening, he'd either study on his own or attend one of the study tables on campus. It was a full but manageable schedule with some free time on the weekends to kick back a little and socialize.

He and Jessica had been at the hub of the party action before. Ben kept a much lower profile these days, often making excuses to stay away altogether. For one thing, he knew Jessica – always a baseball groupie – still frequented those gatherings, and he preferred not to bump into her any more than necessary. Besides, the excess drinking and carrying-on seemed a little juvenile to him now. Although his driver's license said he was not quite twenty-one, he felt much older than the kids around him, having banked a good five to seven years of life experience on every one of them. He'd thoroughly enjoyed the whole college scene the first time around, but he was ready to move on.

Baseball was a different story; he couldn't get enough of it. The coaches pushed the players harder as the start of the season approached, and some of his teammates complained about the work. Not Ben. Every hour in the weight room, every situational drill, every intra-squad scrimmage, and every session in the batting cages brought him one step closer to his ultimate goal.

Just being back on the field was an incredible gift, wrapped in layers of nostalgia and bound by powerful emotional ties. For the first couple of weeks, Ben got chills whenever he heard the sharp, metallic ping of an aluminum bat making solid contact. He thrilled at

101

the sudden release of coiled energy as he sprang to chase down a long fly or sprinted base to base. He loved the smell of the freshly mown outfield grass, the way his well-worn glove fit like a second skin, and the horseplay in the locker room. After his forced hiatus from the game, he was more than happy to live, sleep, and eat baseball again.

The preseason began toward the end of February, taking the team to some warm-weather locales. Then conference games got underway a month later. Ben was playing the best baseball of his life, putting up the kind of numbers he knew should place him in line for a respectable pro contract. Still, he avoided looking too far ahead. Day by day, he kept his focus as much as possible on perfecting his own performance – the only thing he had any control over – figuring the rest would then take care of itself. As the season progressed, though, Ben couldn't help noticing that others were paying attention too.

Kyle nudged him in the dugout during the Sunday game of the Huskies' weekend series at Arizona State. "Dude, did you see who's hunkered down behind the backstop today?" he asked in a tone of awe. "It's Kevin Callaghan, I swear. Kevin… stinkin'… Callaghan!"

Ben had also noticed the high-powered agent, along with a handful of scouts, observing the game. "Yeah, I saw him," he acknowledged, shrugging it off even as a fresh shot of adrenaline fired through his veins.

"I bet he's here to take a look at you, Ben. That would be awesome if you could get an agent like him! Dude, you'd have it made for sure then."

"Knock it off, Rosier. Are you trying to jinx me? I can't afford to get distracted; I gotta keep my head in the game. Besides, Callaghan could just as easily be here for Williams or, more likely, for one of the ASU players. Mike Kelly's sure to be a first-rounder."

"If you say so."

Ben went on to hit an impressive three for four with a triple into the right field corner, and a couple of circus catches on defense. Afterward, Ben discovered Mr. Callaghan's business card, along with one from the Oakland A's scout, had been left to add to his growing collection. Word got around in a heartbeat, and a general melee broke out in the locker room – guys pounding Ben on the head and hurling accolades and insults at him in equal measure. Everyone, except Derek Williams, joined in the celebration, sharing in their teammate's success as if it belonged to all of them equally. That plus their victory over the Sun Devils made for a rowdy group on the bus afterward.

Despite not having a good game himself, Kyle followed suit. "You know you owe me big time for that fly ball in the fourth inning," he told Ben from the seat behind. "I could have gotten to it easy, but I decided to let you take it so you could show off for the scouts."

"Oh, so tripping over your own feet, that was just an act, I guess," Ben called back over his shoulder.

"Of course. Convincing, wasn't it?"

"Very!" Ben said, laughing. "You could be in the wrong game, Rosier. Maybe you should pursue a career in Hollywood instead."

"Hey, I'm seriously considering it. I have the looks, obviously, and I'm starting to think I'll never become famous as a ball player. But you, old pal," he continued, reaching forward on both sides of the seat to give Ben's shoulders a vigorous shake, "you have a legit-imate shot at the big leagues. What round were you drafted out of high school?"

"Way late; in the forty-second."

"I bet you go at least by the fifth this time. Callaghan must think so too or he wouldn't be interested."

Kyle hadn't said anything that wasn't true. Barring any last-minute disasters, Ben fully expected to be drafted, and probably in the early going too. Still, signing a pro contract would be only the first step of his steep and slippery climb to the top, a trail already strewn with the battered bodies and broken dreams of thousands who had made their attempt on the summit before him.

The odds against reaching the upper echelons of the sport were staggering. In a dark and cluttered corner of his mind, Ben knew this. The trick was never to go there and to refuse cynics the chance of sowing seeds of self-doubt anywhere near his ego. Confidence was key, but there were always a few who made it their mission to take down anyone who rose above them. Derek Williams was one of them.

-18-
Rivalry

During boarding, Derek Williams dodged in front of Kyle to take the spot next to Ben for the flight back to Seattle. "You don't mind, do you, Lewis?" he asked, sitting down without waiting for a reply.

Ben shrugged. "Suit yourself," he answered, aiming at a neutral expression.

"I always do."

Ben expected Derek to state his business and wondered what he was up to when he didn't. It's not like they were friends – more like sworn rivals living under an uneasy truce. They'd first clashed over the coveted turf in center field, with the prize ultimately going to Ben. The consolation of playing right fell to Derek. As teammates, they were forced to spend time together every day on the field, but they never chose each other's company off it.

Derek popped on his headphones and didn't say a word while the rest of the passengers loaded, the flight attendants gave their safety instructions, and the 757 taxied out to the runway for takeoff. After they'd been airborne about ten minutes, he finally broke his silence. "Congratulations on a good game back there."

Ben shot him a sideways glance. "Thanks. You too."

"Yeah, I did have a good game, didn't I? But you're the one who got noticed... this time. By Kevin Callaghan, no less. You're really on your way."

"It's a start," Ben replied warily. "I'm sure you've collected a pocketful of interested scouts and agents too."

"That's a solid fact, but *I* don't like to make a show of it."

"Hey, I couldn't help that the guys found out about Callaghan."

"Uh-huh. If you say so. Well, I suppose you need all the positive strokes you can get. You must feel pretty beaten up after what you've been through."

"Excuse me?"

"Being dumped by your girlfriend; that sucks, man."

"For your information, Jessica didn't dump me. I... Oh, never mind. I don't owe you any explanations." Ben reclined his seat and closed his eyes.

"I'm not surprised you don't want to talk about it," Derek continued with a low laugh. "It's gotta be humiliating. But, there's something you should know; Jessica's with *me* now. She's movin' on and movin' up."

Ben shook his head slowly, a wry smile tugging at the corner of his mouth. "I should have seen that coming," he said, mostly to himself, remembering that it was Derek who Jessica had turned to when she deserted him the first time around.

"Yes, you should have," Derek said with a deadpan stare. "A guy like you can't expect to hang on to a fine-lookin' woman like that for long. I'm not sure what she ever saw in you, but she's *so* over it now." The seatbelt sign turned off with a ding. Derek unbuckled and got up, adding, "Try to take it like a man, Lewis... if you can manage that."

Ben bit his tongue to keep from saying something equally caustic in return. They still had several weeks to go in the season, and he had to be able to work alongside this jerk. As for Jessica, he didn't plan to lose any sleep over her. If she wanted to date the guy, that was her business.

Derek, still wearing a superior smirk, strutted down the aisle. He pulled Kyle to his feet and pushed him off toward the now-vacant spot next to Ben.

Kyle went willingly enough. "Hey, Dude, what was that about?" he asked when he got resettled.

"Nothing important," Ben answered, stretching back to get comfortable. "He said he wanted to congratulate me on a good game, but his kind of support I can do without."

~~*~~

Ben powered his way through May, the team playing a series each weekend and sometimes a couple of games mid-week as well. Every day off had to be dedicated to catching up on his studies. His immediate objective, the June draft, was quickly rounding into sight with only the last home stand to get safely through first. Since he had decided not to return for his senior year, the series against the WSU Cougars would be the culmination of his college career. His parents and brother would be in the stands, cheering him on and ready to celebrate with him afterward. Hopefully, there *would* be something to celebrate. The Huskies were favored to win, but anything could happen in a cross-state rivalry match-up.

Friday's game got off to a good start. The UW pitcher, Tim Coleman, who was completely dialed in, held the Cougars scoreless through the first six innings. Meanwhile, the home team racked up seven hits and three runs. Ben did his part with his glove and by leading off the third with a stand-up double to right. He advanced on a ground out and then scored when Derek Williams sent a wicked line drive screaming over the left field fence. The partisan crowd erupted, cheering wildly as Derek circled the bases.

Waiting to give Williams the customary "high five" when he reached home plate, Ben took in the moment, filing away a snap shot of everything it encompassed. Here, at the end of his college career, the team was finally firing on all cylinders – pitching, hitting, and defense – and rolling towards victory in front of their loyal fans. In his experience, there were very few things that could beat the feeling – a collective, natural euphoria – of having a share in something grand, something larger than himself. It was a big part of why he played the game. Not to take anything away from the satisfaction of personal accomplishment, but team success seemed somehow even sweeter.

Things began to unravel in the top of the seventh, however. Ben winced when Coleman got nailed in the ankle by a come-backer and had to leave the game. His replacement, Pritchard, promptly gave up a single to the first man he faced and walked the next two to load the bases. It was hard to watch. Pitch by pitch, Ben felt his gut twisting in tighter knots of sympathetic tension.

With the lead in real jeopardy, the coach called time to settle down the inexperienced reliever. Pritchard's performance improved after that. He was able to coax a strikeout and a routine fly ball from the following hitters for outs one and two. Fingers crossed, it appeared he might manage to wriggle off the hook. *Just one more out*, Ben repeated to himself. But they would have to register that out against a pretty big bat.

No one wanted to face the Cougars' first baseman Grady Hertzec. He had a .325 batting average and more home runs on the year than any of his teammates. When he stepped up to the plate, Ben took a deep breath and two steps backward. He hoped Pritchard had been paying attention during the pre-game briefing. *Pitch him high and tight,* Ben tried to remind him telepathically. *Tie him up.* It had worked for Coleman, who had kept Hertzec in check so far. Now it was Pritchard's turn.

His first pitch dove into the dirt two feet in front of the plate, and Ben's stomach sank along with it. Fortunately, Wilson did a good job blocking the ball, preventing the runners from advancing. Okay, a 1-0 count was no big deal. The second pitch sailed high out of the strike zone. Ben groaned, knowing Pritchard would have to give the slugger something to hit now; he couldn't afford to go 3-0 on him with the bases loaded. Pritchard's next offering would indeed have been ball three if Hertzec had been able to lay off of it. Instead he chased a pitch tailing away from him, getting only a piece of it and cueing it toward the Husky dug-out: foul ball. Ben exhaled in relief.

The catcher gave the sign for a fast ball up and in. Pritchard nodded, came set, and focused on the target of Wilson's glove. He paused, went into his wind-up, and hurled the ball.

It wasn't a bad pitch. It just caught a little more of the plate than it should have. Hertzec turned on it and, with a sharp ring of the bat, sent the ball careening toward right center field. Ben instantly read its trajectory: not long enough to leave the yard, but it had trouble written all over it, threatening to fall into the no man's land between deep center and right. Ben put his head down and sprinted for the spot he expected the ball to return to earth, hoping it had enough hang time for him to arrive there first. Out of the corner of his eye, he saw Derek Williams on a dead run to back him up.

As Ben approached the fence, he craned back over his shoulder, picking up the ball against the high, hazy sky. Still time to turn and position himself for the catch that would end the inning. Waving his arms, he called Williams off and reached his right hand toward the falling projectile, expecting it to drop harmlessly into his glove.

It only took a split second, but Ben lived it in slow motion. A violent hit to his left shoulder blew him over sideways. He never saw it coming.

-19-
Season's End

Ben hit the ground with a sickening thud. Prickles of light peppered his field of vision, dancing before his eyes like Fourth-of-July sparklers as the sky dimmed and brightened again. Temporarily immobilized, Ben saw his teammate towering over him.

Williams had managed to keep his feet despite the force of the impact. He quickly collected the ball from the ground and hurled it over the cut-off man toward home plate on a bounce. Two runners had already come around to score, but the throw was on target and in time for Wilson to tag the third, ending the inning and limiting the damage.

After finishing the play, the right fielder gave Ben a hand up. "Sorry, man. You okay?" he asked.

"I think so," Ben said shaking out his arm. "What happened? Didn't you hear me call you off?"

"Didn't hear a thing; too much crowd noise, I guess."

Derek set off for the dugout at a jog. Ben followed more slowly and was met halfway by Mr. Keller, the team trainer.

"Are you all right, Ben?" he asked, walking back with him. "Looks like you've got a problem with your arm."

"Just a stinger, I think."

"Could be. You took quite a hit to your shoulder. How about your head? Did you black out at all?"

"No. I'm fine. Just saw a few stars."

"In any case, you're done for the day."

Ben began to protest.

"Don't argue with me, Lewis. You're sitting out the rest of this game and that's final. We'll see about tomorrow after we get you thoroughly checked out."

The Huskies hung on to win the game and, ultimately, the series. But Ben ended the season warming the bench – an unfamiliar experience for him. The loss of strength and feeling in his left arm caused by the stinger hung around long enough to prevent him from playing the remaining two games. It was nothing major – just a small glitch that kept him from closing out his college career on a high note.

Derek Williams fared far better, suffering no ill effects from the high-speed collision. Not only was he deemed fit to play, he was moved over to fill Ben's spot in center where he made the most of the opportunity, catching everything that came into his territory and mooching a little around the edges besides.

"Showboating for the scouts," Kyle called it in the final rehash. He had joined the Lewis family for dinner at Giovanni's after the last game on Sunday.

"Williams has always thought he belonged in center field," said Ben. "I guess this was his chance to show he could handle it."

"And he did… at your expense," Ron Lewis added disdainfully.

"That's a part of the game, Dad. Any time one guy gets a break, it's almost always at somebody else's expense. You can't fault him for taking advantage of the chances that happen to come his way."

"No, but this one didn't just 'happen.' I think Williams got tired of waiting and decided to make his own break."

"I'm with Dad on this one," Scott chimed in. "It sure looked to me like he slammed you on purpose, Ben. What do you say?"

Ben studied the spaghetti on his plate as he wound it round and round his fork, the mass growing ever larger like a snowball rolling downhill. A similar knot formed in his stomach whenever he thought about the mishap in the outfield and its implications. Although his head had already come to the same conclusion as his father and brother, his heart struggled against admitting that his injury had been deliberately inflicted by one of his own teammates. It flew in the face of every ideal of sportsmanship he held dear. Believing it true was bad enough. Admitting it to anyone else would only compound the desecration, adding his own disloyalty to Derek's. So he swallowed his sour suspicions and said nothing.

Jan Lewis jumped in to curtail the awkward silence. "Well, he may have stolen a little of your thunder, Ben, but at least you weren't seriously hurt. I'm grateful for that."

Later that night, Ben put in an appearance at the unofficial team party commemorating the end of the season. Jessica was there, draped all over Derek and dripping with apparent adoration for him. Knowing her as well as he did, Ben guessed the show was at least partly for his benefit. He had no hard feelings, but Jessica hadn't said a single civil word to him since their breakup. Regardless whether her devotion to her new boyfriend was genuine or designed to punish him, Ben preferred not to provide her an audience. He stayed clear of the couple as much as possible, hanging out with Kyle and the rest of his friends instead. It was a great group of guys, and they'd become close over the past three years; sharing a damp dugout, a sweaty locker room, and a common goal had that effect. Now, this might be the last time he would see some of them.

"Here's to Lewis and Williams," Wilson hollered over the general din, raising his glass of brew. "Good luck to both of you in the draft and with your professional careers. Remember, wherever you go, you'll always be Huskies. Make us proud!"

While everyone cheered and joined in the toast, Ben caught a look from Williams across the room. Although he'd pasted a smile on his face, Derek's eyes telegraphed how much he resented once again sharing the limelight with him.

~~*~~

Ben finished off the last few days of class before making a trip home for his brother's high school graduation. He was glad to have something to do while he waited for his future to be determined in the MLB draft, which would be taking place right in the middle of finals week. In some ways, the timing was far from ideal, with so much happening all at once. Yet it seemed fitting that he should be closing the door on one phase of his life while walking into the next.

Ben made it through his English Lit exam on Monday, then headed south again to sit by the phone at his parents' house. On Tuesday, the start of the draft, the nerve-gnawing wait began. Ben burned a couple of hours attempting to study for his remaining finals – a complete waste of time. Although his eyes traveled back and forth across the pages, his mind was hopelessly distracted by the fact that, perhaps at that very moment, his fate was being decided by a bunch of men he'd never met. For the last two weeks, representatives from every major league franchise had been huddled together in hotel suites across the country, formulating strategy. Now, by a series of conference calls, they were divvying up this year's crop of baseball talent like so many bushels of wheat, competing for the premium cuts in the beginning and leaving the less-valuable varieties to the end.

Ben had no illusions about being selected in the first round with the likes of ASU's Mike Kelly or Stanford's David McCarty. Yet, as the minutes steadily ticked by, he couldn't help praying for the phone to ring. The sooner it did, the better his draft position. The better his draft position, the better the contract he could expect to negotiate. He thought his numbers should earn him a spot some-where in the first seven or eight rounds, but there was no way of knowing for sure. He just had to sweat it out along with dozens of others guys in the same situation. And who would ultimately take him? That was anybody's guess. Although he'd been contacted by scouts from four different clubs, indicating interest, he might not wind up with any of them. It could be a team he'd never heard from who chose him in the end.

When the phone rang earlier than he'd dared to hope, Ben broke out in a cold sweat. From the living room, he listened as his mother answered.

"Hello… Oh, hi, Claudia…"

False alarm. Ben rubbed his forehead. He'd never expected anything this soon, so there was no reason to be disappointed.

"…Listen, Claudia. I'm going to have to get back to you about that. I need to get off the phone now. My son's expecting a very important call."

Yes, probably the most important call of his life. For as long as he could remember, playing professional baseball had been his dream, his all-consuming passion, his sacred quest. The tenacious tendrils of that vision had, over time, tunneled their way into every fiber of his heart. So it had nearly killed him to have it ripped away the first time. Now, he was only a phone call away from seeing his fantasy finally realized, that victory made all the sweeter for having known the alternative.

His mother had barely replaced the handset when it rang again. Ben's shoulders tensed.

"Hello," she said. "…Just a minute, please. Ben, it's for you."

Ben jumped to his feet and sprinted to the kitchen. He knew none of his friends would be thoughtless enough to call him at such a time, so this had to be it! He took the phone – and a deep breath – before answering. "Hello."

"Ben Lewis?" asked the man at the other end of the line.

"Yes."

"I'm with the Mariner's organization, son. We've selected you in the second round. How would you like to play at the Kingdome someday?"

Second round! And to the hometown team, too! He could hardly believe it. "I… uh… I think I'd like that very much, sir. Thank you!"

Peals of uproarious laughter erupted in Ben's ear. "In your dreams, Lewis." More laughter.

Now he recognized the voice. "Derek, you've got a lot of nerve," Ben said through clenched teeth.

"I just thought I'd give you a little thrill. Come on, where's your sense of humor?"

"Ha, ha; very funny."

"That's better. I told Jessica you'd appreciate the joke. The two of us are having a little draft-day party at my place, and we wanted to include you in the fun. She's right here with me. Hey, Babe, wanna say something to your old boyfriend…?"

Ben hung up. "Practical joke," he explained to his mother, who had been standing by. "I'm gonna go shoot some hoops." He headed outside, letting the screen door slam behind him. Retrieving the basketball from under the laurel hedge, he pounded it relentlessly into the pavement in front of the garage door as he paced back and forth. He felt like taking off down the street at a run to blow off some steam, but he was still on standby.

Two hours later, the real call came.

-20-
Drafted

Ben hung up and let out an ear-splitting whoop worthy of an Apache warrior.

"Oakland, fourth round," he announced proudly to his family.

A celebratory mobbing ensued. Ben got pounded on the back by his brother even as his mother hugged and kissed him. His dad stuck out his chest and waited for his chance to shake the hand of "my son, the professional baseball player." A champagne toast – a rarity in the Lewis household – came next, followed by a furious round of phone calls to friends and family, broadcasting the news. Neighbors were invited in for an impromptu party, the beer flowing freely.

In the midst of the hubbub, Ben slipped away to use the phone in the den. He dialed Kevin Callaghan's number. While he waited on hold, he unconsciously rubbed the sports agent's embossed business card between his fingers like a lucky rabbit's foot. The thing was already well worn from riding around in Ben's pocket for weeks.

Five minutes went by, and then ten. Finally, Callaghan came on the line. "Ben Lewis? Sure, I remember you. Left-handed center fielder for Washington. Saw you play at Arizona State, right?" He spoke with a driven pace and intensity that marked him as a type A personality – all business and always hungry for the next deal.

"Yes, sir. You left your card for me, so I was hoping you would agree to negotiate my contract."

"What round did you go in, kid?"

"In the fourth, to Oakland."

"Not bad, not bad. I've got a lot of first and second rounders on my plate already, but I think we can work something out. Here's what you do. Expect Oakland to send someone out to meet with you soon. They'll say how lucky you are they selected you and how you should jump at the sweet deal they're offering. Let them talk all they want; just don't sign anything, okay?"

"Okay."

"You still got a year of college eligibility left, right?"

"Yes, I do."

"Good. We can use that to leverage a better deal, as if you might change your mind and go back for your senior year unless they cough up some serious cash."

"I just want what's coming to me. You know, what's fair for everybody."

"A purist, eh? You're only in this for the love of the game, I suppose."

"Not *only* that, no."

"Listen to me, Lewis. Unless you turn out to be some frigging boy wonder (you should excuse my French), you're going to have to pay your dues in the minors for at least a couple of years, where you'll be drawing an embarrassingly low salary, I might add. The pimple-faced high school dropout down the block is probably making more per hour working at McDonald's. Your signing bonus is all you've got to lean on until you make it to the big leagues. And God forbid you should fail to do so, it's your only compensation for your disappointment, see?"

"I understand that, but all I need is a chance to prove myself."

"Sure, sure, and that's what I'm talking about. A hefty signing bonus is your best insurance policy; it'll buy you more time to do just that. Even if you get off to a miserably slow start, management will think twice before releasing a guy they've got a couple hundred grand invested in."

"That makes sense."

"Of course it does. This is business, kid. You stick with me, and I'll look out for your interests. Let me know when you've got an offer in hand, and I'll get to work."

Ben thanked the agent and hung up. He could hear the noise of the party going on down the hall and knew he should be getting back to it. But first he took a minute to let everything that had happened sink in a little. None of it seemed quite real yet.

Forth round: awesome! Callaghan to represent him: outstanding! He was happy at the prospect of going to the A's too. It was a quality organization from everything he knew. Heck, they'd been to the

World Series the last three years straight. That spoke for itself. And since the team (as well as a couple of its minor-league affiliates) was west coast based, he had a better-than-average chance of playing some games close to home where his family – and hopefully Abby – could come.

Abby. That's who Ben really wanted to call. Since he jumped back in time, he rarely permitted himself to dwell on how much he missed his wife. That's how he still thought of her, even though she currently didn't know he existed. He couldn't help imagining her pixie face lighting up at his good news. Some people were stingy with themselves – guarded, careful not to risk too much emotionally. Not Abby. He'd never known anyone so honestly open, at least with him. No matter what happened during the day, good or bad, she had always been there for him, ready to celebrate or console. The fact that he couldn't share this achievement with her – at least not yet – took some of the shine off the trophy. It would all be worth it in the end, though, he reminded himself before rejoining the party.

~~*~~

Ben returned to campus for his remaining finals the next day and then went on to his apartment to pack up his belongings.

"Hey, Rosier, could you use another couch?" he called, sticking his head through his buddy's door on the second floor. "Kyle?"

Kyle appeared, foaming at the mouth with toothbrush in hand. "Just a minute, dude," he said through the froth before ducking back into the bathroom. "You wanna get rid of Big Bertha?" he asked when he returned.

"Got to. There's no room for her at home, and I can't take her on the road with me," Ben explained, referring to the oversized, camel-colored sofa he'd picked up at Salvation Army for thirty bucks the previous fall. "Either you take her, or she's got to go to the curb."

"Not the curb! I love that couch."

"She's all yours, then. Consider it a parting gift."

"Right." Kyle kicked at the edge of the dilapidated Oriental rug spread haphazardly across the floor. "Hey, you never can tell, dude. Maybe I'll catch up to you. If I have a stellar senior year and you really stink it up in the minors, we could both wind up in low A ball together after."

"Sounds great, all except for the part about me stinking, of course. So what have you heard from the guys? Anybody else been drafted?"

"Just Derek so far – in the ninth round by the Padres."

"Right. Coleman or Wilson might still have a shot, though... or there's that sure-footed outfielder by the name of Rosier. I hear he's pretty impressive."

Kyle snorted. "Don't bet on it; he's a real long shot."

~~*~~

Ben brought all of his college gear home in a borrowed van and, with Scott's help, hauled it into the house. Although he'd taken a load to Salvation Army first and sold back most of his textbooks, a miniature mountain remained. It was amazing how much he'd managed to accumulate in the three years he'd been away at school: a burgeoning music and video game collection, miscellaneous books, reams of paper, clothing in various stages of disrepair, and the assorted recreational equipment essential to college fun and games. Most of it would have to stay stacked in boxes along the wall of his old bedroom for now. He could take little with him to his next destination, and there would be no time to sort through the rest before he left.

Within three weeks of being drafted, Ben had a pro contract and a plane ticket in his hand. His agent had done an incredible job, winning for him a signing bonus of $185,000 plus an allowance to pay for his final year of college, if and when the time came. Even minus Callaghan's commission, it was more money than Ben had expected, more money than he could really comprehend or imagine spending at the moment. The bulk of it would go straight into the bank. He wasn't extravagant by nature and, as had been pointed out to him, the money needed to last a while. Even the one splurge Ben intended to allow himself – buying a better car, hopefully the classic Corvette he'd always wanted – would have to wait until he had more time. He was supposed to report to Oakland almost immediately.

So it was his old, reliable Toyota he drove north to Magnolia the day before he was slated to ship out. He figured that, if his calculations were correct, Abby should have arrived in town by then.

-21-
The Albrights

The house *was* spectacular, Abigail had to admit when she first arrived with her father. A stained cedar structure with striking horizontal lines, it showed a Frank Lloyd Wright influence that she liked. Still, what really made the place was the setting. The professional landscaping completely enfolded the house in a mantle of green – dozens of mature rhododendrons and lacy Japanese maples with a lush mix of ferns, hostas, and astilbes crowded around their feet. Even the strategically placed decorative rocks were nearly swallowed up in velvety jade jackets of moss. It was like descending into a fern grotto as they wound down the steep driveway to the house.

"A nice change from Tulsa, isn't it?" her father remarked, softening his normally gruff tone for his daughter.

"I liked Tulsa," she replied defensively, feeling lingering ties of loyalty to the town where she had spent less than four years of her life. "All my friends were there."

"Let's not go over that old, thorny ground again, Gail. You'll make new friends; you always do. And now you'll be attending the best-rated nursing school in the nation. Had to pull some strings to make sure you got into this fall's class. One day you'll thank me."

Judith Albright met them at the front door, not a single ash blonde hair out of place, and dressed as if she'd just returned from a luncheon at the Four Seasons. "Welcome to your new home, darling," she said, holding her daughter lightly by the shoulders and ghost-kissing her on both cheeks. "I trust you had a comfortable flight."

"It was fine," Gail answered, stepping into the wide, travertine foyer.

"And no trouble tying up loose ends before you left school?" her mother continued.

"No, everything's taken care of. I settled all my bills, and the paperwork's done for my transfer." She took in her surroundings: a spacious split-level entry flooded with light from an oversized transom window above the double doors. A beveled mirror and tasteful artwork completed the picture. "Lindsay and her parents send their love, by the way."

"How nice. You must be sure to write them a thank-you note for allowing you to stay on with them so long after your father and I had to leave."

"I will, and Lindsay wants to come out here for a visit next summer if that's okay."

"Certainly," said her father. "Now, let me show you something." Frank Albright put down the two suitcases he'd just brought in from the car and led Gail up a short flight of stairs into an expansive living room at the back of the house. "The *pièce de résistance*," he said with proprietary satisfaction as he gestured toward the soaring windows that dominated the exterior wall. "Puget Sound and the Olympic Mountains: can't buy a view like that just anywhere. Not in the state of Oklahoma, that's for damn sure."

Now at last Gail was truly awed. Man-made splendors, such as the house itself, didn't overly impress her, but glories fashioned by the hand of God were another matter. If she could learn to love this place, it would be for those – for the scenic wonder and diversity found here; for the mountains, the water, and maybe even for the legendary rain that kept things green.

She'd gotten a fresh look at Mt. Rainier from the plane and then, as they'd made a wide turn for the approach to SeaTac airport, the woodsy islands crowding south Puget Sound. Seattle was a big city. Yet, whenever she wanted, a short drive or ferry ride would soon transport her far from the urban sprawl. Even within town, parks, lakes, and pockets of tall fir and cedar trees provided a tangible thread of connection to the natural world.

"What do you think?" demanded her father. "Isn't it exactly as I told you?"

"It's a great house, Dad, and the view is amazing."

They'd come full circle now, and Gail hoped this would be the last move. For her whole life, her father had been chasing after the next step up the ladder of success, with his wife and daughter in tow. Five cities in twenty years – six, if she counted Seattle twice. She'd been born here while her dad was athletic director at a small private college. Then it was on to Shreveport, Bolder, Indianapolis, and Tulsa in quick succession as he'd risen up the ranks of college administration. Landing this job at the University of Washington was a dream come true, he'd said. Maybe now he would be content to stay put.

Regardless, Gail didn't plan to continue traipsing back and forth across the country with her parents. If she liked it here, she might stay on after graduation and put down permanent roots. It was as much of a home as she'd ever had. Although she'd been too young to form more than a few shadowy memories of living here before, they'd been back as a family several times over the years for visits. A few shirttail relatives remained in the area as well as life-long friends like the Campbells and Rustons.

As if reading her mind, Judith Albright broke in on Gail's thoughts. "We're invited to the Rustons' for dinner tomorrow night. When they heard you would be arriving today, they insisted on it. Paul is especially anxious to see you again," she said pointedly.

"Fine," Gail responded, not wanting to make waves.

The Rustons. Her feelings were mixed on that subject. They were like family – as close as if there had been an actual blood bond between them. If only everyone would leave it at that. But she knew at least some of the older generation wished to cement the alliance between the two families by the marriage of their children – a totally medieval concept.

Still, she understood their reasoning. On paper, at least, she and Paul made a perfect pair. In addition to their family ties, they shared futures in medicine and their Christian faith. Paul *was* a great guy – intelligent, kind, ambitious, even good-looking – everything a girl could want. Gail's affection for him ran deep, and, had they been left alone, who knows? Romance might have developed naturally enough. She often wished it had… sometimes prayed it still might.

But even if a seed of love managed to germinate, it would stand little chance of surviving, much less thriving, under the hot spotlight of parental scrutiny. The "encouragement" she and Paul received tended to have the exact opposite effect as intended, at least for Gail. Pressure, most overtly from her father, only made her revolt against the idea. And her mother's contribution to the debate?

"Of course you can do what you want, Gail," she would say placidly. "We're only your parents. You have a perfect right to ignore our wishes and advice if you choose." More subtle, maybe, but equally coercive.

Gail felt guilty after every rehashing of the subject – guilty for making people she cared about unhappy, for allowing her defiant streak to get the best of her, and for not being more open-minded about Paul. Bad feelings all around, but she couldn't help it. The more something was forced on her, the less she wanted it.

It was the same story with Sergeant when she was nine. She had begged for a kitten, but her father decided a full-grown German shepherd would make her a better pet. Sergeant was everything a dog should be – loyal, trustworthy, and fiercely protective – but Gail never learned to love him as she was told she should. It was Sergeant all over again with Paul, only worse because much more was at stake.

After admiring the view to her father's satisfaction, Gail asked, "Can I go to my room now? I'm kind of tired."

"Of course, dear," answered her mother. "It's at the top of the stairs and to the right, the door at the end of the hall. I think you'll find everything you need. Freshen up and have a nap before dinner if you like."

A nap sounded wonderful. She'd been up since dawn, and travel had a way of wearying her out of all proportion. Gail headed up to her bedroom, which, she discovered, was really a complete suite spanning the full depth of the house and including a sitting area, a cavernous walk-in closet, and an attached bath. Lots of windows too, on both the view and the street sides.

Some of the furniture she recognized – things the movers had taken along with the rest of the household from Tulsa. The bed was new, though, and more ornate than the one she'd used before. Her mother had been decorating again. Was it French Provincial this time? Gail wasn't sure. She only cared that she had a reasonable degree of privacy as well as enough space to study, sleep, and keep all her things neat.

In a year or so, maybe she'd see about moving out on her own – an idea her parents had strongly resisted so far. In the meantime, she could hardly complain about the accommodations.

And now, time to test out her elegant new bed. Gail slipped off her Italian sandals and size three jeans, slid between the satiny ecru sheets, and quickly dropped off to sleep.

~~*~~

By the following afternoon, Gail felt far more settled. She'd organized and stowed away all her belongings, taken the full tour of the house and yard, and even gone on a drive to get familiar with the immediate neighborhood. A map of Seattle she found in the glove box helped her get her bearings. Although she already had a general idea how the city was laid out from her previous visits, she was less clear about where things were in relation to the Magnolia district, now her home.

The University of Washington, she discovered, was only a few miles east – a short commute on paper at least – and the amenities of downtown even closer. On the other side of the map, which showed the entire Puget Sound region, Gail traced the varied routes out of town. Should she feel the need to get away, I-5 would take her north toward Canada or south to Tacoma, Portland, and beyond; I-90 headed east across Lake Washington and into the Cascade mountains; and blue dotted lines fanning out from the Seattle waterfront indicated ferry service to Bremerton, Winslow, Vashon Island, and Victoria, BC. Lots of options to explore in the months to come.

Later, along with a change of clothing, Gail deliberately donned a more positive attitude for dinner with the Rustons. The little flutter of excitement building in her chest reminded her that she actually looked forward to the reunion... except for the one niggling point of potential irritation. And that, if her father practiced some restraint, need not ruin the evening. Now that they lived in the same city, seeing Paul more frequently was inevitable, even with his heavy schedule as a medical resident at Children's Hospital.

All right, then. She was capable of setting aside her former prejudices, of opening up to new possibilities. One thing she knew for sure. If Paul was meant to be her soul mate, she didn't want to miss out on happiness by being pig-headed. She would give it every chance. They'd soon find out, once and for all, if there could be anything more than friendship between them.

Gail came downstairs when she was ready and joined her mother in the foyer.

"Your father will be bringing the BMW around in just a minute," said Mrs. Albright, checking her image in the mirror by the front door.

Gail nodded and stepped out onto the porch. As her eyes meandered over the yard, taking in the late-blooming rhododendrons, the white-hot brilliance of reflected sunlight drew her attention upward. "That car is still there," she said.

"What, dear?" asked her mother through the open door.

"See that blue car up on the road? It's been there for at least an hour. I saw it from my room earlier. Does it belong to one of the neighbors?"

"From the looks of it, I hardly think so. I imagine someone passing through broke down and abandoned it there. If it's not gone by the time we get back, we'll have it towed."

"No, there's someone in the driver's seat. I can see that now," Gail said, blocking the glare with her hand. "I wonder if he needs help."

"I'm sure he's fine; he's probably just looking at the view. I wish he'd move along, though, since he obviously doesn't belong here."

While Gail focused on the car parked above, trying to get a better look at the driver, a silver coupe cut across her line of sight and into the driveway, pulling up to the porch. Gail waved when she recognized the single occupant.

"It's Paul!" she announced with surprise.

-22-
Shipping Out

Ben couldn't believe his eyes. He'd been staked out in front of the Albrights' house for only an hour or so, all the while feeling uncomfortably like a stalker and prepared to give up the plan at any minute. And now, there she was: Abby, no more than forty yards away, standing on her front step as accommodating as could be. Quickly, before she noticed him or could disappear, he raised his camera and took her picture, zooming in as close as possible. Then he snapped two more, just to be safe.

He needed a fragment of her to take with him, something tangible to hold on to while he was away. Although a photograph fell absurdly short of the real thing, it was the best he could do for the moment and his only hedge against the nagging fear that he would forget her. His memories of his former life still *seemed* sharp enough. But maybe that's the way it happened – fading so gradually that you weren't even aware of it.

She looked up at him then, signaling Ben's heart to perform an abrupt flip-flop. He suddenly visualized rushing down the driveway and pulling her into his arms. If he could just speak to her, peer deep into the pale sky of her eyes, it seemed impossible that she would not know him, that she wouldn't remember their history together or at least sense a cosmic connection between them.

"Don't be a bloody fool," he muttered. *She'd think you were an escaped lunatic, and you'd never get near her again. Drive away. Now! Before you attract too much attention and her father calls the cops.*

As Ben was about to follow his own advice and go, another vehicle came along and turned into the Albrights' drive. Abby lit up and waved as the car cruised to a stop near the porch. There was obviously someone inside she was very happy to see. A tall, sandy-haired man, probably in his late twenties, climbed out to meet her, sweeping her off her feet and twirling her around twice before setting her back down again. No kiss, at least, Ben noted with some relief. Still, he didn't like the way the stranger looked at her, the way he managed to keep hold of Abby's hand even after finally releasing her from the embrace.

Abby didn't look as if she minded either. In fact, she seemed completely delighted. The two were laughing together now. It was hard to watch, yet Ben couldn't turn away. He treasured any chance to see Abby. But *he* wanted to be the one to make her laugh, the one upon whom that dazzling smile of hers shone. Now his parting image would be of his wife in the arms of some other man.

So who was this guy, anyway? And why did he look so damned familiar?

It was a helpless feeling, leaving without knowing the answers. Ben reluctantly started the engine and slipped the Toyota into gear, easing from the curb. A horn blared, shocking him out of his reverie. He slammed on the brakes as a black Audi veered around him, the driver gesturing his disgust. So much for making a discreet exit. Ben ducked his head as he drove away, hoping Abby hadn't gotten a good look at him.

~~*~~

Ben's every nerve, scalp to toes, jolted to attention when his alarm sounded the next morning. This was it: the beginning of his professional career. He'd been preparing for it all his life, sinking his time, sweat, and passion into baseball as long as he could remember. Now it was all paying off.

Ben had packed nearly everything the day before. One large suitcase waited by the front door along with his jacket, plane ticket and a small carry-on. After showering and brushing his teeth, he added his toiletry tote to a second bag, zipped it closed, and parked it with the other things.

His dad was long gone. Since he had a six AM start at Boeing, they'd said their goodbyes the night before. Scott was coming along to the airport, which left only Ben's mom to see him off from home.

"Are you sure you have everything?" she asked, fret lines wrinkling her forehead.

"Yup, all the essentials: mostly cash and clothes. I really won't need much else since I doubt I'll have time for anything beyond baseball where I'm going."

"I guess this is it then," she said, loosely taking his hand and studying the face of her firstborn.

"Don't worry, Mom. I'll be fine."

"Of course you will. I'm proud of you, Ben, and not just for your athletic achievements. You have strong character and a good head on your shoulders too. Rely on them when things get difficult."

He chuckled softly. "I'm not expecting this to be easy, but it's what I've always wanted."

"I know, and I hope everything turns out as wonderful as you've imagined. Just remember your family loves you no matter what, and you can call us anytime."

"I love you too, Mom," Ben said, stooping to hug her tight. "I'll be in touch as soon as I get settled."

She kissed him on the cheek and reluctantly released him, remaining on the porch until he had driven away with his brother.

"So, you're off to Oakland first, then," Scott commented from the passenger seat. "Is that customary, to be invited to team headquarters, I mean?"

"I guess so, at least for the higher draft picks. I'm supposed to have a physical, meet some of the brass, and get a tour. Tomorrow, I'll be packed off to mini-camp in Arizona, and after that to my minor league assignment. God, I still can't believe any of this is real. Later today, I might be shaking hands with Rickey Henderson or Jose Canseco. Tonight I could be watching them play from the owner's suite at the Coliseum!"

"They're just people, Ben. I hope you're not going to go all weird on them, like some lame groupie."

"I don't know what I'll do; I've never met anybody famous before. I'll probably get tongue-tied at least. I bet the same thing would happen to you, though, if you ran into your hero Frank Lloyd Wright."

"I'd probably have a stroke if I ran into old Frank…"

"Like I said."

"…especially since he's been dead for about forty years."

"Oh."

"You know even less about architecture than I do about baseball," Scott concluded.

Their northward progress came to a virtual standstill shortly after merging into the morning rush-hour traffic on highway 167. Ben thrummed the steering wheel with his fingers, preaching patience to himself while he waited for the stop-and-go traffic to go again. No need to panic, though; he'd allowed two hours extra to catch his plane.

"So, you'll be a college man when I see you next," he remarked to his brother as they crept along. "You must be pretty excited about that."

"Yup. I hope I made the right decision by choosing U-Dub instead of Wazzu, though. I guess I can always transfer later."

"You'll like the U, and maybe you could drive my car some while I'm gone. It's not good for it to sit idle for months," Ben said, running a hand across the dashboard.

"No problem. I'll take good care of her for you."

"In fact, you might as well keep her. I'll be buying some new wheels as soon as I get the chance anyway."

"Are you serious?"

"Sure. Why not?"

"Sweet! Thanks. I was wondering how I was going to afford a car with all my money going towards school. For once I won't mind taking your hand-me-downs."

~~*~~

When Ben phoned home a week later, his mother answered. "Now, tell us everything," she said after her husband joined them on the extension. "First of all, where are you, and are you okay?"

"I'm fine, Mom. I'm in Phoenix, and it looks like I'll be staying here to play on the rookie team for the rest of the season."

Ben continued with an animated report of his brief visit to Oakland – how he'd been picked up at the airport like a VIP and whisked to the ball field. After taking a full tour of the A's impressive facility, he'd undergone a complete physical. "Nothing out of the ordinary, except they took a real close look at my left shoulder and arm," he explained.

"Because of your injury in the Washington State game," concluded Mr. Lewis.

"Yeah, that's right. I told them it was only a stinger and that I was fine now. But I guess they needed to see for themselves. Anyway, everything checked out all right. Then later, I got to hang around the locker room, meet some of the players – Harold Baines, Mark McGuire, and even Rickey Henderson. *I* shook hands with the new stolen-bases champ! He acted like just a regular guy too. I was pretty psyched, but you can tell Scott I played it cool. And – Dad, you won't believe this – I got to take batting practice with the team before the game!"

"No kidding? I sure wish I could have been there to see it, son. How'd you do?"

"I was so nervous I could hardly hit a thing. But just being on the field with those guys, looking up at the grandstands filling with fans... It was awesome. I've really got something to shoot for now."

Although he didn't mention it to his parents, that was the end of the red carpet treatment. When he arrived in Phoenix, no one met him at the airport, and no five-star accommodations awaited him. His first look at the ballpark was anticlimactic, too, after the scale and luxury he'd just seen in Oakland. In the low minors, Ben soon discovered, the facilities were nothing special, and neither was he. He was just another rookie starting at the bottom.

-23-
Rookie Ball

Ben knew living in Arizona would be different. However, the arid landscape, punctuated by cactus and red rocky buttes, contrasted so dramatically with the evergreen trees and snow-capped peaks of western Washington that it might as well have been a foreign country... or even another planet. The fact that his twenty-five teammates were all strangers, some of whom didn't speak English, reinforced the impression.

Baseball served as their common language and the thing most dependably familiar. Yet even that had altered. The lighter, power-packed aluminum bats of college were gone. It was wood and only wood from here on out, making for a more difficult adjustment than Ben had expected. It was like learning to hit all over again.

The intensity of competition proved even more humbling, though. Everybody – his teammates as well as opponents – played at a higher level than he was used to. They had each been stars in their own home towns: big fish in little ponds. Now all of them were small fry again, thrown together into a crowded pool packed with talent, testosterone, and other hazards.

Despite Ben's euphoria over actually being paid to play baseball, he soon found out that working all day every day under the desert sun was no picnic. The pressure-cooker combination of heat, competition, and exhaustion took its toll. At least he and his fellow rookie Athletics avoided the grueling travel schedule so common in the minors – an advantage of the Arizona league where all seven teams called the greater Phoenix area home. No matter who they played during the day, they could always return to their own beds at night.

Ben phoned his family regularly, to report that he was "doing great" and to be cheered by hearing at least one familiar voice. Still, after a few weeks, he so longed for some sign of home that he was almost happy to see a former teammate take the field against him. Almost. It was Derek Williams, playing for the AZL Padres. Since he knew Derek had been drafted by San Diego, it wasn't a surprise that their paths should cross again so soon. At least now it was official; they were opponents, not friends.

Ben had their long-standing rivalry on his mind when he stepped up to the plate in the first inning. Under the circumstances, he would have preferred to make an out in just about any other fashion. But the ball he hit sailed lazily – inevitably, it seemed – toward center field. Williams hardly had to move; it dropped straight into his glove. Ben later returned the favor, although he had to go more out of his way to snag Derek's pop fly in the fourth. The two exchanged looks of barely disguised hostility across the expanse of well-watered grass, but they managed to avoid any closer contact during or after the game.

The next time their teams played each other, Derek remained in the dugout while someone else got a turn in center. In the eighth, though, he came off the bench to take over at first base, a rare circumstance that set up a face-to-face meeting.

"Williams," Ben said with a nod of acknowledgement when safely aboard after singling up the middle.

"Lewis."

That probably would have been the end of the exchange had the Padres' coach not called for a pitching substitution, interrupting the action and leaving Ben stranded at first base for several minutes. "Hot day," he said casually, attempting small talk as they waited.

"If you can't stand the heat…"

"I'm good."

"Are you sure? You look kind of worn-out to me."

"Never felt better in my life."

The replacement arrived on the mound.

"How's Jessica?" Ben asked when he couldn't think of anything else to say.

"She's real fine… except she's got it bad for me. Poor girl misses me so much that she's going to spend all her hard-earned money to fly down here and see me play."

"That should be fun for her – the baseball, I mean."

"It's *me* she's comin' to see."

"Don't flatter yourself, Williams. In case you haven't noticed, Jessica's a serious baseball junkie. Without the uniform, she'd never have given you a tumble in the first place. Lose it and she'll drop you so fast it'll make your head spin." This Ben knew from personal experience. "And for the record, *I* broke up with *her*, so it's not like you were even Jessica's first choice."

Leaning forward with hands resting on his thighs, Ben kept his eyes focused on the new pitcher going through his warm-up tosses. Behind him, he could hear Williams smacking his fist into his glove, again and again. Ben knew then that he had gotten under the guy's skin. *Just one more little dig...* Bracing, he added, "Must be annoying as hell, always coming in second to me."

Derek exploded. He dove at Ben's back, fists and profanity flying.

The coaches and umpires immediately intervened, and Williams was ejected from the game. He left the field kicking and cussing, the eruption ultimately costing him a two-week benching and a hefty fine.

Although Ben's own role in the scuffle escaped the umpire's censure, his coach invoked a little-enforced rule against fraternizing with the opposite team to charge him a nominal amount for trash talking. Money well spent, Ben decided. He'd endured Derek Williams's abuse in silence long enough.

~~*~~

By mid-July, Ben had acclimated – as much as humanly possible – to the suffocating heat and the pace of his new life. His athletic body adjusted naturally to the heavier physical demands, building muscle mass and endurance as needed.

If only his brain could have done the same for the psychological grind and the relentless pressure to perform. Everybody knew advancing to the next level, or just keeping your job, depended almost entirely on putting up good numbers. With every aspect of his game being constantly measured, monitored, recorded, analyzed, and compared, it was hard for Ben to forget it... impossible for him to ignore it. It preyed on his mind, especially when things weren't going well.

He skidded into a minor slump toward the end of the month. Nothing alarming at first – just a pair of uncharacteristic fielding errors and a slight dip in his batting average. Yet it was enough to trip the switch in his brain that started thoughts of anxiety, discouragement, and self-doubt spinning in his head. He worried, so he tried harder. But the harder he tried, the more forced – and unsuccessful – his efforts became. A phone call home didn't help; it only reminded him that his dad's vicarious dreams were at stake as well as his own enormous expectations. Added pressure he didn't need.

Some guys eased the stress and bolstered their confidence with alcohol. Others, in the beds of local girls. Booze and women: both readily available. Ben had long-since been cured of the first. The second was a genuine temptation – one he didn't want to give in to. That meant careful navigation of the mine-filled waters of his off hours. It's not like there were hoards of female fans waiting to intercept players at the ballpark, not in *this* league. But there seemed to be no shortage of women at the area watering holes he and his teammates frequented. There Ben would drink his Coke, keep to his own group, and try to avoid making eye contact with anything in a skirt. Another peek at Abby's photo, which he always carried with him, reminded him why. If that wasn't enough, he'd add a five-mile run, a cold shower, and the distraction of a good sci-fi book. So far, the strategy had gotten him through.

Ben eventually conquered his slump too. After digging himself into an ever-deepening hole for a couple weeks, he regrouped. He remembered what Kevin Callaghan had told him about his signing bonus buying him both time and the benefit of the doubt; he probably wouldn't be sent packing the first time his stats slipped a little. Knowing that relieved the pressure, and he began to play better almost immediately. By the third week of August, Ben had his numbers solidly back in a respectable range, which is why he was so surprised to receive an ominous summons to the manager's office.

-24-
Fall Forecast

"Hey, Lewis. The skipper wants to see you," assistant coach Hondel announced.

The usual locker room racket instantly dropped decibels to a low murmur. Ben was already showered, dressed, and, until that moment, looking forward to a good dinner and a little down time. Now a sudden wave of nausea killed any thoughts of food.

This is how it happened, he knew. They purposely waited until the other guys were leaving before calling you in. Then, when the manager finished delivering the bad news, you could clear out your locker and exit without the further humiliation of an audience watching you do it. That's how Hendricks got the axe the week before. Ben had caught up with him afterward as he headed for the bus stop, luggage in hand.

"Now I know why the coaches finally quit yelling at me for playing so crappy," Hendricks said. "It was because they felt sorry for me. They knew I was going home. The fact that they suddenly started being nice should have tipped me off."

Had *he* missed the signs as well? Ben racked his brain for clues as he stowed the last of his gear away. Hondel *had* given him an uncharacteristic "attaboy" pat on the back the other day. If Oberman, who never seemed to have a kind word for anybody, was nice to him too, he'd know it was all over.

Ben could feel the eyes of his teammates – or former teammates – following him as he made the long, slow walk toward the manager's office. Through the window in the door, he could see Cal Oberman at his desk, bent over some paperwork. Ben attempted a dry swallow and knocked. Was that pity on the man's face when he looked up to motion him in?

"You wanted to see me, Skip?" said Ben, poking his head through the door.

"Yes. Come in and have a seat, son," he said gently. "It's time you and I had a chat."

Oh, God, no! Ben eased into the offered chair, feeling every last red corpuscle drain from his head toward his extremities. His hands and feet were lead weights.

"Don't look so grim. It's not what you're thinking," Oberman went on. "Quite the opposite, actually. I wanted to talk to you about your future with the Oakland organization."

The iron band binding Ben's chest fell away and he could breathe again. "My future? You mean I still have one?"

"Yes, of course you do. I know you struggled last month, and I *was* beginning to wonder. But you fought your way through that slump; you didn't let it beat you. That shows mental toughness, which is something that can't be taught. Either a guy has it by the time he gets here or he doesn't. You wouldn't get much further in this sport without it, though." Oberman paused.

Ben nodded. "Yes, sir. I mean, no, sir."

"What it boils down to is this. Upper management is very high on you, Ben. They've told me you are to be given every advantage, every opportunity to develop your talent to its full potential. That's why we're bringing you back for the Fall Instructional League. I trust that won't be a problem. Not too tired or anything?"

Ben couldn't keep up. He still had the shakes from thinking he was about to be released, and now instead Coach had offered him the six weeks of extra training reserved for top prospects. Of course he would come! "C-count me in! I'm never too tired to play ball."

"Good, good. I like your spirit, Lewis, and it's nice to see you aren't afraid of hard work. I'll fill you in on the details later."

Ben took his cue from Oberman, standing when he did and shaking his outstretched hand. "Thank you, sir. I appreciate your confidence, and I won't let you down."

"For your sake, I hope not." He pinned Ben with a laser beam look. "Plenty of other guys happy to take your place if you do."

"Right."

Ben turned to go, teetering somewhere between relief and paranoia. The coach's last line had been completely unnecessary. It's not like Ben was in any danger of becoming overconfident. Only moments before he'd skirted the brink of total annihilation. Now Oberman had made sure he knew he wasn't out of danger. Never would be, Ben supposed as he closed the office door behind him. If he wanted to play baseball, he'd have to learn to live with the needling uncertainty and the perpetual stress that came with it.

~~*~~

A thousand miles to the north, Abigail Albright approached the Health Sciences Center at the University of Washington to begin fall quarter of the undergraduate nursing program. The campus wasn't completely foreign to her. Her father had given her a private tour when she first arrived in June. Plus, she'd taken one class during the summer, just to get her feet wet, and recently attended a nursing orientation session. Still, her insides felt like a sea of eels as she entered the building to face the first day of her nine o'clock pharmacotherapeutics course.

Her dad had dropped her off at the curb on his way to his office, and it was only eight-fifteen... which was fine. She had hoped to pick a seat and get comfortable before the instructor and the rest of the students trailed in. But the classroom door was locked, leaving her stranded in the foyer with a few other scattered early birds.

One face looked familiar – the girl with the long dark hair, standing near the drinking fountain and hugging her books to her chest. Gail was sure she'd seen her at orientation. So, with the boldness acquired through years of practice meeting new people – the one advantage of relocating so often – she put on her warmest smile and walked over to introduce herself.

"Hi. I'm Gail Albright. You're in nursing too, aren't you?"

The girl looked up, responding. "That's right. My name's Lorrie. Lorrie Knutson."

"Nice to meet you, Lorrie."

"You too. Were you here last year? I don't remember seeing you around, taking prereqs with the rest of us."

"No. I just transferred from the University of Oklahoma, so I'm new."

"That explains it, then."

"Explains what?"

"Why you look even more nervous than I feel."

"I've moved around so much, it shouldn't bother me. But I guess I never completely outgrew the first-day-of-school jitters. And here we are starting off with Pharmacotherapeutics of all things." Gail scrunched up her nose and shook her head. "The name alone is seriously intimidating. I'd rather get straight into the hands-on stuff, the clinical work. Wouldn't you?"

"No way! That's the part that really gives me the shakes. The academic courses don't scare me, but I break out in a cold sweat when I think about surgery or poking a needle into somebody. All that blood… " Lorrie's eyes grew wide, and she clapped a hand over her mouth. "Shit! I shouldn't have said that," she muttered. "You've got to promise you won't tell anyone! If they find out I'm a closet hemo-phobe, I'll be bounced out of here so fast…"

Gail couldn't help giggling at the irony. "Lorrie! Why on earth did you go into nursing if you can't stand the sight of blood?"

Lorrie shrugged, tipping her head to one side apologetically. "It's what I've always planned. Sort of a family tradition, really – my grandma, my mom, my aunt, two sisters… Well, you get the idea. Of course, when we played hospital as kids, there was never any actual blood."

"So, when you figured out what was really involved in the profession, why didn't you change your major?"

"Kind of crazy, huh? But don't worry. I've got it all figured out. I'm going to be a school nurse. I like kids, and there shouldn't be too much gore involved – just vomit and a few skinned knees, which I can handle. So if I can only get through the program…"

"I wish you luck, then, and I swear to take your secret with me to the grave," Gail assured her solemnly, holding up her right hand to formalize the promise.

"Thanks. I think that makes you my new best friend."

"Okay, I'll take the job."

"So, Gail, do you live on campus? Have any disgusting habits? And what's your romantic status? If we're going to be best friends, I have a right to know."

Gail laughed. "Fair enough. Don't think the worse of me, but I still live with my parents, I bite my nails something awful, and my romantic status is… Well, it's ambiguous at best. No, let's say it's yet to be determined. There's this guy named Paul. He's a resident in pediatrics."

"Aha, a doctor! Tell me more."

Gail was soon too busy with her new friends and demanding school schedule to pine any longer for things left behind in Tulsa… or to fret much about her future with Paul either.

She saw him intermittently, most often at church or when their two families got together. But occasionally Paul picked somewhere interesting to go, and they set off on their own, just the two of them. They met once at the Seattle Center, taking in a film at the IMAX and a trip up the Space Needle. Another day they'd driven north and then caught a ferry across the Sound to spend a sunny afternoon exploring Lopez Island by bike.

Gail never referred to these outings as dates, not to herself or to anyone else. And her parents were suspiciously silent on the subject, satisfied that things were moving in the desired direction, she supposed. As she vowed when she'd first arrived in Seattle, Gail kept an open mind about Paul, willing to see what, if anything, would develop between them.

They *had* become closer. That much was clear. She felt at ease with Paul; she enjoyed his company; and they never seemed to lack for conversation. It had all been very comfortable and non-threateningly platonic so far. Paul behaved like a perfect gentleman. He never so much as inched a toe over the line… let alone a pair of hands or lips. A bear hug and a peck on the cheek: his displays of affection had gone no further.

Gail sensed that more simmered just below the surface, though, and that Paul held back for her sake. Being older, he had always been protective of her, and he must also feel the responsibility of preserving the friendship between themselves and their families. Why risk ruining what they already had, which was great, by forcing things to the next level before they were both ready? Yes, better to proceed with caution. Yet Gail couldn't help being curious – and the tiniest bit impatient – to see what would happen when they finally took that next step forward. It seemed inevitable that they would. The only question was when.

-25-
Winter Break

Ben hit his stride that October. He began to play with more confidence and to believe he truly belonged in the pros. By the time his extended season finished, he trusted his performance had been impressive enough to kick him up a couple rungs on the minor league ladder. With a little luck, he would skip over the low A team and head straight for Modesto, California, after spring training next year, or maybe even AA Huntsville in Alabama.

Flying home to Seattle, Ben mentally reviewed his plans for the weeks ahead. He looked forward to shopping for his new (or at least new*er*) car – something sporty yet not *too* flashy – and spending time with his family and friends. But top priority had to be bodybuilding. The training staff in Phoenix now placed so much emphasis on increasing muscle mass that Ben didn't dare take it easy over the winter. If he did, the power he'd managed to put on so far would melt away by the spring. "Use it or lose it." The old adage was all too true in this case, and he couldn't afford to drop even an ounce of hard-earned brawn.

The part-time job he'd arranged at the YMCA would make keeping up with his training regime a whole lot easier. The athletic director, whom Ben knew well from working there off and on throughout his high school and college years, had hired him to teach a baseball technique and conditioning class for older kids during his break. Although he didn't necessarily need the job to get by financially, thanks to his signing bonus, the unlimited access to a well-equipped weight room was a priceless perk.

Plus he liked playing with the kids, something he'd discovered his first year as a day camp counselor at the Y. The feeling was mutual too. Ben had been surprised that summer to find both boys and girls trailing after him like he was some kind of pied piper. They constantly vied for his attention, and in the pool he'd have two or three hanging on to his arms and shoulders at once. Now, he looked forward to passing on his love of baseball to some of those same kids.

Beginning his campaign to reconnect with Abby ran a close second on Ben's off-season priority list. He intended to waste no time getting started. At the first opportunity, he'd head up to the U and see if he couldn't arrange to run into her again. Between the standing invitation to crash on Kyle's couch and the added excuse of visiting Scott, Ben figured he could spend part of every week on campus. So what if he made a nuisance of himself in the process? He had to see Abby.

~~*~~

"Our mystery man is back," Lorrie remarked during a break between classes the following January.

Gail's head popped up from the lecture notes she'd been reviewing. "Really?"

"I'm sure it's the same guy. Come see for yourself."

Gail joined her friend at the window of the second-story student lounge overlooking Pacific Avenue, and followed her gaze to a young man across the street, sitting on the edge of a short retaining wall. One hand was tucked into the pocket of his purple and gold letterman's jacket. With the other, he supported an open, hard-cover book, which didn't seem to hold his interest.

Even from a distance, Gail recognized him. Not that there was anything terribly distinctive about his appearance – a bit above average height she knew from seeing him before, hair a very ordinary dark brown with just enough wave to give it body. Here again she was going by memory since today he wore a knit cap pulled down over his ears.

When she and her friends first passed him on the sidewalk out front last November, it had been his extraordinary eyes that riveted her attention. Not so much the espresso-brown color and heavy lashes; rather their haunted expression. He'd stopped in his tracks and stared so soulfully at her as she went by, that she couldn't turn away. His look conveyed the idea that he carried some vital message, something for her alone… which, of course, was ridiculous. She didn't even know the guy. If he'd singled her out of the group of girls she was with, it was probably only for her blond hair or something equally superficial. Still, just for one moment, she'd felt so drawn to him that she had the crazy impulse to stop and ask what he wanted to tell her. But then she was already running late for her anatomy/physiology class.

Such a small event, yet Gail hadn't forgotten it.

She and her friends spotted the same guy several more times before the end of term – the sightings becoming a running joke – but no one seemed to know who he was or why he kept hanging around. Now it was the start of the new quarter and he was back.

"I'm right, aren't I?" Lorrie prompted. "Gail?"

"Oh… Yes, it's definitely him." Still gazing out the window, she noticed the fog generated by the man's exhaled breath and added, "He must be freezing, sitting out there on that cold concrete."

Lorrie glanced out again. "So-o-o… maybe you should go sit with him, just to keep him warm," she teased. "It would be the compassionate thing to do and, as a nurse, you are sworn to alleviate human suffering wherever you find it." Failing to get a rise out of her friend, Lorrie went on. "Also, he *is* kind of cute, if you're attracted to the strong, ruggedly-handsome-but-darkly-dangerous stalker type."

Gail laughed.

"Oh, good. I was beginning to think you weren't listening."

"Well, I was," Gail said, finally turning from the window. "But I can't believe he's really a stalker. A little odd maybe, but not dangerous."

"I don't know. You must have taken an amazing psychology class down in Tulsa if you can assess this guy's character without ever actually speaking to him."

~~*~~

Once more, Ben returned to his friend's apartment, discouraged and chilled to the bone.

"Dude, your lips are the most gruesome shade of purple!" was Kyle Rossier's greeting. "I swear they are. What the heck have you been doing? Hanging out in a meat locker all afternoon?"

"No. Just walking around campus again."

"Do you know how cold it is out there? Seriously, you'd better find a new hobby – something indoors this time – or get yourself some warmer clothes. One or the other."

Ben turned both palms up and hunched his shoulders in a "wudaya-gonna-do?" gesture. He had no reasonable explanation. Surely only an idiot would sit outside in subfreezing temperatures pretending to read for two and a half hours in hopes that the one single person upon whom his future happiness depended might happen to stroll by with nothing better to do than strike up a conversation – and a relationship – with him, a total stranger. What kind of lame plan was that?

Of course, anything could be made to sound absurd if you tried hard enough. Even baseball, when you boiled it down, amounted to no more than hitting a little white ball with a stick, and then running as if your life depended on it. The worthwhile object of the exercise? To advance by ninety-foot increments until you reached home, which was – let's face it – back precisely where you had started. Is that any way for a grown man to make a living?

Okay, now he *was* thinking crazy, to question the validity of his chosen profession. Maybe his mind had gone numb from the cold. *Stick to the plan*, he reminded himself. It was bound to pay off sooner or later. He had come so close that day last fall…

"So who is she?" demanded Kyle.

"What?"

"Earth to Lewis. I said, who is she?"

"Who?"

"Do you always have to answer a question with another question? Come on, bro. I figure it has to be a woman that's got you acting this way. You don't drive up here twice a week just to see *my* pretty face, or because my couch is so comfortable. So, spill it. Who is she?"

"Okay, okay, you win," Ben said, flopping down on what used to be his old sofa, now his borrowed bed. "She's a nursing student, and I'm in love with her. But there's a huge problem."

"What's that? Is she married or dying or something?"

"No. She doesn't know I exist."

"Is that all? You had me worried for a second. I thought it was going to be something major. Not knowing you exist is totally fixable, dude."

-26-
New Strategy

To answer Kyle's questions, Ben related a semi-plausible story about a love-at-first-sight encounter with Abby based on the day in November when he'd come so close to speaking to her. Supposedly, he saw her, their eyes locked, and he just knew. Saying it aloud, it sounded like pure romantic drivel, even to him. So he could hardly believe it when his friend accepted the explanation without blinking, sporting a dopey grin as he listened to the tale. Ben chalked it up to that fact that Kyle had recently fallen under the spell of a fresh-faced sophomore named Kristy, whom he had been enthusiastically dating.

With Ben sprawled on one couch and Kyle stretched out on the other, the two talked, off and on, into the night. The Sonics were playing on TV. Neither of them cared much about the game, but it gave them something to look at while they brainstormed ways for Ben to improve his chances of hooking up with Abby.

"Hey, dude, you could put on a uniform and deliver flowers to her," Kyle suggested early on. "You'd need her name, though. Have you at least managed to learn that much about her?"

"Yeah. She goes by Gail: Gail Albright."

"Gail. Okay, so this is what you do. You buy a huge bunch of roses or something – girls like that kind of junk – and you march into the medical center like you own the joint. If you look official, I bet a secretary will tell you where to find your girl, maybe even give you her schedule."

"Knowing her schedule would make things a *whole* lot easier. Not bad, Rosier. I like the devious way your mind works. Although, I think it might take a serious bribe or someone working on the inside to pry loose that kind of information."

"Someone on the inside? You mean like a spy?"

"Sure, why not? As long as we're talking subterfuge, we might as well go all the way."

Each chewed that thought over a while.

Half a basketball game and a couple beers later, Kyle returned to it. "Kristy could do it."

"What's that?" Ben asked lazily.

"Go undercover – spy, like you said. She could pretend to be interested in the nursing program. Get a tour. Look around. Sort of infiltrate the place. No! No, I've got an even better idea!" With an explosion of laughter, Kyle sat up to face Ben. "This would be legendary, dude. You check into the University Hospital with some fake illness, right?"

"What kind of illness?"

"Who cares, man? Make up something fatal. Then say it's your dying wish to have little miss student-nursey Gail come hold your hand. They send for her, and you make a miraculous recovery. It's perfect!" Kyle nearly fell off the couch in convulsions of mirth.

Ben pitched a pillow at his head. "Brilliant, Rosier. Pure genius," he said dryly.

In the more rational light of day, Ben found he was no further ahead than before. He reverted to random patrols of the area around the UW medical complex, trusting in persistence and fate to bring him together with Abby at last.

Time was running out, though, he realized as he loitered near one of the entrances just before noon on a chilly Friday in mid February. In a week, he would be leaving, reporting to Phoenix for spring training. It would be months before he had another chance to see Abby.

Ben picked up an abandoned copy of the school paper, casually leafing through its pages as he waited. An article in the alumni news section caught his attention. It concerned a former student who graduated with a medical degree: Paul Ruston. Ben knew that name – as well as the face in the accompanying photo – from somewhere. Their tenures at the U would have overlapped, according to the information given, but it seemed unlikely their paths had crossed on campus.

Ben read on.

...After successfully completing an internship in pediatrics, he now works as a resident at Children's Hospital here in Seattle. When asked about his plans, Dr. Paul Ruston said he would like to estab-

142

lish a practice in this area. *"Although I hope to do some traveling, Seattle has always been my home. My family, friends, and future are here."*

Of course! Things started to click into place. This was the guy Abby had mentioned – the "family friend" her parents were so crazy about. And the man he'd seen at the Albrights' house, whirling Abby in his arms? That had been Ruston too. No wonder he'd looked so familiar; Ben had seen his photograph before, in his previous life. Naturally Abby had been happy to see him; she'd said they were very close.

What was the rest? What else had she said about him? From the recesses of his mind, Ben conjured up Abby's words.

"…and then he died – on Valentine's Day, run down by a truck as he crossed the street in front of the Health Sciences building."

It had happened on this very spot, Ben realized with amazement. Paul had been on his way here, bringing lunch and flowers for Abby, when he was killed.

The hair on the back of Ben's neck prickled. *Oh, God, what year would that have been? And what's today's date?* Quick mental calculations confirmed what his gut already told him – the accident would happen today, any minute now, right in front of him.

Even as this truth registered, Ben felt his eyes being dragged irresistibly upward, away from the paper in his hand to the other side of the road. He didn't want to look. He knew what he would see there: Paul Ruston strolling up the sidewalk without a worry in the world, carrying a deli box and a cheerful bundle of roses wrapped in shiny cellophane.

Exactly. Ben blinked hard at the sight, twice, before accepting its reality.

His stomach wrenched. It was bad enough to hear, after the fact, about a total stranger who had been tragically killed, but infinitely worse to realize you're about to witness the violent death of someone you know, even slightly. And suddenly Paul didn't seem like a stranger anymore. He was right there, alive and breathing less than thirty yards away. This was a real human being – someone with a family and loads of potential, someone Abby cared about.

Ben staggered forward, involuntarily drawn toward the horror about to unfold.

The whole thing was surreal. It was like watching a movie, already knowing it would end in tragedy. It wouldn't matter how many times you rewound the tape, the result would be the same. The hero would die, over and over again.

But this wasn't a movie… and the accident hadn't actually happened yet, not in this timeline.

Ben had nearly reached the street now.

A break in the traffic, and Paul stepped off the opposite curb.

This had to be it.

Sure enough. A delivery van sped toward them, swerving erratically.

Could he really stand by, a spectator, and watch history repeat itself? Impossible. He should do – *had* to do – something!

Paul continued into the path of disaster, oblivious.

No time to think. The adrenaline coursing through Ben's veins demanded action. Instinct took over. He charged into the street, racing two tons of hurtling steel for the other side.

Never before had so much depended on his athletic ability. This was no game; lives were at stake… including his own. But it was too late to turn back; he had committed himself. The only thing to do was go all out.

Ben put his head down and sprinted ahead, straining his body to the limit and willing his feet to fly faster than they'd ever run before.

Only a few strides and he'd be there…

Steel and flesh careened on a collision course.

…just a half-second more…

As the dark shape of the truck loomed large, expanding like an explosion in his peripheral vision, Ben threw himself forward in one final surge, tackling Paul at full speed with the gust plowed by a rusty fender licking at his heels. When the two men crashed to the sidewalk in a crumpled heap, a lightening bolt shot through Ben's left arm.

~~*~~

The professor looked up at the sound of someone entering. "Yes, what is it?" she asked.

"Excuse the interruption, but I'm looking for Gail Albright," said the woman at the door, scanning the packed classroom. "It's an emergency."

Gail jumped at hearing her name and "emergency" spoken in the same breath. "I'm here," she said, raising her hand.

"Come with me, please," said the woman, whom Gail recognized as one of the secretaries from the nursing program's administrative office. "And you'd better bring your things with you."

Gail flashed a worried glance at Lorrie, hurriedly collected her notebook and backpack, and headed for the door, heart pounding. Her first thought was for her father. If he'd had some kind of accident or medical crisis while at work, they would send for her. Or perhaps it was her mother. Once in the hall, Gail asked why she'd been summoned.

"A young man named Paul Ruston has been injured and is asking for you."

"Paul? Oh, no! What's happened?"

"I was told he's been involved in some kind of accident on the street out front. I don't think it's too serious. He's in the ER. Do you know how to get there from here?"

"Yes. Thank you."

Walking as fast as she could without breaking into a run, Gail made what seemed like an endless trek through the long hallways connecting the educational wing of the medical complex with the hospital at the south end of it. When at last she arrived in the ER, she was ushered to Paul's bedside.

Gail saw that he had a bandage at the back of his head, along with some cuts and scrapes. Otherwise he looked good, alert and sitting up. She released the pent-up breath she hadn't realized she'd been holding.

"Paul! What a relief. When they told me you'd been in an accident, I imagined the worst."

"I'm fine, Gail. A few bumps and bruises, that's all. I probably shouldn't even have had you dragged out of class, but I really wanted to see you." He held out his hands for her.

As she took them, she saw the uncharacteristic tremor. He was shaken, despite how he tried to downplay the incident. "I'm glad you sent for me. Now, tell me what happened," she urged, settling on the edge of the bed and giving him her undivided attention.

"Well, I was coming to see you, actually, hoping I could steal you away for lunch. I know we're not officially dating, but I got you a little valentine gift anyway. Those were for you." He grimaced as he nodded to the mangled bouquet in a nearby chair. "Your lunch didn't fare quite as well, I'm afraid."

Gail managed only a half-hearted laugh in response to Paul's attempt at humor. "As long as you're okay."

"I am." He squeezed her hands. "Anyway, I started across Pacific, and the next thing I knew I'd been flattened backwards onto the sidewalk, tackled by a crazy man, it seemed to me."

"What? Are you serious?"

"Completely. Turns out the guy saved my life, knocking me clear of a delivery truck that was barreling down on me."

Gail gasped. "Oh, Paul! What a close call. Thank God you weren't seriously hurt."

"I do. I have. Repeatedly! If it hadn't been for Him watching out for me, and for Ben, I shudder to think…" Paul's voice choked off. He closed his eyes, expelled a deep breath, and shook his head.

Gail gave him a moment before asking, "Is 'Ben' the name of the guy who saved you?"

"That's right." Paul smiled and shifted his focus to something across the room, behind Gail.

She turned to follow his gaze, noticing for the first time the man sitting sideways on a bed fifteen feet away, facing them with his arm cradled in a sling.

"Let me introduce my guardian angel," Paul continued. "Gail Albright, this is Ben Lewis."

-27-
Intersection

Gail's mouth fell open when she recognized him. Ben Lewis. So that was his name. The campus mystery man and Paul's savior were one and the same.

"H-hello, Ben," she said, advancing to meet him. "I've seen you before, haven't I?" The air crackled between them as she extended her trembling hand. He took it with one nearly twice its size, holding it as steadily as he did her gaze. Gail couldn't help noticing that both felt strangely at home in his care.

"Yes… That is, I remember seeing *you* before. I'm glad to meet you, Gail… at last."

"I have to thank you for what you did for Paul," she managed after a pause. "I don't think I've ever met a real, live hero before."

"I'm no hero. Right place; right time. That's all."

"Don't be so modest. Most people couldn't – or wouldn't – have done it, risking their life to save a stranger." Gail scrunched her brow and gestured toward Ben's immobilized left arm with the hand she had finally reclaimed from him. "Looks like you were hurt in the process too. Is it broken?"

"No, just a stinger from landing on my shoulder. I've had one before – a sports injury last year. It should be good as new within a couple of weeks, in time for spring training with any luck."

"So you're a baseball player."

"Yeah. I played here at the U for three years before being drafted by Oakland. This will be my first full year as a pro. Do you like baseball, Gail?"

"I do." She smiled wistfully, thinking back. "I haven't been to a game in quite a while now, but when I was little, my dad used to take me to the college where he worked to watch their team play."

"Where was that? What school?"

"Shreveport, Louisiana. LSU."

"Ahhh. The Tigers. And now you're a Husky. Paul, here, tells me you're studying nursing. How do you like it so far?"

Brightening, Gail launched into her excitement about her early clinical experience. She saw how eagerly Ben took it in – took her in – as if he couldn't get enough. Growing self-conscious, she broke off. "I'm sorry. I've gotten carried away. There's no reason you'd be interested."

"But I am. I like your passion. I'm the same way when I get to talking about baseball." Seconds of deafening silence ticked by as they again stared at each other. "So, Gail Albright; that's a pretty name."

"Thanks."

"Let me see if I can pick the middle name that goes with it. I'm betting it's Marie."

"That's right!" She felt goose bumps rise on her arms. "How did you know?"

He shrugged. "Just a lucky guess. It's my mother's middle name too."

An orderly came in, pushing aside the curtain that framed Ben's bed. "Excuse me," he said, "but you can go now, Mr. Lewis. You've been discharged."

Ben acknowledged the news without taking his eyes off Gail's face. "Well, Gail, it was really great meeting you. And I mean that." Then, crossing the room, he shook Paul's hand. "See you around, Paul."

"What can I say? You told me I already thanked you enough. But I'm serious about staying in touch, okay?"

"Sure. Later, man." Ben slipped out the door.

Gail spent another half hour with Paul before returning to her afternoon classes. Although she might as well have gone home, considering how little she absorbed from her instructors. Her mind kept wandering back to all that had happened – the shock of Paul's accident compounded by the surprise of meeting Ben Lewis. When she finished for the day, she related the story to her friend as they made their way through crowded halls toward the parking garage.

"I can't believe you got to meet our favorite stalker face to face," Lorrie exclaimed. "What did you think of him, other than the fact that he must be incredibly brave?"

148

Eyes straight ahead, Gail tipped her head to one side. "He's a pretty regular guy, I guess," she answered with careful nonchalance.

"Come on. I need details! There's got to be more to this encounter than, 'Hello. It's nice to meet you. Thanks for saving my friend's life.' Give me the lowdown, girl. I want to know if he came across as even remotely dangerous; if he's half as buff close up as he looks from across a crowded street; and if any new sparks flew between you two. You know; the good stuff."

"Don't be ridiculous," Gail scolded, feeling her cheeks burning. "Maybe there's nothing that juicy to tell."

"And maybe there *is*." Lorrie swung around in front of Gail, preventing her escape and forcing people to flow past on either side of them, like a river parted by a pair of immovable boulders. "You're blushing like a freshman on prom night. So, what happened?"

"Nothing really," Gail hedged. "It was probably just the circumstances. He'd been through a life-and-death experience. I was keyed up from the shock of hearing about Paul's close call. Too much adrenaline; that's all it was."

"So sparks *did* fly."

"No! Well, not literally, at least. But there was something…"

"Okay, now we're making progress. Come on, Gail, give," Lorrie prompted, motioning with her hands for more information. "What kind of 'something' are we talking about here?"

"It's hard to describe."

"Try!"

"All right." Gail searched for the precise words she needed. "A charged atmosphere? Alive. Tingling, sort of. Crazy, I know, but I felt it when we shook hands. Then, like before, it was the way he looked at me. Not like a stranger. Not like someone he'd just met. Deeper, as if he already knew everything about me – all my thoughts and secrets. And he guessed that my middle name is Marie. How could he know that?"

"Okay, this is sounding a little creepy now. Is he psychic or psycho?"

"I admit it was a little eerie – especially the name thing – but not creepy. If I believed in reincarnation, I would say we must have known each other in a former life, because he seemed like a friend. And he has to be basically a good person, right? Look what he did for Paul."

"Hmm," Lorrie murmured. She unbarred the way, and the two girls rejoined the jumble of students, visitors, and staff streaming down the corridor. "I still think you should proceed with caution. The tingle you noticed might have been fair warning. I've read people feel a pleasant little buzz like that just before they're *struck by lightning*." She ground out the last three words for emphasis.

Gail laughed. "Don't worry. Like I said, it was probably only the unusual circumstances. I won't be seeing him again anyway. He's a baseball player, and he's about to leave for spring training."

"Ooh, an athlete! No wonder he's so buff. I bet he has money, too… and really strong hands."

"Lorrie! Control yourself. You're starting to salivate."

"You shouldn't talk. I'm sure I saw signs of drooling when you returned to class this afternoon."

Gail laughed again. "You're terrible," she said.

"It *is* too bad he's leaving, though. I'd gotten so I kind of looked forward to the next Ben Lewis sighting, although I suppose some of the intrigue is gone now that we actually know his name. So did you find out why he's been hanging around here so much?"

"Not really, except it's his off season. I'm sure he still has a lot of friends on campus since he used to go here. Anyway, none of that matters. The important thing is he was here to save Paul."

Ben hardly needed his car; he could have floated home that evening on an adrenaline-induced high. *What a day!* After weeks of waiting, he'd finally seen Abby again. Spoken to her. Even held her tiny, alabaster hand. And, oh yeah, he'd saved a man's life too. Things turning out so well overshadowed any downside.

Immediately after the accident – sprawled on the sidewalk with the feeling of that delivery van blowing past him still fresh – the magnitude of what he'd risked *had* gotten to him. He started shaking uncontrollably, his body reacting before his mind could absorb the fact that he just escaped death by a hair's breadth.

Since then, Ben had deliberately pushed that sober note aside. He and Kyle even laughed about it later – the extremes to which guys will go to meet women, and how they should have come up with that winning strategy sooner. Instead of Abby's phone number, however, he'd come away with Paul's, which at least meant he had a round-about link back to her until he could establish something more direct.

In the meantime, he hoped he'd made a favorable impression on her. It was difficult – no, make that impossible – for him to be objective about how this first meeting had gone. Did she feel the electricity spiking between them? When he took her hand, he thought he'd seen signs that she did. But maybe that was wishful thinking. His memories of their history together, which Abby unfortunately lacked, fueled his excitement. Whatever she felt depended entirely on instant chemistry… and on gratitude for his saving her friend's life. That had to count for something.

Just as Cora predicted it would, his prior knowledge of Abby seemed to give him an immediate advantage. Their conversation flowed despite his nervousness… and perhaps hers too. When he mentioned playing baseball, she responded much the same as the day they met the first time around, relating that her father used to take her to games when she was a kid. Ben had enjoyed recalling that pleasant image to her mind. Then he made sure to give her an opening to talk about nursing too. But he probably went too far by "guessing" her middle name. A stupid blunder. He meant to impress but had confused her instead.

One thing was certain, though. Meeting under these circumstances, Abby would never forget him. Ben prayed the same was true about his remembering her. Yet he couldn't help wondering if he would pay a higher price than a banged-up shoulder for saving Paul Ruston's life.

~~*~~

"This young man – what did you say his name was?" Mrs. Albright asked at the dinner table.

"Ben Lewis," Gail replied, picking at her Caesar salad.

"So, he really saved our dear Paul's life?"

Gail nodded. "Paul said if Ben hadn't knocked him out of the way, the truck would have run him down." She shuddered as the image once more flashed through her mind like it had a dozen times since she first heard about it.

"Heavens!"

"Driver had some kind of seizure," Mr. Albright elaborated for his wife. "A close call. Talk of the office this afternoon. Kid's quite a hero. A former student visiting friends on campus, apparently. Baseball player now, Gail says."

"We're all very grateful to the young man, I'm sure. But tell me more about Paul," insisted Mrs. Albright. "You're certain he wasn't hurt?"

"Just a few scrapes and a bump on the head," her daughter reassured her. "He's already been released from the hospital. I think he's pretty shaken up, though, so I promised I would see him again tomorrow."

"I should think you would after he risked his life to bring you flowers. And do sit up straight, Gail. Honestly, sometimes your posture..." said Mrs. Albright, shaking her head as she reached for the small, china bell beside her water goblet. After ringing it, she turned expectantly toward the swinging door that led to the kitchen.

It opened. "Yes, ma'am?" said Mrs. Avila.

"You may serve the entrée now."

Mrs. Avila's roasted chicken with rice pilaf and asparagus was superb. Gail's feeble appetite didn't do it justice. At the first opportunity, she retreated to her room to tackle the homework from her Human Responses class. But her *own* responses to the day's events kept her too preoccupied.

Nothing like a life-and-death crisis to shift things into sharper focus and straighten out a few kinks in priorities. Ben Lewis might be an interesting distraction, but Paul was the one she should be thinking about. She had taken him entirely for granted. He'd always been a part of her life, and she'd unconsciously assumed he always would be. Knowing he nearly died that day made her appreciate how bereft she would have felt if he had. How do people manage to go on, she wondered, after losing a parent, sibling, spouse, or fiancé they loved?

And on some level, she did love Paul. Her relationship with him certainly showed more promise than with anyone she'd dated before. Gail smiled at that idea. Okay, so she might as well admit it; she and Paul *were* dating. What was she afraid of after all? Of acknowledging that her parents might have been right all along? That she and Paul belonged together?

No, it was too soon to go that far. She intended to hold out for something beyond their proven friendship and compatibility. That was a good beginning, a solid foundation to build on. But she craved much more than companionship. She wanted it all, everything that was supposed to come with the marrying kind of love. Before she could commit to Paul, she needed to know romance. She needed to be convinced there would be passion between them.

SECOND INTERMISSION

"Your attention, please," Poindexter droned over the PA system at Crossroads. "All executive staff and senior operatives please report to the council chamber. This is a priority one meeting. Do be prompt. That is all."

Cora paced the room, her comical Betty Boop ensemble a sharp visual counterpoint to her sober expression. She twisted the curls of her glossy black wig in tight knots around her fingers – an old, nearly extinct habit which resurfaced occasionally under stress. "Is this really necessary, Dex? I vote we grant an executive pardon in this case and skip the hanging. No need for the formal council."

Poindexter shook his head sadly, regarding his long-time partner with affection, sympathy, and a trace of condescension. "Rules are rules, Cora. You know as well as I do that every point of protocol represents a crucial safeguard for the system, and therefore, must be followed to the letter. Where would we be if important guidelines could be ignored willy-nilly?"

"No one said anything about willy-nillying!" she shot back, hands on well-rounded hips. "I'm only talking about extending a little leniency to someone who totally deserves it."

"In your opinion."

"Yes, in my opinion. Isn't my opinion as valid as yours?"

"No doubt it would be were it not clouded by emotion. You can hardly pretend to be objective in this case. Mr. Lewis has been something of a pet project of yours from the beginning."

"Pet project?" Cora shook with outrage. "Ohhhhh! Sometimes, Dex, you…"

Seemingly unruffled, Poindexter coolly inquired, "Yes? Sometimes I what?"

The chamber door opened, interrupting their debate.

The balance of the senior staff filed in, joining the at-odds co-directors for a total of twelve. They arranged themselves in their customary places around a large, elongated oval table – administrative staff members on one side, case supervisors on the other, with Poindexter and Cora, appropriately enough, at opposing ends.

Poindexter remained standing after the others took their seats, calling the meeting to order and introducing the business at hand. "As you were notified, there has been another breach of protocol. One of our clients, a Mr. Ben Lewis, stands in violation of the terms of his contract. He has used his knowledge of the future to deliberately change the course of events, which is, of course, expressly forbidden by the non-interference clause. It is this council's duty to determine the facts and take appropriate corrective action."

Cora opened her mouth to protest.

Poindexter quickly held up a hand and added, "Hold your comments, everyone. Mr. Harper is the case supervisor, and we will first hear from him."

Harper, a slightly overstuffed-looking man, stood to address the group, consulting his notes on an electronic pad. "The client in question," he read, "has been under my direct observation for the past thirteen and a half months. Mr. Lewis's initial adjustment went smoothly. He seemed motivated and hard working, so I had every reason to anticipate a successful outcome. Now, though, he has committed what might be considered a serious offense. He saved the life of a man he knew would otherwise have died today. Observe," he said as he started a brief recording of the event playing on the adjacent video screen.

As they watched, Paul Ruston stepped off the curb. The speeding delivery van rounded into view. Ben Lewis dashed into the street, reaching the other side just in time to push Paul safely out of the way. The truck narrowly missed both men, crashing into a light post instead.

A low murmur stirred among the council members.

"This action," Harper continued, regaining their attention, "while it could be deemed heroic, technically constitutes a violation of the terms stipulated by Mr. Lewis's contract. And so, I had no choice but to bring it to this body's attention."

"Seems to be a pretty straightforward case," remarked Poindexter crisply after Mr. Harper finished his report and sat down. "Are there any questions, or can we proceed directly to assigning appropriate consequences and, more importantly, formulating a damage control strategy?"

"Yes, *I* have several questions."

All eyes turned to Cora.

"For instance, can we be sure this was premeditated? Couldn't it have been just a 'crime of opportunity,' where Mr. Lewis was as the scene by chance and acted impulsively? Or maybe what happened is what was supposed to happen. Either way, what is Ben's offense? That he risked his life to save someone else? As far as I can see, he had nothing to gain by it personally. Perhaps we should be giving him a medal, not a sentence."

"I can't speak to his motives," Mr. Harper answered, "since I have only very limited access to the client's thoughts. But I can confirm that Mr. Lewis knew of Paul Ruston's death beforehand, and, therefore, did act with prior knowledge to deliberately change the course of events."

"A client's motivation, good or bad, does not alter the facts," council member Mosby, Minister of Collateral Mitigation, reminded the ruling body. "I agree with Mr. Poindexter; this is a clear-cut instance of interference. We have a duty to impose the standard penalty. Mr. Lewis must, at the very least, be deprived of his previous-life memories immediately. There's nothing more to say on the subject."

Cora looked around the table for a sympathetic face, someone to take up Ben's defense. She finally located an ally in the Minister of Client Welfare.

Ms. Magdalene spoke up. "There is plenty more to say, Mr. Mosby. We haven't yet examined all the evidence. And I can, if necessary, cite chapter and verse from dozens of other cases that establish a precedent for leniency. This council's charter grants us considerable latitude. It instructs us to bear in mind extenuating circumstances, to weigh harm against benefit before taking action, and to judge on a case-by-case basis. Let me remind all of you that we are to exercise compassion where appropriate, not just mete out punishment according to the letter of the law."

"Exactly!" Cora cried, turning expectant eyes on Poindexter.

His starched expression never wavered. "A valid point, Ms. Magdalene," he begrudgingly admitted. "Before passing judgment, we will hear from the other administrative chairs concerned in the case. I trust you all came prepared to present your findings and recommendations. Minister of Risks and Probabilities, would you please begin?"

Part Three:

The Comeback

-28-
Ramifications

Ben rode a wave of triumph home the night of the accident. As he steered his used but recently acquired midnight-blue Vet through familiar streets, it struck him that old Mr. Rutland had been on to something when he'd said saving a life topped anything achievable on a baseball field. Ben felt more alive than ever before, a heightened sense that he mattered, strangely mixed with a new, awe-inspired humility. The meaning of his existence; the role of God in the universe; the relationship of time, space, destiny, and freewill: these esoteric themes rolled lazily around in his head. Not in a dark, fatalistic way. More of a life-is-good perspective. It suddenly seemed to him that every breath was intensely sweet and the future full of promise.

Ben pulled into the driveway, relieved to see the house was dark. Although he had carefully downplayed his injuries when he phoned his parents from the hospital, he still half expected his mother to be waiting up for him. That was the last thing Ben wanted. After the public excitement earlier, he now gloried in a world of private thoughts too superb to be interrupted or explained. He savored his reverie the way he would a fine porterhouse steak, languidly allowing the rich, primal flavors to flow where they would. The pleasant spell still in place, Ben slipped unnoticed into his room and drifted off to sleep.

Any lingering euphoria evaporated the instant he jerked awake again just before four in the morning. He was sucking air as if he'd been running wind sprints, and his skin had broken out in a cold sweat. *Probably a bad dream…* although it was strange that he couldn't remember a thing about it. And instead of fading away, the anxiety grew until an atmosphere of dread, heavy and suffocating as an ocean, pressed on him from all sides.

Ben shot out of bed to take stock. Traces of numbness remained in his left arm. But the deadened feeling of his mind – as if set adrift or out of phase – alarmed him far more. He shook himself in a last ditch effort to shed the confusion. It was no good, though. This was definitely something more than a nightmare, something far more serious. His heart dropped into his belly as the truth dawned.

No good deed goes unpunished.

The cynical saying fit, but he wasted no time dwelling on it. If he was right, he didn't have a minute to lose. Ben crossed to his desk, flicked on the lamp, and rummaged through the drawers until he came up with a pen and a mostly empty spiral-bound notebook, one leftover from his high school days. Opening it, he tore out the few used pages and stared at the clean sheet in front of him. He raked deep furrows through his hair as if to straighten out his thoughts, and then he began writing in his back-angling scrawl:

> *What would the average guy give to turn back the clock and set his life straight? Probably anything short of his right arm… that is if he'd made as much a mess of things as I had. I hit bottom in September of 1997. Then, just when I thought I couldn't go on, when I was at a point so low I had to look up to see outfield grass grow, I received a genuine, world-class do-over. Now I'm praying I still have time to salvage it…*

Ben scribbled his story, starting with the illness that had ruined his plans, and then going quickly on to describe how he met Abby, how she'd become his love, his wife, and his best reason to keep living. It was all too precious to be lost forever, especially the facts and feelings concerning Abby. How could he expect to find his way back to her if he forgot she was his destination, that she was his home base?

Even as he wrote, Ben sensed tiny moth holes forming in the fabric of his memory, places where there once had been something – perhaps something important – now replaced by growing gaps. It seemed he couldn't prevent patches of his former life from being eaten away by an unseen force. An image from boyhood flashed through his mind – a favorite movie called *The Neverending Story*. In it, the young warrior Atreyu races to keep ahead of "The

162

Nothing," a dark void relentlessly consuming everything in its path. That's the way Ben felt about his at-risk memories; he had to save them from being swallowed up by the advancing emptiness.

Head down, he pressed on for hours before finally pausing to shake out his cramped hand and check the time. Already nearly nine o'clock, and he had so much more left to write.

Ben could hear his parents up and moving around the house. They would be anxious to see him, especially in light of what happened the day before. If he didn't make an appearance soon, his mother was bound to check in on him. He couldn't risk that. No one must know about or be allowed to interfere with him getting his story down on paper.

So, temporarily tearing himself away from his mission, Ben ventured out to the kitchen, where he found both his parents at the breakfast table. Greeting them with simulated casualness, he sat down for what he hoped would be a very abbreviated meal… and not too many questions.

A certain amount of explanation couldn't be avoided, though. To expedite matters, Ben reiterated the basic facts of the accident while he slathered a bagel with strawberry cream cheese. Under other circumstances, he might have enjoyed sharing all the details. After all, it had been one of the most profound experiences of his life. As it was, a perfunctory overview was the best he could do.

"And you're sure you aren't hurt?" his mother wanted to know afterward.

"Like I told you yesterday, I just banged up my shoulder a little. It's already feeling a lot better. I'm fine, Mom, really."

But he wasn't fine. He was an emotional wreck, riddled with the gaping wounds created by shards of his past being torn away against his will. And every passing moment cost him dearly – more bits of memory lost forever. Once they were gone, he supposed he wouldn't know the difference. If the amnesia was complete, he wouldn't miss what he no longer knew had existed. That thought gave him no comfort, though.

Ben couldn't bear to sit making small talk for one second longer. He pushed back from the table and blurted out, "I'm going to my room." Only then did he realize he'd interrupted his father. "Sorry, Dad, but, uh… the doctors told me I should get as much sleep as possible. You know, because of what I've been through. And I *am* feeling pretty tired," Ben added, allowing his voice to trail off weakly.

"Of course, honey," said his mother, looking puzzled. "You should get back to bed, then. We'll talk more when you're well rested."

Ben started down the hall before she had finished, rationalizing that he'd make it up to his parents later for being rude. They would be far more forgiving than whatever authority was currently trashing the memory circuits of his brain. Was it a minion of fate, an agent of the dark side, or Poindexter himself? Poindexter had never liked him and would probably take pleasure in messing with his mind.

Back at his desk, Ben set to work again. Still so much important information to set down and God-only-knew-how-little time to do it. He hadn't even begun documenting his experience at the Crossroads Center yet. So he forged ahead, writing about the people he met there and the chance he'd been given to redo the past, ending hours later with the account of how he'd made the leap back to 1991.

Ben set down his pen and stared at the closing words:

That's everything I can remember.

He sighed, some of the tension finally easing from the knotted muscles of his back. Undoubtedly an imperfect account, but finished. He was grateful he'd at least had enough time to complete it instead of forgetting everything all at once without warning.

According to what Cora had told him, the inevitable memory loss, whether gradual or abrupt, was considered a protection against regrets Crossroads clients might otherwise feel. It was a kindness, much like the amnesiac aftereffects of the anesthesia drugs given for surgery. If there had been pain, at least you wouldn't remember it. But with no record, it would seem as if those things had never happened... and they had! Forget that nonsense about the tree falling in the forest. *Yes*, it makes a sound, even if no one is there to hear it! Ben had to believe his former life somehow formed an impression on the universe; it mattered.

Now the story wouldn't be completely lost. It was preserved in black and white for whenever he needed it. But what to do with his log in the meantime... Ben slowly closed the notebook, his eyes coming to rest on the green, cardboard cover marked with the word "Chemistry," written with a marker by his own hand years before.

In little more than a week he'd be leaving, returning to Phoenix for spring training. From there, he expected to be assigned to one of the A's minor-league affiliates, flying to Wisconsin, California, or Alabama. Then, during the course of the season, he might be traded, promoted, or even, God forbid, demoted, requiring yet another move. Basically, he had to plan on a nomadic lifestyle for at least the next couple of years. That meant no privacy and a real chance of some of his things being lost or pilfered along the way.

No, far better to keep his valuables, including the newly written journal, safely here at his parents' house. Although he was sick at the thought of leaving behind the memories it contained, he knew they would be of no practical use to him on the road. Until he returned to Washington in the off season, he'd have no time or opportunity to work on winning Abby back.

Ben's eyelids hung at half mast. He yearned for the sleep he'd lost the night before, the rest he'd surely earned by so much con-centrated effort since. Although his comfortable bed beckoned, Ben resisted. "Stay on track… just a little longer," he urged himself in a whisper.

Crossing to the closet instead of to his bed, he silently slid open the door and pulled out one of several plastic bins stacked in the corner – the one he knew contained awards, term papers, and other artifacts from his time at Edgemont High. Ben paused a moment with the notebook gripped tightly in his hand, reviewing a mental checklist and murmuring a formless prayer that everything would work out as it should.

The Bible passage he'd discovered at the Center came back to him then. "Hang on to that verse," old Mrs. Cuthbert had urged him.

On impulse, Ben grabbed his pen and wrote the words on the green cover: *"For I know the plans I have for you," declares the Lord, "plans to prosper you and not to harm you, plans to give you hope and a future."*

It was an artless attempt to invoke the promise the verse em-bodied, physically tying it to the precious information on which so much depended. It probably didn't work that way, he realized, inex-perienced though he was in the things of God. But he would take all the help he could get.

Ben uneasily tucked the notebook in with the other memorabilia and returned the box to its place in the closet. Icy fingers clutched at his heart. In a matter of hours, all memory of his former life would likely be gone. Already, little more than a skeleton remained to hold the shape of what had once been there, like the fibers of a sponge after the organism itself degenerates – taking up space, but lifeless.

Beyond that, he wondered how much of what had happened in his second chance might also be taken from him. Would he recall the real reason for his quest to meet Abby? Would he even remember sitting down and writing all these things in the green notebook… and where he'd hidden it?

In case he didn't, Ben laid a bread-crumb trail to find his way back, leaving cryptic messages to himself in key locations, pointing the way. Toward that end, he also pulled the now permanently bent and faded photo of Abby from his wallet. He gazed at it once more, lovingly, as he had hundreds of times before. It was the hallowed image that had gotten him through the past year. He hated to part with it. But, now that he had a clear picture of her in his head from this lifetime – one that surely wouldn't be taken from him – he needed the precious photo more as a link to the record of his past. He would clip it to one of his notes and leave it in the nightstand drawer to be discovered later. Before doing so and then collapsing on his bed into a heavy sleep, Ben wrote two words on the back of her picture as a final clue:

Remember Abby.

-29-
Moving On

Ben reawakened much later, refreshed and head free of cobwebs. The big event of the day before – saving Paul Ruston's life – immediately popped into his mind. He marveled at it again, but his thoughts soon moved on to the future. Ben could feel that old, familiar excitement building in his chest. Ever since he was a kid, the end of winter meant only one thing: the beginning of baseball season. This year would be better than ever with him attending his first professional spring training camp.

Remembering his injury, Ben clambered out of bed and stretched, checking his arm for numbness and his shoulder for range of motion. Almost back to normal, he discovered with relief, except for some odd cramping in his hand. When he reached Phoenix, though, he should be pretty much one-hundred percent, which was exactly what he needed to be. He intended to get off to a fast start, wasting no time showing what he could do. Impress management early and often; that was his strategy for climbing his way up the ladder.

Ben leisurely showered and dressed. He had nothing special planned for the day. His job at the Y had wrapped up the week before, and it was still too soon to pack for his departure. A sudden urge to drive up to the U struck him, but Ben quickly discarded the idea. He'd already spent more time lurking around campus that winter than he could reasonably account for. Although hanging out with his friends was some excuse, he couldn't understand why he'd been so obsessed with meeting that girl. Gail Albright was pretty enough, but not really his type when it came right down to it. Besides, it looked like she had something going with Paul Ruston.

Rumblings in his stomach caused Ben to glance at his watch as he put it on. Three o'clock? That couldn't be right. He'd never slept past noon in his life, no matter how late he'd stayed out the night before. Yet the clock radio on his nightstand displayed the same time. Strange.

"Hey, Mom," Ben said, wandering out to the kitchen. "I'm starving. What have you got to eat around here?"

"There you are," said Mrs. Lewis. She turned from the task of paying bills to give her son an analytical eye. "I'm glad to see you looking a lot more rested now. I saved you a sandwich from lunch. It's in the fridge if you want it."

"Thanks. Is Scott around?" Ben asked with his face in the refrigerator.

"No, he left early this morning to go skiing with some friends. He'll be back for dinner, though."

Emerging with the sandwich and a jug of milk, Ben headed for the table. "I can't believe I slept so late. Why didn't you wake me?"

"You said this morning that the doctors told you to get lots of sleep, so naturally…"

"This morning? I didn't see you this morning, did I?" he asked, wrinkling his brow.

She chuckled. "Yes, you did. You sat right where you're sitting now, eating a bagel and talking about yesterday's accident. You don't remember, do you?"

Ben shook his head, bewildered.

"I'm not surprised," his mother went on. "You were only up for a few minutes, and you seemed really out of it."

Ben stared back blankly.

"You were sleep-walking, honey," she said, laying her hand over his, "like you used to do. At least that's what your father and I concluded."

Ben brooded a moment. "Yeah, I guess that's what it must have been. Weird. I haven't done anything like that in years."

"Well, you went through a traumatic experience. I'm guessing the shock was enough to cause that old habit to resurface."

"Makes sense, I suppose." After a pause, Ben shrugged. "Anyway, I feel fine now."

~~*~~

Paul Ruston phoned that evening.

"I know this is short notice, Ben," he said, "and you must be pretty busy, getting ready to leave town and all. But my parents insist on thanking the man who saved their son's precious hide. They want to treat you to dinner at Anthony's Home Port in Des Moines tomorrow. It's on the waterfront, right next to the marina."

"Yeah, I know the place, and I appreciate the thought. Dinner would be fine, although…"

"Is there a problem?"

Ben hesitated. "No. It's just that I honestly don't want anybody making a big deal out of this."

"Still being alive *is* a big deal to me, and what you did is worth celebrating. But I'll cancel the press conference if you insist," Paul said, laughing good-naturedly. "No, seriously, I do understand, Ben. No fanfare, speeches, or reporters; I promise. It would just be me, my parents, and my sister. Oh, and I was going to invite Gail too. Does that sound okay?"

"Sounds nice, actually."

Throughout the conversation, Scott had been reprising a time-honored tradition, distracting his brother with goofy faces and gestures just as he'd done when Ben used to talk to his girlfriends on that same house phone years before. It was insufferable then; now it was a mildly irritating joke.

"Good," Paul was saying. "And you're welcome to bring someone – a date or a friend."

Ben saw his chance for a little payback. "How about I bring my obnoxious kid brother? He doesn't get out much."

Scott shook his head and wildly waved his objection.

Ben turned his back.

"Oh, sure," Paul answered. "The more the merrier. Then I'll see you both at six?"

"We'll be there. Thanks." Ben hung up the phone, smirking.

"What did you do that for?" Scott demanded.

"It's a free dinner at Anthony's! You should be thanking me."

"I don't want to be your sidekick for some dinner party with a bunch of people I don't know."

"Really? Since you've reverted to your annoying-little-brother ways, I thought tagging along after me would be perfect."

Scott groaned. "Call them back and say I can't make it."

"No way. You're going. You'll get a good meal out of the arrangement, and it's right on your way back to the U."

With Scott following in his own car, Ben arrived at the restaurant the next day exactly on time, looking forward to the dinner more than he originally expected. If Paul was at all representative, his family should be a friendly bunch. And he had no objection to seeing Gail Albright again. As long as no one made a fuss, it would be fine.

Finding Anthony's wasn't a problem; he'd taken Jessica there several times in the past. He parked in the lot, got out, and waited for his brother to pull in a couple of spaces down. Scott glared and wordlessly shuffled toward the entrance, his hands in his pockets.

"Come on, bro," Ben encouraged, "it'll be fun."

When they asked for the Ruston party at the reservations desk, a hostess escorted them to the upstairs dining room and toward a large table overlooking the water. To Ben's relief, only five, perfectly sedate people waited for there – no crowds, balloons, or hoopla.

Paul and his father rose when Scott and Ben approached.

Ben presented his self-conscious brother and Paul undertook the rest of the introductions. "Gail you know already, of course, Ben. And this is my sister Hollie…"

Ben acknowledged each of them in turn.

"…and my parents, Mr. and Mrs. Ruston."

Mr. Ruston wrung Ben's hand, saying in a low but intense voice, "Call me Henry, son, and my wife is Beth. You're one of the family now. We can't thank you enough for what you did for Paul. If there's ever anything you need, you just say the word. We're forever in your debt."

Mrs. Ruston nodded, moist-eyed. "God bless you, Ben," she added quietly.

Nice people, Ben decided immediately, and Hollie was very attractive. Gail too, of course. The pair looked like they could be sisters with their similar, fair coloring, although Hollie had a curvier figure. Ben happily took the empty chair between the two, and Scott sank into the one on the other side of Hollie.

"Order whatever you want," insisted Mr. Ruston as the menus were distributed around the table. "You boys are our special guests tonight. Let's start off with an appetizer. We'll take a couple of your seafood sampler platters," he instructed their server.

The group fell mostly silent as they perused the tempting descriptions of the entrées offered on the bill of fare. Quickly deciding to stick with his favorite – the prawns – Ben turned his attention to the view. Like the menu, he knew it well.

Outside the window, a familiar forest of aluminum masts grew from the hibernating sailboats berthed below, row upon row of them, waiting for their next call to adventure. Until then, a jetty built of boulders the size of washing machines safely corralled them, sheltering them from the unfriendly chop of the winter Sound. Maury and Vashon Islands rose from the water in the distance, sculpting a succession of camels' backs into the horizon. Even in the gunmetal gray tones of February, it was compellingly beautiful.

After placing their dinner orders, Mrs. Ruston got the conversational ball rolling again with the prosaic request that Ben tell them a little about himself.

"Okay, but it probably won't be all that interesting," Ben cautioned. "I'm just a local kid from the south end." He went on to give the Reader's Digest version of his family history, his lifelong passion for baseball, and his current situation. "I guess that's about it," he concluded after a few minutes.

"So you've never lived anywhere but here?" Gail asked.

"Nope, not until last summer. Didn't even leave the area for college since I grew up dreaming of being a Husky. I've got to get used to living out of a suitcase now, though. I'll probably be on the road a lot until I work my way into the majors. Even then, I won't be able to put down any deep roots. These days, with free agency, it's really rare for any ballplayer to spend his entire career with one team."

"It sounds glamorous," Hollie exclaimed.

"I don't know about that," Ben responded. "There's a lot of sweat and hard work involved. But it's what I've always wanted to do, so I feel pretty lucky."

"Not a normal lifestyle, though, is it?" Gail countered, pensively. "All that moving around from place to place at a moment's notice; not knowing from one month to the next if you'll be starting over somewhere new, or even if you'll have a job. I don't think I could deal with the uncertainty."

"You're right," Ben agreed. "The not-knowing is a pain. I don't mind the travel itself, though. I suppose it would be different if I had a wife and kids. But for now, at least, it seems a pretty small price to

171

pay." He turned back to address the group as a whole. "And I've heard there can be certain 'compensations' if you make it big," he joked, winking and rubbing the thumb and fingers of his left hand together.

~~*~~

Disappointed. Halfway through her baked salmon with dill sauce, Gail admitted it; she was disappointed when Ben Lewis greeted her with an ordinary smile and a nondescript "hello" upon his arrival. It had been bugging her ever since. Maybe it wasn't reasonable, but she'd anticipated something more after the way he'd practically peered through to her soul the two previous times they'd come face to face. By comparison, his expression seemed flat today – friendly, perhaps even mildly interested, but with no trace of the special connection, the unmistakable look of recognition he'd flashed her way before.

"Nice to see you again," she had answered. How original. If that was the best she could do, she had no business faulting Ben for the lack of a riveting opening remark.

Gail listened to Ben talk baseball with just as much fascination as the rest. Sitting next to him, she couldn't escape the effect of his infectious enthusiasm, his passion for the sport. He sometimes became so animated that he enlisted his hands to do some of the talking, once nearly knocking over his water glass as he reenacted a home-run swing. It was a window onto a world the rest of them knew almost nothing about. His world, and he generously shared it. Yet, Gail noticed, he didn't monopolize the conversation as he easily might have.

Setting her earlier disappointment aside, she couldn't help liking Ben... a lot, actually. That was only natural, she told herself; he was a very likable guy with a lot of good qualities. He was open, articulate, outgoing, full of vitality, and quite different from what she would have expected. Same as in their earlier conversation at the hospital, he came off as more intelligent and far less arrogant than she'd always presumed the average professional athlete would be. At that, she reproached herself – for the indefensible stereotype and especially for imagining a kind of mystical link between the two of them. Just as well there wasn't any, she thought with a sigh. It could have become way too complicated otherwise.

Dessert arrived. Crème Brûlée: her favorite. Gail smacked the brittle, caramelized topping with the back of her spoon, then scooped up one of the sugary shards. As it melted on her tongue, she snuck another sideways glance at Ben Lewis.

Her friend had once joked that he appeared ruggedly handsome and darkly dangerous from a distance. A pretty accurate description close up as well, Gail conceded... at least as to his good looks. And dangerous? That too, judging from the effect he had on her. Nursing students learn early on how to evaluate a pulse, and hers had been running rapid and thready all night. But physical attraction alone was a poor basis for a lasting relationship, as she'd already learned the hard way. As for the rest, all she knew about Ben was that he was a baseball player who would be on the road indefinitely.

Kept at a safe distance: that's where Ben Lewis belonged. Not like now, sitting so close she could hear him breathe and feel the occasional brush of his arm against her own. She sighed again, more deeply this time.

"Is everything all right?" Ben asked, turning to her with his thickly lashed, dark eyes.

"Oh... sure. Fine," she stammered.

No, she didn't have any business even *thinking* about getting involved with this guy. Little chance of it happening anyway. In the first place, he hadn't invited her to. Besides, she might never see him again.

-30-
New Outlook

The view of the marina had long since sunk into darkness. Over the past couple of hours, the daylight hues had gradually drained from the scene, gathering briefly in the western sky for a last blaze of glory before stealing away into the night for good. Only isolated points of brightness dappled the docks now – lights mounted on posts and boat rails, their reflections twisting across the inky surface of the water.

Most of Anthony's other patrons had already gone. Yet no one in the Ruston group seemed in any rush for the evening to end. They lingered over coffee and dessert, swapping stories and laughing at the lamest jokes they could remember. At a quarter to nine, Mr. Ruston raised his glass, inviting the others to join him toasting "the excellent food and the even-better company" they had enjoyed. Afterward, they reluctantly made their way toward the exit.

A sharp breeze met them outside, tearing at their coats and hurrying their farewells.

"Thanks a lot for dinner," Ben told the Rustons as they all huddled together near the entrance. "I had a great time."

Scott echoed the sentiment.

"Our extreme pleasure, boys," said Mr. Ruston, reaching to shake their hands in turn. "It was the very least we could do under the circumstances."

"Please keep in touch," requested Mrs. Ruston. She pecked Ben on the cheek and, along with her husband, started across the parking lot.

Hollie smiled and followed.

"Give me a call when you get back into town, Ben," suggested Paul.

"Sure thing." Then Ben turned to Gail. "Hope I'll see you again too."

"Yes, uh… Well, goodbye, and good luck this season."

A sudden flash and distant rumble announced an approaching storm. A moment later, the first heavy drops of rain pelted onto the roof overhead.

"We'd better get going. Bye," said Paul, grabbing Gail's hand. They trotted off to the Rustons' car.

Ben watched them go, thinking it was too bad he hadn't met Paul and the others sooner. At this stage, there didn't seem much value in trying to cultivate what could only be a long-distance friendship. It would be about as pointless as the Christmas cards his parents received every year from people they hadn't seen since high school. The note inside might say, "We really should get together," but they knew they never would. That's probably how it would be with the Rustons too.

Ben glanced at Scott. "That wasn't so bad, now was it? At least you don't look like a man who's just been tortured for nearly three hours. I thought I even saw you enjoying yourself once or twice."

Scott, hands in his pockets again, looked sheepish but didn't answer.

"Does your miraculous attitude adjustment have anything to do with Hollie Ruston? I noticed she laughed at all your idiotic jokes, and she seemed to find architecture a lot more interesting than baseball."

A slow grin crept over Scott's face. "Then that's probably why she gave this to me instead of you," he replied, showing off a scrap of paper with a phone number written on it.

Ben made a lunge for it and missed.

"Oh, no you don't!" Scott tucked his prize safely away in his wallet. "This one's all mine. Besides," he continued, readying another barb, "Hollie would be wasted on you, or aren't you saving yourself for your true love Abby anymore?"

"Who's Abby?"

"I don't know her, but you must. You told me ages ago that she was 'the one.'" Scott made quotation marks in the air with his fingers. "Don't you remember? You went all weird on me, talking about dreams and fate – spooky junk like that. Said you were waiting for this girl Abby."

175

"You're jerking my chain. When and where did this mysterious conversation supposedly take place?"

"A year ago, up at Crystal, the day we went skiing at the end of Christmas break." Receiving no reaction, Scott prompted, "It was right after you broke up with Jessica... an act of sheer madness, which, by the way, totally reinforces the point I was making. Beautiful women are completely wasted on you."

"Hold on, chowder head. It's coming back to me now. I remember saying that stuff; I just don't seem to remember the girl."

"You made such a big deal about her then. I can't believe you don't even recognize her name now. Guess she wasn't that special after all."

"I guess not." Ben shivered without knowing why. "So, are you going to call Hollie?"

"You know it."

"Treat her right, then. Hey, I gotta get going."

"Me too. Early class tomorrow."

"See you around, kid." Ben gave his brother a quick one-armed hug. "And take good care of the old Toyota," he tossed back over his shoulder as he darted out into the rain.

Ben drove home, his wipers beating furiously in an effort to keep pace with what had escalated into a full-fledged downpour. It had been a pleasant evening. No, more than pleasant – first-class, actually. All except for the odd exchange with his brother at the end.

Initially, Ben thought the business about the alleged dream girl was just a joke intended to make him question his sanity. It would be quite a coup for the intellectual to convince the athlete he'd lost most of his already-inferior marbles. But Scott wasn't that cruel, and when he'd recounted the story, Ben believed him. Contrary to what he'd told his brother, though, he had only the vaguest recollection of the conversation in question. And of Abby herself – if she really existed – he had nothing at all. Just an unsettling blank.

~~*~~

Ben pulled into the driveway at home. Nearly nine-thirty, and yet his mother's car was missing. Then he remembered she'd had something going on at church that night. It must have run late.

Ben let himself in as quietly as the squeaky front door allowed, knowing his father would be in bed already because of his early start time at Boeing. Instead, Ben found him in the living room, enthroned in his man-sized recliner in front of the TV.

"Hey, Dad, what are you doing up? Aren't you going to work tomorrow?"

"Nope," he drawled out, turning the volume down with the remote. "The good old Lazy-B will have to get along without me for a few days. I decided to take some time off while the plane's in the paint hanger and there's not much for me and my crew to do."

"A little vacation, then."

He snorted. "Hardly! I've just got to catch up on things around here. It's a long list. First, I've gotta do something about that dead maple tree before it falls on the house. And the gutters are clogged again. I suppose I should finally take down the Christmas lights too. Plus, the shower head in the upstairs bathroom hasn't worked right for months. Then there's the furnace. It really has me worried, the way it keeps tripping off. It's almost thirty years old, but I'm hoping I can keep it running a little while longer."

"I can help you with that stuff if you want. I've got nothing going on tomorrow."

"Thanks. I was counting on it, to tell you the truth. It seems like there's always more maintenance to be done around this old house than I have time for, and I can't afford to waste money paying somebody else to do things I know how to do myself."

Ben dropped into the other recliner. "Sounds like homeownership isn't all it's cracked up to be."

Ron Lewis nodded ruefully. "When we bought this place – almost twenty years ago, now – your mom and I made big plans for how we'd fix it up. Only half of it ever got done. The rest was pie in the sky, I guess. It seemed a good spot to raise a family, though – close enough to the city to be within commuting distance for me, yet still with a rural feel. We wanted space for you boys to run and explore."

It *had* been a great place to grow up, Ben silently acknowledged. Although new construction had since swallowed up nearly every patch of open ground, back then he and his friends played in big back yards, the park down the street, and a make-shift baseball field carved out of a vacant lot.

"But now…" Ron trailed off as he scanned his slightly shabby surroundings.

Ben followed his father's gaze. The house definitely showed its age. Every room in the place arguably needed fresh paint and new flooring to do away with the scars left over the years by packs of rampaging, neighborhood boys. Outside, he knew the shrubbery was overgrown, and the riotous blackberry vines invading from next door would take over the yard if you turned your back for five minutes. Then there were all the little things you got used to ignoring when you lived in a place – the missing piece of molding next to the fireplace, the sticky lock on the front door, the kitchen cabinets that no longer closed properly.

"Now the house isn't so perfect anymore?" Ben suggested.

"Right, and some of those projects I dreamed up when I was younger…" He shook his head, a scornful overtone coloring his voice when he continued. "Remember the rec room I was going to make by finishing off the basement? Well, that's never going to happen. And I guess you're a little too old now for the tree house I promised you and your brother."

Ben grinned at the thought. "Never too old for tree houses, Dad," he said.

His father waved his hand dismissively. "Anyway, at this point my goal is just to keep the grass mowed and the rain off our heads."

They both fell quiet as the movie resumed after the commercial break – *Silent Running* with Bruce Dern, a Sci-Fi classic – but Ben's thoughts stayed with the former topic. He hated hearing his father sounding so discouraged, and he envisioned magnanimously buying his parents a brand new home like some celebrities do after making it big. That day was still a long way off for him, though.

"Sorry I haven't been more help around here recently," Ben offered, feeling how inadequate it was.

"Never mind. You boys have your own lives now, and that's as it should be." He returned his full concentration to the screen, signaling the end of their rare heart-to-heart talk.

A few minutes later, Jan Lewis opened the stubborn front door with a bump of her shoulder. "I'm home," she called from the entry, pausing to hang her coat in the closet. "Nasty weather out there to-night," she added cheerfully as she came into the living room. She kissed her preoccupied husband on the forehead on her way to taking a seat at the end of the couch nearest her son. "How was your dinner party?" she asked softly, leaning toward him.

Ben kept his voice low as well. "Great, actually. The Rustons are really nice people. You'd like them."

"Well, then, I hope I get a chance to meet them sometime."

"And the more I get to know Paul, the better I feel about saving his life. Did I tell you he's a pediatrician?"

"You said a doctor, yes."

"So think of all the good he'll do in the years to come."

"True, but isn't every life equally valuable? What if you'd known ahead of time that Paul was something very ordinary instead? Say, for example, a truck driver. Would that really have made a difference in how you reacted?"

"No, at least I don't think so. I still can't imagine standing by and watching someone die. I'm just happy he didn't turn out to be an axe murderer. That's all I'm saying. I'd rather be responsible for extending the life of a man who's going to amount to something good. It makes the risk seem more worthwhile."

"I have no doubt Paul Ruston's life was well worth saving, but you could easily have sacrificed your own in the process." She brought her palms together at her lips and exhaled. "Thank God it didn't come to that."

"I know," he said thoughtfully, "but, if you consider the big picture, it would have been a good exchange."

"Oh, Ben!"

"Really, Mom, who except my own family and friends would miss one extra ballplayer in the world? But a lot of sick kids might suffer for lack of a good doctor."

"No, that's not what I meant. What you said gave me chills because it reminded me so much of the scripture we studied at church tonight. It's one of those God-incidence things you probably don't believe in."

Ben rolled his eyes. "All right. So what does this verse say, anyway? I can see you're dying to tell me."

"Oh, I couldn't quote it word for word, but it's in the first part of Romans five, verse six or seven, I think. You have a Bible. Why don't you look it up for yourself?"

-31-
Spring Training

Despite having rarely cracked open his Bible in recent years, Ben knew exactly where it was. His mother had trained him from an early age that it belonged bedside. Of course she'd also trained him, less successfully, that it was intended for daily use – morning devotions and nightly prayers. Ben felt a sting of conscience, one which he deftly pushed aside. He preferred to focus on how the path he'd chosen fulfilled his father's expectations rather than where it might have fallen short of his mother's.

She had piqued his curiosity this time, though. Opening the nightstand drawer, Ben immediately spotted a corner of black, embossed leather jutting out from under a few loose papers and photographs. He pulled out the book and slowly ran a hand across its familiar pebbled surface. With his fingertip, he traced his name engraved in gold at the bottom of the front cover, and then flipped it open. Hand-written inside, he read, *Presented this day, May 11, 1981, to Benjamin Lewis by Calvary Community Church. Jer.29:11.*

Every fifth grader was given a Bible at the end of the Sunday school year, he recalled. Back then, his mother had seen to it that he and his brother made it to church regularly. Later, when he made his own choices, he'd drifted away. Or maybe more accurately, he'd been pulled loose from those first tentative moorings of faith by things that dazzled his imagination more. It was a case of careless neglect rather than deliberate rejection, so he still considered himself a Christian by default… when he thought about it… which wasn't often.

Ben returned his attention to what he'd come to do, to find Romans. New Testament, right? Somewhere toward the back, then. He used to be able to rattle off all the books in correct order. "Matthew, Mark, Luke, and John…" he began, surprised to hear a far-off echo in his head of the little tune they'd been taught in Sunday school to memorize them by. "Acts, Romans..." There it was. Flipping to chapter five, he skipped down to the second paragraph.

Very rarely will anyone die for a righteous man, though for a good man someone might possibly dare to die. But God demonstrates his own love for us in this: While we were still sinners, Christ died for us.

The part about daring to die for a good man – that must be what his mom had meant. Without thinking about it at the time, he *had* dared to die for Paul, who, according to everything he knew, was a really good guy. An interesting parallel, although being cast in the role of savior felt even more uncomfortable than when Gail Albright called him a hero. It was too much to live up to. He didn't want the responsibility of shouldering either of those impossible titles.

Ben grabbed something handy from the drawer to mark the page as he tucked the verse away in his mind. He then put his Bible back in the nightstand... where it belonged.

~~*~~

After claiming his luggage at Phoenix's Sky Harbor International Airport, Ben hailed a taxi. Since bringing a car had been discouraged, he'd left his at home for the time being. But he had already floated the invitation to Scott of his taking a spring-break road trip to Arizona as a potential way of retrieving his wheels before the end of camp. In the meantime, he'd be stuck using the bus or his own two feet to get around. The cab was a once-only splurge.

Ben arrived at the Athletics' facility feeling like he was on the cusp of something great. He'd dreamt of this all his life. Spring Training was a singular rite of passage, an assembling of the tribe, and, for those who were invited, a mark of membership in a fraternity with a proud history stretching back through the decades. Rookie mini-camp the previous year had been just that – a miniature version comprised of a bunch of neophytes. This was the real deal with all two hundred or so veteran players under contract with the A's organization showing up to prep for the long season ahead.

To an outsider, the group might have seemed a strange kind of brotherhood. On one hand, they were all teammates, and baseball culture says that the good of the team always comes first. Meanwhile, the unspoken truth was that each of them was locked in a mortal struggle against the others for his professional survival. Every player knew that the only way to rise to the top was to usurp the position of the man above – to take his job – and yet he also lived with the certain knowledge that the guy below him had exactly the same objective in mind.

Ben and his fellow athletes accepted this tension as the natural order of things, no more to be questioned or complained about than gravity. Besides, it was the beginning of a bright, shiny new season when anything was still possible and no one was thinking about getting cut.

Ben hauled his luggage into the minor league clubhouse, saying hi to a few familiar faces along the way. He located his locker and began carefully stowing his gear, inspecting every item as he went and adjusting the fit of his equipment as needed. Then he tackled the job of taping some bats so they would be ready when play began.

"Jell-O, over here," he called out, spotting Angelo Capra looking lost. Capra was a good guy. Ben knew him from his rookie team, and they had signed up to bunk together at Spring Training to avoid the perils of a random roommate assignment. Angelo lumbered toward the nearby locker Ben pointed out for him, bent under the weight of a backpack, a super-sized suitcase, and a duffle bag straining at the seams.

"Hey, man, keep it down. I was hoping to lose the nickname this year," he said dropping his burden in a heap on the floor and collapsing on the bench beside it.

"Like that's going to happen. Some guys have it a whole lot worse, though. At least you're named after food instead of something you couldn't mention to your mother."

"Yeah, but 'Jell-O'? Who's going to be intimidated by that? Who's going to want to put *that* joker in a major league starting line-up? It'll never happen!"

"Take it as a sign you'll be sticking around. Nobody bothers to hang a moniker on a guy who's just passing through."

Angelo sighed. "I can't believe you've made it this far without picking up a nickname yourself."

"I'm lucky. You can't do much with 'Ben Lewis;' it's too plain. So, I guess you haven't checked in at the hotel yet either," he said nodding toward Angelo's luggage.

"Nope, I came straight here. They've got team busses shuttling back and forth. I'll catch one when I'm done."

"See you there, then. Maybe we can grab some dinner."

"Sure. So, what's next after I offload some of this stuff?"

"You're supposed to check in with the training staff. I hear they have health questionnaires for us to fill out, plus they'll give you an appointment for your physical." Ben returned the bat he'd been working on to its compartment. "That's where I'm headed now."

"Hey, did you see Hudson yet?" Capra asked as Ben stood to go.

"No, why?"

"Man, he's as big as an ox. He was out there showing off his physique and hyping his new training regime when I came in. I don't know what kind of body building he's into, but the results are amazing."

"He was only a .220 hitter last year. Big biceps won't help him hit the ball any more often."

"Maybe not, but when he does hit it, it's gonna fly a country mile."

Ben passed his physical the next day with hardly a hitch. The doctor who examined his every joint and sinew frowned when he heard about the recent shoulder injury. But since he couldn't find any lingering trace of trouble, he cleared Ben for play.

The first few days of training weren't too intense – stretching, running, soft-toss in the batting cages, and other light drills inter-spersed with orientation sessions, soup-and-sandwich lunches in the clubhouse, cool-down, and then more stretching, all finished by three o'clock. Within a week, though, they were up to speed with full-squad workouts occupying all four fields, live batting practice, and a slate of repetitive drills designed to fine-tune every aspect of the game.

"We run everywhere," Ben explained when he called home, "from the morning team meeting to defensive drills on field four maybe, then to fly ball drills on field one, and back indoors for a weight training rotation."

"Sounds rough," sympathized his father.

"No, it's great! It's just the way I imagined it would be."

"Are you rubbing shoulders with the major leaguers?"

"No, everything's kept pretty separate. They have their own locker room and work out on different fields."

"Rank has its privileges. Pretty soon it'll be your turn, Ben, and all the young kids will be envying you."

"I know. I'm working hard and trying to be patient. Games start in less than a week so they're splitting us up into temporary teams. I'll be working out with the AA Stars, at least to begin with."

"The Huntsville, Alabama team, right?"

"Yeah, but there's no guarantee I'll end up going there when camp breaks. It's still really early."

"Sounds like a good sign, though. Keep us posted on your progress."

"I will. Well, I'd better get going. Love to Mom."

-32-
The Next Step

Like an avid gardener working the newly warmed earth, Gail dug enthusiastically into her studies that spring. At last, it seemed they were getting to the core of their curriculum, to the essence of what nursing was all about. If there had been any doubt in her mind before, she was now certain she'd made the right career choice. She thrived on the professional atmosphere of the healthcare environment and gloried in the high ideals pioneered by those who had gone before.

Stories of Florence Nightingale had long ago captured Gail's preadolescent imagination. At the age of seven she first pictured herself following in that great lady's footsteps, and she'd held true to her original vision ever since. She shrugged off the subtle pressure to set her sights on a more advanced degree – specifically, her high school guidance counselor's suggestion that she should shoot for medical school instead. It seemed to Gail that nurses most directly provided compassionate care to patients, and every set of initials earned beyond RN was a level further removed from the aspects of medicine that appealed to her most.

With her professional life on a solid path, Gail reexamined her less-concrete personal plans with a new sense of purpose. Before, she had been more or less content to drift like a raft on a meandering river, trusting that God and the perpetual flow of time would ultimately carry her where she needed to go. But something had inexplicably changed because of the accident. Although only Paul – and Ben Lewis – were directly involved, she had been unbalanced by the trauma as well, her small boat rocked by the wake it created.

Weeks had passed, and still her emotional equilibrium felt out of whack. Her insides had been shaken like a snow globe, only the swirling flakes stubbornly refused to settle back into their proper places. She was restless, and impatient to have things decided with Paul one way or the other. If he was the man she was supposed to plan a future with, then why not get started? If he wasn't, she should know that as soon as possible too.

Since he was free, Paul picked Gail up for church the next Sunday. Afterward, they drove back by way of Ballard, buying lunch at a sandwich shop to eat in the park-like setting at the locks. They strolled down to the water and picked a spot on the inviting stair-stepped lawn overlooking the ship canal that connects Lake Washington and Lake Union with the Sound. Boat traffic was brisk, Gail noticed, with a variety of colorful craft straining for open water, their occupants in high spirits. No one could resist an unseasonably warm March day, with everything bursting into bloom at once, least of all sun-starved Seattleites. It seemed outdoor enthusiasts of all kinds had only been awaiting this engraved invitation to emerge from their winter hibernations.

Gail could appreciate the feeling. She had certainly weathered harsher climates elsewhere, but no place with more sodden, steel-gray days. It wasn't so much the total quantity of water that fell from the sky here, she had decided, but the number of weeks and months it took to reach that total. That's what grated away at your spirit: the constant drip, drip, drip. If the Inuit people had a hundred different words for the snow that constantly surrounded them, then the same should be true for the variations of Pacific Northwest precipitation. She'd noticed the forecast wasn't given in black and white – rain, or no rain – but in shades of gray: partly cloudy, scattered showers, patchy morning fog, and her personal favorite, drizzle. No wonder that a clear blue sky was celebrated like a national holiday, especially in early spring.

As she and Paul ate their lunch on the lawn, Gail tilted her face upward, closing her eyes and luxuriating in the delicious warmth like a sleek, black cat stretched out on a sun-drenched windowsill. After spending a winter in Seattle, she'd never take a day like this for granted again.

When their simple picnic was finished, Gail and Paul crossed to the opposite bank using the narrow walkways atop the closed gates of the locks. Water roared seaward over the spillway just beyond, throwing spray high into the air. Gulls cackled an incessant chorus overhead.

"Shall we see if there are any salmon in the fish ladder?" Gail suggested.

"There won't be. Sorry, wrong time of year," Paul explained.

So they rambled westward along the channel, continuing all the way to the end of the sidewalk. Far downstream, past the open railway drawbridge, Gail could just glimpse a sliver of the Sound. She pulled the sharp, salt air deep into her lungs and let it out with a satisfied sigh. "What a magnificent day!"

"Certainly is," Paul agreed, catching and squeezing her hand. "It's almost time for me to take you home, though. My shift at the hospital starts at four."

"I suppose we should head back to the car, then." But instead, Gail turned toward Paul. She had decided to move things forward, hadn't she? Well, this was a perfect time and a perfect setting to test the romantic waters. She looked up into his open face, nuzzled closer, and smiled. She wanted to be kissed; she was sending all the obvious signals.

He hesitated. "Are you sure?"

Gail nodded, and he bent to meet her lips.

~~*~~

"It's about bloody time!" Lorrie cried when Gail told her over lunch the next day. "Well, then, how was it? Worth the wait, I hope."

"It was nice," Gail reported brightly before taking another bite of her lukewarm, cafeteria lasagna.

"*Nice?*" Lorrie repeated, stringing the word out with yards of sarcasm.

"Okay, very nice!"

"That's it? You're not exactly gushing. I take it you didn't feel the earth move, and no fireworks either?"

"Don't be so disappointed. *I'm* not."

"You expect me to believe that?"

"Well, not much disappointed, anyway. I wasn't really expecting fireworks. It's kind of awkward, after being friends so long, to suddenly switch gears like that."

"Listen," said Lorrie, wagging her fork at her friend. "There's absolutely *nothing* sudden about your relationship with Paul. It's been creeping along at a snail's pace – a crippled, elderly snail – ever since I've known you. I enjoy an old-fashioned romance as much as the next girl, but this one's so puritanical that it almost puts me to sleep."

Gail's eyebrows jerked to attention. "So sorry to bore you!" she shot back, crossing her arms over her chest.

"Now, don't go gettin' your panties in a bunch, Gail. I'm your friend; I'm on your side."

"I'll try to remember that if you will."

"I just want to see you passionately in love and insanely happy – with Paul, or with somebody else if necessary."

"Me too, but it doesn't happen overnight."

"Sometimes it does; it did with me and Larry. But I'll try to be satisfied that you kids have finally taken at least a baby step forward. I sure hope you pick up steam from here, though. None of us are getting any younger, you know."

"A little steam would be good," Gail agreed. "I'll see what I can do."

The green light she had given Paul that afternoon at the locks signaled an instant transition in their relationship. They were definitely a couple now. Gail couldn't help being excited by the newness of it, the possibilities. Yet she felt safe knowing Paul wouldn't push the physical aspect beyond a certain point. They understood and respected each other, which was a promising start.

It was impossible to keep the status change from her parents, much as Gail would have liked to. "Don't get your hopes up," she chided her father when she came in from kissing Paul goodbye on the front porch one evening.

"What did I do?" he asked with palms up and shoulders hunched.

"I saw that look. Listen, Dad. I like Paul a lot, but it's way too soon to start planning the wedding. Understand?"

"Just glad you're finally giving good old Paul a chance. He'll take care of the rest."

Gail sighed. "We'll see about that. We'll see."

-33-
Looking Ahead

"Hi," Gail said when Paul arrived at Ivar's, the seafood restaurant on the waterfront where they'd arranged to meet for lunch. "What have you got there?"

Paul came around to kiss her on the cheek before settling into the seat opposite.

"This?" he said holding aloft a rolled-up magazine. "It's the latest edition of *Baseball America*. My father took a subscription so we could follow Ben Lewis's progress. Thought you might get a kick out of seeing it." He unfurled the colorful periodical and laid it on the table in front of her.

"I will," Gail agreed, immediately dropping her eyes to study the cover. It featured a Rangers outfielder – someone she'd never heard of before – with a look of hawk-like concentration, leaping to make a catch against the fence. "So how's Ben doing?" she asked casually.

"It's kind of hard to tell. Every issue has a whole new laundry list of statistics on him and every other pro ball player in the country. With all the numbers and abbreviations, it's like trying to read a foreign language. But the main news is that spring training's over, and Ben's been sent to play in Modesto, California. That much I was able to decipher."

"Is it a good assignment? A promotion, I mean?"

"Uh-huh. Here." Paul flipped the copy open to a dog-eared page and pointed to a circled section. "See, the Modesto A's are the 'advanced A' affiliate of the Oakland minor league system. If I've got this straight, that's two levels up from the rookie team he played for last season. I think it usually takes a few years to get to the majors, so we shouldn't expect that too soon."

"It would be fun to watch him play. I don't suppose the games are televised, though."

"Not around here anyway, and, according to their schedule, the team plays all their games in California except for a few in Reno."

"No chance we'll get to see him this year, then."

"Not unless you're traveling south. Maybe next season. If Ben makes it to triple A, he could wind up playing in Tacoma and we'll plan to go."

The waitress came to take their orders.

"We're going to need a few more minutes," Gail told her. "I guess we'd better figure out what we want," she said to Paul when they were alone again. She closed *Baseball America* and handed it back to him.

"No, you can keep it. Dad's done with it, and we'll get another one in a few days anyway."

"Okay, thanks." Gail tucked the magazine in beside her purse and turned her attention to the menu.

~~*~~

As they left the restaurant, Paul checked his watch. "I've still got an hour before I have to head back to the hospital. Let's poke around the waterfront a little."

Gail smiled and nodded. "I'd like that."

"Which direction do you want to go?" Paul asked.

Shading her eyes with her hand, Gail looked one way and then the other. "Let's start here," she said, pointing to the intriguing store next door. Totem poles framed the entrance, and the sign read *Ye Olde Curiosity Shop.*

"Haven't you ever been in there before?"

"No, never."

"Then today's your lucky day," Paul said leading the way. "But be prepared for some pretty strange sights."

"Like what?"

"Well, they've got all kinds of imports and cheesy souvenirs, which are for sale, but also museum pieces and... hmm... shall we say anatomical oddities? ...which aren't." He opened the door.

Gail stepped over the threshold and took in the scene. The shop seemed part global emporium and part sideshow, packed to the gills with a bizarre variety of merchandise and memorabilia. An assemblage of Native American art climbed high up one wall and spilled down across the next. A forest of antlers and a mounted buffalo head hung precariously from the ceiling. Tables and counters displayed everything from saltwater taffy, made locally, to exquisite Russian lacquer boxes; from chunky ethnic jewelry to vials containing Mexican jumping beans.

As she and Paul navigated through the narrow aisles, Gail paused to gawk at a leathery-skinned mummy named Sylvester. Next Paul pointed out a curio cabinet full of ornately carved ivory tusks, and another displaying a half dozen "genuine shrunken heads."

"Are they real, do you think?" Gail asked.

"Probably. The guy who started this place back around the turn of the century was a world-class collector."

"Okay, but what about that?" Gail challenged, nodding toward a trophy "Jackalope" hanging on the wall. It was a rabbit-like creature sporting, next to the more-expected set of long ears, a small pair of very natural-looking antlers.

"Sure," said Paul, not quite able to keep a straight face. "It's a rare example of an animal – now extinct, I believe – thought to be a cross between a jackrabbit and an antelope."

"Nice try, but I'm not buying it."

"Of course not; it isn't for sale at any price. See, that's what the sign says."

Gail laughed.

After viewing the preserved "mermaid" and the two-headed calf, Gail and Paul exited the shop and turned left, strolling north along Alaskan Way. Against the background smells of seawater, kelp, and creosoted pilings, Gail picked up a smoky whiff of food grilling somewhere nearby. A photographer snapped pictures of tourists boarding a sightseeing boat at pier fifty-four. Noise of street-level traffic punctuated the constant hum of tires droning by on the elevated viaduct off to the right.

Distracted by all the activity and the eclectic parade of people passing on the sidewalk, Gail didn't at first notice that Paul had fallen silent. When she glanced sideways, though, she saw furrows of concentration creasing his brow. "What's on your mind, Paul?" she asked. "You look worried."

"Hmm? Oh, sorry. No, not worried exactly." He halted, pulled her to one side, and peered into her light eyes. "I *have* been thinking a lot about the future, though."

Gail's throat tightened. "We agreed to take things slowly, Paul. Remember?"

"Don't panic. I wasn't talking about us. I meant me, what I'm going to do once I'm finally done with my education. Here, let's sit down a minute," he said leading the way to a vacant bench.

"I thought you'd decided to set up shop here in Seattle."

"That was the plan. But ever since the accident, I've had second thoughts. I guess talking about Ben earlier reminded me again that I almost died that day."

"But you didn't."

"Exactly. I was spared, and for what? I can't help thinking I'm still alive for a reason, for something more important than building up a practice and a comfortable life for myself."

"What on earth would you do instead? You're a doctor, Paul; of course you'll practice medicine. That's been your passion all along, what you've spent years training for."

"No, the way I feel about medicine hasn't changed. I'll always be a doctor. I just can't shake the impression that God spared me that day because He has some specific work for me to do. I've got to figure out what it is and do it, that's all. It might not mean throwing out the original plan altogether, only modifying it."

"Do you mean missions or charity work?"

"Maybe. I don't know yet. But it's like this extra time I've been given doesn't really belong to me. Do you see?"

Gail couldn't argue. Quite the opposite. She knew she ought to applaud his selfless attitude, to praise his altruistic view of the future. After all, Paul's spiritual and moral convictions were leading reasons why she'd decided to give a relationship with him a chance in the first place. What he had just told her only confirmed his good character.

She should admire him all the more for it. And she did.

She should also count herself lucky to be part of his life.

Intellectually she understood this, even believed it. So why did she feel betrayed instead? And guilty besides?

-34-
Modesto

The morning after he arrived in Modesto California, Ben and his new teammates piled off the bus for their first inspection of the ballpark that would be their professional home for the next five months. Looking around themselves, no one said much… and not because they were in awe. John Thurman Field wasn't the sort of place that took anyone's breath away. There were four bases, a pitcher's mound and a grassy outfield. Otherwise, it bore little resemblance to the great, green, circular cathedral of baseball less than sixty miles to the west: the Oakland Coliseum. Ben couldn't help thinking how close he was to that Mecca in terms of physical distance, and yet how far away measured by time and other intangibles.

After getting a look at the facilities, finding a roommate and a place to live were the next priorities. The organization gave all the players a three-day paid hotel stay and a list of potential, long-term accommodations to get them started. They would be on their own after that.

Ben paired up with Angelo Capra again. The apartment they leased together wasn't exactly a palace, but then they had a very limited budget to work with; Ben didn't want to dip into his signing bonus if he could help it, and Angelo didn't have one to dip into. So they felt lucky to come across something decent they could afford. A couple of the guys were still looking, continuing to pay hotel fees out of their own pockets in the meantime.

Modesto seemed like a nice enough city – not too big yet close to metropolitan attractions. In that way, it was much like the town of Puyallup where Ben had grown up. The location had some other advantages, as he remembered in his glass-is-half-full moments: the more moderate climate, for example. He would be spared the tyrannical heat he'd endured the previous summer in Phoenix as well as the Deep South humidity Huntsville would have undoubtedly supplied. And Modesto was comparatively close to home – another plus. When Ben had called to let his family know where he was headed, his dad used that line of reasoning to put a positive spin on the assignment.

"We can hop on a plane and be there in a couple of hours – come watch you play. How about in June, just as soon as your mother's done with the school year? Maybe we'll even combine it with a getaway weekend in San Francisco."

"Yeah, that'd be great, Dad."

There was only one *real* reason Modesto was a letdown; it wasn't Huntsville. Ben would have gladly born any inconvenience for the chance to leapfrog over the single A division and land on Oakland's double A team, another step closer to the majors. He'd put up good numbers in camp. Apparently not good enough, though. The double A promotion had gone to Barry Hudson instead, who had edged him out in the power hitting stats. But whatever Ben lacked in brute strength, he vowed to make up by trying harder than anybody else. He poured everything he had into the game – subjugating himself to the routine of training, working until his muscles vibrated with fatigue, precision tuning his mental strings for competition. Hard work: that was the all-purpose cure.

Once the season began, Ben quickly shrugged off his disappointment over being sent to Modesto. A few weeks in, it was a distant memory. The important thing was that he was still playing baseball every day and getting paid for it to boot. He was moving in the right direction: up – unlike at least one of his teammates. That's who he felt sorry for, the guys whose careers had stalled out.

"This will be my last year in baseball," Cosmo Gonzales, a fellow outfielder, told him matter-of-factly one day during the pregame warm-up. "Unless something breaks for me soon, I'm on my way out. I'll have to quit if they don't let me go first."

Ben studied him sideways, both of them sitting on the grass stretching their hamstrings. "I don't know how you can even think about giving up, Coz. You sound so resigned to it too."

"Not resigned, just realistic."

"If my time ever comes, they'll have to drag me out of here and lock the gate behind me. I sure wouldn't quit voluntarily."

"That's the way I used to feel, but things change."

On cue, they switched to stretch out the other leg.

"I've got a wife to consider now," Cosmo continued. "We've talked about having kids, but we can't afford to on what I'm making. Even if Maria goes back to work fulltime after, things would be tight."

"It would all be worthwhile if you made it."

"But what if I don't? What if I get traded or released instead? You hear about guys who move six or eight times in one season. That's no way to raise a family, dragging them back and forth across the country chasing my next job. I've been busting my butt in the low minors for over four years now, and I've got nothing to show for it. I'm ready to cut my losses and get on with my life."

Ben had no idea how to respond. Along with the rest of the team, he got to his feet for arm circles and rotator cuff stretches. "So, what will you do?" he asked a minute later.

Gonzales shrugged and sighed. "Maria's father owns a video store back home in El Paso. He's offered to take me on, to show me the ropes before he retires. He wants to leave the business to me. It's a good opportunity."

"I'm sorry, Coz."

"It's okay, really." He gave Ben a wan smile. "Time to grow up, that's all. At least I had my shot. A lot of guys don't even get that."

Ben had to believe his own story would turn out differently. Unquestioning self-confidence was critical. What else would persuade anyone to embark on a quest where the odds against success were about a million to one? To begin to doubt was to flirt with disaster, to give in to the dark side. Baseball was something like a religion in that way; without faith, you were lost.

For better or for worse, Ben soon said goodbye to the presence that daily reminded him of that unsettling conversation. Cosmo Gonzales was cut from the team and went home to El Paso at the end of April.

~~*~~

The Modesto Athletics played in the ten-team California league, which kept Ben and his teammates traveling throughout the southern two-thirds of the state, and periodically across the border into Nevada for a series against the Reno Silver Sox. Week-long road trips took them to cities like Bakersfield, San Bernardino, and Palm Springs, with shorter jaunts to their nearer opponents in Stockton and San Jose. The schedule was punishing with only a rare day off at home. Some, like Ben, thrived on the steady work. Those who did not, seldom complained, knowing someone else would jump at the chance to take their place if they couldn't hack it.

At Modesto's first game against the High Desert Mavericks in Adelanto, Ben spied Derek Williams in the opposing lineup, as expected. He already knew his old rival had garnered the same promotion he had and now played for the Padres' advanced A team. When Ben wasn't *playing* baseball, he was *studying* baseball, keeping up with player assignments, trades, and statistics. Plus he'd recently talked to his old buddy Kyle, who always knew the latest scuttlebutt.

"Dude, I ran into your ex after our game the other day. She was looking mighty fine, I must say," Kyle told him on the phone. "Said she's still dating Williams. Sounds like you'll be seeing a lot of him too since you're playing in the same league."

"Yeah, I know. We're like matter and antimatter; we shouldn't be allowed anywhere near each other, but I can't seem to shake the guy. Let's not talk about him. How's Scott? Do you ever see him around campus?"

"Sure. I'm watching out for the little bro like you asked me. He's cool. Sometimes we hang together too. Wish you were here, though. The team isn't the same this year without you."

"I wish you were here instead, Rosier. We could use your perfectly adequate skills in left."

"To make you look good by contrast, I suppose."

"I'll take all the help I can get."

The month of June turned into a veritable hitting bonanza for Ben. Like discovering a seam of gold-laden ore between layers of ordinary bedrock, he suddenly broke into one of those enigmatic, preciously scarce hot streaks, exploiting it for all it was worth. His fielding continued nearly flawless, but now his batting average and power numbers were way up too.

Ben couldn't define the difference. He wasn't as superstitious as a lot of ball players who might have credited the success to a new haircut or wearing their socks inside out. Nothing had changed except that he was seeing the ball extraordinarily well. It now looked as big as a grapefruit when it came floating off the pitcher's hand toward the plate. There he waited, muscles poised for action and itching to turn loose his swing. Ben was suddenly hitting .500, producing doubles instead of singles, shooting for the fence instead of the outfield gaps.

He knew it wouldn't last forever; hot streaks eventually played themselves out. When the Midas touch vanished, he would be reduced to mere mortal status again. But Ben reveled in every minute that the force – or whatever kind of magic it was – remained with him. He hoped it would hold long enough to earn him the next rung up the ladder, and for his parents to see him at his best.

He was still in peak form when they flew down at the end of the month. As soon as he came onto the field that day, Ben spotted them in the sparsely populated stands. He gave them a little two-fingered, boy-scout-style salute of acknowledgement. Three hands waved back, the third belonging to Jessica Martinelli.

-35-
Visitors

Wearing sunglasses, tight shorts, and a beauty-queen smile, Jessica looked like the poster girl for a "Vacation in Sunny California" campaign. Her olive complexion always gave her a head start on her summer tan. So, unlike some of the pasty-white tourists from their native north, she was not ashamed to show some skin in public. She sat with her long, athletically trim legs stretched out across the bench in front of her and her bare arms propped on the one behind, managing to transform the uncomfortable bleachers into her personal chaise lounge.

"Friend of yours?" Angelo asked Ben after seeing the exchange of salutations.

"Sort of." They broke into a jog for their warm-up lap around the field. "That's my ex-girlfriend next to my parents. The parents, I expected. Jessica, I didn't."

Angelo gave a low whistle modulated by the rhythm of his footfalls. "That's one choice female. But why would she be here if she's your ex?"

"She dates a guy we both know from the University of Washington. He plays for High Desert. I'm sure she's here to see him, not me."

"Your ex-girlfriend with your ex-teammate? Hmm. Sounds awkward."

"No big deal. Jessica and I were over a long time ago."

It was the first of a three-game home series against the High Desert Mavericks. With Derek Williams in town, Ben probably shouldn't have been surprised to see Jessica among the spectators. But he *was* surprised, and not altogether pleased. Her presence was bound to be a distraction at the very least.

Whenever the grandstands were packed, the sweep of fans tended to blend into one amorphous array of humanity – just a generic backdrop speckled with dots of noise and color. That's the way Ben preferred it. It was good knowing his friends were there supporting him, yet better if his attention wasn't diverted by actually spotting one of them. But he knew that John Thurman Field wouldn't come close to reaching its capacity for a Tuesday game. Individual faces and voices would stand out, especially those of someone like Jessica, who was difficult to overlook even in a crowd.

It turned out she was less of a distraction for Ben than for others. Derek, he noticed, conspicuously upped his strut-and-swagger game, scoring extra style points to compensate for faulty execution. Defensively, he bobbled a ball in the seventh inning, allowing the runner time to take an extra base. When Derek tried to pull off the same trick in the ninth, attempting to stretch his long single into a double, Ben gunned him down at second. Modesto won, four to three.

After a quick shower, Ben found his parents waiting behind the stands in the open-air concession concourse. Jessica was still with them, and no sign of Derek Williams yet. Keeping an eye out for him, Ben gave his mom and dad each a hug.

"Good game, son," said Mr. Lewis.

"Thanks." Ben turned to the third member of the party. "Hi, Jess," he said warily. "I didn't expect to see you here."

"I thought I'd surprise you," she said, smiling up at him through thick, dark lashes. "No, actually, Derek made me promise that I'd visit him as soon as I was out of school."

"I figured."

"It saved me some money coming here instead of flying all the way to LA to see him play at his home field."

Movement at the door to the visitors' locker room caught Ben's attention. "There's your boyfriend now," he said nodding in that direction.

Derek spotted them immediately. His face hardened into a stony glare.

"Oops, I'd better go," Jessica said, dashing off to meet him.

Ben turned away from the couple's reunion and back to his parents. "Where's Scott?" he asked as they started making their way toward the parking lot. "I thought he was coming with you."

"He wanted to," answered Mr. Lewis, "but it turned out he had to start his summer job right away instead of next week like he'd hoped. They wouldn't hold it for him. And he did just see you a couple months ago in Phoenix."

"Yeah, it was cool he could drive my car down and hang out for a few days. Well, now that you're here, what do you want to do first?"

"I'd like to see where you live, if that's okay," said Mrs. Lewis, "and then we're going to take you out to dinner. You'll need to choose the restaurant, though, since we don't know our way around."

With his father following in the rental car, Ben gave his mother a lift in his, toning down his driving style accordingly.

"So what's the deal, Mom?" Ben asked her *en route*. "Why do you have Jessica in tow?"

"She flew down with us and is staying at the same hotel too. When I told Mrs. Martinelli we were planning this trip, she suggested it."

"It seems kind of weird, though, since we're not together anymore."

"We got rather attached to Jessica when you two dated so long, and I've been friends with her mother for years. All that doesn't stop just because you two broke up, you know."

Ben made a face. "I suppose not."

"Besides, if anybody was going to be uncomfortable about the arrangement, it should have been Jessica, and she said she was fine with it. You don't really mind, do you, Ben?"

"No, but her boyfriend might not be too crazy about her hanging out with my family, considering our history."

When they arrived, Ben gave his parents the short tour of his very ordinary apartment, the only highlight being the chance to meet his roommate. Angelo declined the invitation to join them for dinner, so the other three piled into the rental car and set off in search of food, winding up at The Windjammer, one of the nicer restaurants in town.

Halfway through the meal, Mr. Lewis cleared his throat and announced, "Ben, your mother and I have something to tell you, some pretty big news that we thought we should deliver in person."

Ben's mind raced. "You're not getting a divorce," he stated emphatically.

200

"No, no, it's not that drastic," his father assured him, waving away Ben's worst fear, "but it will be a big change. We've decided to sell the house."

"Sell the house? Why?"

"It's gotten to be too much upkeep for us," his mother answered. "That's the main reason. And we just don't need such a big place anymore, now that you boys are grown and gone most of the time. Don't worry, though; we'll always have room for you to stay with us when you come home." She paused, but when Ben said nothing, she went on. "We're buying a beautiful new condominium in West Seattle, near Alki beach. Wait until you see it! It's got all the amenities – a gym, a billiard room, concierge service, even an indoor pool – plus great views of the city across Elliot Bay from the rooftop deck. It's going to be like living in a luxury hotel." Again, she waited. "Say something, honey. You look like you're in shock."

Ben had frozen – mouth open and fork suspended in midair – unable to speak. "A condo?" he finally managed, his face scrunched up in disbelief. "When did all this happen?"

"Now, Son, you knew your mother and I planned to downsize eventually…"

"Yeah, when you retired!"

"…and the opportunity came up a little sooner than we expected, that's all. There's this developer buying big tracts of land all up and down our street. He's going to tear down some of the older houses, like ours, which sit on half-acre lots, so he can build a bunch of new ones on quarter-acre lots. It's going to be a 'planned community' with sidewalks, playgrounds, metro bus service, and even a new elementary school. I know it sounds a little crazy – leveling a whole neighborhood to start over – but that's the economic reality. With the population growing so fast in our area, the land is more valuable than the houses. Most of our neighbors are selling too – the Beals, Robblees, Capettos, and old Mr. Johnson. It's too good a deal to pass up."

While Ben tried to wrap his head around the idea that his parents – his predictably suburban mom and dad – had suddenly decided to sell and relocate to some swanky urban condo, they took turns filling him in on all the advantages of the move: maintenance-free living, a shorter commute, easy access to sports and cultural events in town, more freedom to travel. Despite seeing how excited they obviously were, all Ben could think about was that "coming home" would never be the same again.

"The only real drawback of the new place," Mrs. Lewis continued, "is that there's pretty limited storage. So, we've already started sorting and getting rid of stuff. Scott's going to work on clearing his things out over the summer, but we'll probably have to rent a storage unit for yours temporarily."

"Why? When do you have to be out of the house, Mom?"

"By the first of September – before your season's over. I'm sorry, Ben."

~~*~~

The Mavericks won the next night to even up the series, Derek Williams turning in a stellar performance for his team and his girlfriend. This time, Ben was the one distracted and off his game. The news from his parents hit him hard. Until they informed him they were selling it, Ben had no idea how attached he was to his childhood home. It was just an ordinary house, an inorganic object, a shell. Yet to learn he would never spend another night under its roof... It felt like someone had died, and he hadn't even been given the chance to say goodbye.

If he had a regular job, it might have been easier to take. Then he could get excited about moving on, finding a home of his own. With his nomadic lifestyle, though, it made little sense to buy or even to rent a permanent place in Seattle when he would spend so little time there. Ben had always assumed he could just bunk in with his parents for the off seasons until his future was more settled. Now that would mean a guest bedroom in an impersonal condominium instead of home, with all his belongings around him.

Ben put the issue out of his mind before the final game of the series against High Desert. It was important for him to concentrate solely on baseball and to rebound from his lackluster appearance the previous night. He wasn't prepared to give up his hot streak yet. He also wanted to play well for his parents' last day in town. Their plan was to drop Jessica off at the Oakland airport in time for her flight later that night, and then they would go on from there to spend the weekend in San Francisco before returning to Seattle themselves.

Ben got off to a fast start, hitting a solo homer his first time up. Derek Williams didn't fare as well in his initial plate appearance. He quickly fell behind 0-2, swinging uncharacteristically wild at the first two pitches, a strike at the knees and ball high and out of the zone. Regrouping, he let the next two balls pass unmolested to even the count. When the umpire rang him up on the following pitch, bellowing "ste-e-e-ri-i-i-ke" over a pitch that barely nicked the outside corner of the plate, Derek went ballistic. He broke his bat over his knee and got into the umpire's face with his harsh opinion of the man's eyesight.

The outburst finished Derek's day. He was ejected from the game and sent to the showers. Before he left the field, however, Ben saw him cast a malevolent look into the stands, in Jessica's direction. Although the Mavericks ended up winning the game to take the series, Derek Williams wasn't around to enjoy it. Ben didn't see anything of his old rival afterward either, only what he took to be his handiwork. Someone had "keyed" his car, Ben discovered in the parking lot. He stared at the jagged score mark in disgust, clenching his jaw and his fists.

"Oooow! Nasty scratch," he heard Jessica say from behind.

Ben wrenched his head around to her, and then slowly back to the defaced door panel.

"Derek?" she suggested.

He forced his muscles to relax and took a deep breath before answering. "Probably. It seems like the kind of thing he would do, especially with the mood he was in."

Jessica came around to face Ben, leaning against the car and biting her lower lip. "My fault, I think. I sort of broke up with him right before the game."

"No wonder, then. I figured something must have set him off for him to totally lose his cool like he did."

"I told him I still liked him, but that I wanted to date other guys too, since he's not around much. He didn't see the point in that arrangement, so I guess we're through. You don't think I was being unreasonable, do you?"

"Hey, none of *my* business," Ben said, holding up his hands to fend off any more unwanted information. "Listen, Jess, I've got to run. I'm supposed to meet my parents back at their hotel."

Jessica laughed. "I know; that's where I'm going too."

"Oh, yeah. I forgot."

"I told them you'd give me a ride. So how about it? Just for old time's sake?"

Ben floundered for a polite way to say no.

A car horn sounded. They both turned to see Mr. and Mrs. Lewis driving by, waving as they exited the lot.

"Now you'll *have* to drive me, unless you want to call me a cab."

Ben shrugged. "Hop in."

It was only a fifteen-minute trip. Jessica started off by admiring Ben's car and complimenting his play on the field. He kept his responses short and to the point. Then, when they turned in at the hotel, Jessica reached across and lightly slid her left hand down Ben's forearm to cover his right on the shifter.

"It's really good to see you again, Ben," she purred.

Her touch triggered a knee-jerk reaction in his system, instantly flashing back to their former intimacy. Guarding his expression, Ben carefully pulled into a parking spot. There he killed the engine and firmly returned Jessica's hand to her side of the car. "It's nice to see you too, Jess, but I don't think this is such a good idea."

"Why not?" she asked facing him and leaning in. "We've always been attracted to each other. That hasn't changed."

Ben opened his mouth to protest.

She cut in. "Don't deny it; you know it's true."

"But we're not together anymore."

"And why is that, Benji? For the life of me, I can't think of one good reason why we ever split up in the first place." She combed her fingers up through his hair. "Can you?"

No, he couldn't explain it either, at least not with that dark, musky scent she always wore filling his nostrils and going straight to his brain. He remembered breaking off with Jessica, but, at least for the moment, not why he'd done it. Maybe it *was* sheer madness, as Scott had said.

"Think about it," she murmured, trailing the tip of her little finger down Ben's jaw line and across his lips. "And call me... any-time."

-36-
Summer of '92

Gail kept busier than ever through the summer months. Along with the two classes she elected to take that quarter, she began working part time as a nurse tech at a GI clinic, for experience and for some extra spending money. She pulled and filed charts, escorted patients to the exam rooms, took blood pressures, and the like. Gail enjoyed everything about her job, especially that it moved her one step closer to her career goals.

She and Paul carved out time together whenever their schedules allowed – an occasional day off in common, but more often a couple hours squeezed in here or there. Paul channeled the remainder of his free time into the quest to discover his calling. Like a tenacious bull-dog, he'd latched onto the idea that God had spared his life for some specific, but as-yet-unrevealed, purpose. He couldn't rest until he knew what it was; and he could talk of little else.

"The possibilities are limitless!" he told Gail one day. He had joined her on campus after her classes, and they'd walked over to the Hub for a bite of lunch. They took their food to a small table and sat down. "Physicians are in high demand," he continued, his words spilling out rapidly. "Once I started looking around, I couldn't be-lieve how many agencies – religious as well as secular – employ doctors. Hospitals and clinics, of course, but also research institu-tions, public facilities for the handicapped or mentally ill, not to mention an endless list of charitable organizations working in this country and abroad. It's hard to know where to begin."

"Shouldn't you start by praying about it, before getting too car-ried away?" she suggested.

"That goes without saying. But I want to be proactive too. I feel like I need to do my part, not just sit back and expect the answer to drop into my lap. I'll focus on options in pediatrics, of course. That narrows the field. Right now, though, the thing that excites me most is foreign missions."

"Foreign missions," Gail repeated softly. She dropped her eyes to her shrimp salad, concentrating on the task of distributing a drizzle of Thousand Island dressing evenly over every torn lettuce leaf. She noticed Paul had leaned forward, and she felt the uncomfortable weight of his gaze on her face. He would be expecting her to join in his enthusiasm and wondering why she held back. Still, she didn't answer.

He continued, more solemnly. "You know, nurses are needed every bit as much as doctors in all the same settings I'm considering."

"I'm sure they are," Gail answered evenly without looking up from her meal.

"Well, what do you think? Would you consider doing something like that after you graduate?"

She gave a one-shouldered shrug. "I don't know. I haven't really thought that far ahead."

Paul reached across to take hold of her hand. "We'd make a good team, you and I," he said intensely. Then he immediately backed off. "I'm sorry, Gail. I know I promised I wouldn't pressure you, but the future seems so clear to me, at least that part. Think about it. I'm sure you want to do the right thing; you're not a selfish person."

He gave her far too much credit, she thought. Suddenly she felt *very* selfish, her standard reaction to the subject of foreign missions. An accusing voice, which she took to be her over-developed conscience, told her she wouldn't be a first-class Christian until she cheerfully left everything behind and winged her way to some third-world country to care for lepers.

But the guilty truth was she really didn't want to go. She admired missionaries tremendously, for their passion and commitment. She even envied the unique fulfillment they seemed to find in their work. Yet when she tried to imagine herself in their places, she just couldn't see it. Her heart wasn't in it.

That could change, though, right? God was in the business of changing hearts. And Gail strongly believed that if He intended her to marry Paul and follow him to the mission fields of Mozambique or wherever, she would never be happy doing anything else. Maybe she just needed a little more time… and a little more faith.

Gail arranged to take the last week of August off from her job at the clinic. Summer quarter was over, and her best friend from Tulsa, Lindsay Macon, was flying in for a visit during the break. Gail bubbled with excitement for the long-awaited reunion, the chance to compare notes on their personal lives and on their respective nursing programs. Plus, she looked forward to introducing Lindsay to her closest friends and favorite places around Seattle.

With the day of Lindsay's arrival approaching, Gail kept her fingers crossed and an eye on the dubious long-range forecast. The only thing people from out of state seemed to know about Seattle was that it rained all the time. Not true, of course, although sometimes it felt certifiably so. Still, that wasn't the side of northwest living Gail wished to play up for her friend. She hoped to show off her new home town to its best advantage, and all the local attractions would benefit from the cosmetic lift of fair weather.

It poured buckets Saturday when Gail went to SeaTac airport to meet Lindsay's plane.

"It's not always like this," Gail reassured her.

Then it rained all day Sunday as well. It hardly mattered. The friends spent the time catching up on the missed details of each other's lives. That, at least, didn't depend on clear skies.

Monday was dry but still overcast, so they postponed their visit to Mt. Rainier. Seeing the mountain and checking another national park off her list had been Lindsay's specific request, yet there wasn't much point in going all that way if the star attraction remained shrouded in clouds.

The sun finally broke out on Wednesday, and the girls headed south first thing in the morning. They took highway 410, skirting the border of the park to Chinook Pass, where Gail had a short hike planned. Paul had introduced her to the Naches Peak trail, so she knew from experience how impressive Lindsay's first close-up view of the mountain would be from there. They rounded a bend in the path, and suddenly there it was, the craggy, glacier-encrusted peak standing tall against the sky and perfectly reflected in a tiny alpine lake surrounded by wildflowers.

"Wow," Lindsay murmured. "That's amazing. Beautiful!" She reached for her camera.

"You won't find a view like that in Oklahoma," Gail heard herself boasting, a sentiment almost word for word what her father told her when she arrived in Washington. Funny how she'd done such a quick about-face. A year before she'd complained about being dragged to yet another new city. Now she realized she wouldn't give up her life in the northwest for Tulsa or anywhere else.

After admiring the vista and returning to the car, they continued south, entering the park proper at Stevens Canyon. Gail pulled off the road a short time later for a detour on foot to another favorite spot. A wooded trail and narrow bridge guided them to a protected island of evergreen trees called The Grove of the Patriarchs. Spared from forest fire for a thousand years, the cedars and firs had grown to vast age and immense girth. Gail and Lindsay took photos of each other in front of one particularly impressive specimen and then asked a passerby to snap a picture of them together.

"Thanks a lot," Gail told the helpful stranger. Glancing at her watch and turning to her friend, she added, "We'd better go. We still have a long drive ahead of us and we'll want to spend some time at Paradise before we head home."

"Paradise?"

"Yeah. It's a visitor's area on the south flank of the mountain with a lodge, trails, and some spectacular alpine meadows. Last summer, Paul and I climbed from there up to Panorama Point at about seven thousand feet. Paul's been all the way up to ten thousand, to Camp Muir. That's the base where most of the attempts on the summit start."

"Hey, I'm game for anything. I came prepared," Lindsay declared, striking an L. L. Bean catalogue pose in her safari hat, sturdy hiking boots, and knapsack stocked with canteen, binoculars, sunscreen, and a week's emergency rations.

"You sure did. I think a little *over* prepared," Gail said shaking her head. By comparison, she carried only her wallet, keys, a granola bar, and a water bottle in a fanny pack. "We haven't left civilization, you know. We've barely been a mile off the road in any direction so far. You must have been a boy scout in a former life," she joked.

"Maybe, but I'm having fun." They turned back the way they'd come. "So is Paul going to climb all the way to the top of Mt. Rainier someday?"

"He wants to, or at least he did. I don't think it's as important to him anymore. His priorities have changed. With all his talk of working as a doctor overseas, it's probably more likely he'll wind up climbing Mt. Kilimanjaro."

"I can't wait to meet this guy."

"You'll get your chance on Friday."

~~*~~

Paul was the one who had suggested a group outing to the Seattle Center. He had the whole day available. So did his sister Hollie and Ben's brother Scott, whom she had been dating since February when they met at Anthony's. Scott had offered to bring his friend Kyle as a date of sorts for Lindsay. Even the weather cooperated spectacularly with clear skies and the temperature predicted to hit ninety.

After meeting at the Albrights' house, the group carpooled to the Center to do all the typical touristy stuff for Lindsay's benefit. They rode the Monorail to downtown and back. They sampled the food and rides at the Fun Forrest amusement park. Then they cooled off standing downwind in the over spray from the International Fountain, faces forward and arms outstretched. A visit to the dinosaur exhibit at the Science Center followed, and finally the obligatory pilgrimage six hundred feet up to the observation deck of the Space Needle for a panorama of the city and beyond. Lindsay was properly impressed.

When they returned to the house, the group of six, dressed in shorts and sneakers, joined Mr. and Mrs. Albright for dinner around the large oval table set with linen, crystal, fine bone china, and fresh flowers.

"So, Scott," Mrs. Albright ventured during the course of the meal. "Gail tells me you are the brother of the young man who is credited with saving Paul's life back in February."

"That's right. He's a hero in my book."

"Mine too," Paul chimed in.

"And some sort of professional athlete, I believe," Mrs. Albright continued to Scott.

"Yeah, a minor league outfielder. He just got a promotion, too."

"That's baseball, isn't it?" questioned Mrs. Albright. "I know so little about sports."

"Yes, Judith, as I've told you before," Mr. Albright chided.

Gail redirected the conversation. "So, Scott, that's pretty great news about your brother."

"Yeah. Ben's having an awesome year. He got called up to double A last week, so he's in Huntsville, Alabama now."

"He's got to be totally psyched about it too," added Kyle.

Paul asked, "Isn't the season almost finished, though?"

"It is for most of the minor leaguers," Scott explained. "A few will go to the majors with the September call-ups, when the teams are allowed to expand their rosters. For the rest, it'll be over in about another week."

"Will Ben be coming home soon then?" Hollie asked him.

"I don't know. Last I heard he was probably going to play in the Arizona Fall League. So we might not see him until the holidays. Then he should be around for at least a couple of months."

After dinner, the six young people retreated downstairs to hang out and shoot pool. Paul and Lindsay played the first game with Kyle and Gail watching from the sidelines. Scott and Hollie wandered off together, hand in hand, across the lawn to where the terraced hillside fell away toward the shimmering Sound beyond.

"Thanks for coming along today, Kyle," Gail said as they boosted onto stools by the bar. "I think Lindsay had a lot of fun."

"Likewise. She's awesome. Too bad she lives so far away."

"I know. I've been trying to convince her to move here when she graduates – showing her all the great things Seattle has available."

"I'll take that as a compliment..."

"No, I... Never mind."

"...and I do happen to be available at the moment. I was seeing someone for a while, but it didn't work out."

"That's too bad. I'm sorry."

"No worries. Anyway, it was very cool to meet you finally, Gail, after hearing so much about you from Ben. He was so stoked to hook up with you at the beginning; I was surprised when it didn't go anywhere."

"Ben was 'stoked' to meet me?"

"Totally, ever since that first time he locked eyes with you on campus. He told me all about it – the instant, cosmic kind of thing he thought you two had going on. He about went crazy trying to find a way to meet you after that."

"I didn't know. He never said anything."

"I told him he should have, but maybe he felt awkward about it because of Paul. Oh, well. I guess it wasn't meant to be after all, kinda like me and Kristy."

"You're up," Paul said coming across the room to pass the cue stick off to Kyle. "Good luck. You'll need it." Taking Kyle's vacated seat, he turned to Gail. "Your friend Lindsay, there, is a shark."

"Hmm? What did you say?"

"I said Lindsay is a shark. Killer instinct, that's what she's got. I had no chance."

"Uh-huh," she said absently.

"Hey, is something wrong, Gail? You look upset."

Gail shook it off and smiled at him. "No. I'm fine! So, how did your game with Lindsay go?"

The party broke up about seven, Paul and Scott both needing to be at work early the next morning. Scott kissed Hollie goodbye and then ducked into the washroom while the rest started making their way up the half flight of stairs to the front door. Kyle, who had arrived last, drove off first followed by Paul and then his sister, leaving the driveway empty. Lindsay turned back into the house just as Scott emerged onto the porch.

Gail asked him, "Where's your car?"

"Oh, it's up there," he answered, indicating the vehicle on the side of the street above. "The driveway was kind of full when I got here and I didn't want to block anybody in."

Gail lifted her eyes. A lump rose in her throat when she saw the old, blue Toyota parked on the shoulder, shafts of amber light skipping off the glass and chrome in all directions. She blinked... twice. A curious tingle ran up her spine to prickle the downy hairs at the nape of her neck.

"You must have an appreciation for classic cars," Scott remarked as she continued to stare. "Girls aren't usually that impressed with the old Corolla. Hollie won't even…"

Gail interrupted. "You've been to this house before; I saw your car parked exactly where it is now. Months ago."

"What?" Scott tilted his head sideways and wrinkled his brow. "Not me. That's why I needed directions. It must have been another one just like it, or maybe it was my brother you saw. The car was his until last summer."

-37-
Introspection

Ben Lewis. Why did his name keep cropping up every time she turned around? Here she was trying to focus on her relationship with Paul, and reminders of Ben (not only his existence but his inexplicable link to her) entered the conversation when she least expected. Not that he was to blame. Paul himself was the worst offender, frequently reiterating how grateful he was to Ben or commenting on the most recent set of statistics from that baseball magazine. Then today, Ben was mentioned no less than three times by three different people – first by her mother at the table, next during the odd exchange with his friend Kyle, and finally by his brother in reference to the Toyota.

Nothing strange about what her mother had said; that was just Mom's polite dinner conversation, as much a part of her hostess-mode conventions as insisting on the good china for a bunch of sunburned, underdressed college kids.

Kyle's remarks were more difficult to shrug off. They confirmed what she had sensed from Ben himself – that he originally believed in a strong connection to her. He'd nearly convinced her of it too with the way he looked at her the first couple of times they met. Then he'd lost interest by that night at the restaurant. No, that wasn't quite right. It wasn't so much that he'd lost interest, or that he'd stepped aside for Paul's sake either. He had acted as if they were only minor acquaintances (which of course they were), as if he didn't remember having any special bond with her in the first place.

Why? Was she so completely forgettable? Or had she failed to live up to his expectations when they finally spoke? Could a fixation, like Kyle described Ben as having, be turned off as easily as a light switch? Very peculiar.

But it was seeing that rusty blue Toyota that had really given her the shakes. Sure, there had to be thousands just like it on the planet. Yet somehow Gail knew – knew down to the ends of her toenails – that it was the very same one she'd seen before, and Ben Lewis must have been the guy behind the wheel.

You could call it a coincidence... but it didn't feel like one. You could call it stalking... except Ben couldn't have even known her when he first turned up at her house that day last June. Maybe his hanging out on campus, after they'd first locked eyes with each other there, *did* have something to do with her. But it was ludicrous to suppose Ben could foresee that hurtling himself in front of an out-of-control delivery van would lead to them finally meeting. No, it felt more like the actions of fate, something beyond time and human control – an appointment with destiny, if you like.

A sudden gust of wind swept up off the water, coursing between the houses stacked above the bluff and rattling the first parched leaves loose from the maple trees. It lifted the thick, flaxen mane from Gail's shoulders and forehead. It tugged at the open door. Only then did Gail realize she was still standing with her hand on the knob, staring up at the road and the empty swatch of blue sky above it, long after Scott had driven away in the troublesome Toyota. "Get a grip, Gail," she muttered. "You're slipping into pure fantasy now."

"Sounds interesting," Lindsay said, coming up behind her. "Tell me more. Are you having exotic daydreams about your handsome Dr. Paul?"

"Not about Paul."

Lindsay raised an eyebrow.

Gail felt her cheeks flush. "I mean, no exotic dreams about him or anyone else either!" A quizzical frown waltzed across Gail's face. "Do you really think Paul is handsome?"

"Don't you? Gail! He's like a taller, blonder version of Tom Cruise. You must have noticed."

"I haven't thought much about it one way or the other, maybe because I've known him all my life. Besides, someone's physical appearance isn't what's most important."

"True, but Paul seems to have a lot else going for him. He's a really good guy from everything you've told me, and you can't help admiring him for wanting to go into the mission field. Plus, he clearly adores you. What more could you want?"

214

"Nothing *more* exactly, but sometimes I wonder…"

"What?"

"Oh, I don't know." Gail rubbed her temples. "You're right; there's absolutely nothing wrong with Paul. He's perfect and I'm an idiot for questioning it."

~~*~~

Ben rationalized that he would certainly have tried to get home at the end of the season if he still had a home to go to. But an unfamiliar condo in Seattle? No, that wasn't a big draw. Besides, as he had explained to his parents back then, there wasn't much free time before he was due in Arizona to play in the fall league. So instead of flying from Huntsville to Seattle, he returned to Oakland to reclaim his car and the bulk of his belongings, which he'd been forced to abandon when he was called up to double A. From there, he'd driven south to Phoenix to play some more baseball.

Afterward, he'd found an excuse to delay and a couple detours to take. But he'd made it home in time for Christmas as promised. Or to his parents' new place, more correctly. The condo was everything they'd said it would be – sleek, sophisticated, efficient, centrally located – yet a little impersonal to Ben's mind. He'd expected to at least recognize the furniture. But no, that had all changed as well. Understandable when he considered it objectively. Even he could see that their bulky, colonial-style things from the ranch house in the suburbs wouldn't fit this new, minimalist setting. The scale would be all wrong for one thing. Probably the design, too, although he was no judge.

A few vestiges of the past remained, however. Mom's beloved collection of original artwork graced the tall walls, reframed and skillfully color keyed to blend with the new furnishings. The Christmas tree, set up in the main living space, wore the same ornaments the family had used ever since he could remember. And, in the guest room, one old soldier from his childhood survived. Ben's scarred, utilitarian nightstand looked like a poor misfit between the two modern platform beds, as out of place as a Klingon in full battle dress would be at the Lewis family reunion in Dubuque. All the same, Ben was glad to see it.

"Yes, we decided to keep that here for you," his mother said, seeing his eyes come to rest on the bedside table. "We had to put most of your things in storage, as I mentioned, but I thought you might want this closer by." She paused, giving time for a reply that didn't come. "Well, I'll leave you to get settled then. You can pick whichever bed you like, and we saved dresser drawers and closet space for you." She started to go, then turned back to hug her eldest tightly, kissing his cheek. "We're so happy to have you home with us again, honey. You've been away a long time."

Ben put one arm across her back and patted her shoulder lightly, mechanically. The warmth of her words and embrace opened a small crack in his armor, but he refused to give in. Although he'd grown weary of carrying around the silent resentment he felt against his parents for selling the house out from under him, he wasn't ready to lay it down. Not yet. Not until he made sure they were at least aware of it. It was childish; he knew that. Still, he couldn't help it. So he let his mother leave the room without offering her much return for her unabashed affection.

When she had gone, Ben put down his bag and poked around the twelve by fourteen foot room, petulantly finding fault wherever he turned. The beige walls were boring. The closet was impossibly small. And the view out the rain-splattered window? Unimpressive: a dreary street scene half blocked by a tree. It was quiet, though, for being in the city. He acknowledged that much. At least the builders hadn't skimped on sound-proofing.

Ben flopped back onto the bed against the far wall and glared at the high, concrete ceiling with exposed ductwork and track lighting. He told himself for the hundredth time since leaving Phoenix that any sane person would be grateful for a little time off after the non-stop schedule he'd been keeping for months. Instead, he worried that taking a vacation from baseball would break his momentum. That, plus the whole business with the change of house, had put him in a funk. And maybe there was something else.

Only eight weeks, he reminded himself. Less than two months to fill before the new season started. He didn't have to spend it cooped up in this cramped condo. He could hang out with friends instead. Scott lived in a student housing apartment with a roommate, but Kyle, now a fifth year senior, still had the same solo bachelor pad with the accommodating oversized couch. He could crash there and probably get access to the athletic facilities on campus once winter quarter began.

Ben glanced at his watch. A little late to phone anyone, he decided, but in the morning he would let his friends know he was back in town and make some plans. Besides Scott and Kyle, he'd try to get in touch with Paul Ruston as he'd promised last February. And what about Jessica? Hmm. That was tempting, although he still wasn't convinced that hooking up with her again was a good idea. Their relationship had faltered before, sort of foundered under the weight of unrealistic expectations as best he could remember. Was there any reason to think things would turn out differently if they tried a second time?

He hadn't exactly lacked companionship in the meantime. There were plenty of attractive, female fans willing to serve as surrogate girlfriends for lonely ballplayers far from home. He'd gone out of his way to avoid them his first year, although now he wasn't exactly sure why. Then this past July in Modesto, he found himself drawn to a willowy blonde named Annie, who he'd noticed hanging around the ballpark after the games.

It wasn't a great love match; that was clear almost from the beginning. "We'll just have some fun together," Annie had said with sparking blue eyes, "no strings attached." Sounded good, but then she started demanding more – time, exclusivity, promises – things Ben wasn't prepared to give. He wouldn't make that mistake again. Better to keep things casual; socialize in groups; never date a girl more than twice; and don't let things go too far. Then no one could get the wrong idea, and no one would get hurt. That was his working theory anyway.

Yet, deep down, Ben recognized that he actually *did* want more, needed more… just not with Annie. He envied his married teammates who had wives to go home to, who always had someone to share the good times and the bad. Ultimately, he wanted that kind of committed connection too, with the right woman. She was out there; no question in his mind. In fact, he felt as if he already knew her on a certain level. He sometimes sensed her skirting around the edges of his subconscious, just beyond sight of his mind's eye. But she would always vanish, like a wisp of smoke, before he could capture more than a hazy image.

Ben pushed off from the bed and stalked the confines of the small room. *Baseball!* That was his true love, he reaffirmed. For now, at least, that's where his focus belonged, not distracted by female phantoms.

Staring at the handset on the nightstand, Ben took the wallet from his back pocket and opened it. He pulled out the creased and tattered 3x5 card that served as his portable mini-phonebook. Jessica's number remained prominently at the top of the list, leftover from the years they'd dated. The blue ink was blurred from getting damp at some point, but it was still legible. Not that he needed much prompting; those seven digits, memorized long ago, came back to him at a glance. Jessica might even be home now, for the holidays, or else Mrs. Martinelli could tell him how to reach her.

He fanned the card back and forth, absently tapping it against the wallet and thinking. Maybe he *should* call her. Their relationship hadn't been perfect, but it was possible he'd given up on it too soon. Jessica obviously thought so; she was willing to try again. What could it hurt to at least explore the option?

THIRD INTERMISSION

"Whoa! Hold on a minute!" Cora, dressed in a '50s poodle skirt, paused the video feed. Her saddle shoes paced the private lounge where she and Poindexter had retreated after the day's work was done. "Things are getting completely off track here, Dex. Abigail seems determined to ignore all signs of her connection to Ben while she forges ahead building a life with Paul. Meanwhile, Ben is falling back into Jessica Martinelli's clutches. I can't bear it!"

"I wish you wouldn't watch these progress updates, my dear," said Poindexter. He crossed his legs and wagged his head back and forth. "It's not healthy. You only succeed in torturing yourself."

"I can't help caring what happens to our clients."

"Especially Mr. Lewis, it seems," he muttered under his breath. "Really, Cora, I don't know why you are so concerned. He appears to me to be doing remarkably well. His career is going gangbusters and even his love life is looking up."

"But Ben belongs with Abby!"

"You cannot know that for certain. Just because he married her the first time does not mean that it was for the best. I believe there were problems between them. Perhaps he would be happier with somebody else. After all, that is the business we are in – giving people a chance to make different choices than they did before. Miss Albright may seem superior according to your criteria, but Miss Martinelli has some very nice… compensations."

"Compensations! Is that what you call them? I should have known you would prefer her type."

"That is neither here nor there. It is Mr. Lewis's opinion that matters. He is acquainted with both young ladies, and it looks as if he prefers Miss Martinelli."

"He wouldn't if he remembered what she did to him in his first life! She doesn't love him now anymore than she did then, and she'll drop him just as quickly this time if he fails to live up to her ambitions."

"That may well be, but it is none of our concern," said Poindexter with infinite patience. "You know we have little control – and just as little responsibility – for the ultimate outcome."

"The council bears responsibility for deciding to remove Ben's memory prematurely," she reminded him.

"He was shown great leniency, over my objections as you will recall. He should never have been given time to document his past."

"I thought it showed quick thinking and resourcefulness."

"Commendable traits, in general. In this case, however, it seems more akin to cheating at the game, and the council agreed that he should not be allowed to profit by it."

"You have made sure he won't. His poor, unsuspecting parents," Cora said shaking her head in disapproval. "I suppose they have no idea why they were suddenly seized by the irresistible urge to move into a condominium without adequate space to keep their son's belongings."

Poindexter failed to stifle a chuckle. "I should imagine not."

With a huff, Cora left off her pacing, coming to a halt a few feet away from him. "We think so differently that there's obviously no point in discussing it any further. We'll only make each other angry."

"I quite agree with you, my dear. I am sorry for your misgivings, which I trust will be laid to rest by and by. These situations have an astonishing habit of sorting themselves out in the end."

"Although not always the way we think they should. That's why I'm still nervous for Ben."

"Understandably so," he said sympathetically, rising to his feet. "Now, as for Mr. Lewis' character, will it help if I agree to defer to your excellent judgment? I am inclined to admit he is, after all, an admirable young man who no doubt deserves to be wonderfully successful and supremely happy. There, will that do?" Poindexter stretched out his hand to Cora, waiting until she reluctantly took it. "Let us simply trust he also has the good sense, as I did, to choose the woman who is right for him – one he can love and respect for a lifetime and one who is sharp enough to keep him on his toes."

Cora raised a finger in objection. "But, my dear Poindexter, you didn't choose me; I chose you."

"Ah, yes. And look how well it has turned out."

-38-
Christmas

Christmas turned out a more traditional celebration than Ben had imagined possible, given the new surroundings. When it was just their family of four gathered together, doing the things they always did, it didn't seem to matter so much where they were.

Mom's Christmas Eve pork roast – served, as always, with mashed potatoes and homemade applesauce – tasted just as good eaten off the new glass-topped dining table as it had from the old maple one. This year's taller tree, made possible by the condominium's high ceilings, recaptured the towering proportions of Ben's youthful memories. Gathered around it, they opened their presents that night, taking turns from youngest to oldest, as was their custom. The empty stockings – the matching patchwork ones his mother made for each of them long age – hung from the mantle of the slate-fronted fireplace, ready to be filled by Santa's stand-in as soon as "the children" were in bed. That was his father's job, Ben knew. Just as he knew without asking that there would be hot chocolate, French toast, and bacon for breakfast in the morning.

Scott stayed the night, bunking in with Ben, something the brothers hadn't done since they were kids. It felt like a sleepover as they lounged on their beds on opposite sides of the darkened room, talking into the wee hours. They took turns trading stories saved up from their separate lives during the months apart. For Ben, that meant baseball. For Scott, it was school and his social life – mostly Hollie Ruston.

"I work like a dog on my studies all week," he said, "so that I can spend most of the weekend with her. She's even got me going to church again, which makes Mom happy."

"Sounds serious."

"It just might be." Scott sat up and leaned toward his brother, silhouetted across from him. "Hey, you should come with us tomorrow."

"To church?"

"Sure. It *is* Christmas, in case you need a special reason. Dad will beg off, of course, but Mom's going. It's a long drive back to Edgewood, so she's been attending the Rustons' church with me some since the move. The contemporary music might not be her favorite, but I like it. I think you will too if you give it a chance."

"All right, all right. You can stop with the hard sell. I'm not such a lost cause, you know. In fact, I've been going to chapel pretty regularly this past year."

"Chapel?"

"Yeah. Every place I've been assigned, some player or other will organize a short devotion before practice for whoever's interested. Very informal. Anyway, it feels kind of good to be reminded that there's something out there bigger and more important than baseball. Keeps things in perspective."

"I never thought I'd hear you admit that. You've been 'all baseball, all the time' for as long as I can remember."

"Yeah, well, I guess I've gotten a little more philosophical since that close call last February. Something like that makes a guy stop and think."

"So what's your new philosophy? Have you got life all figured out?"

Ben laughed at the irony. "No, I think if anything I'm *less* sure of myself. Before, my life seemed pretty clear cut; I knew what I wanted and I went for it. Now, I see the paradox. The thing is, I have to give baseball a hundred percent to have any chance of success. Right?"

"I suppose so, considering how competitive it is."

"Exactly. But, if I invest everything I've got into baseball, will there be anything leftover to build a life with afterward? That's the question."

"So, you admit there is such a thing as life beyond baseball?"

"I'm starting to hope so. There has to be, because at some point – a decade or more from now, if I'm lucky – the ride will be over."

~~*~~

222

"Are you looking forward to this?" Paul asked as they drove south on I-5 the Tuesday night after Christmas.

"Yeah, it should be fun," Gail answered. Staring out the car window at the nearly full moon, she rubbed her new heart-shaped, filigree pendant between her fingers. It was a Christmas present from Paul... and such a relief. When she'd seen the tiny box from Zale's, she'd been seized by dread, fearing it might be an engagement ring. She wouldn't have been ready for that, but the necklace was perfect.

Now they were headed for *Zoolights*, the holiday light display at Point Defiance Zoo in Tacoma. Paul had suggested the evening, mostly as a fun outing, but also as a way of getting together with Ben Lewis, who was back in town. That's the part Gail would rather have done without. Of course Paul had no clue that it could be awkward for her, since she'd never discussed with him the strange connection she felt to Ben. She didn't intend to either. What would be the point?

At least she had been able to override Paul's original idea of taking a van and going all together.

"I know Lorrie and Larry have plans for later that night, so they'll need to drive by themselves anyway," she'd told Paul. "And Ben's bringing a date too, isn't he?"

"Yeah, an old girlfriend he just got back in touch with, he said."

"So, they'll want their privacy as well."

"I suppose a little privacy would be nice for us too," he'd agreed, squeezing her hand. "We have so little time together. Okay, we can just meet up at the gate, enjoy the lights, and go our separate ways again afterward."

So that was the plan.

They arrived at the zoo a few minutes before seven. As Paul pulled into a parking space and turned off the engine, Gail slipped on her fuzzy knit hat and mittens.

"Are you sure you're going to be warm enough in those?" Paul asked. "There's a thicker pair in the glove box."

"I'll be fine. These are warmer than they look." She flashed him a wide smile. "Besides, it will give you an excuse to hold my hand."

"Good thinking."

They got out of the car and headed for the entrance. As they approached, Gail spotted Ben already waiting there with a stunning, dark-haired girl draped on his arm. They were talking with their heads close together, the clouds of condensation from their breath merging in the cold night air.

Ben looked up, then, and waved. "This is Jessica Martinelli," he said after he and the other two had exchanged greetings. "Jessica, this is Gail Albright and Paul Ruston. Dr. Ruston, I should say."

"No, that's way too formal," Paul responded, offering his hand. "Nice to meet you, Jessica. Please call me Paul."

"I'd be delighted to," she answered in a husky voice, placing her trim, gloved hand in his.

Gail noticed Jessica didn't extend her the same courtesy. In fact, Jessica barely acknowledged her existence. The same thing happened to Lorrie moments later when she and Larry arrived and were introduced. Ben went out of his way to be friendly to both, but Jessica aimed her considerable charms exclusively at Larry.

Gail exchanged a look with Lorrie. It was going to be an interesting evening.

"Well, shall we go in?" Paul suggested. "On a night like this, we'll have to keep moving or freeze where we stand."

They bought tickets and passed through the gate, halting just inside.

"It's like a fairy land," Gail commented, looking over the park.

The night and a million tiny lights had transformed the zoo landscape into something truly magical. Each tree and bush glowed a different color. Animated animal shapes romped on all sides.

In a captivated silence, the three couples strolled down one of several paved walkways, all outlined with rope-lights to guide them, looking left and right to take in the other-worldly setting. They soon came to a scene fabricated entirely from blue, green, and white lights depicting the Tacoma Narrows Bridge, the foothills, and Mt. Rainier in the background.

"Oh, there's the Flame Tree," said Paul, pointing to where a group had gathered further along the way. "It's kind of the star attraction. Let's take a look."

So they moved on, joining the others collected around the tree, which had metamorphosed into a giant, mushroom-shaped confection. On the massive trunk and major branches burned a solid blanket of pistachio-colored lights, and its spreading canopy blazed with hot pink. The sight matched Forth-of-July fireworks for effect, eliciting "oohs" and "ahs" from on-lookers.

After a minute, Jessica announced, "I'm cold. Can't we go inside someplace?"

Gail wasn't surprised. Jessica's perfectly coordinated hat, gloves, coat, and boots looked like they were designed with fashion, not practicality, in mind. Apparently, even Ben's arm around her shoulders couldn't make up for what her clothing lacked.

"The South Pacific Aquarium is supposed to be open," Paul suggested. "We could go there next."

"I think it's this way," said Larry, leading off down the path with Lorrie in tow.

With a shrug, Gail added, "I guess we can see the rest after we warm up a little."

Tropical heat enveloped them as soon as they entered the building – a sauna compared to the arctic conditions outdoors. Gail immediately pulled off her mittens and unbuttoned her coat to compensate. But the aquarium had far more to offer than a reprieve from the cold. Dozens of brightly colored tropical fish species swam safe from predators in the lagoon exhibit. In a separate, larger tank, only a glass wall separated groupers, jacks, sharks, and a quarter million gallons of sea water from the visitors.

A boy of about four pointed and squealed at the sight of a black-tip reef shark cruising toward him. In mock terror he screamed again and hid behind his mother's legs, obviously delighted with what he saw and with the sound of his own voice echoing off the hard concrete and glass surfaces.

The acoustics amplified the murmurings of the couple of dozen people into something comparable to a crowd at a basketball game. The noise escalated still more when a high-pitched scream cut through above the general din.

"Help!" a woman shouted repeatedly. "Somebody please help me!"

Other voices hushed, and all heads turned toward her. It was the mother of the same little boy Gail had noticed a moment before, only now the child lay on the floor, pale and gasping for air.

With Gail and the others following, Paul rushed over. "I'm a doctor," he informed the frantic mother. "What happened?"

"I don't know," the woman sobbed. "All of a sudden he sort of fainted. Now he can barely breathe. You've got to help him!"

Paul knelt beside the boy and made a quick assessment – pulse, skin, eyes, and mouth. "Somebody call 911," he shouted over his shoulder, eliciting a swift response from a zoo employee with a two-way radio. "Does your son have any allergies?" Paul demanded of the mother.

"He's deathly allergic to peanuts, but I never give him…"

"I'm guessing he got hold of something without you knowing, because he's showing all the signs of anaphylactic shock. Do you carry an EpiPen for him?"

"Yes! Yes!" Her hands shaking, she fumbled through her capacious handbag, soon giving up the search and dumping the contents out onto the floor.

Paul instantly singled out the tubular container from amongst the clutter and grabbed it before it rolled out of reach. He opened it and slid the device out. "You should administer it," he told the mother, offering the EpiPen to her.

"I c-can't!" Her voice quavered as badly as her hands. "You'll have to do it… p-please!"

Grasping the injector in his fist, Paul stripped off the safety latch and sank the tip firmly into the boy's thigh. The child, who hung on the brink of unconsciousness, didn't make a sound. After a count of ten, Paul removed the EpiPen and rubbed the injection site. Everyone else held their collective breath… waiting. But still the boy didn't move.

"The medics are on the way," reported the zoo employee who made the call. "They'll meet us at the main gate."

"We should get your son into their care as quickly as possible," Paul told the mother.

"I'll carry him," Ben volunteered. He stooped, gently scooped the child into his arms, and headed for the door. A path opened through the crowd to let him pass. The mother and the others fell in behind, rushing to keep up with Ben's long strides.

~~*~~

"He's going to be all right," Paul announced after the aid car pulled away. His friends and a score of strangers who still awaited the outcome broke into spontaneous applause.

Gail exhaled deeply. "Thank God!"

"His name's Caleb by the way," Paul continued, smiling. "His blood pressure's back to normal and the swelling that was blocking his airway has gone down. They're taking him to Mary Bridge Hospital, just for observation."

With the news, people began to drift off, chattering as they went on their way.

Dark eyes sparkling, Jessica gushed, "It was absolutely *thrilling* the way you saved that boy's life, Paul. I've never seen anything like it."

"Don't be so impressed. If she hadn't panicked, Caleb's mom could have done it herself. Or any second year nursing student," he added, winking at Gail.

"Better you than me," she answered.

"Hey, I think I could have handled the situation just as well," Lorrie boasted. "As long as there wasn't any blood involved," she whispered to Gail.

"I hate to break up the party, but we've got to get going," Larry said. "My brother is expecting us to show up at his place in Tumwater soon."

"I'm going to follow Caleb to the hospital," Paul explained. "It's not strictly necessary, but his mother asked me to. Ben, I wondered if you could give Gail a lift home?"

"Sure. Be glad to."

"What?" exclaimed Gail, taken by surprise. "No, really. That's not necessary. I mean, thank you, Ben, but I'll just tag along with Paul. I'm in no hurry."

"Unfortunately, darling, I *am* kind of pressed for time," Paul told her. "I've got to work tonight, remember? I'll have to go directly there when I'm done at Mary Bridge. Let Ben drive you so that I know you'll get home all right. For me, please?" he added.

"It's no trouble," said Ben. With a nudge of his elbow, he added, "Is it, Jess?"

Jessica promptly turned up the corners of her mouth and said, "Of course not. No trouble."

Gail was no more pleased with the arrangement than Jessica, but she hoped her smile was more convincing. "I guess it's settled then," she said cheerfully.

-39-
Drive Home

"We had plans," Jessica complained at the door of the Martinelli house in Puyallup.

"I know," Ben said, "but it couldn't be helped."

"You didn't have to volunteer so eagerly."

"How else was she supposed to get home? Paul was tied up, and the others were headed in the opposite direction." Feeling his shoulders beginning to tighten, he took a deep breath. "It's a small sacrifice, Jess. We can get together tomorrow or the next day just as well."

"I suppose so," she huffed. "I still don't like it, though."

"I don't expect you to. Now, pull that bottom lip back in where it belongs so I can kiss you goodbye. I'll call you tomorrow." He gave her a quick peck and then jogged to the car where his unscheduled passenger waited. "Sorry for the delay," he told Gail, sliding in behind the wheel.

"No problem. I just feel bad your plans have been disrupted."

"Yours have too."

She shrugged. "It comes with the territory. Paul's duties as a doctor will always take priority. That's the way it has to be, and I understand."

Ben carefully avoided his old neighborhood as he wound north towards the nearest freeway onramp. Presumably, by now his former home (and several others) had been bulldozed into oblivion. He had no desire to see it. He preferred to preserve the untarnished memory of things as they used to be.

After merging into light traffic on I-5, Ben tried to get the stalled conversation going again. Glancing over at Gail, he said, "It's a good thing Paul was there tonight. None of the rest of us knew what to do, and that poor kid could have died without immediate help."

"You did your part."

"Carrying Caleb to the aid car? That was nothing."

"I didn't mean that. You forget, Paul wouldn't have been there to save Caleb if you hadn't first saved Paul. In fact, everything he does with his life from now on is thanks to you in part."

They drove on in silence for a minute, Ben mulling over what she'd said. "I've actually thought a lot about that lately, about how interconnected things are. No one can make a move on this planet without affecting somebody else for better or worse. I mean, as you said, because I saved Paul, Paul could save Caleb. Now Caleb will grow up and…"

"Yes, now Caleb *will* grow up! How cool is that?"

"*Very* cool. Go ahead, then. You make up a future for him, now that it's decided he has one. What do you imagine Caleb will do with his life? Anything exceptional?"

"Sure. Why not? What if he invents the cure for cancer?"

"I like it; inspired choice."

"Then you'll be promoted to 'super hero' for playing a part in saving millions of lives, not only Paul's and Caleb's."

"Awesome. I'm sure I'd look great in tights and a cape."

Gail giggled. "I can picture it now."

"But here's the downside to your logic," Ben said, getting set to throw her a curve. "What if the kid grows up to be another Hitler instead?"

"No! Not our sweet, little Caleb!"

"Somebody probably thought 'little Adolph' was sweet at four too."

"Never; the moustache would have given him away."

Ben snorted.

"I know, I know. Bad joke. So, let me get this straight," Gail continued, twisting her hair around her finger. "Are you wondering how much responsibility you would bear for indirectly unleashing the next fascist dictator on the world?"

"That's right."

"Tough question."

"It is. You be the judge, though. What's your ruling?"

"Hmm. I say you're not to blame as long as you acted with pure motives. You can't be held responsible since you couldn't possibly anticipate or control all potential consequences."

"So, I'm officially off the hook?"

"Definitely." Making the sign of the cross in the darkness between them, Gail said in a low, somber voice, "I absolve you of all guilt, my son."

"Now you're priest as well as judge? Excellent." Sensing she was enjoying the game as much as he was, Ben went on. "Okay then, I have another quandary for you to consider. Are you up to the challenge?"

"Sure. Fire away."

"Well, we agree that big events have far-reaching consequences. According to the same cause-and-effect theory, though, I submit that even the small stuff has an impact. Take what happened tonight. All poor little Caleb did was eat a peanut he shouldn't have, and everything changed from there."

"A few people were inconvenienced; that's all. Nothing significant."

"Ah, but we don't really know that. For example, you're here in my car instead of in Paul's because of it. Think of the possible implications wrapped up in that one fact alone. What if I get into a crash, or what if he would have otherwise? Doesn't it shake you up a little to know you could end up living or dying based on a stray peanut catching the eye of a four-year-old?"

Gail erupted in laughter. "Next you'll tell me you're afraid to blow your nose for fear of setting off a chain reaction leading to the end of civilization and life as we know it!"

"Exactly! So you see what we're up against!"

They were both laughing now.

"Oh, my," Gail finally said, recovering. "I had no idea you were such a comedian, Ben... and a philosopher."

"Hey, those of us who think deep thoughts gotta have a sense of humor too or we'd go mad."

"It comes in pretty handy for the rest of us too."

Ben stole another look at Gail. Passing headlights illuminated her pixie features, stretched wide in an unguarded smile. It had been a long time since he'd enjoyed talking to anyone as much. His worries had been for nothing. He'd expected this drive to be awkward, alone so long with a girl he barely knew. Instead it was turning out to be a pure pleasure... and she felt like anything but a stranger.

After a couple of pensive minutes, Gail commented, "This whole scenario – you know, the unforeseeable consequences of saving someone's life – reminds me of an old Star Trek episode. Did you ever see the one where they travel back in time, to earth around 1940, and Captain Kirk saves the life of a woman he's fallen in love with?"

"A pacifist who then goes on to prevent the U.S. from entering World War Two…"

"…ultimately changing the outcome of the war and everything that follows, yes! So you *have* seen it."

"Of course. I know them all. I can't believe you're a fan too."

From there, they transitioned seamlessly to more serious subjects. Ben told Gail how the recent loss of his childhood home rankled him. She told him how she'd hated being forced to move every few years growing up. And so on. The conversation simply flowed, as lively and unbroken as the chatter of a tumbling brook.

Ben cut over to highway 99 south of town. He drove slowly, wishing they weren't so close to reaching their destination.

"I saw you at church with your mom on Christmas morning," Gail was saying. "It was so crowded that I couldn't get over to say hi. I'm glad you came, though."

"Yeah, I saw you too, with Paul and the Rustons. Sure is a big church. Different from what I grew up with, but I liked it."

"I met your mom a few Sundays before that, when she came with Scott. She seems really nice."

"She is. If I didn't turn out like I should have, it's not her fault. Dad's a good guy too, but he left most of the day-to-day discipline to Mom."

"It's sort of the opposite in my family. My father always has to be in charge of everything, and my mother just goes along. Not that I want them fighting, but once in a while it would be nice to know she understood me and that she was in my corner. You know what I mean?"

"Uh-huh." After sailing along the downtown waterfront on the viaduct, Ben exited to Elliot Ave. "I think being a parent has to be about the toughest job in the world. There's no instruction manual or formal training for one thing. And most couples have kids when they're too young to know what they're doing. My parents were *my* age when they had me, and I sure don't feel ready to be a father yet."

"I suppose people do the best they can, but they're bound to make mistakes. We probably will too, when we have kids. Uh, I mean, w-whenever either of us has children," Gail stammered, "separately... sometime in the future."

As he took the ramp onto the Magnolia Bridge, Ben smiled at the implications of her slip-of-the-tongue. "So, do you want kids someday?"

"I do, but I guess I'm a little scared too. It's a huge responsibility. What about you?"

"The same." Ben unconsciously negotiated the surface streets as they talked: left on Howe, left again on 32nd. "It would be easier not to, for sure, but I think you'd be missing out on a lot. Besides, kids are cool. I get a kick out of the ones who come to the ballpark. From the goofy stuff they say, I kind of wonder what's going on in their little brains."

Right on Magnolia Blvd.

"I bet you'll make a good dad, Ben."

He glanced over at her. "You think so?"

"Yeah, I do."

"Thanks. Well, here we are." As Ben pulled down the Albrights' steep driveway, a shudder quaked through his neck and shoulders. Icy fingers swept every hair of his forearms to attention. "Whoa!"

"What's the matter?" Gail asked.

"I've got a serious case of déjà vu or something going on here."

She sharply drew in her breath, answering with a catch in her voice. "Me too."

Ben turned off the engine and stared straight ahead through the first uncomfortable silence of the night. His mind whirled with questions and with odd glimmers of things just beyond his reach. He stole a look at his companion and found her eyes riveted on him. When she spoke, it wasn't an accusation. It sounded like she was struggling to make sense of the same circumstances that bewildered him.

"We were so busy... busy talking," she said haltingly, "that I forgot. I didn't even think about giving you directions, so... h-how did you find my house so easily, Ben? You drove right to it... as if you'd been here a hundred times before."

He shook his head slowly and answered, "I have no idea. I was just wondering the same thing."

-40-
Intrigue

He hadn't been able to give Gail any plausible explanation. He'd desperately wanted to – for his own sake as well as hers – but he didn't have a clue how he'd known where she lived. Driving to her house had come automatically, like something ingrained – one of those muscle-memory skills that he no longer had to think about because he'd repeated it so many times before. His body just knew what to do.

Ben stretched out on his bed at the condo without bothering to remove his shoes. Even now, after time to think, he couldn't shed any light on Gail's questions. And he couldn't blame her for being upset. He was slightly freaked out himself.

"I don't understand," she had said. "You're a nice guy, Ben. At least… at least I *think* you are. But every time we meet there's some kind of mystery involved. Tonight was great until this. On top of what Kyle told me and the thing with your brother's car… Well, what am I supposed to believe?"

"Kyle? What has he got to do with it?"

"Never mind that now. Just answer the question."

Ben clutched after a scrap of clarity to offer her, some shred of sense, any reasonable grounds for her to stay with him. He was losing her. The closeness of only a minute before was slipping away. A chasm cracked open between them, and still nothing came to him, not one single word of illumination or reassurance to ease the lines of confusion on her face.

Gail had waited for him to respond, and when he didn't, she'd turned from him and gotten out of the car.

"I'm sorry," he'd managed just before she shut the door. Not enough. Not nearly enough.

Still shaken, Ben closed his eyes and focused on deep breathing. Gradually the knots in his stomach uncoiled themselves. Gradually the tightness in his chest eased. Logic eventually conquered emotion, and he formed a plan.

First thing in the morning, he'd restart his training regimen. He had to get his feet back on solid ground, to get back to what he knew and trusted: baseball, hard work, and proven friends. He would call Jessica too, like he'd promised. At least with Jessica, he knew where he stood. She was straightforward and uncomplicated. No intrigue.

All the weirdness – memory gaps, déjà vu, etc. – seemed bound up in his tangled relationship with Gail. She was a disruption he couldn't afford, though. She didn't belong to him anyway; she belonged to Paul and would probably end up marrying him. Sharing his home and future. Having his babies.

But he shouldn't go there; it would only make him crazy. He shouldn't imagine what might have been with altered timing and circumstances. No, for the sake of his sanity and his career, he had to give up any thoughts of Gail. In fact, he should avoid seeing her altogether. He was accustomed to self-denial, to giving up things he badly wanted in favor of his ultimate goal. This was no different.

And he wasn't the only one who had made sacrifices. His parents had forfeited countless hours and thousands of dollars over the years to give him a shot at his dream. Evenings, weekends, and summer vacations all had revolved around baseball because of him, with Scott probably getting the worst of the deal since he had no say. His family had paid a high price. It was his responsibility to make sure it hadn't been for nothing.

Ben's alarm went off at seven. He got up at once, pulled on a shirt and basketball shorts, quietly slipped out the front door, and took the elevator to the gym in the basement. Not surprisingly, he had the place to himself. After his usual warm-up stretches, he attacked the limited weight machine array with a vengeance, and then followed with a five-mile run on a treadmill. At ten, he returned to the condo, finding his mother at the kitchen table drinking her morning coffee and working the daily crossword puzzle.

"There you are," she said.

"Yeah, I was trying out your so-called 'fitness center' downstairs."

"So I see," she said observing his semi-saturated tee-shirt. "You don't sound too impressed."

His breath shot out in a scornful laugh. "I'm not. It's pretty rudimentary equipment – okay for the average person, I suppose, but not exactly what I'm used to."

"No, I suppose not. Well, I'm sorry it didn't measure up," she said, a hint of annoyance creeping into her voice. "Still, you apparently managed to work up a good sweat in spite of the sub-standard facility."

"Sorry, Mom," he said, softening his tone and coming over to rub her shoulders. "I don't know what's wrong with me. I'm going to take a shower and then see if I can find a batting cage open somewhere. I'll feel better after I bash a few dozen balls around."

~~*~~

The first time the Albrights' phone rang that morning, it was Paul. "Hi, I just finished my shift," he told Gail when she answered, "and I just wanted to be sure you got home okay last night."

"Yes, fine, no problem," she assured him, taking the handset from the kitchen with her as she strolled to the living room.

"What did you and Ben find to talk about on that long drive? You two don't seem to have much in common, so I was a little worried."

"Oh, I don't know. Nothing in particular, I guess."

"I hope it wasn't too uncomfortable."

Standing at the windows, she stared off across the silvery-gray water to the southwest. She could just make out the Winslow Ferry in the distance, clearing Wing Point on Bainbridge Island and heading for Seattle. "No, it was fine, really. Fine."

The second call came a half hour later. Gail answered it again. "It's for me, Mother. It's Lorrie," she called out, this time carrying the phone upstairs with her. "Are you home already?" she asked her friend. "I thought you and Larry were staying in Tumwater until tomorrow."

"We are, but I couldn't wait till then. I had to talk to you about last night, especially your ride home with Ben."

"I'm glad you called." Gail sighed as she shut the door to her room behind her. Her hand automatically went to the light switch. Then she thought better of it.

"What's the matter?"

"I'm tired; I didn't get much sleep," she answered, beginning to pace a circle around the perimeter of her bedroom suite.

"Aha! We'll get back to that, but we'd better start at the beginning. So? What do we think of Jessica Martinelli? You go first."

"She's beautiful, that's for sure."

"Come on, Gail. You can do better than that. I know you disliked her as much as I did."

"I wouldn't say I disliked her," she hedged.

"I know you wouldn't. That's why I said it for you."

"Okay, so I'll admit that it's unlikely Jessica and I will ever be good friends, but then I didn't see any sign that she wanted my friendship, or yours either."

"No!" Lorrie snorted out a laugh. "She's all about the boys. I wanted to smack her right across those pouty lips for the way she flirted with Larry. Right in front of me too! And it was positively nauseating how she hung on Ben."

"Well, he's welcome to her." Gail paused. "Although if that's the kind of woman he goes for, I can't say much for his taste."

"That's more like it. You should vent a little now and then. You keep holding stuff in and eventually you're gonna explode."

"I think Ben deserves better, that's all."

"You're right; he does. Know what else? I think you're jealous."

"Jealous?"

"Yes, jealous. You're jealous of Jessica, which means you're attracted to Ben. Who could blame you? He's a certifiable hunk."

"You're imagining things, Lorrie. Even if I were interested in Ben – which I'm not saying I am – it would never work. His career and my life... they barely coexist in the same universe."

"So you *have* thought about it."

"Only long enough to realize how impossible it would be. Besides, I wonder if he might be some kind of stalker after all. Remember I told you that I thought he had been to my house before? That I'd seen his old car here once? Well now I'm certain because he drove right to it last night without any directions."

"You're kidding!"

"It's true. Then he pretended to be as surprised as I was that it happened. Add the fact that he was always hanging around campus and knew my middle name, and what have you got?"

"Okay, so there is an element of intrigue, but that's been there all along. You weren't particularly bothered by it before."

"I know, and honestly I'm not much bothered by it now either. I think it's just an excuse. Part of me wants to find fault with him because the truth is…" She continued in a lower voice. "The truth is I really do like him. If I could forget Paul and all the other complications…" She trailed off.

"Go ahead!" Lorrie encouraged. "Forget *all* of it, just for a minute. What then?"

Gail flopped back on her bed. "Oh, Lorrie, we were having the best time last night. We talked about anything and everything – serious stuff, crazy stuff! I haven't laughed that much in ages. I felt like I understood him – deep down, you know? – and that we did have some kind of special connection after all. Then things turned strange at the end and I got spooked. Now I'm just confused."

"…which is why you didn't get any sleep last night."

"Right." Gail rubbed her forehead. "So, am I an idiot for wanting to see Ben again? No, don't answer that; we shouldn't even be talking about this. It seems terribly disloyal to discuss another man behind Paul's back, especially since we're practically engaged."

"Yeah. I've been meaning to talk to you about that, Gail. Are you really going to marry Paul and traipse off to Zambia with him?"

"It's Zimbabwe. He's going to Zimbabwe. That's what he finally decided."

"Whatever. I just hope you won't agree to go until you're absolutely sure that's the life you want."

"At the moment, I'm not sure of anything."

~~*~~

Red meat and physical exercise: that was Ben's chosen antidote for the angst he'd fallen into over Christmas. So it was a relief when winter quarter opened at the U and he received permission to use the athletic facilities on campus. Back in a proper gym, he resumed a stringent training schedule, determined to keep busy and to put on a couple more pounds of muscle before reporting for spring training.

Some of his teammates, like Barry Hudson, whom he'd seen again when he was in Huntsville, swore by the new "supplement" that had been circulating. There wasn't any official policy for or against the pills, and nobody seemed to know exactly what was in them, only that they worked like a charm, building more muscle mass than all the protein shakes and bench presses in the world ever could. Ben had passed on the temptation to try them… so far. Like everybody else, he was looking for a competitive edge, but he was careful about what he put into his body. Besides, he believed that too much bulk would compromise his speed, which was at least as important as strength in his position.

Ben spent many nights on Kyle's couch – for camaraderie as well as for convenience of location. His buddy worked out with him sometimes too, although in his case it was just for old times' sake. Kyle was done with competitive baseball, having used up his college eligibility without being drafted into the professional ranks. Now he planned to finish his business degree and get a job.

Back in Seattle after spending the holidays with her mother, Jessica claimed her share of Ben's time as well. She'd taken an entry-level position at the Post Intelligencer after graduating and now lived with a female co-worker in an apartment on Capitol Hill, a short drive from the U. Ben picked her up and dropped her off there, but never spent the night. He'd laid down new ground rules when they'd started dating again, hoping to keep things light. So far, it seemed to be working; they were getting along well. If the relationship ultimately became more serious, fine. But for now, he wanted no expectations, no complications.

As for Gail Albright, Ben kept his resolution not to see her again. He steered well clear of the medical complex when on campus. He invented an excuse to skip a party at the Rustons' in January, assuming Gail would be there. He stayed away from their church for the same reason. Now it was February, and Ben had decided to run the risk just once. Paul had particularly invited him to be there Sunday when he spoke about his mission plans. It was a huge congregation. Ben figured if he arrived late and slipped out quickly afterward, he stood a good chance of avoiding Gail entirely. If he couldn't manage that, he would keep the meeting brief and impersonal. Either way, that would be the end of it since he was leaving for Spring Training the following day.

-41-
Paul's Plan

Gail couldn't believe how quickly the time had flown by. She was already six weeks into the winter quarter of her second year of nursing school. If all went well, she would graduate in another four months. Then only a board exam would stand between her and her license. Gail still hadn't determined what she would do after that. She liked her job at the GI clinic, but pediatrics and surgery also interested her. Then, of course, there was the mission option always hovering around. By contrast, Paul had his plans completely worked out.

Back in December, after mock fanfare played on an imagery trumpet, he'd said, "I have an announcement to make." They were on their way to a restaurant in Bellevue, and Gail had been staring out the window, daydreaming. Now, with her full attention, Paul continued. "I've signed on with an organization called *The Least of These* to serve as staff physician at an orphanage in Zimbabwe."

Gail's mouth had dropped open. "Just like that," she said after a moment. "Isn't this kind of sudden?"

"What do you mean? I've been praying about it and researching my options for months. You know that. Once the answer became clear, I didn't hesitate. I signed the paperwork yesterday, and I'll be leaving in October."

Gail stared at him, incredulous.

Seeing her reaction, Paul pulled to the side of the road and reached for her hand. "I thought you'd be excited for me," he said. "What's the matter?"

"I..." Gail shook her head. "I guess I expected we'd at least discuss your decision before you made it final. I thought you might want to consider my opinion. Weren't you hoping I'd be going with you?"

"Yes, of course! You know that's what I want. And I didn't forget you; the orphanage needs nurses too. They said they'd be glad to have you."

Gail felt the muscles of her jaw tighten. Her hand turned to lead in his. "So, you discussed me with total strangers at this agency, but you neglected to discuss this agency – whatever it's called – with me, the woman you say you want to marry."

"Why are you so upset, Gail? I only signed the papers yesterday, and I'm telling you about it now."

"*After* the fact, when nothing I say could make the slightest difference."

"I'm sorry, darling, but the truth is that the decision was between me and God. It would have been wrong to take your direction over His. Don't you agree?"

Gail pulled her hand away to roll the window down a few inches. She'd let the icy rain spatter her upturned face as she sucked in the cold air. After a long minute, she closed the window again and said, "Yes, Paul. In principle, I do agree. But if, as you've said you believe, God means for us to be together, we must both come to the same conclusion. It would have been nice to know it was a joint decision; that's all."

It was as close as they'd ever come to a full-fledged fight. Neither of them had raised their voices or lost their tempers – all carefully controlled – yet it took a while to recover their normal easiness. Although Gail couldn't help feeling slighted by how he'd handled it, she ultimately concluded that Paul was right. He'd had to make his own choice, guided by his conscience, the same as she would soon have to make hers.

With each succeeding week, she felt the weight of her unmade decision growing heavier, to where it seemed to overshadow every minute of every day. She couldn't expect Paul to be patient forever. He would leave for Africa in only eight months now, and naturally he hoped to have things resolved long before then. That wasn't unreasonable. She'd had plenty of time to think, yet her feet were bogged in mire and she couldn't seem to make any headway.

For better or for worse, Gail hadn't seen Ben Lewis since he'd driven her home from Tacoma that night right after Christmas. She could only presume he was intentionally avoiding her, since he hadn't been back to church and had neatly dodged the invitation to

Paul's party. Apparently, Ben had decided he would rather ignore than explore the strange link between them… if it even existed. As time passed, that seemed less and less likely. Still, Gail needed to know for sure, to see him at least once more. But for all she knew, he'd already left for spring training.

That's what she was thinking coming into church with Paul one dreary Sunday in mid-February. Then, during one of the songs, she spotted Ben in a pew on the far left. Her heart thudded against her chest. Had he come because he wanted to see her before going away? Blushing at her presumption, Gail realized she should be hoping he came out of devotion to God instead. If he was there to see any human being, it was probably Paul, because he was speaking that day.

Ben happened to look her direction. He acknowledged her with a solemn nod and then turned away again.

"I'm up next," Paul whispered, reeling in Gail's attention. "To tell you the truth, I'm a little nervous."

Patting his arm, she said, "You'll be fine!"

He stood as the music came to a close and made his way forward down the aisle. Pastor Greer announced him, and Paul gingerly approached the podium. "Uh… good morning," he began. "I, uh… appreciate this chance to talk to you today."

Gail's stomach churned in sympathy for him. She knew how she'd feel in his shoes. Nothing scarier than public speaking, in her opinion. She'd rather swim shark-infested waters.

Paul plunged ahead, his eyes fixed on the 3x5 note cards clutched in his hand. "When I started to consider going into the mission field, I was shocked to learn that the AIDS epidemic has orphaned nearly two million children in Zimbabwe alone." Then he set his notes aside, took a deep breath, and looked out at the audience. "It tears me up inside to know those kids have not only lost both their parents, but many of them are infected themselves and left without proper medical care. It's an overwhelming problem. What can one person possibly do?" He paused. "Well, I intend to find out…"

Gail relaxed as Paul hit his stride. He was speaking from the heart now – about the work of the orphanage, about his place in it, about the incredible need for more help. It moved her. And she wasn't the only one, judging by the expressions on the faces of those around her.

Paul wrapped up a few minutes later. "...I'm excited about the challenge before me, and I would appreciate your prayers and support. Thank you." His face radiant, he left the podium and returned to his seat, carried along by a thunderous round of applause.

"That was great, Paul!" Gail whispered when he sat down beside her. "I'm so proud of you."

"Thanks," he said, squeezing her hand. "Was it really okay? I hardly knew what I was saying. I lost my place on my notes, and then the words just started pouring out from someplace inside."

"You were wonderful, like you've been giving speeches all you life," she assured him, meaning every word.

They settled in to listen to Pastor Greer's sermon. Afterward, everyone rose to go.

"I noticed Ben Lewis is here today," Gail casually tossed out. As she hoped, Paul picked up the line.

"Let's try to catch him," he suggested.

The two snaked their way through the crowd of people, slowed by friends and well-wishers they met along the way. The fleeting glimpses Gail caught of Ben showed he was making better progress. Then he disappeared through the exit leading to the large foyer beyond. By the time she and Paul reached the foyer themselves, Ben was at the front door. Paul called out to him, and Ben froze in his tracks, looking guilty, as if suddenly pinned down by a prison spotlight while trying to escape through the barbed wire fence.

"Over here," Paul said waving as he closed the intervening distance, Gail following.

Ben turned. "Hi Paul, Gail," he said neutrally.

"I'm glad we caught you," continued Paul. "Where are you off to in such a hurry?"

"Yeah, um, sorry about that. I wanted to hear your presentation, but I have a lot of packing left to do. I ship out tomorrow."

"Oh, that's too bad," Paul said. "I was hoping we could get together again – maybe double with you and Jessica."

Pastor Greer came up to join them at that point. "Excuse me," he said. "Sorry to interrupt. I won't keep you more than a minute, Paul. I just wanted to get you thinking about an idea I had for a fundraiser for your trip..."

Until the other two completed their conversation, Gail and Ben were left facing each other in silence. Even had they been able to speak freely, Gail would have been at a loss. Her questions weren't the kind that translated easily into words. If nonverbal cues were reliable, however, the hard set of Ben's mouth spoke volumes. She couldn't read his eyes. For a moment, she thought she saw a spark of warmth. Then they went dark and cold as storm clouds. Those same eyes that had communicated so eloquently in their early meetings today were veiled with heavy curtains that shut her out. Although Ben stood right in front of her, literally close enough to touch, he'd taken himself miles off and completely out of reach.

Paul, having finished with Pastor Greer, broke in on Gail's thoughts. "How does that sound to you, darling?" he asked.

"Sorry. What?"

"Pastor Greer's suggestion of a fundraising banquet. What do you think about it?"

"Oh. It… it sounds like a great idea."

"Good, I think so too. Now Ben, since you're leaving tomorrow, let us take you to lunch as a kind of send off."

"Thank you, but I can't."

"Gail, help me twist his arm a little," Paul suggested.

"Oh, yes, please do join us, Ben. You'll be gone a long time and…"

"No, really," Ben interrupted, looking at Paul rather than her. He tapped his watch. "I appreciate the offer, but I'm extremely pressed for time. I should get going."

"Of course. Hope you have a great season, then. We'll be rooting for you."

Ben shook Paul's hand and then mumbled, "Goodbye, Gail."

She answered without looking up. She didn't need to see his detached expression again.

Ben pivoted and strode out the glass double doors, shoving them so hard that they hit their stops, and then breaking into a jog.

Cold air rushed in though the void, stinging Gail's face and throat. She stood frozen in place, watching Ben thread his way between parked cars and out of sight.

She'd asked for one more chance to determine if there was anything between them. Well, she'd gotten her answer, clear and decisive, although not the one she'd privately hoped for, she now realized. Nevertheless, it was obviously time to move on.

Spring Ahead

Ben felt better as soon as the plane left the ground for Phoenix. Ahead, the promise of another year playing the game he loved, and each minute in flight meaning he left the off-season turmoil further behind. He figured a thousand miles ought to about do the trick.

He'd come to terms with his parents selling the house; that wouldn't eat away at him anymore. But it had been a mistake to risk seeing Gail once more. Just when he thought he'd successfully extinguished the last smoldering ember of interest there, things got stirred up all over again. Not by what she'd said. They hadn't exchanged more than a few, impersonal words. It was the way she looked at him, the pleading expression in her pale-blue eyes. He'd had the irrational impression that she was reaching out to him, silently begging him for a lifeline, which he'd refused to give.

Now he was back to square one for the task of putting her out of his mind. Funny that the woman he was supposed to be dating, he had to remind himself to call. Yet the one he needed to forget in order to save his sanity, he couldn't stop thinking about. Not healthy, but baseball would soon cure him.

Although it wasn't his first, spring training still thrilled him. The atmosphere was like nothing else on earth – the exhilaration, the positive energy, the daily challenge, the intense training balanced by practical jokes and horseplay. Ben felt privileged to be a part of it, and even luckier when, four weeks in, he was sent to work out with the major leaguers for the duration. He didn't delude himself into believing he would actually make the team, not with someone like Dave Henderson already patrolling center field. Still, he figured it meant management believed he was within striking distance.

His performance took a hit with the transition. Sharing the field with the likes of Rickey Henderson and Mark McGwire took some getting used to. Then there was the humiliation of facing big-league pitching for the first time. Ben's batting average plummeted. It took days for him to recover from the initial shock, and much longer for his numbers to rebound. Yet he wouldn't have traded the experience for anything.

Anxiety levels ran to record highs the day the regular-season assignments were due to be posted. A fortunate few at the top didn't have to sweat it; they knew they were headed for Oakland. The others, like Ben, didn't get much sleep the night before. The worst nightmare would be not finding your name anywhere on the chart. If you didn't have a team, it meant you were going home for good. Ben suffered no such fears; he knew his star was on the rise. The suspense came in wondering how high it had taken him.

For the answer, he waited his chance to glimpse the bulletin board.

His buddy Angelo got a look at it first. "Lewis, congratulations; you're goin' to Tacoma," he called back over his shoulder.

"Seriously?" Ben strained for a view between the heads of those in front of him. Finally a pathway opened so he could move up beside Angelo, who was pointing to the triple A club roster. There it was, his name in black and white. Ben gave an ear-splitting whoop, grabbed his friend by the shoulders, and shook him.

"What about you Jell-O?" he asked next, searching the list again. "Are you comin' with me?"

"You should be so lucky. Nah, it's Huntsville for me."

"Not bad, not bad. A nice step up. But this means we'll both have to break in new roommates. That's a bummer."

"Somehow I think you'll get over your disappointment."

Triple A Tacoma Tigers: exactly what he'd hoped for. He was headed back to the Pacific Northwest to play in front of his friends and the hometown fans. Short of actually landing in Oakland, which would have taken a minor miracle, he couldn't have wished for anything better.

Ben grabbed the phone as soon as he got back to the hotel late that afternoon, impatient to share his good news. He called his parents first, and then left messages for Kyle and for his brother, who were both out. Lastly, he rang Jessica.

"That's great, Benji!" she squealed in response to his announcement. "You're almost at 'The Show.' That's what they call it when you get to the major leagues, isn't it?"

"Right, pretty much."

"Well, I always knew you could do it. Even back in high school I could tell you were going to be great. One more little step left and it will be just like we always planned."

"It's a giant step, not a little one, Jess. I'm a lot closer now, that's true, but there's still no guarantee I'll make it to the Bigs."

"Don't say that!" she scolded. "You have to keep telling yourself that anything less than a major league contract is impossible. You don't tolerate failure any better than I do."

"I'm as ambitious as you are, true, but I have to be realistic too."

"Not if it means you're willing to give up!"

"Who said anything about giving up? I just got a huge promotion, remember?"

"Sorry, Benji. It's really good news. We'll be able to see each other all the time. And you'll be making a lot more money now, won't you?"

"Yeah, triple A pays quite a bit better."

"Then you can finally take me out to some nice places. No more all-you-can-eat nights at the Ranch House Restaurant. You could afford an apartment of your own this time too, instead of sharing with a roommate."

"Probably. I hadn't really thought that far ahead yet."

"Then I could stay over sometimes," she suggested in a throaty voice.

"Jess, we've talked about this. I'm not looking for a commitment right now."

"Honestly, Ben, you've gotten awful old fashioned in your ideas about sex. This is 1993. I'm not asking you to marry me. That can wait until our careers are further along. But we've been back together for a while now, and I think we're ready to take the next step. I want to be with you – really *with* you – you know, like we used to be."

Images of what it 'used to be' like with Jessica came crashing in, instantly breaching the mental dam Ben had constructed to safely contain them. If possible, he would have exiled those memories to another planet – or at least a country on the far side of the globe – as a mandatory precaution against temptation. He wasn't proud of the way they'd carried on back then, and he liked to think he had better self-control now. But Jessica was going to make it difficult.

"Ben, did you hear me?"

"Oh, yeah."

"Well, what do you say?"

"Say? I uh… I say we'll have plenty of time to discuss it later."

~~*~~

Gail emerged from her room, dressed for an evening out with Paul. When she passed the study, she paused in the open doorway. "I'm leaving now, Daddy. Don't wait up."

Franklin Albright sat hunched over his paper-strewn desk, the lines of his face carved years deeper by the harsh light of the goosenecked lamp off to one side. He glanced up from his work and smiled. "There's my beautiful princess," he said, rising and coming around for a closer inspection. He took Gail's hands, turned her this way and that, and tucked a stray wisp of hair behind her ear. "You should dress up more often, Angel. Suits you."

"I don't usually have any reason to dress up."

"I'll speak to Paul about that. His job to give you a reason."

"But if I marry him, I'll have even fewer chances. Not many formal occasions in the mission field, I imagine."

"Don't be ridiculous, Gail; you're not going to Africa," he said matter-of-factly. "You'll wait to marry him until he returns to civilization."

Gail's hands flew to her hips. "Oh, so that's the way you've got it figured. Now I understand. I wondered why you were still pushing me into Paul's arms after he decided to take up mission work instead of private practice. Listen, Dad, I'll go to Africa with Paul if I want to! He's asked me, and I'm thinking about saying yes. The decision is mine, not yours," she concluded firmly.

Her father smiled indulgently, but said nothing.

"Anyway, what makes you think Paul will be coming back?"

"Seen the way he looks at you, kiddo. If you're here, he's coming back. Trust me. Besides, Paul's ambitious. Twelve months stagnating in the bush and he'll be itching to move on."

Gail started down the hall, her father following. "You've got him all wrong. Paul's very committed."

"Sure he is. He'll soon miss the comforts of home, though, and being at the heart of the action. Politics. That's where I see him in twenty years. With you at his side, Kitten. Still, this little 'mission' of his won't be a waste. Tremendous cachet in charity work. They'll declare him a damned humanitarian when the time comes. You wait and see."

Gail shook her head. "An interesting theory, but way off base. Paul could be gone for years. Me too if I marry him."

A sobering statement. Intellectually, Gail had known it all along. Yet, when she spoke the words aloud, it finally sank in. She realized that if Paul left without her, she would miss him terribly. Unacceptable. On the other hand, if she went with him, wouldn't she miss everyone else, all she left behind, just as much… or perhaps more? It seemed a no-win situation. She'd been unconsciously hoping to find a perfect, pain-free solution, but there wasn't one. Despite what her father said, she couldn't have it both ways; she couldn't keep Paul and also the life she'd built in Seattle. She had to choose.

With this day in view, Gail had decided months earlier to do her honors thesis on the topic of nursing in the mission field, intending to learn more about it for her own sake and also to show Paul she was seriously considering the option.

"That's great!" he'd said when she'd told him. "I'm sure you'll get caught up by the idea like I did once you explore it a little further. I can help you too. The information I compiled during my own research will be exactly the kind of thing you need for your thesis."

It had been a good start, and the more she studied the project, the more viable the possibility of serving overseas seemed, especially now that she'd put her fascination with Ben Lewis behind her. Moving to the other side of the globe had some advantages – a chance to get on with her life and be useful to others at the same time.

As she dug deeper, the places she read about became more real, as well as the people in need. Gail could begin to picture laboring there in the mission field alongside Paul, caring for sick kids and making a fulfilling career for herself. Yet her classes in her final quarter, which emphasized the looming transition to professional practice, kept drawing her back to other options. Gail continued to wrestle with the choice before her, and the clock ticked louder every day.

Saying 'no' to Africa and to Paul required nothing further, but if she consented to go with him in October as his wife, there would be a lot to do in a short time. She started making a mental checklist. A simple wedding needed to be arranged – nothing elaborate, just a small gathering. She would have to register with the agency, get some clothing appropriate for their destination, acquire the correct travel visas and inoculations… Gail drew up short, feeling pressure building inside her chest, like it would burst if she went on. Was it excitement? Anticipation? Or panic? Probably a combination. Completely natural, she decided, since she hung on the brink of making the most important decision of her life.

Paul always seemed perfectly calm by contrast, calm and confident. He knew exactly what he wanted – Gail envied him that – and he was busier than ever, finishing his residency while planning the benefit banquet to be held in early July. *The Least of These* provided logistical and advisory support but required every participant to raise funds for their own transportation and living expenses. The banquet, as proposed by Pastor Greer, would be the centerpiece of Paul's capital campaign.

Paul gave Gail a progress report as they took a walk through her neighborhood in late April, making the loop down to Perkins Lane and back up to Magnolia Blvd. The sun was out, but the breeze off the water still had a bite to it. Gail had her windbreaker zipped up close under her chin.

"I'm hoping Ben Lewis can come to the banquet," he told her. "I'd like him to be one of the guests of honor."

Gail nearly stumbled at the unexpected mention of Ben's name. It had been days since she'd allowed a conscious thought for him. With her eyes on the uneven ground ahead, she said, "That's a nice idea, but I don't see how he could. He can't take time off in the middle of the baseball season, can he?"

"It's just one evening, and he won't need much travel time since he'll be so close by. He's playing in Tacoma this year. Didn't I tell you?"

"Tacoma? No, you never mentioned it."

"I'll invite him in any case. He's a big part in why I'm going to Africa, and I'd like the chance to publicly acknowledge him for it."

"He didn't want a big fuss made about saving your life, remember."

"I know, but it wouldn't be right to overlook that fact either. And despite what he says, we all like having our accomplishments recognized."

"Still, you shouldn't embarrass him."

"He performs in front of a crowd every day. I can't imagine he's very easily embarrassed. Don't worry. I won't go overboard. In the meantime, we need to find a free day to drive down and watch him play."

"Do you really want to?"

"Of course! You did too, as I remember. So now's our chance."

"I guess I've sort of lost interest. Plus, I'm really busy right now – midterms coming up, studying for board exams, my honors thesis."

They paused for a view overlooking the Sound.

"So how's your thesis coming along," Paul asked. "Are you learning lots of encouraging things about mission work?"

"I am," Gail admitted for the first time. "I think I've even caught some of your enthusiasm for it."

"That's wonderful, darling!" he said pulling her into an embrace. "I was sure you'd come around." He kissed her firmly.

She kissed him back. She liked seeing him so happy, but... "Wait, Paul," she said drawing away a little. "Don't overreact. I haven't said yes yet."

"I know," he answered with a Cheshire cat grin, "but soon, I trust." He gave her another quick kiss. "Gail," he continued more tentatively, "if you *do* decide to go with me to Zimbabwe, there'll be some necessary preparations. What I mean is, these things take time."

"Yes. I'm very much aware of that, believe me."

Tick, tick, tick.

~~*~~

Ben quickly settled in at Tacoma. Being so close to his roots minimized the adjustment, and he soon felt at home with his new team, with Cheney Stadium, and with playing at a higher level. One of the guys he'd gotten to know during spring training – Aaron Metcalf, a utility infielder – already had a two-bedroom apartment and was looking for someone to help pay the rent. So, despite Jessica's suggestion – or perhaps because of it – Ben moved in with him instead of getting his own place. He reasoned that a roommate with conservative standards would be a handy excuse if he needed one to keep Jessica at arm's length… especially if his own resolve weakened.

It seemed everyone he knew turned out for the Tigers' games those first few weeks. His parents and Jessica were regulars. On weekends, Kyle often showed up, with or without a date, and Scott too, usually with Hollie Ruston. Word had gotten around quickly, and friends from high school as well as college teammates waited for Ben after the home games, congratulating him on a timely hit or teasing him for the boner he'd pulled in the outfield that day, as the case warranted. They all wanted their programs autographed, which Ben was happy to do.

It was a honeymoon period all the way around. Ben was playing well. He felt comfortable and confident, knowing he was contributing to the team's success and to his own future prospects. In turn, the coaching staff gave him every opportunity to develop, grooming him by training and experience to advance as far as his talent would take him.

The extra pay helped too, especially with Jessica. She had expensive tastes and felt entitled to have them indulged, now that Ben could afford it. Not that he had much free time to take her out. Instead, he placated her with an occasional gift – usually something pink or glitzy – and the promise of a better class of nightlife in the off season.

Everything seemed to be going Ben's way. Then, on an ordinary Tuesday in mid-May, he showed up in the clubhouse at the usual time. As always, he first checked the daily line-up card, expecting to see his name where he'd become accustomed to finding it – starting in center field and batting fourth.

It wasn't there.

"Hey Charlie, what's up?" Ben asked the first member of the Tigers staff he spotted. "How come I'm not playing today?"

Rather than answering the question, the bench coach pointed toward Ben's locker. There hung a note saying, "Lewis: report to the Skipper."

Gut check time. Every similar summons over his short professional career had had the same effect. Ben dumped his gear off, dried his instantly clammy palms on his pant legs, and made the slow walk to manager Bob Boone's office to meet his fate.

-43-
Up and Down

The door stood ajar. Ben knocked and poked his head in. "You wanted to see me?"

Boone waved him in. "Lewis, yes. Time to pack a bag, son," he said opening a drawer. Withdrawing something and sliding it across the desk, he added, "You're leaving us for a bit."

Ben picked up the packet. It was a United Airlines ticket jacket with his name on it. His perspiring fingers stuck to the paper as he opened it to check the destination: Oakland. Ben stared in disbelief.

A wry grin broke over the manager's face. "Seems Dave Henderson's absent due to a family emergency, and Oakland's bench is a little thin right now – half a dozen guys puking their guts out with some kind of flu. So LaRussa called to ask if you could help them out for a few days."

"Me? LaRussa asked for me... specifically?"

"Yup. I guess he liked what he saw during spring training. Anyway, we've got you booked on a flight out later today. If you're lucky, you'll get to Oakland in time to see a little action tonight and be in the starting lineup tomorrow. That won't be a problem, will it?"

"No! I'm there." Ben wandered back toward the locker room in a daze. A chorus of cheers, whistles, and high-fives greeted him, courtesy of his Tiger teammates, who had just learned of his temporary call up. Ben hurricdly collected his gear and, with a last thumbs-up gesture, made tracks back to his car.

As soon as Ben got to his apartment, he phoned his parents with the news. His dad shouted into the phone so loud it hurt. He offered to spread the word for Ben, telling everyone to watch the games, which, since the A's were playing the Mariners, would be televised locally.

"That's a stroke of luck," he said. "It would be tough getting time off work on such sort notice, but there's no way I'm going to miss seeing your major league debut."

"That's okay, Dad. You'll have a better view on TV anyway. And I'll only be there a few days this time, just until one of the regulars gets back. You can come in person when I'm called up for real."

"It's a deal. We'll all be rooting for you, son. Make us proud."

"Don't expect too much. Mostly, I'll just be trying not to embarrass myself while I keep Dave Henderson's spot warm for him."

Ben threw a few things in a suitcase, drove to the airport, and caught his plane to Oakland, all the while feeling as if at any moment he would wake to find that none of it was real, that he was still a gangly kid in a little league uniform, dreaming of playing in the majors someday. He'd visualized this for most of his life, and now the moment had finally come.

The game was already well along when Ben arrived at the ballpark straight from the airport. He was directed to the locker room and found an A's uniform waiting for him. The roar of the home crowd echoed down the tunnel as he suited up, lacing his cleats with shaking fingers. Ben knew without looking that there would be at least ten times as many fans in the stands as he'd ever played in front of before… plus the TV cameras. Thanks to his spring training experience, he was familiar with the team and the system he'd be joining. But the Oakland Coliseum, that was the scene of myths and legends, the big stage, the site of so many of Ben's own fantasies.

When he was ready at last, Ben navigated through the passageway to the A's dugout, the crowd noise building louder with each step forward. Coming out into the open, he resisted the temptation to gawk slack-jawed at his surroundings like some star-struck tourist. "Business as usual," he coached himself.

Ben checked in with manager LaRussa before slipping unobtrusively into an open seat next to Brent Gates. He secretly hoped he'd be allowed to stay there, have a chance to get his bearings a little. The game was almost over anyway.

No such luck. Before Ben had thoroughly warmed a spot on the bench, he was sent in to get his feet wet as a pinch runner in the bottom of the eighth. One out with the A's sitting comfortably in the lead; that eased the pressure somewhat. Ben tried to block out the foreign surroundings, focusing instead on the sport that had become second nature to him. Baseball hadn't changed, only the venue. The thousand games he'd played on the field and the thousand more he had rehearsed in his head – they'd prepared him for this moment.

Ben stepped out onto the freshly mown grass of the generous foul territory along the third base line and jogged across the infield to claim his spot at first base, hearing his name announced as he did so. Taking a cautious lead, he looked for the signs, and then kept a sharp eye on the opposing pitcher. His suspense didn't last long. Sprinting for second with the crack of the bat, Ben was out long before he got there on an inning-ending double play.

He stayed in the game for the top of the ninth, taking the traditionally quieter right field post while the far more-experienced Ruben Sierra shifted to center. As Ben suspected, though, his area code didn't matter. The rule is that the ball always finds the new guy. Accordingly, Mike Blowers, Seattle's third baseman, soon sent one sailing deep into Ben's newly acquired territory. It was a routine fly – a can of corn – only distinguishable from all the other fly balls he'd caught in that this one was a *major league* fly ball. Ben backpedaled, position himself, and waited. With the reassuring, muffled slap of leather against leather, the ball dropped safely into his glove. He squeezed it tight a moment to be sure, exhaled, and airmailed it back to the infield.

The final two batters grounded out harmlessly, and the game was over. Ben gladly put up with some mild initiation abuse from his temporary teammates in the clubhouse before taking a cab to the comfortable hotel room provided for his use. He didn't sleep much that night, however, thanks to a combination of nerves and the knowledge that he would have to make his hitting debut the next day against the Mariners' hard-throwing, left-handed ace Randy Johnson – sort of a baptism by fire.

Wednesday night, he struck out looking his first time up, swinging the second, and managed only a weak pop out in his final at-bat. The rest of the lineup didn't fare much better against the "Big Unit" and the A's lost three to one.

Thursday night's contest produced better results: a victory for the home team to take the series, and an improved showing for Ben personally. While his outfield play continued solid, he showed encouraging signs of life on offense. First time up, facing right-hander

Erik Hansen, he struck out, same as the night before. But on his next opportunity, Ben unloaded on a 2-2 fastball, lacing a line drive all the way to the wall in left center. He ran for all he was worth, slid into second with an RBI double, and later scored. In the eighth, he did the job assigned to him, moving the runners along by laying down a sacrifice bunt to help cement the win for Oakland.

After the game, Tony LaRussa pulled Ben aside. "Nice work tonight, son," he said. "Dave will be back in the lineup tomorrow, though, so you're going home to Tacoma."

Ben nodded.

"You handled yourself real well out there, Lewis. I don't think it'll be long before we see you again. Who knows? Maybe later this year with the September call-ups."

"That would be amazing, sir. Thank you."

LaRussa shook Ben's hand and dismissed him.

While Ben packed up his gear, catcher Terry Steinbach came over to present him with the ball used that night for his first major-league hit. Looked like the whole team had signed it too. Overcome, Ben mumbled his gratitude and tucked the priceless souvenir into his duffle bag.

He left Oakland ecstatic for having had the opportunity to play, and disappointed it was all over so soon. He also felt relieved that he'd come through the adventure unscathed: no errors, no disasters. Next time would be easier with an ounce of big league experience already under his belt, and he would walk a little taller for it in the meantime.

~~*~~

Feigning illness wasn't that much of a stretch; Gail really did feel queasy at the thought of facing Ben Lewis again.

She hadn't wanted to come to the Tacoma Tigers' game in the first place, but Paul insisted. Not that she had any right blaming him. He was an innocent bystander – innocent and clueless, thanks to her. She'd kept him totally in the dark. Maybe she should have been honest with him from the start about the strange business with Ben. If she had, she could have been spared a lot of awkwardness – today's included. And Paul would never have mentioned that name to her again, let alone dragged her to witness a demonstration of Ben's athletic prowess.

"Are you feeling any better?" Paul asked her twenty minutes down the road.

"Much, thanks to your air conditioning." She took another sip of the bottled water Paul bought for her before they left Cheney Stadium. "I'm sorry you didn't get to hang around and talk to Ben, like you wanted."

"That's okay. Another time."

"I don't know what came over me. I felt fine until the end."

"Probably a combination of the heat and a little dehydration. Not surprising when you sit out in the sun for three hours. Next time, we'll have to be sure to take plenty of water and to get seats higher up in the stands where there's shade."

"Yes… if we go again."

"I'd like to. I thought it was fun. Ben sure put on a show today, didn't he? That home run and a couple great catches. The one in the fifth inning especially. I didn't think there was any way he'd be able to get to that ball before it hit the ground. But he can really fly; I'm living proof of that. And then diving at the last second the way he did. Impressive."

"Uh-huh," Gail murmured, hoping to let the topic die. *Please, no more about Ben Lewis!* No more talk about him. No more thinking about him. No more friendly get-togethers and certainly no more watching him exercise his muscles. A thorn in her side: that's what Ben had become. A prickly reminder of a foolish attraction that she should never have allowed to get hold of her in the first place. But she *had* allowed it, perhaps even encouraged it, which meant it was her own fault that disconcerting reminders of him still loitered on dusty shelves in her head, despite her efforts to clean house.

"Oh, I never told you what my dad said about you a while back," Gail began lightly, by way of changing the subject. "You'll get a laugh out of this, Paul. Basically, he thinks your plan to go into missions is no more than a whim. He expects you to last about a year before returning to civilization, as he calls it, and he actually envisions you winding up in politics someday." She forced a chuckle. "What do you say to that?"

"Humph. Your father must have a pretty poor opinion of me if he thinks I'll give up so easily."

"No, just the opposite. The way he sees it, you have too much potential and ambition to bury yourself in Africa for long. I told him he was all wrong, that you're very serious about this."

"Thanks for setting him straight."

After a brief lull, Gail continued. "It did make me wonder, though, how long you *do* intend to stay at the orphanage. Five years? Ten? The rest of your life?"

"Indefinitely, I guess. It's a year-by-year commitment from a legal standpoint, but I'll stay either until I'm no longer needed or until God makes it clear He's moving me elsewhere."

Indefinitely. He might as well have said forever; it could amount to the same thing. Doctors are *always* needed, and the world would never run out of orphans. "Don't you think you'll miss your family and friends, being away so long? What about your parents? What if they need help as they get older or just want to see their grand-children? Won't it be hard to be so far away?"

"Their grandchildren?" Paul eyed her and smiled. "I like the way you think."

Gail huffed. "Just projecting possible scenarios. Now, be serious."

"All right. I'm sure it will be hard for them, but my parents believe in what I'm trying to do. They support my decision to go. Yours would too, wouldn't they?"

"Not my dad; he's already given me his views on the subject. And my mother, of course, would agree with him."

"But it's your decision."

"Right. That's what I told him."

"Good. Look, Gail, well-meaning people like your father will urge you to play it safe, and they'll be happy to supply you with plenty of rational reasons why you shouldn't go. But you need to recognize those reasons for what they are – tempting excuses – and don't allow yourself to be swayed by them. Nobody chooses missionary work because it's easy, convenient, or smart by worldly standards. You choose it because you're called, and because it's the right thing to do."

"I understand all that. I just want to be sure I *am* being called."

~~*~~

Ben had noticed her in the stands – Gail, with Paul by her side as usual. Generally, he avoided picking individual faces out of the crowd, but something had compelled him to study the bleachers while he waited for the relief pitcher to throw his warm-up tosses in the top of the eighth. Even from his remote location in center field, he knew at once it was her. It became impossible *not* to see her after that, with her platinum hair shining in the sun like a beacon. No matter where he looked, that bright spark of light drew his eye.

He'd spent the rest of the game distracted, thinking what he should do if Gail and Paul approached him. Only Jessica waited for him, though, and she was hard enough to handle.

"Good game, Benji," she said twining her arm through his and falling into step with him as if they were joined at the hip.

"Thanks. Guess I did all right. Where's your car?"

She pointed across the parking lot. "I'm so proud when you hit home runs and everybody cheers. You should do that more often."

"I'll keep it in mind," he muttered, walking her in the direction she'd indicated.

"So, can we go to your place, Benji? Or will that nosey roommate of yours be there again?"

"I expect he will be; it's his apartment. Besides, I need to make it an early night. Road trip starts tomorrow, remember?"

"All the more reason for us to spend some time together first, before you leave the country."

"It's just Canada, Jess, not the ends of the earth."

"I know, but I'd still like to give you a proper sendoff," she said slipping her fingers under his shirt and plowing them up the taut skin of his back.

Ben corralled Jessica's straying hand. "Not here," he said firmly.

She jerked around to face him, riveting him with flashing eyes. "Where, then? When? Huh? We're never alone; you see to that! I'm not poison, you know. And if you don't want me, I'll find someone else who does."

"Take it easy," he said, stroking her hair. "I'm sorry. Of course I *want* you." He kissed her gently. "Any man with a pulse would want you. But we've talked about this. We can't go back to the way things were because we've both changed. For the better, I hope."

"You keep saying that, Ben, but really *you're* the one who's changed. I'm still me."

259

She was right he realized when he thought about it *en route* to Vancouver the next morning. Jessica hadn't changed much in all the years he'd known her. Then as now, she was strong willed, overtly sensual, socially ambitious, and determined. She wasn't malicious about it, at least not that he'd ever observed. She simply wanted what she wanted, and she wasn't very patient with anyone or anything that stood in her way.

Ben had admired her for it. At one time, he saw himself as cut from the same cloth. Success was all-important, and whatever didn't fit his formula for achieving it got kicked to the curb without a second thought. Lately, though, things didn't seem so black and white, and it had been harder to maintain his single-minded focus. The blinders that kept him on his narrow path had slipped a little now, allowing a kaleidoscope of tempting colors to leak in from the sides. Baseball remained number one, unquestionably, but it was no longer the *only* thing that interested him. That probably made him a healthier human being. Did it also mean he was losing his edge?

~~*~~

After Vancouver, the team moved on for a series in Calgary against the Cannons. That's where Ben received another unexpected summons from Bob Boone. Again his nerves teetered on a tightrope, anticipating what it could mean. Was he headed back to Oakland so soon? No, that was too much to hope for, especially after getting a look at his manager's face. No smile this time.

"Sit down, Ben," Boone said.

"What's up coach?"

"No point in beating around the bush."

Ben swallowed hard.

"The thing is, you've been traded."

"Traded?"

"That's right. To the Padres organization."

Ben's mouth fell open.

Boone went on. "It's a lateral move for you. You'll be playing for the Stars. I'm real sorry to lose you, son, but you've got to catch a flight to Las Vegas," he said, handing Ben a plane ticket.

With a mere handful of words, Ben's brief time with Tacoma, as well as his much longer association with the A's organization, came to an abrupt end. He wandered back to the locker room to pack and say goodbye. The guys there were no longer his teammates. In fact, the next time he saw them, they would be his opponents. He no longer lived where he had ten minutes before, and he might not have the chance to collect his belongings until his new team traveled to Tacoma. His entire future had been unceremoniously rearranged in the blink of an eye.

He'd done nothing wrong; Boone had assured him of that. Probably the opposite. Playing well had brought him to the attention of the Padres, and they'd decided to go after him to complete the back end of a larger deal between the two clubs. Ben had become the guy you're always hearing about, the proverbial "minor league player to be named later."

Nothing personal; just part of the game. That's how Boone had summed up the trade. But it still felt like a kick in the gut. Halfway to Vegas, Ben remembered one more reason to be wary of his new assignment. Last time he'd checked, Derek Williams also played for the Stars.

-44-

Over and Out

Gail exhaled deeply as she left the lecture hall for the last time, having just turned in her *final,* final exam. She was certainly relieved, but not as elated as she had expected. Shouldn't she be buoyed up by a sense of accomplishment and anticipation for the future? Instead, she felt a little sad to think that this chapter of her life was almost over.

"How'd you do?" Lorrie asked when she caught up with her.

"Oh, fine, I think."

"Fine? You probably aced this test like all the others. I don't know why I bothered to ask."

"Did you think it was particularly difficult?"

"Perfectly miserable! Grueling. Impossible! But that's just me. Maybe if I studied day and night like you do…"

"I'm sure you passed with flying colors." They started down the hallway. "You always agonize, and it always turns out you had nothing to worry about."

"Then you think it's too soon for me to start getting nervous about next month's board exam?"

Gail laughed. "Definitely! Let's enjoy graduation first. Besides, we'll be ready for boards; we've been preparing for months."

With a devilish grin, Lorrie asked, "Isn't it interesting how his name keeps coming up? Interesting and highly significant, I'd say."

Gail wrinkled her brow. "Who are you talking about?"

"Ben Lewis, of course. You just mentioned him."

"I did not!"

"Yes, you did. You said, 'We've *Ben* preparing for months.' You were thinking about him again, weren't you?"

"Stop it, Lorrie! You shouldn't tease me. How can I consign that whole embarrassing episode to the past if you and Paul keep bringing up *that person's* name? Paul's completely innocent, but you... You should know better."

"Okay, okay, I can take a hint. I'll change the subject. Will that make you happy?"

Gail nodded curtly.

"All right, then. So, have you seen any good baseball games lately?"

Gail clapped her hands over her face and gave a muffled scream.

"Jeeze Louise, Gail! I wouldn't have made that crack if I'd know you were going to freak out on me. When did you become so sensitive, anyhow?"

Gail dragged her fingers slowly downward and away. "Sorry. You hit a sore spot, though. Paul's dragging me to another baseball game in Tacoma in a couple of weeks, when Ben's new team comes to town."

~~*~~

Derek Williams narrowed his eyes into a knife-edged squint when Ben entered the Stars' clubhouse. No boisterous greeting for his old college teammate. Not even a neutral nod of recognition.

Ben took his cue and kept his distance. It was going to be like old times, then. And not in a good way. But that's exactly what he'd expected from Derek.

The tepid reception Ben received from the rest of the guys was a surprise, though. Not that they had any reason to be overjoyed at his coming. He didn't really know any of them except by sight and reputation from playing against them. Perhaps he'd displaced someone they'd considered a friend. That could account for it. Or, more likely, Derek had filled their heads with negative misinformation. Ben wasn't overly concerned. He made friends easily. It might just take a little longer this time; that's all.

The thing with Derek himself was completely different. It had to be dealt with. They couldn't go weeks and months avoiding each other, not in the confined quarters of locker rooms, dugouts, and team buses. No, they would have to find a way to normalize relations, to put aside their differences so they could play ball together, literally. Ben was willing to let bygones be bygones for the sake of team unity, but he would need Derek's cooperation.

Over that first week, Ben made an effort. He said hello when he arrived at the ballpark. No response. Along with the rest of the guys, he offered a high-five after Derek hit a home run; Derek skipped right over him. In fact, Derek ignored him completely, which took some doing since they were playing side by side again – Ben in center and Derek in right, same as before. That was undoubtedly part of the problem since, Ben learned, his old rival had occupied the coveted center field spot until he showed up.

Ben had nearly resigned himself to living with the silent treatment when things were brought to a head by the first road trip after his arrival. As fate would have it, he was assigned to room with his old nemesis. No avoiding each other now, so Ben took the plunge that first day in their shared Portland hotel room.

"This is ridiculous," Ben said, barring Derek's path to the door. "We have to clear the air. This bad blood between us is hurting the team."

Derek shot him a murderous glare. "You've got no right to tell me what's good for the team. You've only been here a week. Now get out of my way."

Ben stood his ground. "Look, Williams, I didn't ask to be sent here. I'd have much rather stayed in Tacoma, but you know I had no choice. We'll just have to be professional about this and make the best of the situation. Truce?" He held out his hand.

"Spare me your sanctimonious 'let's be friends' crap! Someone takes what belongs to me, and he's going to pay. In the meantime, Lewis, I don't need you telling me how to do my job, understand?" Derek pushed past and out the door.

It seemed as if the confrontation somehow, brutally but effectively, broke the ice, and Derek's glacial manner slowly began to thaw. They could at least speak to each other when necessary, which meant they could work together. Good communication between teammates was important. They relied on each other. They had to be able to trust each other too.

Ben was also encouraged that their next destination was Tacoma. He'd be able to pick up his belongings and see his most supportive fans again: his parents, Scott, Jessica, and Kyle. They were all back at Cheney Stadium for the first game, cheering him on and joining him for a victory dinner afterward to celebrate his winning hit.

264

The second game – a matinee – was just as hotly contested with the two teams matching each other run for run all the way through. In the bottom of the ninth, the score was tied again at four with the Stars hoping to contain the Tigers' threat to force extra innings. Ben's former roommate Aaron Metcalf stepped up to the plate with two outs and the potential winning run on third. Since Metcalf wasn't known as a power hitter, the outfielder was drawn in slightly. The strategy made sense, since allowing a fly ball to drop in front of one of them – in no man's land – would be just as bad as a ball dropping behind. Either way, the runner on third would score and the game would be over.

Things looked good for Las Vegas when Metcalf fell behind 0-2. But he hung around, fouling off several pitches until he'd worked the count full, and reviving Tacoma's hopes of putting a quick end to the game. With two outs and two strikes, something had to give soon. The next crack of the bat would probably decide it. The crowd noise rose with anticipation.

Adrenaline coursed through Ben's every vessel and sinew. It was the kind of situation he lived for. The game was on the line, and anything could happen – a decisive strike to mow down the batter and end the inning; an anticlimactic ground out; or a ball hit sharply somewhere, hopefully to him. His muscles tightened, poised for action. He had to be ready to react in a split second – no room for hesitation. Speed could mean the difference between success and failure, between winning and losing.

In seeming slow motion, the ball catapulted from the pitcher's hand toward the plate. Metcalf started his swing and Ben saw him solidly connect. Even as the crack of the bat reached his ear, he was off toward deep right center field. It was a fly ball rather than a liner, so, despite being somewhat out of position to start with, he had an honest chance. Halfway to the fence, Ben craned back over his right shoulder to spot the ball. Once he had it in his sights, he didn't dare look away and run the risk losing it in the sun.

Back and back he ran blindly. He knew there wasn't much of a warning track, so he depended on his teammates and his inner radar to tell him when he was closing in on the unforgiving plywood wall. Then he heard Derek Williams shout.

"You've got room! You've got room!"

Reassured, Ben then gave his total focus to making the catch.

Two more long strides and he leaped, glove stretched to its highest limit to intersect the ball. Hurtling through the air at full speed, he slammed into the wall. His left shoulder hit first and buckled in an explosion of pain. His head impacted a split second later, and then everything went black.

~~*~~

The ball fell out of Ben's glove to the ground and the runner trotted home from third to win the game for Tacoma. But the cheers of Tiger fans quickly died away, and a respectful hush descended over the ballpark as all attention turned to the crumpled, motionless figure at the base of the wall in center field.

"Ben!" Gail gasped. "Oh, Paul, he's really hurt."

Paul put a firm arm around her shoulders. They were on their feet now, along with everyone else, waiting. The Stars training staff had rushed out at once, and one of them was motioning for more help. Still Ben didn't move.

The announcer's voice came over the PA system. "I'm sure our thoughts and best wishes go out to the injured Stars player. That's Ben Lewis, folks, local boy and one of our own Tacoma Tigers until recently. He's getting the best care possible, I promise you. So I trust he'll be up and around again real soon."

Some players from both Ben's current and former teams collected in a circle at second base, dropping to one knee in prayer.

As Gail and Paul watched, Ben was strapped to a board to stabilize his spine, carefully loaded onto a stretcher, and taken off the field. Minutes later, they heard the siren of the aid car as it pulled away. The players quietly dispersed and the uncertain fans began to slowly file out as well, their heads bowed and voices low as if leaving a memorial service rather than a ball game.

"Come on, Gail. We might as well go too," Paul suggested.

"Shouldn't we do something? Call someone?" she demanded. "His family should be notified!"

"I'm sure that's already been done. I'll call Hollie when we get to your place. She might have heard something from Scott by then."

"But do you think it could be serious? He wasn't even moving."

"He hit that wall pretty hard. No doubt a concussion, since he lost consciousness, and possibly a broken bone or two."

Gail groaned.

"Don't worry. As bad as it looked, I doubt there could be anything life-threatening."

Gail allowed Paul to lead her down the stands and out of the stadium. They drove back to Seattle, to Gail's house, in subdued silence, and Paul phoned his sister from there. He relayed the secondhand report bit by bit as he heard it.

"Ben's conscious…"

"Thank God," Gail murmured.

"…but he definitely has a concussion… a broken collar bone… and a shoulder dislocation with probable torn ligaments. Right, Hollie, thanks. Let us know when you have more news. Bye." Paul hung up the receiver. "Well, I guess Ben won't be playing any more baseball for a while. The collar bone's straight forward enough, but he could have some lingering effects from the concussion and it's hard to say about the shoulder."

"Will he need surgery?"

"It would depend on how much damage has been done. I gather they're still evaluating."

"Poor guy. He must be in a lot of pain."

"I'm sure he is. But from what I know about Ben, it's the setback to his career that will be hardest for him to take."

~~*~~

Torn rotator cuff. Surgery required. Out for the season. Difficult rehab. An uncertain future. Not what Ben wanted to hear. Even drugged and nauseated by pain, he clearly understood that his road to the major leagues had just taken a major detour.

Everything else was a blur, though, including how he'd ended up in this mess. He was playing a game at Cheney Stadium; that much he remembered. Then, according to what he'd been told, he crashed into the wall trying to make a catch and lost consciousness. Since waking at the hospital, he'd been stripped down, examined, scanned, poked, and prodded in every possible way, leading to the gloomy prognosis just given to him.

A nurse peered in. "You have visitors, Mr. Lewis."

Ben's parents came in, his mother hurrying to his uninjured side.

"We came as quickly as we could, honey. How are you feeling?" she asked, grasping his hand in both of hers.

"I've had better days," he mumbled. "Pretty stupid stunt, huh Dad, running into a wall?"

"Not the brightest thing you've ever done, that's true. So what comes next, son? How long until you're back on your feet?"

Ben grimaced. "On my feet is one thing; on the field is another. They say if I'm lucky, I'll be ready to go in time for spring training next year."

"And if you're not so lucky?"

"It could be longer, Dad. A *lot* longer."

-45-
A Banquet

The Padres organization spared no expense toward restoring their prized new acquisition to playing condition. As soon as Ben recovered enough to travel, they packed him off to see Dr. Andrews at the American Sports Medicine Institute in Birmingham, Alabama. Andrews was, without a doubt, the best in the business, but the news coming out of surgery still wasn't good. The doctor had discovered scar tissue from a previous injury and some additional new damage – a small tear to the labrum – all of which meant rehab would be more difficult and take up to a year instead of the estimated six months.

Ben accepted the news stoically and moved on to his next destination, the Padres' spring training facility in Peoria, Arizona. There he met with Dr. Matthews, the rehabilitation coordinator, a balding man in his late forties.

"You have a long road ahead of you, Mr. Lewis," Matthews said after doing his own evaluation. "I hope you're up to the challenge."

"I'll do whatever it takes, Doc."

"Good. We'll need to get you started on some light exercise right away. Nothing very strenuous at first. The goal will be to maintain as much of your strength and range of motion as possible while your collar bone and repaired ligaments knit themselves back together." He illustrated by tightly interlacing his fingers. "Then, in four to six weeks, the real work begins. I won't sugarcoat this, Ben. Rehab isn't for sissies. It'll probably be the hardest thing you've ever done in your life. But we're here to help you. It's our job to make sure you come through this stronger than ever and ready to play at the highest level again."

"That's my goal too, and I'm not afraid of hard work."

"Then I'm sure you'll do very well. Any questions before I turn you over to the staff?"

Ben thought a moment. "I was wondering, since I can't really get started on much until things heal up, would it be okay if I went home for a week or two?"

"Where's home, son?"

"Seattle. There are a couple of important events coming up: a fundraising banquet for a friend of mine and a party for my parents' silver anniversary. Before this happened," he said, indicating his bum arm, "I assumed I wouldn't be able to make it to either one, but it would mean a lot to me if I could."

"Hmm," the doctor murmured, pursing his lips. "It would have to be cleared by management, of course, but I don't see it being a problem as long as you're consistent with your exercises while you're gone."

"I will be, I swear."

"Then let's see what can be arranged."

Gail assessed her reflection in the full-length mirror. Her dress was new for the occasion. Well, old actually. A simple, dusty-blue silk sheath she'd discovered at a vintage clothing shop near Pioneer Square. It fit her lithe frame like a glove and reminded her of something Audrey Hepburn would have worn, except for the color which was tailor made for a blue-eyed blonde. Gail borrowed her mother's pearls and swept her hair up into a twist at the back of her head to complete the effect.

This was a big night for Paul, and she wanted to look her best, especially since he had insisted she sit at the head table with him. The place would be packed, the enormous multi-purpose building at the church converted into a banquet hall for the event. Pretty much everybody she knew – and a few hundred she didn't – would be there, each paying seventy-five dollars a plate to hear about Paul's plans and contribute toward his expenses.

There was a tap at her door. "Gail, it's time to go," her father said from the hallway.

"Coming."

She was riding with her parents. That had been Paul's suggestion since he intended to get to the church hours earlier than there was any reason for her to appear.

When they arrived, the Albrights pulled up to the covered entry and turned the BMW over to one of the college-aged youth group members pressed into service as valet parking attendants. Although still early, dozens of people were already milling around in the multi-purpose space *cum* banquet hall – friends of the Rustons and those responsible for setting up. The clatter of industrious activity echoed through the space as volunteers placed chairs around the last few tables, organizers called out final instructions, and the technical staff tested the sound system.

Gail was awed by the total transformation. The building, where sweaty teenagers had probably played basketball the night before, didn't look anything like a gymnasium now. The hoops had disappeared into their enclosures. Large carpet squares covered the hardwood floors, except for an area in front of the stage left exposed for dancing. Round tables, complete with fresh flowers, candles, and crisp, white linens, arrayed the rest of the space – enough to accommodate four to five hundred people, Gail estimated at a glance.

She spotted Paul – easy to do since he was taller than everyone else – and started in his direction. His formal attire seemed to accentuate his height, giving him an aloof, almost regal, appearance. For a moment, Gail could see what her father meant that time about a political future. The way Paul looked tonight, he fit the role to a T. But, despite what anybody else might envision for him, she knew his heart was firmly set on helping AIDS orphans in Africa. That's what this event was all about: making his dream a reality. Consequently, Gail approached it with mixed feelings – thrilled for Paul, but still unsure how or even if she fit into the plan.

"Hello, darling," Paul said, slipping one hand around the back of her neck and kissing her firmly. "You look amazing."

"Thanks. So do you. I've never seen you in a tux before."

"And you probably never will again... except maybe on our wedding day," he added with a wink. Not waiting for a reaction, he towed her excitedly toward the steps at the front. "Let me show you where you're sitting."

Gail resisted. "Not up there!"

"Sure! Why not? I told you you'd be at the head table with me."

"I guess I didn't picture it being on a stage."

"Don't worry. No one's going to expect you to make a speech. I have to, though, and I'll need you beside me for moral support."

271

Gail obediently trailed him up the stairs, behind the long, formally dressed and skirted table, and toward the far end, reading the place cards as she went by each empty chair. First was Pastor Greer. Beside him, someone named Connie Hamilton – the representative from the mission organization, Gail guessed. Mr. and Mrs. Ruston's seats were next in line, then Ben Lewis's, her own place, and lastly Paul's closest to the end by the podium.

"You've got me sitting next to Ben Lewis?"

"That's not a problem, is it?"

It was, but she certainly couldn't get into an involved explanation as to why. Too late for that now. "No, I suppose not. I'm sure it'll be fine." She forced a weak smile.

"Good! I want everything to be perfect tonight. Did I tell you we're sold out? The publicity has been great, and people from work and the community have been really supportive. So every one of those seats will be filled tonight," he said looking out over the expanse of still-vacant tables.

Gail did likewise and imagined a sea of expectant faces gazing back at them. She felt her throat constricting. "Doesn't it terrify you, Paul, to have to speak in front of so many people?" she choked out. "I'd faint on the spot."

He took up her hand and stroked it. "Then it's a good thing I'm the one doing the talking," he said, a tremor of emotion in his voice. He shook it off and went on cheerfully. "This is going to be a night to remember, Gail."

They returned to the floor, and, with a peck on her cheek, Paul left to attend to the last-minute questions thrown his way by several others. Gail slowly scanned the cavernous room, searching for someone she knew. Instead, a familiar baritone voice startled her from behind.

"Hello, Gail."

She spun around to find Ben Lewis, his appreciative eyes appraising her from a few feet away. She couldn't help returning the favor. He looked... He looked gorgeous – there was no other word for it – in his tux, with his athletic build and dark features. Even the sling supporting his left arm didn't destroy the effect. "Ben, I... uh..."

"Yes?" He waited, an unreadable expression playing across his face.

"I… I'd like to introduce you to my parents," she said, happily striking on the idea.

~~*~~

Ben followed as Gail wove between tables toward a middle-aged couple standing near the door. *Meeting her parents?* How had he let this happen? He was supposed to be steering clear of Gail tonight… and for the rest of his life. That was the plan. But what had he done instead? As soon as he arrived, he'd seen her standing there alone, centered in the glow of an overhead light, like some kind of fairy queen illuminated by a moonbeam. Without thinking, he'd taken the most direct route to her side.

At least Gail seemed willing to be civil. After the way their most recent meeting last winter had terminated, he hadn't known if she would even speak to him should their paths unavoidably cross again. Now, here she was presenting him to her mother and father, for whatever that was worth. Ben could have picked Mrs. Albright out of a crowd by her unmistakable resemblance to her daughter. Mr. Albright, a stocky man with a hard jaw line, only betrayed his relation to Gail by the way his expression softened when he set eyes on her.

"We heard what you did for our dear Paul," Gail's mother said smoothly after the initial introductions. "And I believe we met your brother last summer."

"Yes, Scott told me. He'll be here tonight too. He's a good friend of Hollie Ruston's."

"You're a pro ball player," stated Mr. Albright, pressing Ben's hand in his solid grip.

"That's right. Still in the minors, though, and now I've suffered a little setback," Ben said, inclining his head toward his bad left shoulder.

"So I see. Tough break, but I wouldn't worry. Playing sports always pays off. A stepping stone to other things too. That's how I got my start in college administration. Did Gail tell you?"

Ben glanced around to take his cue from Gail, but she wasn't there. If he'd wondered how she felt about him, he had his answer. She'd dumped him on her parents and made her escape first chance she got. "N-no, sir. Your daughter and I haven't spent that much time together, and the subject never came up."

"I started out as an athletic director. Worked my way up from there. Always had a soft spot for sports, though. Especially baseball. Used to take Gail to the games when we were at LSU..."

The banquet hall was filling quickly, and the volume produced by the voices swelled with it.

Mrs. Albright stood passively by while her husband described his successful climb up through the ranks to his present position. Ben nodded and contributed when he could, but he was distracted. He'd spotted Gail again... at Paul's side, naturally, talking with some people Ben didn't recognize. She appeared a somewhat more animated version of her mother. It seemed both were willing to play the dutiful-wife role to dominating leading men. No, that wasn't fair. He wasn't impartial enough to judge Gail's relationship with Paul.

Ben continued to watch her surreptitiously – that wide, welcoming smile as she listened; the light, quick grace of her gestures; her satiny smooth hair and skin. She was like a bright, exquisite bird that should always be allowed to fly free. He hated to think of Paul or anyone else trying to clip her wings or, worse yet, cage her.

Gail and Paul, having apparently finished their conversation with the others, turned and came toward him. Ben immediately neutralized his expression, which he realized had settled into a scowl.

Paul extended his hand as he approached. "I'm so glad you could make it after all, Ben," he said with warmth. "You're looking much better than when Gail and I saw you last, when you were being carried off the field in Tacoma."

"Yeah, well, I figured running into that wall was the only way I could arrange to get back home for tonight."

"Then I'm even more in your debt than before." Paul laughed and turned to address the Albrights. "I'm going to have to steal my good friend away now. It's almost time to get started. Come with us, Ben. I'll show you where you're sitting."

It turned out he was sitting right next to Gail.

Second Course

Gail resigned herself. She'd have to say something to Ben and get it over with. "I'm sorry I abandoned you back there. Paul had some people he wanted me to meet, and this is his night."

"Of course, if Paul needed you…" Ben didn't complete the thought.

"How did you get along with my parents? I hope Daddy didn't bore you."

"No, he kept me so entertained that I barely noticed you'd gone." Ben then turned to talk to Mrs. Ruston on his other side.

Ouch. She deserved that, Gail admitted. It was just as well that's the way Ben had decided to play it; it would be easier for them both. She shifted in her seat, rotating more toward Paul. Shortly thereafter, Pastor Greer made his way to the podium, giving her even more excuse to turn her back to Ben.

"Good evening, everyone, and welcome," the pastor said into the microphone. The general din immediately died by half. "We're about ready to go, so please take your seats."

He waited another minute for the crowd to settle.

"This is a very special night, as you know. We're gathered here to offer our support to our friend and brother Paul Ruston, to hear more about the mission God has called him to undertake, and to provide the means necessary to send him on his way." Applause rose from the crowd. "But there's no reason we can't have a good time doing it, right?" More cheers and applause. "I've visited the kitchen, and I think I can promise that you're in for an excellent meal to start. Then we'll have a bit of a program, followed by music, dancing, and socializing. You can mix and mingle to your heart's content. So, if you'll bow your heads for a moment, I'll ask the blessing and we'll get started."

After the prayer, the pastor invited them to begin the meal with the green salad and rolls already on the tables. An all-volunteer army of wait staff, dressed in black pants and white shirts with bow ties, began circulating, ready to clear the salad plates and serve the chicken fettuccini.

Gail was too keyed up to fully appreciate the meal. She hated feeling so conspicuous, under hot lights in front of hundreds of people. Her discomfort doubled with being caught, quite literally, between Paul on one side and Ben on the other – two very different men with very different threads of attraction drawing her in opposite directions. It wasn't a matter of choosing between them, though. Only the one wanted her, and it was useless to waste any more time hypothesizing about the other. Ben's presence simply muddied the waters. Yet, she reminded herself, no future with Paul would even be possible if not for Ben.

If she was keyed up, Paul was even more so. Gail saw the bright excitement in his eyes at the close of the meal. "Almost time for your speech?" she asked as the waiters began clearing the dessert dishes away.

"Not yet. Connie Hamilton is going to make a presentation first."

"Are you nervous?"

"Only about one part of it, the last bit."

"Is that when you have to ask people to commit their support to you?"

Paul grinned and nodded. "Pretty much."

Just then, Ms. Hamilton stopped on her way to the podium. "An excellent turnout tonight," she observed to Paul. Then, addressing the larger gathering, she said, "Good evening. My name is Connie Hamilton. I'm here representing *The Least of These*, a charitable organization founded on the words of Matthew 25:40. We take seriously the idea that service rendered to the least of God's children is service to the Lord himself. And you would be hard pressed to find human beings in conditions lowlier than those of the AIDS orphans of Zimbabwe."

The lights in front dimmed, and a hush fell over the room as she brought up the first of her slides showing gaunt, half-naked children in a Harare slum, their sad eyes enough to break anyone's heart. Gail was instantly riveted, like the rest of the audience.

"The first case of AIDS was reported in Zimbabwe in 1985. In the eight years since, the disease has spread throughout the population like wildfire, leaving devastation, poverty and nearly two million orphans in its wake. These children need our help."

Ms. Hamilton continued by delivering shocking life expectancy and infant mortality statistics. She informed her listeners about the cultural and political climate that contributed to the problem, and about current efforts to stem the tide with education and behavior modification. Finally, she revealed a glimmer of hope. Her slides showed the shining faces – children and staff alike – representing the many orphanages established to care for the innocents set adrift by circumstances far beyond their control.

"This epidemic shows no mercy, but we must. Paul Ruston has answered the call to do his part. Won't you do *yours* by supporting him? Thank you."

The throng below sat in meditative silence for a long moment before a sprinkling of applause began, quickly growing into a rumble and then thunder. Paul stood to thank his sponsor, shaking her hand and then claiming the podium as she relinquished it. As he stepped to the microphone, Gail trembled with a mixture of pride and nervous fear on Paul's behalf.

"Thank you, Ms. Hamilton," he said as the applause continued. "You've truly opened our eyes."

Paul dropped his gaze and arranged his notes, waiting. An expectant stillness stole over the company, and yet he waited longer, as if unaware of or unconcerned that more than four hundred people hung on his next words.

"Last year, on the fourteenth of February," he began solemnly, "I came within a split second of death." He let the revelation sink in. "If not for the heroics of a total stranger, I would have died in the street that day, a random casualty of the hazards of twentieth century life. But God had other plans for me…"

Paul described his journey since – the strong call he felt to serve and the winding road that finally led him to sign on with *The Least of These*.

"…That pretty well brings you up to date. A year ago, I had no idea I would be standing here talking about a mission that will take me to the other side of the world. I thank God for preserving my life

277

that day and for giving me a clear purpose for the future. I have many *people* to thank as well.

"First, I want to thank my parents, Henry and Beth Ruston, and also Pastor Greer, for their faithful support and guidance over the years. Please stand." After a hesitation, they did as Paul requested and were publicly recognized by a round of enthusiastic applause.

"Next, I want to extend my gratitude to Connie Hamilton and the people at *The Least of These* for giving me this opportunity." He motioned for her to rise as well, and the clapping warmed in appreciation.

With a growing knot in her stomach, Gail began to suspect Paul meant to publicly thank – and embarrass, in her case – everyone at the head table in turn, which was the last thing she wanted.

"Now, please join me in acknowledging the best guardian angel a guy ever had – my friend Ben Lewis, who quite literally saved my life that day last February." The crowd roared as Ben reluctantly stood at Paul's insistence.

"And finally, I wish to thank everyone here tonight..." he said with a sweeping gesture.

Gail breathed a sigh of relief; she would be spared after all.

"...the volunteers who spent countless hours to make this evening possible, and all of you who bought tickets to contribute financially. It means so much to me," he said, patting his chest. "Give yourselves a round of applause." Paul led by example, raising his hands and clapping for them.

"There's just one more thing I want to say." He paused. "God never sends missionaries out into the world alone; He always goes with them. But He also understands our need for human companionship. In the beginning, He gave Adam the gift of Eve. God willing, I too will have a helpmate at my side when I leave for Africa in six months. Let me introduce you to an amazing young woman whom I happen to be in love with – Miss Gail Albright."

Gail sat petrified, unable to move.

Paul turned to her and dropped to one knee. A shout of approval went up from the room. He drew a ring from his pocket and held it aloft. The ovation grew louder, nearly drowning out his next words. "Abigail Marie Albright, will you marry me?"

~~*~~

278

No! No! No! Ben wanted to shout, but no sound came out. Instead he stared helplessly, mutely, as everything around him except Gail receded into deep shadow. She seemed frozen in time as well. Or was she hesitating? Resisting? *Good! That's it, Gail. Don't be sucked in by the moment. Don't let him carry you away... away from me.*

But then Paul slid the ring on her finger, and they kissed. She'd said yes, apparently, and it was official; Gail belonged to Paul. The whole thing had happened three feet in front of him, and he'd done nothing to stop it. Nothing!

Then she glanced back at him, and for a moment their eyes held. Did he read a certain sadness there? A small regret, perhaps, for what might have been? No, he'd only imagined it, for now she was focused on Paul again, wrapped up in his arms.

The air had turned to swamp water and his shirt collar a noose. Ben couldn't breath; he had to get out. He forced himself to his feet and staggered down the stairs toward the exit. Faces swam around him. A cacophony of voices echoed in his ears. People and furniture conspired to block his path. Ben pushed past them all, out the door and into the night.

-47-
Before Dawn

Almost before Gail realized what had happened, Mr. and Mrs. Ruston were engulfing her, calling her "daughter." Her own parents approached as soon as she and Paul made their way off the stage. They were all smiles as well. Her father winked and whispered in her ear, "Congratulations, Kitten."

Gail didn't even remember saying yes. She must have, though, because there was Paul's ring on her finger – solid, definitely real, the unfamiliar band pressing into her skin. Things had happened so fast. The glare of the lights; Paul's proposal taking her by surprise; all those people watching, cheering; everyone waiting for her to answer: it was one big blur, and she was still in a daze.

Now friends and well wishers pressed around them. Church members said what a fine thing Paul was doing, and how wonderful that Gail would be going with him. Total strangers remarked what a privilege it had been to share in the couple's big moment. Teary-eyed old ladies gushed about how much they loved romantic endings.

The overwhelming current of goodwill buoyed Gail along. There was no resisting it. She nodded and smiled and agreed she was lucky to be marrying "such an exceptional young man." People treated them like royalty. For that one magical moment in time, she was a princess waltzing with her handsome prince as their admiring subjects looked on.

~~*~~

Breaking out onto the sidewalk at last, Ben sucked in a lungful of fresh air – warm, but still infinitely better than the suffocating atmosphere inside. He gave the parking attendant the ticket for the car without a word, then waited like a man in a trance. Before long, Ben became aware of someone squeezing his arm.

"Ben? Ben! Are you okay?"

Ben turned and blinked away the cobwebs. "Hey, Scott," he said flatly. "I'm fine."

"You don't look fine. I thought you were going to keel over back there when you got up and headed for the door. Are you sure you're okay?"

"I said I'm fine!" Ben rubbed his forehead. "Sorry. Just a little too much excitement for me. I'm going home."

"You want some company? I'll come over if you do. Hollie can catch a ride with her parents or with Paul."

"Right, good ol' Paul," Ben repeated sardonically. "Gail said this was his night. I guess she must have known what was coming."

The attendant pulled up in the blue Toyota that Ben had borrowed back from his brother, it being easier to drive one handed. Leaving the engine running, the young man hopped out and dropped the keys into Ben's palm. "There you go, sir. Have a nice evening," he said.

Scott studied his brother's ashen face. "Do you really think you should be driving? Honestly, Ben, you don't look so good."

"I'll talk to you tomorrow."

"Whatever you say. But take it easy, all right?"

"Yeah. No problem."

Somehow, he managed to get safely home to the condo and to his own room. His parents had been watching a movie when he came in, and he'd just said he had a headache and was going to bed early. That seemed to satisfy them. And he did try to sleep, but his mind still reeled from what had happened earlier. He was tortured by unanswered questions.

First and foremost, why had Gail's engagement hit him so hard? His devastation seemed out of proportion to all logic. Sure, he was strongly attracted to her – until that night he hadn't realized how much – but he'd never entertained any serious thoughts of marrying her himself. He had in fact, months before, made up his mind to avoid further contact with her. Yet, less than an hour ago, he'd reacted as if there'd been some kind of definite understanding between them, that she was supposed to know she belonged to him and to his future, not to Paul. That was crazy, of course. But it was also the only thing that explained why he'd felt so betrayed, why his world had come crashing down the moment Paul slipped that ring on her finger.

The further back in their history his mind wandered, the more gaps and mysteries cropped up. For example, why had he been so inexplicably determined to meet Gail in the first place? He couldn't remember. And, more importantly perhaps, what could account for him letting her go so easily despite their undeniable connection. Looking back, he had basically walked away, given her up to Paul without a fight or even a pang of regret. But why? It wasn't like him to back away from a challenge when something important was at stake. It didn't make sense; he had to be missing something.

After tossing and turning for another hour, Ben flicked on the bedside lamp and fumbled through the nightstand for his Bible. He pulled it from the top drawer and let it fall open to the page book-marked with an old photograph. The picture, not the passage, caught his attention. His hands began to tremble and his mouth went dry when he recognized the subject. The snapshot was worn and creased, but there was no doubt in his mind. It was Gail. He flipped the photo over. The inscription in his own handwriting read, "Remember Abby."

Ben shot out of bed and pulled on some clothes. Before leaving the room he grabbed his wallet, keys, and the photo of Gail.

~~*~~

Gail rolled onto her side, checking the clock radio next to her bed again. Two-fifteen. She couldn't sleep; she was still too keyed up. Paul had been right when he'd told her it would be a night to remember. It certainly was.

Obviously, he'd had it all planned out ahead of time to make sure it would be special for her, for them. And everything had gone according to his script – "perfect" as he had ordained. The banquet was a huge success topped off by a fairytale ending. It was exactly the kind of romantic, true-life story she liked reading about. Paul was the ideal leading man, who had taken to the spotlight like a thoroughbred to a fast track. And, once she got over her initial self-consciousness, Gail had enjoyed being treated like a minor celebrity as well.

It was still hard to believe she and Paul were engaged, though. Not that she hadn't thought about it a million times before, but it was real now. The half-carat solitaire on her fourth finger proved it. She raised her left hand to where she could see it in the moonlight coming through the window. It was a beautiful ring, although Paul had guessed wrong about the size. It was uncomfortably tight. For that reason, she wriggled it off and slipped it back into its box for safekeeping.

She'd done the right thing, agreeing to marry Paul. Everyone thought so. Both families were delighted; it's what they'd been hoping for all along. And the proposal had obviously thrilled people at the banquet, becoming an unexpected cherry to top off the fine affair. Most importantly, though, Paul was ecstatic. When he'd turned his eager, adoring eyes to her, she couldn't say no. She couldn't bear to disappoint him, to embarrass him in front of all those people. Making him happy instead had to be the right thing. She might not be one hundred percent sure of *herself*, but she believed in Paul with all her heart. And he was confident enough for them both.

Their engagement seemed to displease only one person: Ben Lewis, although she couldn't think why he should care. Something had made her turn to see his reaction, and he looked physically ill. Maybe that was the real problem after all because he disappeared right afterward. She hadn't seen him again.

Ben pounded on the apartment door for the forth time. "Come on! Open up!" he demanded.

A groggy Kyle Rosier appeared at last. "Dude, do you have any idea what time it is?"

Ben pushed past him and closed the door. "Two-thirty," he said brusquely. "But I need your help. Scott's too. I called him and he's on his way."

"Middle-of-the-night cloak-and-dagger stuff. Awesome."

Another knock announced the arrival of the third member of the conclave. Scott came in disheveled and yawning. "Okay, I'm here. So what's the emergency? Does this have anything to do with Gail Albright getting engaged?"

"Gail Albright is engaged?" Kyle asked. "When did that happen?"

"Earlier tonight, to Paul Ruston," answered Ben. "And yes, this has *everything* to do with her." The three drew mismatched chairs together to form a tight huddle. Then Ben produced the crucial photograph and showed it to the other two.

"It's Gail," Kyle said.

"On the front porch of her house," added Scott. "But when was it taken? It looks old."

"I don't know when it's from. I found it just before I called you. Turn it over."

Scott did so. "Remember Abby," he read aloud. "What does it mean?"

"It means Abby and Gail are the same person! Tonight, when Paul proposed, he called her by her full name: Abigail. But I didn't put the pieces together until I found this picture. I think I must have known her before somehow as Abby. The ironic part is, with my brain so full of holes, I can't do what I wrote there. I can't remember her! Some kind of amnesia, maybe. I'm hoping you guys can help me plug the gaps. Scott, you mentioned to me – it was the night we had dinner at Anthony's with the Rustons – that I supposedly once raved on and on about a girl named Abby. Right?"

"Yeah, you told me about her months before that, saying you broke up with Jessica because this girl Abby was 'the one.' You made a big speech on the subject of fate and dreams and junk like that. But when I mentioned it later, at the restaurant, you acted as if you had no idea what I was talking about."

"And I didn't. That's what I'm telling you; my memory is Swiss cheese!" Ben got up and made a restless circuit around the kitchen table before returning to his seat. "Big chunks are missing, mostly stuff to do with Gail... uh, Abby... I think. But somehow I've barely noticed until recently. It's insane!"

"Dude, maybe you should see a doctor and get your head examined."

"You're probably right, Rosier, but I don't have time. I have to be back in Arizona in a week, and before I can get home again, Gail might be married and gone. You two will have to be my headshrinkers for now."

"At your service, man," said Kyle.

"Likewise," Scott agreed.

Ben exhaled. "Okay, then, what else can you tell me about that original conversation, Scott?"

He shook his head. "Not much. It was a long time ago – over two years now. We were up skiing at Crystal right after we got back from Mexico."

"That would have been January, '91. How is that possible? Gail was still in Tulsa then, at the University of Oklahoma. So how could I tell you about someone that I hadn't had a chance to meet yet?"

Scott pondered a minute. "This part I do remember. You said you were 'waiting for her,' as if she hadn't arrived yet. So that fits. And you also told me I would never believe where you met her, all kind of mysterious like, as if there were cosmic secrets you couldn't reveal or something. Does that help?"

"Not sure. It still doesn't make much sense, but maybe after I have a chance to think about it a while..." Ben turned to Kyle. "Now, old buddy, what I need from you is to hear what you know about my quest to meet Gail. For me, the details are pretty sketchy, but I'm hoping you have a more complete picture."

"Hey, this brain is a vault," he said pointing to his head. "Important stuff goes in and nothing leaks out. Oh, no offense."

"Never mind. Just tell me what's in that vault of yours."

"Well, you were acting real weird for starters – hanging out here for no particular reason, wandering around campus until you about froze to death – so I knew something was up. A woman, I figured, and you finally admitted it. You said you were in love with this nursing student named Gail, but that she didn't know you existed."

"Interesting. Did I happen to clue you in on how I'd fallen in love with a total stranger?"

"One of those... those love-at-first-sight things." Kyle gestured in the air as if trying to summon back Ben's words. "You passed her on the sidewalk, looked deep into her eyes, and you somehow knew you were meant for each other. I think that's the way it went."

"Doesn't sound too plausible, does it?"

"Not really. Seemed to make sense at the time... but I was drinking a lot of beer back then. Anyway, you were totally determined to meet her, so we spent half the night brainstorming stupid ideas for how to arrange it. In the end, though, it happened because you saved Paul Ruston's life... which of course you were in position to do because you were still, pathetically, hanging out in front of Gail's building, hoping to run into her."

"Of course."

"When you came to my place that night after playing hero, you were totally stoked that you'd finally met her. That's all you could talk about – how Gail was an angel, and you two had made a solid connection. You could hardly wait to see her again. Do you remember any of this?"

"Only vaguely."

"Then you totally dropped her after that. Next time we talked, it was as if she'd never been anything special to you. I could never figure it out."

"Yeah," Scott chimed in. "That dinner with the Rustons was only two days after the accident, and you acted like you barely knew her. In fact, you seemed as interested in Hollie as in Gail."

Ben rose and paced the room again, the other two watching him expectantly. Finally he said, as much to himself as to his friends, "So what happened the day after the accident that changed everything?"

-48-
The Day After

It was after five when Ben returned home from the meeting at Kyle's apartment. Although he knew more than before, he still felt caught in a bog of unanswerable questions. Nothing added up, yet he was too exhausted to slog any deeper into the quagmire. He silently stole to his room and dropped directly into bed, surrendering to sleep.

The clock on the nightstand read 9:47 when he opened his eyes again, but Ben was in no hurry to get up – not until he had a plan. He discarded his first impulse, which was to rush to Gail and persuade her to change her mind about marrying Paul. That would be a mistake. What could he tell her at this point? That his gut and some disjointed memory fragments insisted she belonged with him instead? She already thought he was slightly crazy; that would seal the deal. No, he had to get his facts – and his head – straight before attempting it. And he had less than a week.

Neither Scott nor Kyle had known anything about the day after the accident, which seemed the pivotal point in time. That's when everything changed – his memory and his attitude toward Gail. Before that date, he apparently thought of her as Abby, and believed with every fiber of his being that they were destined for each other. Afterward, he knew her only as Paul's friend Gail – a girl who had no particular significance to him.

What had happened in between? Maybe his parents could give him a clue. It was Saturday. Hopefully, they would be around and he could ask them a few subtle questions. He didn't want to make a big deal about it, get them worrying for nothing. If he told them what was really going on, they'd insist he see a doctor… who would probably fit him for a straightjacket and check him into the nearest asylum. Better to fly below the radar for now at least.

As he dressed, Ben strategized how to approach his parents – one or both of them, whoever was home. He would adopt an attitude of casual curiosity. Nothing suspicious about that. And he could pass off any memory gaps as the result of the trauma he'd been through at the time. With a little luck, he'd learn what he needed to know without giving himself away. He had to try... and soon. His presence being required back in Peoria in just a few days, there wasn't a moment to lose.

Ben emerged from the guest suite and saw his mother in the living room, talking to, presumably, his father, who was out of view. Good, he'd have a shot at both of them without delay. "Morning Mom," he said, coming down the short hallway. "Morning... Jessica? What are you doing here?"

"Morning, honey," said Mrs. Lewis, tilting her head to invite her son's kiss on her cheek. "I was about to come get you. Jessica says you made plans."

Ben closed his eyes and raked his good hand front to back through his mop of dark hair. "Shopping," he groaned, remembering his promise to Jessica.

"Yes, shopping!" Jessica repeated. "And whatever else I want to do. You're mine all day; that's what you said."

It seemed ages ago and in another life.

~~*~~

From her bed, Gail squinted warily through eyes still clouded by sleep. Something felt different or out of place this morning, and she half expected to find herself in an unfamiliar room, or at least that the furniture had been rearranged while she slept. Then she saw the small velvet box on her nightstand and her eyes popped wide. That's what had changed. She had finally agreed to marry Paul. The proof, she knew, rested in that fuzzy, black package.

Gail sat up cross-legged, flipped on the lamp, and pried open the box with the excitement of a child at Christmas. She was struck afresh by the ring's perfection... and Paul's taste in selecting it. It was definitely too tight, though, she confirmed, trying it again. Worse than the night before, in fact, but then her fingers were often a little puffy first thing in the morning. She frowned. It was disappointing not to be able to wear it. Yet, if she forced it on, she might not be able to get it off again. Better wait and have it properly sized, she decided. She'd talk to Paul about that later.

First, though, she had a couple of overdue phone calls to make. Here she had been engaged for over twelve hours and neither one of her two best friends knew it!

Gail tiptoed down the hall in her pajamas to use the phone in the study. Closing the door, she curled up in her father's chair, behind his massive desk, and dialed Lindsay's number. Gail knew she could count on a favorable reaction there since Lindsay was an established fan of both Paul and the idea of mission work. As anticipated, she bubbled over with enthusiasm when Gail apprised her of the news.

"…And of course you're going with him! This is nonsense, what your father says about waiting for him to come back. If it were me, I'd already be packed!"

"Over packed, you mean," Gail said, laughing. "I know you'd jump in with both feet. You're always up for an adventure. I was really kind of hoping to stay put for a while, though… but I don't believe in long-distance relationships either. There's no point in Paul and I being together if we can't be, uh… together."

"That's truly profound, Gail," Lindsay teased. "You always were a deep thinker. Seriously, though, you name the time and place of the wedding, and I'm there."

Lorrie didn't take Gail's announcement as well.

"What business did you have saying yes?" she scolded. "I know you were leaning that direction, but you told me you weren't ready to commit yet."

"I didn't think I was. Then, when he asked me, it just seemed like the only possible answer. So I must have been more ready than I thought. If you'd been there, Lorrie, you'd understand. It was an incredible night and Paul was amazing – distinguished, charming, masterful, eloquent. He had the audience eating out of the palm of his hand."

"You too, apparently."

"I was impressed; that's for sure. And proud of him. I couldn't help getting a little swept away, but you *should* be swept away by getting engaged, right?"

"He set you up!"

"What? No! Paul wouldn't do that. He just wanted everything to be really special."

"All the same, he created a situation – the right mood, the glamorous setting, the drama of a public proposal – where there wasn't any way you could refuse him. I know you well enough – and so does he, obviously – to see that you couldn't humiliate him in front of all those people by saying no."

Gail hesitated. "To be honest, I don't remember saying 'yes' either." She quickly added, "I don't doubt that I said it, but at the time I was kind of... kind of petrified, I guess – from the proposal and from being caught in the spotlight. I must have looked like a deer frozen in a car's headlights."

"Gail, that's not love; that's stage fright! *Not* a sufficient reason to consent to marriage!"

"I'm sorry you don't approve, Lorrie, but I happen to love Paul!" Gail shot back.

In a more appeasing tone, Lorrie asked, "Yes, but are you *in* love with him? There's a difference, you know. And what about Ben?"

"What's *he* got to do with this?" Gail challenged, her voice rising in exasperation.

"What about your feelings for him? Or did one magical night erase all that?"

"No," Gail admitted softly after a silent minute. "He was there, actually, sitting right on the other side of me when Paul proposed."

"That must have been cozy. How did he take it?"

"He looked like he was going to be sick, and then he ran out."

"There! That should tell you something."

"Yeah, like he ate some bad shrimp for lunch."

"Or that he cares for you too. Did you ever think of that?"

"Why do you always take Ben's part? Do you like him so much better than Paul?"

"I'm sure Paul's a great guy, but you haven't convinced me he's the love of your life. I wouldn't be much of a friend if I stood by and said nothing when I believed you were about to make a colossal mistake. Look, this isn't like your paisley blazer. When you decided you had to have that hideous thing, I kept my mouth shut because I knew if you came to your senses you could simply get rid of it and buy one that suited you better. Husbands can't be changed as easily. You have to get it right the first time."

~~*~~

Jessica's arrival blew Ben's plans out of the water. He had two choices: waste an entire day entertaining a woman he could no longer pretend an interest in, or risk raising warning flags for all to see by sending her away for no apparent reason. Ben chose the latter. Jessica had to go, but if there was going to be an unpleasant scene, he didn't want it played out in front of his mother.

"Okay, Jess," he said as if resigned. "I'll just grab my wallet."

"That's better," she chided. "You'll see; it'll be fun. Bye, Mrs. L.," she added, starting for the door.

"Goodbye, dear."

Ben hung back and whispered to his mother, "Are you going to be here for a while?"

"Yes, all day as far as I know. Why?"

"I need to talk to you."

"But I thought…"

"I'll be back as soon as I can."

"Benji," Jessica called, "are you coming?"

"Right behind you."

"We'll take my car," Jessica said in the elevator. "That way we won't have to transfer the shopping bags later. You can drive, though," she said handing him the keys. "Since it's an automatic, you can manage even with your arm in that sling."

Ben waited until they were in the car with the doors closed. "Jess, I'm sorry to do this to you, but I can't go shopping today." Before she could object, he charged ahead. "The truth is, I don't think there's any point in us continuing. Dating, I mean. You said yourself that I've changed, and you were right. We don't want the same things out of life anymore. So let's just admit this isn't going to work and go our separate ways."

The stunned look on her face quickly morphed into fury. "Oh, no! You can't do this to me, Ben. Not again! I've got too much invested in you. Now that you're finally close to making some serious money, you're going to dump me? I don't think so!"

"Ya know," Ben said, jerking his wallet from his back pocket, "if it's my money you want, you're welcome to it! Here's a nice little return on your investment." He pulled out a thick stack of twenties – all the cash he had on hand – and dropped it into her lap. "Although,

thanks to this banged up shoulder, that might be about the last of it."
Ben opened his door to get out.

"Wait!" Jessica cried.

Ben hesitated.

"Please?"

He resettled wearily into the seat, leaving one foot on the pavement. The will to fight had suddenly deserted him, as it had her, judging from her tone.

"What do you mean," she asked, "that this might be the last of it?"

"I mean there's a real possibility I won't ever play professionally again," he answered matter-of-factly, acknowledging for the first time that it was true.

"Why didn't you tell me?" she asked.

"I guess I didn't want to admit it to myself." Also true. "I'm not giving up or anything. If there's a chance, I'll work my way back, but nobody's giving me any guarantees."

"Then you could wind up doing what? Teaching school?"

"And coaching. That's the plan whenever baseball is over for me. Actually, as long as it doesn't come too soon, I'm kind of looking forward to it." Another true and surprisingly liberating statement, he discovered. "Something tells me you couldn't deal with that, though. That's okay; you can't help it. But I need a woman who doesn't care about the money, who's not impressed by celebrity, who doesn't even want to be the center of attention." He smiled wistfully, picturing a certain lady who fit that description perfectly. "She'd probably rather spend an evening volunteering at a soup kitchen than attending a fancy society ball."

"Holy crap!" Jessica exclaimed. "Whoever you're imagining, it sure isn't me."

They sat quietly for a minute.

"Thanks," Ben added.

Jessica contracted her brow. "For what?"

"For listening... and for taking it so well. I wish you all the best, Jess. I really do. But I gotta go now, okay?"

"Okay, I guess." They both got out of the car and Jessica started around to the driver's side, meeting Ben at the back end. "Do you want your money back?" she asked, offering him the neatly folded bills.

"Nah. You keep it. Buy yourself something real nice on me. Consider it a going-away present." Ben winked, kissed her on the cheek, and jogged off toward the elevators.

~~*~~

Lorrie's brutally frank words still hung in the air half an hour later. They'd successfully dragged Gail's head down out of the clouds, for which service she didn't feel a bit grateful. For one moment, she'd been happy. For one moment, she'd had peace. After months of uncertainty, she had finally felt settled about her future. Now Lorrie had stirred the pot again, dredging disturbing doubts and questions up from the bottom where Gail had deliberately sunk them, hoping it was forever. Instead, they were now floating in front of her face again. "A colossal mistake. Get it right. Are you in love with him? What about Ben?"

Gail hadn't budged since hanging up on Lorrie. She sat rocking herself in her father's springy office chair with her knees hugged up to her chest, eyes closed, and thinking, going over all the pros and cons of her decision one more time, second guessing herself until she couldn't stand it any more. She opened her mouth to vent some of the pressure, not knowing whether what came out would sound more like a laugh or a scream. It sounded like a shrill ringing noise. No, that was the phone.

Gail picked it up automatically. "Hello," she said.

"Good morning, darling. How's my beautiful fiancé?"

"Oh, hi, Paul." It struck her then that she didn't even have an affectionate nickname or comfortable endearment to call him. She'd have to work on that.

"You don't sound too chipper. Anything wrong?"

"No, no. I just didn't sleep well. Too much excitement, I think."

"It was a great night, wasn't it? Hey, how about I drive over later and take you to lunch? Anywhere you say. I can't wait to see you, and to show you and that ring off a little."

"Four hundred witnesses last night weren't enough?"

"No! I want the whole world to know. What do you say? Can I pick you up at one?"

"Sure, lunch would be fine. But could we stop by the jewelers on the way? There is a little problem with the ring."

"What? Don't you like it?"

"Of course, I do! It's absolutely perfect, like I told you. All except the size. It's a little too tight."

"Then we'd better get it taken care of right away."

After saying goodbye, Gail took a deep breath and let it out. Good. Seeing Paul again was just what she needed to remind her why she'd made the choice she had. Her own changeable emotions sometimes got the best of her; she couldn't trust them. But Paul was a rock. She could depend on *his* stability. He never wavered.

-49-
Following Leads

"So, what happened that day, Mom? Last February, the day after I saved Paul Ruston's life?" Ben asked as soon as he returned upstairs. He'd abandoned his plan for subtlety in favor of the direct approach, hoping to save time. His conversation with Jessica had launched him forward, and he wanted to keep the momentum going. At this point, he was ready to face what lay ahead, but the key to that future remained hidden in the past.

"Wait a minute, Ben. What happened with Jessica?"

"We broke up. For good this time."

Mrs. Lewis absorbed the news without betraying any emotion. "Is… is she going to be okay?"

"Probably. She took it more gracefully than I expected. I think she actually understood that she would be better off with someone else in the long run – someone who wants the same things she does."

"So, what brought this on?"

He shrugged. "It was time. No point in dragging things out any longer." Ben intended to leave it at that and then changed his mind. As long as he was being direct, he might as well be honest about the rest. "Besides," he added, "I'm interested in someone else – Gail Albright."

His mother's eyes blinked wide. "Nice young woman," she said after composing herself, "but I thought she was pretty attached to Paul Ruston."

"They aren't married yet, so I still have a chance. Now, can we get back to my question? I need your help. What do you remember about that day?"

"I don't understand why this is so important to you all of a sudden… or why you're asking me what you should already know."

"Don't freak out on me, Mom, but I have a few gaps in my memory from around that time. The result of the trauma, I'm sure. So, help me fill in the blanks. Tell me everything you can remember about the day after the accident. Will you do that for me?"

"Sure, but…"

"Trust me. It's important."

She folded her arms and studied her son with a shrewd eye, before sighing and giving in. "Well… I remember you got up and ate some breakfast with us. Around nine, I imagine."

"Good. Then what happened?"

"You were acting strangely."

"In what way?"

"You weren't yourself. Distracted. Agitated even. We talked a bit about what happened the day before. You said your shoulder was sore, but it wasn't serious. Then, after a few minutes, you got up, interrupting your father to announce you were going back to bed. You said the doctors told you to get plenty of sleep, but I'm not sure that's what you did."

"Why?"

"Because I remember seeing some light showing from under your door, like your desk lamp was on. I suppose you must have slept at some point, though. You certainly seemed a lot more rested when you came out of your room hours later."

"So, that would have been mid-afternoon?"

"Uh-huh. Two or three o'clock. The funny thing was you didn't seem to recall being up earlier, eating and talking with us. Your father and I put it down to sleepwalking, but I guess it might have been trauma as you suggest."

"Hmm. Is there anything more? Anything else you can tell me?"

"No. No, I don't think so. You seemed perfectly fine after that. Back to your old self. So, what does it all mean, Ben?"

"I wish I knew."

~~*~~

Ben took a walk down to the waterfront to think. He needed fresh air, needed to escape the walls of the condo and the persistent looks of maternal concern.

The interview with his mother had been a disappointment, shedding very little fresh light on the day in question. Most of what she'd said – that he'd come out of his room in the morning, acted strangely, and didn't remember it later – he already knew from what she had told him at the time. And he recalled the suggestion that he could have been sleepwalking. The only new clue was her suspicion that he wasn't in bed the whole time in between. Yet it hardly seemed likely he could have been doing anything life-altering either.

Ben was stumped, at a dead end. He sat down on a vacant bench at Alki beach and pulled the old photo of Gail from his wallet again. It had been in and out of the plastic picture protector half a dozen times already since he'd discovered it the day before. It fit perfectly he'd noticed right away – cut to size and with the same permanent curvature as the wallet, like it had resided there before. It probably had, he realized with a pang. But knowing that didn't give any direction for what he should do next.

"Hello, Ben," someone behind him said. "Oh, sorry. I didn't mean to startle you," she added.

Ben turned to see a woman decked out in dark glasses and an outrageous fluorescent green running suit. Her brown ponytail, which sprouted out the back of a Mariners baseball cap, flipped back and forth as she continued to jog in place.

"Hi," he said, thinking she looked vaguely familiar. "I'm sorry, but… Do I know you?"

"Sure you do, hon," she answered with a twangy east-coast accent. "Well, sort of. I'm an old friend of your mother's, but you wouldn't remember me. Do you mind?" she asked, pointing at the empty seat next to him.

"Be my guest." Ben moved over to make room.

She flopped down beside him and puffed out an exaggerated breath. "Feels good to take a load off, if you know what I mean. I'm not as young as I used to be." Her eye caught on the photograph Ben still held. "She's very pretty. Your girlfriend?"

"No, unfortunately she's somebody else's fiancé."

"Oh, that's too bad… for you I mean."

"You can say that again."

"Of course, it's none of my business, but maybe you should do something about it if it makes you so unhappy."

"I plan to, just as soon as I can figure out what to say to her."
Why he was spilling his guts to the woman, Ben couldn't explain.
But at that point, he was desperate enough to grasp at straws, even if
those straws were offered by a virtual stranger with questionable
taste in clothing.

"How about telling her the truth?" his outspoken benchmate suggested.

"The truth? That's kind of the problem. The truth is too weird to
believe."

"It's stranger than fiction. That's what they say, hon." After several seconds with no response, she went on. "So this weird truth you
need to explain to this girl – what's her name?"

"Gail. Abigail, actually."

"Okay, so this thing you need to tell Abigail, don't you have any
evidence to back it up?"

"Just this picture."

"And where did it come from?"

"I found it in a drawer with a bunch of old papers and things."

"I see." She paused, looking right and left as if worried about
being overheard. "It's just a thought, now, but maybe there's something else in that drawer that could help you. Have you checked?"

"No, I haven't."

"Well, what do I know?" she said dismissively. "It does seem to
me, though, that when you discover treasure somewhere unexpected,
you should dig around a little to see if there's any more. But, like I
said before, it's really none of my business. Anyway, I should get
moving." Once more, her gaze darted this way and that. "It was nice
to see you again, Ben, and good luck with Abby." She popped to her
feet and started off.

"Wait," Ben called after her. "I didn't catch your name."

"Oh, it's Cora, dear," she tossed back over her shoulder.

Cora. The name rattled around his mind a moment in an oddly
familiar way. Then Cora's advice sent him hurrying home.

Ben headed straight for his room. He hauled out the nightstand
drawer with his good arm, dumped the contents onto the bed, and
sorted through the jumble – address book, *Hotrod* magazine, baseball
cards, pens, pencils, photographs, rubber bands, movie ticket stubs, a
program from one of Scott's high school band concerts. Ben ultimately discarded everything as meaningless except a folded half

sheet of college-ruled paper bearing a couple lines of his own hand-writing:

2-15-92
Important note to self:
Don't panic. You haven't lost your mind, only your memory. Everything you need to know about the past and Abby can be found in "chemistry."

"Jackpot!" he muttered under his breath. The wacky woman at the waterfront had been right. Here was evidence that he wasn't crazy. Another piece of the puzzle. Ben read the note again, more analytically this time. He'd written it the day after the accident, apparently aware that portions of his memory would desert him. He was supposed to discover it later, have his fears eased, and be directed to the rest of the story. But what on earth had he meant by "chemistry?" It was only a teaser, not the whole answer. He could curse himself for having been so cryptic.

Ben spun around, looking for somewhere else to search. Yet there wasn't a thing in the tidy guest room that could help him – nothing his, nothing of the past.

Ben grabbed the phone and dialed Scott's number. An hour later they were in Burien, at *Safe and Secure Storage*, unlocking the door to unit 107.

~~*~~

"Thanks for lunch, Paul," Gail said as they waited for the check.

"My pleasure." He eyed her with concern. "You're awfully quiet today. Are you sure you're okay about the ring? Looks like it's still bothering you."

She'd been fiddling with it again, she realized and quieted her hands. "No, it's fine. I'm just embarrassed I made such a fuss about nothing. I suppose that rude little man at the jewelry store is right. It's sized correctly. I just need to let it settle in, get used to how it feels. I've never worn a ring full time before."

"He may be right, but I still intend to complain about his attitude. He had no business speaking to you so condescendingly."

"No, really, I'd prefer to let it go. Let's not talk about it anymore, all right?"

"Whatever you say, darling."

Always so polite. Always considerate and protective. Dependable. That was the quintessential Paul. Which should reassure her, should give her confidence for a secure future and a solid marriage.

That's what they'd discussed over lunch – plans for the wedding and the other things that needed to be accomplished in the coming weeks. Well, mostly Paul discussed and she nodded. She'd thought through all of it before. With school finished and board exams now out of the way too, she would have more time. If necessary she'd give up her job at Dr. Bingham's office a little sooner than she'd intended.

"I can handle it," she'd said. "Everything's under control."

What a relief to have things finally settled, Gail told herself, to have a concrete plan for the future. Now she knew exactly where she was going and what she'd be doing for the next several years at least.

The months ahead would be the most exciting time of her life – getting married, traveling to a distant land, putting her medical training to use at last – so why did she feel her *joie de vivre* bleeding away? She could see it seeping like water, drop by drop, through her tightly cupped fingers.

Nonsense! came the immediate rebuttal from a more sensible part of her brain. If she felt a little drained, it was simply an understandable letdown from the romantic high of the night before. If she had a case of cold feet about marrying Paul... Well, then she would get over it.

Gail breathed in the fresh air as they left the restaurant and gave herself a figurative shake. If Lorrie hadn't planted doubts in her mind, she wouldn't have needed even that much to get back on track.

Her heart's desire was to follow God's plan for her life, wherever it took her. She'd never wavered about that. And she'd been praying for months that He would guide her whether to say yes or no to marrying Paul and entering the mission field. Now, presumably, she had her answer, although not in so many words. But nobody should expect a *literal* sign from God. A growing conviction further confirmed by scripture or circumstances was more likely, and surely that's what she'd been given. She had already been leaning toward saying yes, and then all the circumstances fell into place at the banquet. She just wished she could be a hundred percent certain…

Gail's pensive mood persisted on the drive home. When they stopped at a light on Market Street, she absently turned to look at the yellow moving van that pulled up next to them. Then she froze, her mouth gaping. It was unbelievable. There, on the broad side of the truck, written in bold letters two feet high, was a public service message advising, "Just… Say… No!"

Gail erupted in helpless laughter. A dam broke. A flood of tears mingled with mirth escaped down her cheeks.

"What is it?" Paul asked.

She could only point at the sign that had set her off.

"So? Say no to drugs. What's funny about that?" The traffic light turned green, and he drove ahead. "Gail, what's the matter with you?" Paul persisted. "You're practically hysterical."

Absolutely, she admitted to herself, and then she gladly surrendered to it. Her whole body shook uncontrollably – from laughter one minute and sobs the next. Was it shock? Relief? Temporary insanity? Or a long overdue catharsis? Gail didn't care. Whatever it was, it felt wonderful – conceding weakness, letting go after holding things in so long, releasing the pent-up pressure from the shaken bottle of soda.

"Shall I pull over?" Paul asked.

Gail drew a shuddering breath and managed a feeble smile. "No, I'll be fine. Just take me home."

Paul nodded, tight-lipped, and drove.

By the time they arrived twenty minutes later, Gail's wild flight of emotion had settled back to earth. Her mood was still a little restless for what lay before her, but her head was clear, her thoughts more sharply focused than they had been in a long time. The popular saying was wrong, she decided. The real calm came *after* the storm, not before. High waves swept away the clutter and left only bare, honest sand in their wake.

"Now, do you mind telling me what that was all about back there?" Paul asked as he braked to a stop in the driveway. "You're worrying me. I've never seen you out of control like that before."

"Do you have time to come in for a while?" she asked instead of answering his question.

"Sure, I'm in no hurry."

"I need to freshen up a bit," Gail told him when they reached the porch. "Why don't you say hello to Mother and I'll be down in a few minutes?"

Abandoning Paul as soon as they were in the door, Gail dashed upstairs to her bedroom suite. She went straight to the sink, drenched her face in cold water, and then confronted the image in the mirror. She could forgive the disheveled appearance; there were more serious flaws to address if she peered a little deeper. Apparently, the woman looking back at her was even less spiritually attuned than Gail had suspected before. But was she really so blind that it took something the color and size of a school bus to get her attention? A billboard large enough to blot out the sun to make her understand? It would seem so.

"Well, you've really made a mess of things, haven't you?" she accused her reflection. "Time to clean it up."

~~*~~

"I shouldn't be helping you," Scott grumbled as he dragged down the first carton. "This creates a serious conflict of interests, you know. If you succeed in stealing Gail away from Paul, it's going to be very awkward for me. Have you thought about that? How am I supposed to face Hollie after you destroy her sainted brother's happiness?"

"Think of it this way," Ben answered. "If my theory is correct, we'll actually be preventing him from marrying the wrong woman. Besides, you're helping the handicapped. I couldn't possibly manage these bins and boxes on my own at the moment."

"So what exactly are we searching for?"

"Something to do with chemistry – a text book, lab notes, test tubes. I don't really know. Hopefully we'll recognize it when we see it."

The first box housed baseball trophies garnered from little league on up. Clothes filled several more, as well as the drawers of an old dresser. As the pair continued the hunt, they discovered a giant tub of Legos, a duffle bag of outgrown sports gear, and Ben's movie, music, and video game collections. They gave each container a cursory inspection before moving on.

Scott groaned when he hauled the next box off the shelf and eased it to the concrete floor. "This one must be full of rocks," he said. Opening it, he corrected himself. "No, college textbooks."

"Now we're getting somewhere! There should be one from the chemistry class I took sophomore year." Ben began yanking out the heavy volumes with his good hand, checking and discarding each one in turn. "I remember the bookstore wouldn't buy it back afterward because they weren't going to be using that edition again. Here it is!" he said latching onto the massive, mustard-colored tome and handing it to Scott. "Flip through and see if there's anything hidden inside."

Scott held the book aloft, opening it upside down and ruffling the pages. A folded piece of paper floated down, and Ben snatched it up eagerly.

"Blast! It's blank," he reported. "Isn't there anything else?"

Scott leafed through again, more methodically this time. "Nothing, sorry."

"Okay, let's move on then."

Back went the textbooks, and down came a plastic bin filled with assorted papers.

"High school stuff," Ben pronounced upon open it.

"Did you take chemistry in high school too?"

"Yup. My senior year so there could be something. See what you can find."

They examined each item together, Scott's hands and Ben's eyes doing the work. It was slow going, but three inches deep into the pile they hit pay dirt. They checked at the sight of a green, spiral-bound pad with the word "Chemistry" emblazoned across the front.

"God, please let this be it," Ben murmured, picking up the notebook reverently.

"What's this Bible verse doing here on the cover?" Scott asked, pointing.

Ben scanned the lines. "That clinches it. I never would have written something like that in high school. It has to be more recent." His hand trembling, Ben opened the front cover and slowly turned the pages, one by one, until he found what he was looking for. With Scott peering over his shoulder, Ben began reading aloud:

What would the average guy give to turn back the clock and set his life straight? Probably anything short of his right arm... that is if he'd made as much a mess of things as I had. I hit bottom in September of 1997. Then, just when I thought I couldn't go on, when I was at a point so low I had to look up to see outfield grass grow, I received a genuine, world-class do-over. Now I'm praying I still have time to salvage it.

"The date!" Scott nearly shouted. "Do you realize what you just read, Ben? It says 1997. That's four years from now, Bro!"

"I know," Ben whispered, before reading on. "I know."

It came as a gift. No charge. And I appreciate how lucky I am. Except I'm discovering there is a kind of cost after all, which I'm belatedly paying.

To be fair, I was forewarned. A year ago, I barely thought twice about exchanging my lackluster past for a chance at resurrecting my dream. But, now that they're at risk, I suddenly realize some memories from those discarded months and years are too precious to part with: the satisfaction of helping one of my students succeed, friendships with Jeff and the others at the Center, and most importantly, every mental picture of Abby from a time she knew and loved me. The thought of those treasures being sucked irretrievably down a black hole...

Well, I simply can't let that happen. While I'm still able, I have to write down how I got to this point – what took place the first time around and everything that has changed since...

Ben calmly closed the notebook. Maybe it was the verse on the front cover that reassured him, or the fact that the account was in his own handwriting. For whatever reason, the little he'd read so far didn't shock him. Instead, the words proved – at least to him – that he hadn't lost his mind. Here was vindication, the explanation he'd been lacking. He sensed he was on the verge of coming full circle, of returning home to a place he'd long forgotten but never stopped missing.

"Let's go," Ben said. "We've got what we came for."

-50-
Into the Light

"You realize you can't tell anybody about this," Ben said at last, referring to the story he'd finished reading from the notebook a full five minutes before.

The brothers, sitting side by side in Ben's Corvette, stared out the windshield at the concrete pillars and walls framing the underground parking garage of the Seattle condo, the mundane setting for more than one significant event that day.

"Who would I tell exactly? Like it says in there, no one would believe it. I'm not sure *I* do, for that matter."

"That's okay. You don't have to. I'm guessing that in a few months you won't remember it anyway. I might not either. That seems to be the general rule. But for now at least, I know what happened... *and* what to do next."

"You're going to see Gail, I suppose," Scott said dubiously.

"Of course. She's my wife! At least she should be."

Some of the other things he'd learned from his log – facts about his previous life – had blindsided him. His own behavior shocked him more than anything else. He hardly recognized the guy described as being so discouraged that he gave up all will to live. Thank God he'd been given a second chance. No matter what happened this time (and he was fully aware that both his career and his chances with Gail were in significant jeopardy), Ben couldn't imagine sinking so low again.

He hadn't been shocked to learn that he and Gail were once husband and wife. On some level, he'd known already. The conscious memories were gone, but a deeper kind of comprehension remained. He'd always felt an unmistakable connection to Gail even when he'd most stubbornly denied it, felt irresistibly drawn to her while vowing to stay away.

"There's still something powerful between us," he told Scott, "and we can build on that."

"Oh, I get it, all right. But good luck convincing *her* of that."

Ben ignored the comment. "Can I keep your car a couple more days?"

"Permanently, if you want. It's no trouble to me driving this sweet ride instead," he said stroking the custom steering wheel.

"Don't get too used to it; I'll want it back when I can drive a stick again." Ben reached over to shake Scott's hand. "Thanks for everything. I don't know what on earth I would have done without your help."

"No problem. I hope things work out for you and Gail. I really do."

"I appreciate that." Ben opened the door and boosted himself from the deep bucket seat, while Scott brought the V8 rumbling to life. With the green notebook tucked tightly under his arm, Ben climbed into the Toyota and soon followed his brother from the shadowy garage into the daylight.

~~*~~

Music wafted through the house, faint wisps wending their way into Gail's room upstairs. She had been brushing the tangles out of her hair but paused to listen. Something from *Phantom of the Opera*, she concluded. Mother had apparently forced Paul to the baby grand again and was now no doubt sitting in her wing-backed chair, eyes closed, basking in the luxury of having him play her bidding. Not that Paul ever seemed to mind. He was generous with his talent. Would there be a decent piano available for him at the orphanage, Gail wondered? She could picture how much he would delight in entertaining the kids. He deserved to have that joy. That and more. But then, life wasn't always fair.

Taking a deep breath, she started down the hall as Paul transitioned into another piece from the same musical. Gail recognized the familiar, melancholy tune. Her mind automatically supplied the accompanying lyrics: *Think of me. Think of me fondly when we've said goodbye. Remember me once in a while; please promise me you'll try. Think of all the things we've shared and seen; don't think about the way things might have been...*

306

She'd heard enough, and it wasn't kind to keep Paul waiting. Gail marched down the stairs to the main floor. Before she reached the music room, however, the doorbell rang.

"I'll get it, Mother," she called out, detouring to the foyer another half flight down.

She should have checked through the peek hole to see who it was. She should have, but she didn't. Instead, she opened the door straight away and discovered Ben Lewis on the other side.

"Ben!"

"Gail, I…"

"What are *you* doing here? I'm sorry. I didn't mean that the way it sounded. I'm just… just surprised to see you."

"I would have called first, but I don't have your number."

Gail couldn't think. Ben was gazing at her like she was a long-lost friend back from the dead, as if he intended to memorize every square inch of her face in case she vanished again. That soulful expression, those compelling eyes… "Uh… Were you looking for Paul?" she finally asked.

"No, not Paul. I came to see you. Could we go somewhere and talk?"

"Talk? No, I can't. Paul's here, actually."

"Oh, I suppose I should have realized. Tomorrow, then? Would you meet me after church? Alone. It's important."

"What's this about, Ben?"

Footsteps approached.

"It's hard to explain. I'd rather…"

The door swung wide. "Ben!" said Paul with a broad smile. "It's nice to see you again so soon. To what do we owe this pleasure?" he asked, resting his arm around Gail's shoulders.

"I… I was in the area and thought I'd stop by… to congratulate Gail – and you too, of course, since you're here – on your engage-ment. I didn't get the chance last night."

"Thanks. We're pretty excited about it, aren't we, darling?" Gail flushed and nodded. "So, where did you disappear to so suddenly, anyway?"

"I wasn't feeling well," Ben mumbled. "My shoulder had started really bothering me."

"That's too bad. You missed a heck of a party. Hey, why are we standing around here in the doorway? Come in and stay a while,"

Paul said with an inviting wave of his hand. "That's all right, isn't it, Gail?"

Gail started. "Oh! Sure, but..." Her mind raced. "But Ben said he didn't have time to come in. I already asked him."

"That's right," Ben confirmed at once, making a show of checking his watch. "I've got to be somewhere in half an hour, so I should get going. But listen, Paul, I want you to know that I admire what you're doing, your mission, I mean. If I don't see you again before you go, have a safe trip, and I hope your work in Zimbabwe is a great success." Ben put out his hand, and Paul shook it firmly.

"Thanks, but shouldn't you be wishing Gail the same?" he asked, chuckling. "She *is* coming with me, you know."

"Yes... I know... and I do. All the best, Gail."

"Thank you," she said, her voice faltering.

Ben gave Gail a final, pleading look before walking away. He'd barely taken his eyes off her the whole time, she realized, even when he was talking to Paul. It was almost like... No. No, it was exactly the same as when they'd first met all those months ago.

~~*~~

Ben wrestled all night with the weight of unfinished business. He'd been so close to his goal – Gail standing right in front of him – and then he'd been forced to back off without stating his case. Had she understood? Would she meet him in the morning? If only they'd had time to finish before Paul interrupted.

Not that he should be blaming Paul. Dear God, he'd felt like such a hypocrite wishing the man a nice trip while at the same time plotting to steal his fiancé. Some kind of friend. The ironic part was Ben could imagine that Paul, consummate good guy, might even forgive him for it, which would make it all the worse. Wasn't there something in the Bible about heaping burning coals on your enemy's head by being excruciatingly kind? It would be easier if Paul flew into a rage and slugged him instead. *If* he succeeded with Gail, that is, and that was a big if.

A huge chunk of his future hinged on what took place during the next several hours. The suspense was nearly unbearable. It was like the most critical ballgame of his life was about to begin. The stakes were high because they'd be playing for keeps. Winner takes all.

When he stepped up to the plate in the morning, he'd take his best shot with Gail. Hold nothing back. If he was going to strike out, he'd much rather go down hacking than because he was afraid to get the bat off his shoulder.

~~*~~

Gail awoke from the best night's sleep she'd had in a long time, feeling rested and at peace with what she'd done. It had been the right thing, despite the pain. She'd cried like a baby and made a general fool of herself, apologizing again and again. But Paul had been very decent about it, even admitting he was partly to blame for putting her on the spot at the banquet. In the end, it came down to the question Lorrie had asked her. The answer was no, she wasn't in love with Paul, at least not enough to justify a wedding and "till death do us part." He deserved a wife who could love him more, passionately and without reservation.

It was a little scary walking away from Paul and a life of worthwhile work without a single solid idea where she was going. Yet it was exhilarating too, like raising a sail and launching across uncharted waters, wind take her where it would. For now, though, she was going to church. As for seeing Ben Lewis afterward, she still hadn't decided.

~~*~~

Ben arrived at the church well ahead of the hour and sat at the back of the sanctuary where he could watch for Gail. She entered ten minutes later. By herself. *Yes!* That was a good start. His heart skipped a beat when she glanced his way. But then she took a seat further forward without betraying that she'd even seen him. Ben exhaled and sank deeper into his seat. At least she'd come. That was enough for now.

Right after the opening hymn, the lector read the day's scripture lessons, including a familiar passage from Jeremiah 29. *"For I know the plans I have for you," declares the Lord, "plans to prosper you and not to harm you, plans to give you hope and a future."*

The words smacked Ben right between the eyes, as if God had spoken especially to him. Knowing the uncertainty he still faced with his career and with Gail, the king of the universe had personally arranged to remind him that his future was in good hands. It wasn't the first time. But it *was* the first time he'd really listened.

Ben felt an inexplicable wave of well being flood through him, filling him to overflowing. He couldn't take in anything more and suddenly wanted to be alone.

Slipping out the back, he made his way to the parking lot. There, he leaned against the fender of his brother's car, tipped his face toward the sun, and closed his eyes. The pain in his shoulder was gone, and so were the fears for what the coming hours, weeks, and months might bring. God had a plan to prosper him, and now Ben understood that the promise had nothing to do with wealth, career, or even his love life. It was simply an invitation to trust.

He had no idea how long he remained in that attitude of quiet communion, but when Ben opened his eyes, Gail was emerging through the doors into the light. A warm breeze lifted her corn-silk hair, framing her face in a flowing halo of pale gold. She scanned the parking lot and then moved in his direction.

His pulse raced ahead at the sight of her determined progress toward him. Foot by foot, stride by stride, she drew closer, figuratively as well as literally. It wasn't a prophetic vision on the order of Jeremiah's, but Ben's heart told him it meant more than her willingness to have a conversation. Although she couldn't possibly know it, it constituted the first step of a potential homecoming for them both – the fulfillment of vows made long ago.

~~*~~

Gail waited for her eyes to adjust to the brightness. Then she saw him, bronzed by sunlight and standing next to that scruffy blue car – the one he apparently used to drive but that belonged to his brother now. Again she questioned the wisdom of speaking to him. That's all she'd mentally committed to do, however – to find out what he wanted. There couldn't be any harm in that. So she started toward him with resolve.

Ben met her partway. "Hi," he said in his mellow baritone.

Again, that soul-piercing look. Again, that feeling of connection. Gail couldn't speak, only stare back at him.

"Paul's not with you?" he asked.

"He had to work today." That was true enough.

Ben allowed some people to pass by before continuing in a lower voice. "If you don't mind my asking, what happened to that diamond ring he put on your finger the other night?"

Gail blinked at the question and tucked her naked left hand behind her back, saying, "It didn't fit. Now, what was so urgent, Ben? Why do you need to talk to me?"

He grimaced. "How much time have you got?"

"Seriously?"

"Seriously. It's a long story."

"About...?" Gail prompted uncertainly. "Give me *something* to go on here."

He hesitated and then blurted it out. "About you and me. That's what it comes down to. Us, actually." He held her gaze.

"Oh... I see," Gail murmured. And she was beginning to.

"Look, Gail, I probably have no right to ask, but come away with me this afternoon. Please. Just to talk. Let's hop on a ferry and get out of town for a few hours. After that, you can tell me to get lost if you want. You can marry Paul and walk out of my life forever if that's what will make you happy. I promise I won't bother you again."

Gail at last broke eye contact and turned away. She needed time to think. But it was no use. Although there had to be a dozen perfectly valid reasons to refuse, the only objection she produced to sailing away with Ben that afternoon sounded pathetically lame. "But you don't even like boats," she accused. "You get seasick!"

Ben grinned back at her, exasperatingly attractive crinkles gathering at the corners of his eyes. "Oh, I think I can manage a ferry ride on a calm day. But I'm touched – touched and impressed – that you remember I'm prone to seasickness."

"Why shouldn't I remember? You must have told me."

Ben slowly shook his head. "Not in *this* lifetime, Abby."

"What...?" she began. Then images of the two of them – together, in each other's arms – flickered through her mind. Was it past, future... or just wishful thinking? And there was that peculiar déjà vu feeling again, tingling up her spine.

"Come on. I'll explain," he said, leading the way back to the Toyota.

Gail followed him without knowing exactly why, only that it felt as if a benevolent breeze were blowing her gently *but persistently* his way. When she settled into the oddly familiar car beside him, he covered her diminutive hand with his and everything seemed to fall into place. That's where she belonged... with Ben... where she had always belonged.

POSTLUDE

"There, my dear. Didn't I tell you all would come right in the end?" Poindexter chided, leaning back in his chair with his hands clasped behind his head. "Mr. Lewis worked things out for himself, as you see. You never had any business fretting... or interfering."

Cora, reprising her Star Trek costume in Ben's honor, scooted herself sideways onto the desk. "Interfering?" she repeated as if the word and its meaning were totally foreign to her. "I'm sure I have no idea what you mean."

"You are not the only one who keeps an eye on the video progress reports, you know. Your disguise wouldn't have fooled a child, let alone someone who knows you so well. I instantly recognized your singular taste in apparel."

"Well," Cora whimpered with a little sniff, "maybe I did try to help things along just a little. Still, it can't really be called interference, can it? Since it made no difference in the outcome, I mean. As you said, Ben worked things out for himself. He'd already made up his mind about Abby before reading the notebook I helped him find. And the same can be said for her; she decided against marrying Paul and in favor of exploring her attraction to Ben, all without knowing the story of their past life together."

"Which is precisely my point," he said, raising his eyebrows. "There was absolutely no occasion for you to stick your fingers into the pie."

"But I like pie," said Cora, swiveling around to dangle her crossed legs in full view. "Don't be angry, Dex. I can't bear it when you scowl at me."

His expression softened. "Well, since no harm was done, I don't suppose we need say anything more about it." He abruptly rose and retrieved his clipboard. Making rapid notations and checkmarks there, he added, "I believe we can now consider Mr. Lewis's case closed."

"What about his baseball career? We still don't know if he succeeds with that."

"His career?" Poindexter pulled Cora to her feet and wrapped her in an amorous embrace. "My dear, you of all people should know that Mr. Lewis's second chance had very little to do with that. It never was about baseball at all."

-51-
Ben's Postscript

Every year on our anniversary, Abby and I reread our story from that old spiral notebook – my original log, plus the rest that we added together. We do it to keep the memories fresh and to remind ourselves how fortunate we are. It's still tempting to pass the whole thing off as fiction, except that all the pieces fit, and nothing else can explain the things we both experienced and know to be true. So, we accept it without understanding it. We marvel at it. We keep it to ourselves like a secret, hoarded treasure.

After we found our way back to each other, Abby followed me to Phoenix, which still amazes me. It took a huge leap of faith on her part, but then faith is one of her specialties. She got a job at a local hospital and stood by me through my long rehabilitation. Although I did finally fight my way back into playing condition, I never got another shot at the majors. The cumulative damage to my shoulder left me shy of peak form, and nothing less cuts it at that level. I kicked around the minors for a few more years, Abby accompanying me to each new town without complaint, until we both decided we would be happier returning home to Seattle for good.

No regrets. No bitterness. No recriminations. That's how I look back on my baseball career. I lived my dream, however briefly, not achieving everything I once hoped, but enough. Whatever else I do in life, I can always be satisfied that I played hard and competed honorably. No home in the Hall of Fame, but I came away with rich memories, a band of lifelong buddies, and a little money in the bank besides.

Baseball's reputation may have gotten a little tarnished, what with the '94 strike, steroid-tainted records, and monster salaries. But the game itself is the same as always. I still love it, and now I enjoy passing my passion for the sport on to the younger generation.

Teaching has turned into a perfect second career, allowing me to use the lessons I learned in the first to help mold the kids I mentor. I keep my hand in baseball too, coaching at the high school and playing on a community team. I may not be in the same shape as I was in my twenties, but I can still run down a fly ball with the best of them.

Our son Brian, who's twelve now and turning into a pretty good little short stop, never tires of hearing anecdotes from my playing days. But I suspect he wishes my professional baseball career had been more impressive for the sake of bragging to his friends.

Recently, he came into my office and picked his favorite item off my desk – the signed baseball from my one and only major league hit. Tossing it from hand to hand, he asked me, "Don't you ever get mad that you got hurt and couldn't play anymore, Dad? Especially when it wasn't even your fault."

His question reminded me of my old nemesis Derek Williams, whose baseball career had bottomed out even quicker than my own. When I heard he was finished by an injury too, I admit thinking there was some poetic justice in it, but that was about the last thought I ever wasted on him.

"I guess it used to bother me some," I told Brian truthfully, "but I'm happy with my life. I have a great family, a comfortable home, and a job I love. I don't need anything else."

"Yeah, but you were an awesome athlete before. Grandpa Lewis showed me some of the old video tapes."

"Too bad your grandpa doesn't have video of the athletic move I'm proudest of."

"Which one is that?"

"The time I saved your Uncle Paul's life. Believe me, Brian, that was more important than anything I could have accomplished in baseball," I told him. And I meant it.

Paul went to Zimbabwe as he'd planned (only without Abby), and he's been working there with the orphans ever since. He and his wife spend time with us every summer on their month-long leaves. It's a treat for Abby and me to see them both, and they've become great favorites with our kids too, earning their honorary titles of Aunt Lindsay and Uncle Paul. We count them every bit as much a part of our family as Scott and Hollie, our children's more official aunt and uncle.

316

Not only has Paul's work meant the world to the hundreds of kids he's helped, but, by taking the position at the orphanage, he freed another doctor to make equally important contributions elsewhere. A few years ago, Abby and I put the pieces together.

When our oldest, our daughter Lisa, was eleven, she was diagnosed with Crohn's disease. It seems that although I'd received a reprieve, I'd still managed to pass a genetic tendency for the illness on to my innocent child. Then as now, I would take it back if it meant sparing her. But that's impossible. So, I blamed myself. I got angry. Then I got busy, researching on the internet to see what the current treatment options were. What I discovered was that science had come a long way. Much more effective medications are available now, thanks in large part to a researcher by the name of Dr. Jeff Kendall.

Dr. Jeff. I knew that name well from reading the account of my stay at the Crossroads Center, where we apparently became good friends. When I left him, he was leaning toward the option of going back in time to be staff physician at an orphanage in Zimbabwe. I'd always considered it a freakish coincidence that it was the same plan Paul settled on. But what if it wasn't coincidence? What if, by saving Paul's life, I had inadvertently changed Jeff's plans as well? My guess is that, with the position at the orphanage filled, he must have turned instead to his other love: research.

I wish I could thank Jeff personally for what he's done for our family. The drugs he and his research team developed have kept Lisa nearly symptom free. She will lead a very normal life, thank God.

It's just one more ripple on the surface of the pond. Cause and effect, like Abby and I talked about on that winter drive home from Tacoma so many years ago. None of us can foresee what far-reaching consequences a simple act of kindness may have, what influence for good one life will…

"Are you still philosophizing?" Abby asks over my shoulder.

I can hear the unwavering affection in her voice, the kind that says she knows my history and all my secret flaws and loves me anyway. I am a very lucky man.

She closes my laptop while distracting me with a suggestive kiss on the side of my neck. "It's late, Ben," she whispers in my ear. "Come to bed."

THE END

One Ballplayer's Retrospective

by
Christopher Rosenbaum
technical advisor for *Leap of Faith*

Baseball is a beautiful game, one that has been stitched into the fabric of my life since I began playing when I was eight years old. I spent seventeen years on the field and sixteen of them as a catcher behind home plate – a fitting name, for no matter which field, that patch of ground always feels like home to me.

It was an early goal of mine to play professional baseball – not an easy feat but one I was fortunate enough to accomplish. After a successful collegiate career, with two NCAA National Championships and an Academic All-American honor, I was signed by the Los Angeles Angels of Anaheim. Again, I had some triumphs – enough to keep me going – but after three seasons in the minors, suddenly it was over. Despite all the time and hard work I had invested, I was released.

As realistic as I had been regarding my talent, knowing I wasn't as good as many of my peers, it was still painful to hear I was no longer wanted. What do you do when the one constant in your life is being taken away?

Although I had hoped that day wouldn't come so soon, I knew I would eventually need to face life after baseball. This was something I'd accounted for, and getting a business degree was always part of my plan. However, the economic downturn left my MBA-wielding self as just one among the masses of twenty-somethings competing for a dwindling number of investment banking and corporate finance jobs.

It was time to reassess my options.

Baseball organizations are always looking to differentiate themselves and find competitive advantages. I was no different. So what was my competitive edge? While I might be ordinary in the world of finance, I was unique to the baseball industry in that I could pair my expertise learned through playing a cerebral position at an elite level with an MBA education that gave me knowledge in the areas of business and leadership. I realized this combination could open doors for me in the front office part of baseball.

So that became the new plan: break into baseball's executive side. My job would still be to help an organization win, but this time using my head – combining my baseball knowledge with my business skills – instead of actually setting foot on the field.

I secured an internship with the Boston Red Sox organization and set out to work my way up in this game once again, channeling the same dedication to my craft used in my playing days in a different direction. After that first whirlwind year, I became a full-time advance scout for the Washington Nationals organization, where I've been ever since. Having played professionally gives me a unique perspective and an advantage in this, my second baseball career.

I cannot be more grateful for the support and guidance provided by family, friends, and coaches through the years. But, Looking back, was it all worth it? – the enormous effort and countless sacrifices made so I could play professional baseball?

Especially in light of the disappointment of a premature end to my playing days, it would be easy to become jaded remembering below-minimum-wage salaries, endless bus-rides through the night, debilitating injuries, and grueling rehab. And yet baseball has given back so much to me. I've had opportunities and experiences most only dream of.

The game that I loved growing up has transformed into an ongoing livelihood and vocation for me. However, the true beauty of baseball lies within its *unchanged* core, where pitches are still balls or strikes, runners are out or safe, and batted balls are either fair or foul. There is no clock; every team gets an even chance to win, to claim victory by the collective sum of their individual efforts.

So, like Ben Lewis, I have no regrets. To borrow a thought from the final chapter of this book, *I lived my dream, however briefly, not achieving everything I once hoped, but enough. Whatever else I do in life, I can always be satisfied that I played hard and competed honorably.*

Although I sometimes wonder how my life might have ended up had I gotten that opportunity to break in to finance, I'm ecstatic to have found a way to stay in the game I know and love so well. For me, baseball provides a special sense of home – an extended family of players, coaches, and staff who become best friends and mentors, people who share experiences that will last a lifetime.

Thank you for reading

Leap of Faith
Second Chance at the Dream

If you enjoyed this book, please look for Book 2 of
Shannon Winslow's Crossroads Collection:

Leap of Hope
Chance at an Austen Kind of Life
featuring Hope O'Neil,
whom you met in chapters 12-13

Shannon Winslow's other novels:

The Darcys of Pemberley
Return to Longbourn
Miss Georgiana Darcy of Pemberley
For Myself Alone
The Persuasion of Miss Jane Austen

Learn more at
www.shannonwinslow.com